COLD
VICTORY

Also by Karl Marlantes

Matterhorn

What It Is Like to Go to War

Deep River

KARL MARLANTES

COLD VICTORY

A NOVEL

Atlantic Monthly Press
New York

FIRST EDITION

Published simultaneously in Canada
Printed in the United States of America

This book was set in 12-point Adobe Caslon by Alpha Design & Composition of Pittsfield, NH.

First Grove Atlantic hardcover edition: January 2024

Library of Congress Cataloging-in-Publication data is available for this title.

ISBN 978-0-8021-6142-0
eISBN 978-0-8021-6143-7

Atlantic Monthly Press
an imprint of Grove Atlantic
154 West 14th Street
New York, NY 10011

Distributed by Publishers Group West

groveatlantic.com

24 25 26 27   10 9 8 7 6 5 4 3 2 1

Dedicated to all who fight to preserve rule by just law—particularly those in Ukraine.

Historical Timeline

September 17, 1809   Russia defeats Sweden, takes control of Finland

November 7, 1917   Communist revolution, Russia becomes Union of Soviet Socialist Republics (Soviet Union)

December 6, 1917   Finland becomes a democracy and declares independence from Soviet Union

January 22, 1918   Finnish civil war starts, communists defeated, but large numbers remain loyal to Soviet Union

September 1, 1939   Germany and Soviet Union join to invade Poland starting World War II

November 30, 1939   Soviet Union invades Finland (the Winter War)

March 12, 1940   Moscow Peace Treaty, Finland forced to give 9% of land to USSR, 422,000 Finns flee west to democratic Finland

June 22, 1941   Germany invades Soviet Union ending Soviet-German alliance

June 25, 1941   Finland joins forces with Germany eventually regaining all its lost territories (the Continuation War)

December 7, 1941   United Kingdom, an ally of the Soviet Union, declares war against Finland

December 11, 1941   US declares war on Germany, as an ally of the Soviet Union the US eventually will sever relations with Finland, but never declare war

June 9, 1944   With Germany facing defeat, the Soviet Union launches a massive attack against Finland, retaking the 9% of formerly ceded Finnish land and 2% more in bitter fighting, a now exhausted Finland asks for peace

September 19, 1944   Moscow Armistice, Finland forced to turn on Germany, give up 11% of its land, its largest naval base west of Helsinki, and pay crippling reparations

December 8, 1944   US reestablishes diplomatic relations with Finland

December 10, 1946   Louise and Arnie arrive in Finland

February 10, 1947   Paris Peace Treaty formally ends USSR and UK war against Finland and permanently gives the Soviet Union all Finnish land conquered in the Winter War

Part One

Tuesday, December 10, 1946
Ferry Terminal, Turku, Finland

She'd followed Arnie Koski a long way from Edmond, Oklahoma. Louise Koski was now standing on the open passenger deck of the Stockholm-Turku ferry as it formed a channel through the thin, early December ice leaving floating shards reflecting the wan sunlight in its wake. The angle of the somber sun in a clear comfortless sky was only a held-out fist above the southern horizon.

Wrapping herself against the cold in her stylish but inadequate coat, Louise watched the low snow-covered shoreline slowly pass behind on both sides as the eighteenth- and nineteenth-century buildings of Turku grew into distinct shapes, interspersed with occasional gaps where a now-bombed-out building had stood before the war.

Arnie came up from behind and hugged her. She snuggled into his chest, shielding herself against the slight but icy wind. Arnie was wearing civilian clothes under a heavy wool army greatcoat. He kissed her hair, and she turned to look up at him. His eyes shone with the excitement that he wouldn't allow himself to show on the rest of his face. "Is it like coming home, somehow?" she asked.

"In a way."

Three words made an average sentence for Arnie.

They entered the open water of the harbor and the icebreaker that had been preceding them moved aside to let the ferry nose into the terminal.

The line going through customs wasn't long. Travel between Finland and Sweden was only just beginning to revive so soon after the war. A Finnish customs official examined their passports and Arnie's diplomatic papers. The customs official looked up at them. "Is this all of you?" he asked in accented English.

"Just two," Arnie replied.

Louise felt a twinge. She was thirty and despite several army doctors declaring that she was perfectly healthy, she'd already suffered two miscarriages in five years of trying. She desperately wanted children, and the clock was ticking. The family remained, as Arnie said, just two.

When they emerged from the terminal, a young man in his early twenties with thick blond hair walked up to them, his breath showing a bright white cloud. He asked in English, "Lieutenant Colonel Koski?"

Arnie nodded and answered yes in Finnish.

"Pulkkinen," the man said and grabbed both of their suitcases. Pulkkinen silently led them to a khaki 1942 Chevy Fleetmaster sedan with diplomatic plates. The white star of the US Army was still on the driver's door.

Louise pulled herself closer to Arnie's ear. "Loquacious," she whispered.

"If you think Dad was taciturn . . ." he whispered back. He left the rest unsaid, which made her smile. Like father like son.

Pulkkinen stowed the luggage in the trunk and held a rear door open for her. Louise expected to be in the back seat; Arnie would want to pump the driver for as much information as he could. The leather of the rear seat was cold. She didn't look forward to the three-hour drive to Helsinki.

Constantly clearing the window condensation with her coat sleeve, Louise watched the bleak landscape of farms interspersed with tracts of snow-dusted trees slide by. It was only three in the afternoon and already the sun was setting.

Arnie was talking in his fluent Finnish with Pulkkinen. She could feel Arnie's excitement for his new posting, military attaché to the American legation in Helsinki, Finland. It wasn't just his new posting; it was hers as well. Every woman knew that all high-level diplomatic jobs took two people—and this was their first one. His end was gathering military intelligence. Her end was providing the social lubricant and connections that made his job easier. That meant what her mother called socializing. Just months before, she'd been an ordinary army wife. Could she do the job?

She was immensely proud of Arnie. It was a real coup, a position like this as a light colonel. But she worried that she would let him down. Several of the wives at the State Department briefing had gone to East Coast colleges like Vassar and Sweet Briar. She'd gone to the University of Oklahoma. Many had been to Europe before the war. She'd never ventured east of the Mississippi River. They came to the briefings dressed exactly right, seemingly without much thought or effort. Her *Emily Post* was getting dog-eared. Then there was the actual job, essentially being a secondary and subtle channel for any information that Arnie might find useful—or want to communicate—picking up on slight changes in tone, nuances of conversation, and cultivating the contacts that would help Arnie do his job. Her problem, however, was knowing what useful information was. The State Department briefings had been long on protocol: who got seated where at parties, how to address the wife of an ambassador versus the wife of a career diplomat, when not to shake hands, what to wear when. But the single brief lecture on what was actually happening in Finland, what America wanted—what the Soviet Union and Finland wanted—had been cursory. To her disappointment, she found that State was no different than the army. There was an unspoken assumption that the wives wouldn't be interested, so they were spared the details. Their husbands could fill them in if they really wanted to know.

That attitude on the part of State and the army, however, did not ease any of the pressure. If this assignment went well, Arnie could make full colonel, paving the way to general. If not, she remembered the wife of another military attaché, half-sloshed at a cocktail party in Washington before they left, offering "helpful" advice. "Screw this up and your husband's career is over."

Louise was all too aware that many a promising army career had been cut short by an awkward wife who lacked social skills. The French, whose literature she had studied in college, had a single word for it that she hoped would never be applied to her: gauche. But the French spent their entire childhoods learning how to be French. She only knew how to be polite in Oklahoma, and trying to learn diplomatic protocol in a couple of weeks of lectures was like trying to learn a foreign language without ever being able to practice speaking. She would never be fluent.

Right now, however, her free-floating anxiety about whether she was up to the job of making this assignment work was ambient background for a related and more specific worry. Would their household items, which they'd shipped over a month ago, especially her clothes, be waiting in Helsinki? If not, that would mean buying several dresses, and it would be with their own money. What would they think of her—and Arnie—if she had to go to a fancy embassy party in—she looked down at her sensible wool skirt—this? Were there even dress shops in Helsinki?

They passed a crossroads in the dark and Pulkkinen pointed to the road on the right. "Porkkala." A single word. No emotion.

"Porkkala?" she asked.

Arnie turned to look back at her. "The Russian navy base."

"A Russian navy base? Here? We're no more than twenty miles from Helsinki. No one said anything about it in *our* briefings."

"With another base in Estonia they control the sea approaches to Leningrad," Arnie said. "Part of the deal."

The "deal" referred to the Moscow Armistice, which was signed on September 19, 1944, ending the fighting between Finland and the Soviet Union. She had heard of the agreement in the briefings, but Arnie had had to explain its consequences in more detail on the ferry. The deal had been very bad for the Finns.

In November 1939, the Soviet Union, then an ally of Hitler's Germany, had invaded Finland. The Finns fought bravely and alone against enormous odds in what became known as the Winter War, inflicting massive casualties on the Soviet juggernaut, stopping it cold, and earning the accolades of the entire free world. Accolades, however, were all they got. With no help from the West, exhausted and out of hope, they signed the first armistice with the Soviet Union in the spring of 1940, giving up over 10 percent of their land.

Fearing the Soviets wanted even more, they again sought help from neutral Sweden and the Western Allies to shore up their defenses. Again, they got none. So, when Nazi Germany invaded the Soviet Union in June of 1941, the Finns joined with Germany to take back the territory they'd lost. They regained all of it. They however continued, some would say foolishly, to help their German ally lay siege to Leningrad. Leningrad never fell, and Stalin never forgot.

In June 1944, when the Germans were falling back on Berlin and facing the Allied landings in Normandy, Stalin took his revenge.

With overwhelming superiority in men and equipment, fueled with massive matériel support from the United States, the Red Army drove the Finns back toward Helsinki. But by September 1944, the campaign had cost the Soviet Union close to a million casualties. For every dead Finn and German, there were four dead Russians. Stalin decided it would be better for the Soviet Union to make peace than to continue to pay the enormous price of conquering Finland by force. The Finns, spent and starving, their German allies facing sure defeat, signed a terribly punitive second armistice. This one cost Finland even more land than the previous one in 1940 and, in addition, the entire Porkkala peninsula just west of Helsinki, along with its large naval base. It further imposed brutal "reparation" payments that amounted to 60 percent of Finland's prewar GDP. Bad as this deal looked, however, because of Finland's fierce resistance, it was still independent, the only Eastern European country that hadn't succumbed to the Red Army. Yet.

Stalin was still set on establishing a Communist government friendly to the Soviet Union but for the moment sought to do so from within. His weapon was the Communist Party of Finland, which until the 1944 treaty had been outlawed. But with Soviet support, it now held about a third of the seats in the parliament. It was Stalin's velvet glove. The iron fist in that glove was the threat of invasion from a massive army in Finland's lost territory in the east and the First Mozyr Red Banner Naval Infantry Division based on the Russian-occupied Porkkala peninsula just twenty miles west of Helsinki.

If any political or foreign policy decision offended Joseph Stalin, he could cut the thread holding the Damocles sword of war that hung over Finland's head. Driving in the cold twilight, Louise knew that she and Arnie were heading right under that sword.

They reached Helsinki around five, well after dark. Too few inadequate streetlights, composed of single electric bulbs, struggled to cast light on the nearly empty streets. Louise unconsciously expected the city to be lit up for Christmas like American cities. Helsinki emanated cheerless austerity.

Pulkkinen helped check them into a hotel near the American legation office. Louise guessed the hotel had probably been built in the last century. The small lobby smelled of decades-old carpet.

There were no bellhops, and Pulkkinen helped Arnie haul their bags into the lobby.

A bit flustered, Louise whispered, "Do we tip him?"

Arnie smiled. "I assure you he's well paid. Way better than most."

She gave Pulkkinen a big smile and said, "Kiitos paljon!" Thank you very much, one of her few Finnish phrases.

Pulkkinen merely looked at her. Then he nodded slightly, coming back to what Louise could only graciously describe as a reserved stare. Then, Pulkkinen said, in what sounded to her like an upper-crust British accent, "It has been a pleasure, Mrs. Koski."

Louise looked at Arnie, who was suppressing a grin. Arnie reached out a hand to Pulkkinen, saying thank you and a few other words. Watching Pulkkinen return to the car, Louise said quietly, "How wonderful he speaks English! At least when he speaks. Do you think we'll be able to use him to help us get settled?"

"We can ask. He works for Max Hamilton, the charge d'affaires of the legation." He paused. "We pay him, but we may not be the only ones. Just be careful what you say around him."

"Oh, Arnie. I'm sure he's on our side. He seems really friendly."

"I hope you're right. But the Finns fought a civil war in 1918 as bloody as our own. The Communists lost, but I'd guess at least a third of this country still *wants* the Communists to take over. The Soviet Union is here to make that happen. And *we,* my dear, are here to help make it not happen."

Standing with Arnie on the cold sidewalk, watching the big Fleetmaster pull away, Louise suddenly felt alone and exposed. It was the first time in years that she hadn't been surrounded in safety by the US Army. She pulled herself in closer to Arnie. "Don't you think we might be a little late to the party?" she said softly. She looked up at him. "I mean, Russia is fifty times the size of Finland with a huge army on Finland's border. I now find out they also have a navy base practically in their capital. What do *we* have here to fight that?"

Arnie paused, then said quite seriously, "A 1942 Chevy Fleetmaster sedan. It means far more than you might think."

When Louise leaned over their room's double bed to unpack her suitcase, her rear end touched the wall. A single window sat over a noisy steam radiator on the other side of the bed, its paper roller shade pulled all the way down, making the room seem even smaller. She resolved to move out of the hotel as soon as possible, but there was no embassy staff to help find housing. That would be entirely up to her.

In fact, there was no embassy and no ambassador. Because the Finns had joined with Germany to fight the Soviet Union, the United States came under intense pressure from its Soviet ally to declare war on Finland as Great Britain had done. Not wanting to go that far, the United States simply broke off diplomatic relations with Finland on June 30, 1944. Until peace between the Soviet Union, Great Britain, and Finland was official, with a signed peace treaty, diplomatic relations couldn't be reestablished. The United States could not send an ambassador, nor could it set up an embassy. Instead, it had the legation with its tiny staff preparing for the day when full diplomatic relations would be restored.

Wednesday, December 11, 1946
Helsinki Hotel

The next morning, Arnie completed his nearly inviolable morning exercise routine in the hotel basement, a fierce combination of intense moves like burpees and push-ups, all done to exhaustion. After eating the simple breakfast served by the hotel in another part of the basement, Louise and Arnie reported to Max Hamilton, the US chargé d'affaires, at his office, which was located in a converted mansion that sat among large, now-bare deciduous trees near a park crisscrossed with walking lanes and intersected with narrow paved roads.

Hamilton appeared to be in his early fifties, and Louise found him to be charming, East Coast, well educated, intelligent, and probably wealthy. Arnie had told her, just before they went into Hamilton's office, that it was a blessing that Finland didn't want an embassy; it avoided his having to report to an ignorant political appointee instead of an experienced career diplomat like Hamilton.

Louise wasn't so sure, because she quickly saw that Max Hamilton evinced one of the downsides of the career diplomat. Anytime she'd ask a question of substance, he'd smile and deflect pleasantly and politely, saying nothing of importance.

She'd asked if the United States would offer financial help or loans to Finland, even though they'd fought with the Germans. He'd answered, "We're really not into the banking business. Do you need any help finding a personal bank here in Helsinki?" She'd tried again, asking him how strong the Communist Party of Finland was and how dependent it was on the Soviets. He'd answered, "It is, of course, an active political party. One of many. It's probably best if we keep our opinions about the internal policies of a host country's political parties to ourselves." She wasn't sure if she'd been rebuked.

She kept her frustration hidden behind what she called her polite-face smile. Beneath it was good old Oklahoma irritation. How in hell could she do her job if Hamilton wouldn't answer her questions and none of her good clothes were here?

She listened while Hamilton and Arnie discussed the details of his job. Finland was directly under the likely path of American B-29 bombers flying out of England and Greenland to bomb Russia should war erupt. Soviet air and naval bases needed to be located and their capabilities determined. Emergency landing sites needed to be established. Possible invasion routes and key roads, rail lines, bridges, and their load capacities needed to be identified. Probable strategies needed to be understood. Any threat to Finnish independence that would move Finland into the Soviet camp, whether posed by the Red Army, Soviet intelligence organizations, or the pro-Soviet Finnish Communist Party needed to be uncovered.

When she'd sensed that Arnie had exhausted all of his detailed questions, she plunged in to help Arnie with the part of his job that he was neither good at nor inclined to do: managing up. She turned on the charm. If Hamilton wanted just to make congenial small talk with her, then she'd, by gum, make use of that. So, she joined the game he was playing and began lobbing conversational tennis balls across the net that were easy to hit back. She quickly learned that Hamilton was an enthusiastic member of Phi Delta Theta fraternity from Washington and Jefferson College in Washington, Pennsylvania. She made sure he knew she was still an enthusiastic member of Delta Gamma sorority. Within ten minutes he was telling funny stories about Foggy Bottom in the old days and had even unbuttoned his suit coat. It ended with

Hamilton calling his wife, asking her to have coffee with Louise at the legation that afternoon to help Louise get settled.

Back on the street, Arnie said, "Thank you. You know how I hate buttering up."

"You're welcome."

"Did you have to make him fall in love with you?"

"Just fall at my feet, my dear." She tucked her arm in close to the crook of his own. He in turn pulled her in closer to his side, making her want to hurry back to the hotel.

When they got there, however, Arnie immediately disappeared to his new assignment, leaving Louise a bit frustrated. Temporarily thwarted from what she considered her most important task, she turned to her own assignment, finding an apartment. The first order of business on that front was the impending meeting with Hamilton's wife. That meant ironing the dress she was wearing. The other two dresses she'd packed were a conservative cocktail dress and a housedress, neither suitable for meeting Mrs. Hamilton for coffee at the legation offices.

She did some of her best planning ironing clothes and the to-do list was already long. Arnie would need clothes, too, if their crates didn't arrive. They needed stationery for thank-you notes. Telephone service. Groceries. There must be a fish market. Helsinki was on a harbor after all. Did Finland have department stores?

Army wives were used to getting things done alone, especially when a war was on. They raised their children alone. They made all the difficult decisions—where to go to school, what to do about the teacher their child hated, getting the children to church, making sure they remembered their absent fathers and knew who their father's parents were—all tasks she wished she could have been doing herself. About the only difference between being an army wife and a widowed or divorced single mother was the steady paycheck and the hope that someday the loneliness would end without having to go down to the local bar—and dealing with their husbands when they came back from war forever changed.

Having found housing off base several times during the war and again in the suburbs of DC when Arnie spent seventeen weeks at Strategic Intelligence School, Louise thought she would only be mildly challenged by it being her first time outside of the United States.

In the past, finding housing had been easy compared to the things she'd done working in her father's lumberyard as a teenager. By the time she was in high school, she had been helping contractors with purchases and dealing with their complaints, helping with the books and preparing the taxes, and, on occasion, when her father was short of help in the yard, even doing jobs like pulling out higher grades of lumber from recently arrived mixed pallets to sell for premium prices. This involved moving hundreds of pieces of lumber, some of the larger two-by-twelves weighing over sixty pounds. She smiled, remembering using nearly a jar of her mother's Pond's Cold Cream on her hands and having to roll sideways out of her bed in the morning for about a week because she was so stiff.

In college, she'd been elected president of her sorority. Managing meals, house maintenance, recruitment, complicated social events, and the quarrels, jealousies, and emotions of eighty-seven girls, followed by six and a half years of military life, most of it spent in wartime, she assumed would have prepared her for her current assignment.

It hadn't. None of her previous experience had been in a country reeling from a recent war. Finding housing in the States had been hard, but there hadn't been thousands of homeless refugees pouring into the city. And the language was totally alien. Although she'd majored in education, she'd minored in French in college and the language had been easy for her. Trying for several months to learn even rudimentary Finnish had left her feeling tired and inadequate. Yes, she could find the bathroom, count to one hundred, and figure out how to buy a bus ticket, but engaging in an intelligent conversation would have to wait. That would be another item on the list she thought, finding a Finnish language tutor. On top of it all, there were less than six hours of daylight, and daylight was gloomy at best.

Every day, Arnie left their hotel early and returned late, always in darkness. The Finns called their country Suomi, which Arnie had told her was derived from some pre–Finnish language word for "bog," adding in his careful way that it was only one theory of several. Others were that Suomi meant "land of the lakes" or just "the land." After several days of trudging around the war-torn, bleak city, she thought darkly that the bog theory was the more likely.

Not that Louise hadn't expected housing to be difficult to find. Housing all over Europe was scarce because of the bombing. Helsinki, too, had been bombed—by the Russians—using American bombers. Much of Helsinki had been saved from severe damage because the Finns had lured the bombers away from the city by lighting fires and placing searchlights on the islands just off the coast. The actual cause of the housing shortage was the four hundred thousand Finns who had fled their homes in Eastern Finland rather than live under Soviet domination and another one hundred thousand discharged soldiers.

Then, there were the orphans, thousands of them.

Saturday, December 21, 1946
Kaarina Vanhatalo Varila's Apartment

Finland's recent history became personal to Louise the Saturday before Christmas. She and Arnie were invited to the home of Kaarina Varila. Arnie's aunt Aino had urged Arnie to locate the daughter of her mother's cousin, a Vanhatalo, who she thought might still live in Helsinki. It had been this cousin who first took care of Aino when she was released from a Russian jail in 1905, just before she emigrated to America. Arnie had told Louise that Aunt Aino had been arrested by the secret police for being a Communist linked to a terrorist organization that tried to bomb a Russian army barracks. Louise had found this hard to believe. Aunt Aino made bread and told earthy jokes. Her brother, Arnie's father Matti, was a member of the Astoria Golf and Country Club and as staunch a Republican businessman as Louise's own father.

To find this Vanhatalo cousin, Arnie had gone to the Finnish police. The police, staunchly anti-Communist and therefore pro-American, had been happy to help, despite their government's precarious and careful positioning regarding the Soviets. They soon determined that Aino's cousin had died during the war, but they'd located the woman's daughter, Kaarina, under her married name, Varila. Arnie made contact and they'd been invited to dinner.

* * *

Kaarina lived with her adult son, Pietari, who opened the door to their knock. In his early twenties, he looked like his mother, who was standing behind him in a dark-blue wool dress that brought out her blue eyes. She was wearing old-fashioned cotton stockings and lace-up shoes with two-inch heels. She was a big-boned woman, not at all fat, with a wide face, thick dark blonde hair, and what to Louise was amazingly clear soft skin for a woman probably in her early fifties. She and Pietari very formally shook hands with Arnie and Louise and ushered them in.

The house was spotlessly clean—and simple. Louise was becoming used to there being no electric Christmas lights but was taken aback by the lack of what she considered to be essential household items. Standing in the living room, Louise could see into the kitchen. The floors were made of wood, so often scrubbed they had the appearance of a ship's deck. There was no hot water faucet at the kitchen sink. A single-bulb light fixture hung from the middle of the kitchen ceiling. In the living room, a floor lamp stood by a stuffed armchair, where an open book rested on a small end table. The feeble light barely reached the walls of the room, giving it the feel to her of a cloudy afternoon.

Louise smiled brightly, remarking on the beautiful handmade rag rugs scattered on the living room's wood floor, trying to hide her reaction to the seeming poverty of the place so as not to embarrass Kaarina. Somehow, she'd expected Kaarina's house to be like that of her in-laws and Arnie's aunt and uncle, in Astoria, Oregon, full of soft furniture, flooded with electric light—and warm.

The house was heated by a single cylindrical metal wood stove in a corner of the living room. The room itself couldn't be much warmer than the midfifties Fahrenheit. She imagined that the bedrooms had no heat at all. There was a fireplace with a mantel, but it was clear that it hadn't had a fire for some time. She imagined any wood would be burned in the corner stove; the heat was too precious to waste going up a fireplace chimney. On the fireplace mantel were two photos of young couples in late-nineteenth-century wedding clothes. There was also one of Kaarina as a bride in an ankle-length narrow wedding dress standing next to a handsome well-built man in a heavy wool suit, presumably her husband. There was a fourth photograph of three grinning towheaded boys.

Kaarina touched one of the old wedding pictures. "My parents. Father died twenty years ago. Mother," she hesitated, "in 1940." She pointed to another photo. "Me and my husband, Niko." She paused just enough to keep the sadness in. "And there," she said quietly, "Pietari when he was six, and his brothers, Oskar and Risto." Louise suspected what would—and did—come next: lost in the war.

Kaarina turned to look at Pietari who was talking to Arnie. Pietari was a lean, robust young man in his early twenties. No longer a towhead, his hair was a thick caramel blond. "Well, not all were lost," she said, smiling at him. "Pietari fought the Russians when he was eighteen. After the Russians forced us to fight the Germans who were trying to make it to Norway, he fought Germans." She paused. "Now, he fights himself." She looked on her son for a moment. "And he hates Russians *and* Germans." She gave Louise a quick smile. "Complicated."

"I know you didn't want to be on Germany's side," Louise said.

"Not all of us," Kaarina replied. "That's *not* so complicated. The Russians demanded we give up several of our eastern provinces. We refused. The Russians invaded. We fought hard, but in the end, they were too big and they took our land." She paused. "No one helped us. But you sent millions of dollars of military aid to the Russians."

Louise was wondering if Kaarina was somehow blaming her for US foreign policy.

"So," Kaarina went on, "when Germany attacked the Soviet Union, we accepted German help and took back our land. When the Germans started losing to the Russians, the Russians invaded us again in 1944.

They took back the land they'd taken from us in 1940. We signed an armistice so they wouldn't take the whole country. Part of the armistice agreement was that we turn on our German allies. Which we did. The Germans headed for Norway burning everything in their path. That's why Pietari fought both Russians and Germans."

Kaarina's tone revealed none of her feelings, leaving Louise wondering where Kaarina stood politically. She could have been pro-German, even a Fascist. Or maybe she was a Communist like Arnie's aunt. Louise didn't dare ask. She already felt she was treading on eggshells.

Dinner was potatoes, cabbage, parsnips, and one roasted chicken, about half the size of a chicken they would have had back in Edmond. Dessert was just enough rice pudding topped with preserved lingonberries.

Louise's Finnish wasn't sufficient for her to keep up with the conversation, but Kaarina had worked for Thomas Cook and Sons as a young woman, so her English was quite good, although accented. She spoke to Louise in English, but despite that, the conversation still lagged as Pietari's English was only rudimentary. The conversation flowed, however, when Kaarina, Pietari, and Arnie would lapse into Finn, leaving Louise feeling left out.

Kaarina brought coffee to Arnie and Pietari, who were on facing armchairs by the empty fireplace. It was clear they were talking about the war, Arnie quietly asking questions, ever the professional, and Pietari quietly and succinctly answering them.

"Come sit in the kitchen," Kaarina said, handing Louise her cup. "It's warmer."

Kaarina led her to two simple wood rocking chairs next to the brick cookstove. Iron doors indicated there was an iron firebox inside the bricks. The bricks were warm. It reminded Louise of Arnie's comment before she first met his parents. "Be patient. Finns aren't cold, they just warm up slow."

Louise settled back in the chair, feeling for the first time that evening that maybe there was some hope of Kaarina liking her. Then she took a sip of her coffee and nearly gagged. She stopped just short of spitting it back into the cup, but managed to swallow, trying to hide her reaction.

"How do you like the coffee?" Kaarina asked, her face deadpan.

Louise had been around Arnie's relatives enough to know that Finnish humor and deadpan went together often. She was being gently teased.

"OK. I'll bite. What is it?"

Kaarina chuckled. "It's made from mushrooms. Chaga. They grow on birch trees. I haven't had a good cup of coffee since 1939. I'm told there was a shipment arrived in Turku last February, but you need ration cards to get any. They're rare."

"Uh . . ." Louise didn't know whether to put the cup down or keep sipping at it. "It was rationed at home, at least for the first part of the war."

"It wasn't rationed here during the war."

"Really?" Louise responded.

Looking at her like she was from another planet, Kaarina said, "There wasn't any."

"Oh." She didn't know if she'd just missed some rather dry and ironic humor behind "it wasn't rationed here" or if Kaarina was being serious and resentful that Americans had coffee during the war. "Gosh. I wish I'd known." Should she offer to see if she could get some from the legation? Or would that offend Kaarina? She scrambled. "Uh, how do you make it?"

"I'll show you."

Kaarina went to a large pot sitting on the floor next to the stove and removed the lid. Soaking in water were ugly organic lumps that looked to Louise like black stove clinkers.

"You give them a good squeeze after a couple of days." Kaarina smiled. "Then you drink it and wish for coffee."

They returned to the rocking chairs. Louise took another sip and gently sat the cup on the brick edge that lined the iron cooktop.

"No need to drink any more," Kaarina said. "It will go back in the pot for later and not wasted."

Louise nodded. There was silence.

"I'm so sorry you lost your husband and sons."

There was now awkward silence, just as with Arnie's family when she'd gotten too personal too soon. She glanced into the living room, wishing Arnie were there to bail her out, but Arnie was still fully engaged with Pietari.

"I'm sorry. I didn't mean to . . . I just wanted . . . I mean it must have been so hard."

Kaarina looked at her for what seemed a very long time but that must have been no more than a few seconds. Then, something softened. "It was hard," Kaarina said.

"Yes."

"Still, losing a husband and sons is not so bad as a child losing parents."

"I hope I never have to find out," Louise said quietly.

Kaarina smiled. "You live in a safe golden land."

"Yes, we do. We're very fortunate."

There was more silence, but not as awkward.

"No children?" Kaarina asked. "Or are they with a babysitter?"

"No, just the two of us."

"Do you want children?"

"Yes, we do. Very much." Then she added, "I've"—she hesitated—"miscarried twice." She was briefly flooded with the memory of holding the cold body of her stillborn daughter close to her sobbing chest and breaking heart.

Kaarina seemed a little taken aback at the word "miscarried." Louise looked down at her Chaga, realizing she may again have shared too openly for a first-time meeting with a Finn.

Kaarina, however, seemed to recover. "You're still young," she said without emotion.

"Thirty. Not so young."

"Well, from my perspective . . ." Kaarina chuckled, trying to make Louise feel better.

"I suppose you're right," Louise said with a slight smile.

"Did you ever think of adopting?"

Now Louise was a bit taken aback. "No. Not really."

"We have thousands of orphans."

"I know."

"I work with them, you know."

"I didn't know."

"At an orphanage. Down near the harbor." She looked through the kitchen door to the mantel and its photographs. "It gives me comfort but also heartbreak. There are so many, and there is so little to give. We're a bit overwhelmed." Kaarina smiled.

Louise smiled politely, wondering if Kaarina was simply telling her a fact or was wanting her to donate money, help at the orphanage, or adopt someone.

She chose help. "Gosh. I could help. I mean once we get settled. I'm pretty good with kids," she added hurriedly. "I could maybe help them with their reading."

Kaarina simply nodded, then said, "They can learn to read in school." She smiled. "If you want to help, we have more pressing needs."

"Sure. I'd love to come by. I like to pitch in. Do things. I mean, being the wife of a military attaché . . . diplomat's wife . . . I could use a project. Maybe two." She felt a flicker of excitement. "What do you need?" she asked.

"Money."

"Uh, Arnie and I aren't—"

"I wasn't asking you for money. I was just saying what we needed."

Louise felt her cheeks reddening. "Of course. I didn't think you were asking us personally." But she knew that she had thought that and that Kaarina knew it, too.

Back at the hotel, Louise sat dumbly on the bed, waiting for Arnie to get out of the bathroom. She was looking at the wall just two feet from her face, brooding over the awkward moments in the conversation, simultaneously playing it out in her head with how the conversation would have gone if she'd been smoother. She should have jumped on Kaarina's need for money, but she'd kept silent after her embarrassing misinterpretation of Kaarina's statement about it, fearing she would seem too pushy. She was also a bit further troubled because the thought of adopting kept popping up.

When Arnie came out of the bathroom, half-undressed, he stopped.

"What's wrong?" he asked.

"Nothing."

Arnie waited.

"Oh, Arnie," she finally wailed. "Why am I always putting my foot in my mouth?"

"You're from Oklahoma?" Arnie answered with a question.

She couldn't help but smile.

He sat down beside her, put his arm around her, and gave her a couple of short affectionate tugs on her shoulder. Then he said, "Nice wall."

She chuckled.

"Now, what's wrong?"

She relayed the awkward conversation with Kaarina and ended it with, "I *do* so want her, all your relatives, to like me."

They both sat there, silent, Arnie's hand across her back and holding her shoulder, staring at the wall in front of them. Then in a flat, low voice, Louise said, still looking at the wall, "Are we going to have to spend Christmas in this stupid hotel room?"

They did, but she felt OK about it. Arnie found a tiny little Christmas tree and she'd decorated it with the jewelry she'd brought with her, Arnie's civilian neckties, and little paper rings she'd fashioned from newspaper and paste. On Christmas morning, they sat next to it, both grateful to be quiet and alone together in the little hotel room.

Since the visit to Kaarina's, Arnie had only been back in the room to sleep. She'd spent every day looking for housing. She got no help from an overwhelmed American legation staff, and lunch with Mrs. Hamilton had been pleasant but not very helpful. Mrs. Hamilton did invite them to a nice dinner, one they had to cram into a relentless round of Christmas-season embassy parties.

Before they left America, she'd imagined herself at sophisticated parties and dinners. Instead, she found herself in an antiquated and cramped hotel bathroom trying to get dolled up for parties where she felt like the most provincial and unsophisticated woman in the room. And still with only one nice dress. She had to check herself from explaining to the other wives that it wasn't her fault. She really did have nice clothes—somewhere. She used to envy Arnie's easy clothing choices. It was either a uniform or his suit—with an accessory choice of wristwatch or no wristwatch. Now she was in the same position. She hated it.

* * *

Even though the parties were often fun and interesting, she felt they were a bit dampened by her constant awareness that she had to guard her speech. She just never quite knew if she was being pumped for information or simply asked about herself out of polite curiosity. During the day, that guarded feeling was amplified by a nagging feeling that she was being watched. It wasn't like there was some sinister man in a raincoat and fedora darting into alleys and turning his back at department store windows. First, there *were* no department store windows. Just weren't. No, it was something—something so subtle that she couldn't bring herself to mention it to Arnie for fear of looking paranoid. But there was the time she returned unexpectedly to the car and saw Pulkkinen quickly slip what looked like a small notebook into his coat pocket. Then there was the man reading the newspaper just across the street from the hotel. Twice. Waiting for a bus or taxi? It was *cold* outside.

The briefings in Washington hadn't all been about how to set a table either. There had been the rather sobering discussion of what to do if your husband didn't return when you expected him. You didn't just go to the local police. At one of the after-session cocktail hours the wife of a former military attaché to Spain when Carlton Hayes was ambassador related how, responding to a knock on her door, she'd opened it to five local police, huge men in weird three-corner hats. They'd handed her an order to be out of the country in twenty-four hours. She and her husband had hurried to Ambassador Hayes's house to be told, not without a great deal of sympathy, that Generalissimo Franco was exceedingly upset with the help the American embassy was giving to Jews coming across the Pyrenees. Her husband had been recognized. Hayes had to sacrifice someone.

When Arnie became a military attaché, Louise knew that she became more than an army wife. She became the wife of a spy—a known and legal spy but a spy, nevertheless. She also knew that if Arnie or she made some false move they could be deported—or worse. All of it both excited and scared her.

Because there had been no US presence in Finland for most of the war, there were no sophisticated radio or human intelligence networks. Lack of the latter meant that personal connections would be a major source of information, and Louise would play a large part in making those connections. In addition, she would need to be constantly alert for any small slip or behavioral nuance at a party or luncheon that she could report to Arnie.

Knowing all this, when Arnie told her about the invitation to a New Year's Eve party at the Soviet envoy's residence, Louise had frozen, temporarily unable to move, an equally frozen smile on her face. She knew that the party would be opening night for her. What she didn't know was that party would engender a series of events that would test Louise to her very soul.

Tuesday, December 31, 1946
The Soviet Envoy's Residence, Helsinki

The night of New Year's Eve, Louise had managed to steer Arnie to several parties before going to the one at the Soviet envoy's residence. Now, despite being purposefully fortified by several drinks, walking through lightly falling snow, her arm linked with Arnie's, she began to worry she'd had too much fortification. She was afraid she'd say the wrong thing. Just being around army officers and their wives, having drinks, she knew a great deal that most governments would want to classify. Suppose something that would hurt the United States slipped out. Maybe something she thought was harmless. But, if she wasn't sociable, she'd be that awkward wife that hurt her husband's chances for promotion.

They reached an open gate with two sturdy brick pillars about five feet high on either side. Up a stone path was the large front door to the Soviet envoy's residence, an imposing brick building. Before the 1944 armistice agreement, it had been the German embassy. It was lost on no one that the Soviets made it the residence of their envoy extraordinary to send a clear signal of Soviet triumph. To the victor go the spoils.

Two guards stood at each side of the door. Arnie touched Louise's mitten.

"What?" she asked.

"Just be careful. Remember, the walls have ears."

"Mum's the word," she said brightly. She wished she felt as brave as she sounded.

Arnie presented his identification to one of the guards, who to Louise's delight came to attention and saluted him. The other guard opened the door.

They walked into a large, brightly lit room filled with the babble of a party in full swing. Looking for familiar faces and finding none, Louise realized they must be the only Americans. There were numerous elegantly dressed women in formal gowns and men in black tuxedos and a large number of Russian army officers, already well-oiled and as loud as any Americans.

"Geez, Arnie," she whispered. "It looks like the whole Red Army is here."

"Most likely part of the Allied Control Commission," he whispered back. "More accurately referred to as the Soviet Control Commission. When the Finns signed the treaty with the Soviet Union, England also made peace. They formed the Allied Control Commission, two hundred Russians and fifteen Brits, to make sure the Finns were complying with the terms."

"Are they?"

"There's a whole Red Army on the border, just waiting for an excuse to come across. They're complying alright."

Overhead was a high ceiling and carved plaster coving. The large room had classic clean lines, which she liked. However, it had been filled with Russian furniture that had the ostentatious bad taste of a sirdar's throne room. Heavy velvet drapes, dark green and maroon, framed tall windows. Just outside the windows, light reflected off falling snowflakes into the room. There were several tables loaded with ornate silver and gold canapé trays. Bowls of caviar rested on ice in prerevolution silver containers decorated with scenes of wolf hunts. There were dozens of champagne and vodka bottles. The champagne labels were varied and in French. The vodka labels were in Russian, identical, all from the one official government vodka factory. The walls had been decorated with hammers and sickles, making it clear that everything was done for the benefit of the working class. The irony was not lost on Louise.

A small orchestra of two violins, two trumpets, two saxophones, a clarinet, trombone, tuba, and snare drum was playing sedate dance music, strictly on the beat. Behind them on a pedestal was a large electric clock with a second hand jerking toward midnight.

A soldier in a dress uniform took their coats and wraps. Then a beautiful young woman in a turquoise silk cocktail dress that tastefully highlighted every curve, presented them with a silver tray holding several crystal flutes of champagne.

She moved on, and Louise watched Arnie watching her leave. It amused her. Given the way this young woman looked and dressed, it would worry her if Arnie *didn't* watch—within reason.

Louise noticed two men looking at them, one around forty, obviously informing the older about something. The older man smiled and started toward them, the younger man in tow. It had to be Aleksandr Abramov, the Soviet envoy. Louise tensed. This man personified the power of the Soviet state, power that not only menaced Finland, but with each news article she read about what was happening in Germany and Eastern Europe, menaced democracy, menaced her.

"Envoy Abramov," the younger man said in accented English, "may I present Colonel and Mrs. Koski of the American legation."

Louise smiled as brilliantly as she could and held out her hand, remembering to keep it soft, but not limp. She was relieved when Abramov took it gently and, looking directly into her eyes, said in accented English, "Mrs. Koski. Welcome to Finland." He immediately turned to Arnie, who put his own hand out, which Abramov seemed to grasp like he was going to pull Arnie out of a hole or something, repeating the greeting.

Abramov parted hands with Arnie who had been enduring the vigorous pumping of the man's handshake with a near-frozen smile.

Indicating the younger man beside him, Abramov said, "Colonel and Mrs. Koski, may I present Colonel Oleg Sokolov. He is responsible for security here in Finland."

Holding her hand out for Sokolov, Louise smiled, looking directly into his eyes as she'd been taught. He took her hand and smiled—with his mouth—observing her rather than looking at her with cold Uranian-blue eyes. She had an awkward moment, not knowing when to withdraw her hand.

"Mrs. Koski. My great pleasure." He spoke English, but with a Russian accent, reminding her of Arnie's father, whom she liked very much.

Then Sokolov raised her hand and bowed just enough to kiss it. That had never happened to her before. It felt like being in a Tolstoy novel.

Sokolov, still holding her hand, looked directly into her eyes. She felt that he knew this was a first for her. His knowing this about her, reading her so easily without her saying a word, made her feel vulnerable and uneasy. At the same time, she felt a stirring of excitement. There was something about this man. He was like one of the bad boys her mother would never let her date—but, oh, had she wanted to.

Arnie came to her rescue, holding out his own hand. "Colonel Sokolov. I understand you were there when the Red Army took Berlin."

Sokolov released Louise's hand and smiled at Arnie, in the same way he had with Louise. "You have been doing your homework, Colonel Koski." He shook Arnie's hand.

"It's a pleasure to meet one of our allies," Arnie replied.

The brief *Gone-With-the-Wind* moment was gone.

It was the first time Louise heard Arnie talking like a diplomat. Maybe somewhere in those seventeen weeks of Strategic Intelligence School there'd been classes on charm like the ones they'd given the wives.

Abramov broke into the introductions, saying to Louise, "I apologize. My wife is somewhere or I'd introduce. I hope you understand. She is hostess." He chuckled. "Many social emergency to solve." He smiled and turned to Arnie. "Welcome. And best wishes for the new year." He nodded and, gesturing to the party, said, "Please, enjoy yourselves." He left, Sokolov following.

Arnie very quietly said to Louise, "Sokolov is MGB. Ministry of State Security. Secret police. Viktor Abakumov's crowd. It used to be called the NKVD." He gave Louise a meaningful look. "They make the gestapo look like amateurs."

She felt herself tighten, trying to check the uneasiness that came from hearing the names spoken aloud.

A particularly gorgeous auburn-haired woman with exotic, slightly slanted eyes approached them with another tray full of champagne flutes. It wasn't lost on Arnie that the drinks were being served by beautiful Russian women. Alcohol loosened tongues; it was the lifeblood of diplomacy and espionage. The girl brushed her hand on Arnie's sleeve when she took his glass. Then she walked away, balancing the tray on one hand and herself on high heels.

Louise looked up at Arnie impishly, signaling she knew he was watching the girl's backside.

"Also MGB," Arnie said. "They drilled us on honey traps at Strategic Intelligence School. I'm surprised they didn't make us take a vow of chastity in front of the Senate."

"The last place a vow of chastity would be taken," Louise answered with an eye roll. Then she said, "That's four for both of us."

Arnie would have preferred not to hear Louise announce drink number four, even though they'd long ago agreed that he would follow her lead when it came to drinks at any party. He was feeling uncomfortable, and drinking helped.

Arnie had been in uniform since he'd entered West Point, the summer of 1932, but now, because his dress uniform hadn't yet arrived, he was in a rented tuxedo. Unlike civilians, career military people wear their resumés on their shoulders and chests. Any career military person would have seen from Arnie's ribbons that he'd been in combat and had fought courageously, as attested by a Silver Star and a Purple Heart. The silver oak leaves of a lieutenant colonel on his shoulder would have immediately placed him—and Louise—in the appropriate place in the social pecking order.

The Russian military men were all in uniform. Arnie had been told they eschewed civilian tuxedos as symbols of class decadence. The irony wasn't lost on him, however, that wearing uniforms only made fine gradations of class totally and easily readable, as well as telegraphing who was more powerful. Almost all the military men working for Western embassies wore civilian clothes. No one would know if Arnie was a colonel or a decorated combat veteran—or even a civilian. Without any of the props, he realized he would have to establish himself in the eyes of others by talking about himself. He felt awkward doing that. In addition to his stereotypical Finnish introversion, he'd been told all his life not to brag. A fine standard in a culture where everyone knew if you had what it took to be a good logger or fisherman. Courage and skill were exhibited openly. Not so at cocktail parties.

Arnie, however, knew tooting one's own horn, as his mother used to call it, was important, and not just here in Helsinki. He also knew he didn't have the social skills—skills Louise seemed born with—to do that subtly. He looked at her fondly. It was another of the many reasons he'd married her—along with knowing she had his back with his other weak points. "You're right," he said. He held his glass up in a partial salute, drained it, and put it down firmly on a nearby table.

*   *   *

Arnie and Louise watched the crowd with forced smiles.

"I hate this," Arnie said, not breaking his smile.

"I never really liked it either, even though in college I did this all the time."

"But you were good at it."

"Sure. In Oklahoma. But I knew what I was doing. Everyone else was from Oklahoma, too."

"At least you got some training. Socializing wasn't in the West Point curriculum."

"You should have been a Delta Gamma."

"You wouldn't let me in."

Louise laughed, then looking around, said, almost to herself, "Arnie, look at that couple over there, the Russian uniform. They're about our age."

Arnie looked at the woman first. She was striking—tall and elegantly thin with long lustrous black hair—and she carried herself like a dancer, fitting one of the two stereotypes with which most Americans viewed Russian women: they were either hardened road workers in shapeless dresses and scarves, or they danced at the Bolshoi. She had almond-colored eyes like creamed coffee.

Arnie shifted his gaze to the man he presumed was her husband. Red Army. A podpolkovnik, the equivalent of a lieutenant colonel, his equal. Lots of medals, including the big one, Hero of the Soviet Union, their Medal of Honor. If typical, the man had been at war continuously for seven years. He looked at the man's face and took in a short breath.

"What?" Louise asked. "She's not *that* gorgeous."

"No," Arnie replied. He pulled her a little closer. "I know that man."

"You what? How?"

"I'm trying to remember."

Then it all came back.

*   *   *

May 8, 1945, just outside of Linz, Austria. Arnie's Seventy-First Infantry Division had just reached the Enns River. Arnie had been driving a jeep, his M2 carbine on the passenger seat, Sergeant McCormick in the back with a Browning Automatic Rifle. They'd been looking for a way to cross the Enns. They'd also been looking for the first signs of their Soviet allies. Linking up with the Russians would be proof that the Germans were now surrounded, with total surrender or annihilation their only choice.

McCormick shouted, pointing across the river. Soldiers, perhaps an infantry company in size. At first there'd been the fear, scrambling to get the jeep between them and the soldiers across the river, the quick calculations, coming so fast it hardly seemed like calculating. Chambering rounds. Bobbing up for a quick look and back down. Bobbing up again.

The soldiers on the other side of the river were standing still, looking at them, not throwing themselves on the ground, scrambling for firing positions. Then he and Mack looked at each other, both with mouths slightly open. They rose slowly. They were looking across the river at the famed Red Army.

He remembered their boots, no laces, straight up above the calves, trousers tucked in, belted, quilted overcoats. Oddly, to him, the soldiers had a curious lack of steel helmets. Most were wearing light wool garrison caps, the kind that could be folded flat when not in use, but about a third were still in their winter caps of fur with the earflaps tied together above the crown.

A man in a greatcoat stood up on the passenger side seat of a Lend-Lease American jeep and raised a Shpagin burp gun above his head, easily identified by the round magazine that made it look like an American Tommy gun. As with American combat troops, officers looked identical to everyone else, but he could tell by the assumed authority that this man was the group's leader.

Arnie came out from behind the jeep, his carbine raised above his head. Then the man with the Shpagin opened fire into the air. Arnie ducked and McCormick hit the ground, but the Russian soldiers began shouting and cheering, pounding each other on the back, some also firing rounds into the air, many waving their arms.

The man who'd fired the Shpagin was gesturing downstream, spreading one arm wide and then back to join the other forearm. Arnie pumped his carbine up and down to acknowledge he understood.

"Mack, I think there's a bridge."

Arnie always remembered that moment as the moment he'd declared personal victory over Germany. He also remembered it as the last day of good feelings between the soldiers of the East and the West. Now, the Red Army controlled Eastern Europe from the Adriatic to the Baltic, and it didn't look to Arnie like they would be leaving anytime soon—not without a fight.

Arnie was also remembering the swollen bodies and dead horses, the bottom half of a corpse, trailing intestines, all slowly turning as they floated down the river.

Louise saw that Arnie had that *look*, the one where she knew he was seeing images that he wasn't talking about. She elbowed him gently. "Talk," she said.

She watched his eyes come from gazing far away to look at her, once again present with her. "They were ski troops," he said. "Like the Tenth Mountain. Heading for the Austrian and German Alps. We beat them to it."

"I met him on the Enns," Arnie continued, bringing her back to the present. "After the Tenth crossed the Po in Italy, I was transferred to the staff of the Seventy-First because they were heading into the Alps. I was trying to find some intact bridges. I remember thinking, They look just like us. Kids. But with bad teeth and knee boots without laces." He smiled. "And they smelled."

"As if you didn't," Louise said.

"No. Truly. You have no idea. You could smell them across the river."

"Oh, Arnie."

It annoyed Arnie when Louise did the "Oh, Arnie" comeback. It felt to him as if she thought he were exaggerating or being funny. Louise had no concept of what he was trying to communicate, nor could she, nor could anyone who hadn't seen combat. That left him feeling isolated.

It would never be OK to tell Louise about the memories of that day. Every night those images turned in his mind before falling into restless sleep. During sleep, however, the dreams were always of Italy, floundering without his skis through snow mixed with blood like macabre rust-red shaved ice of snow cones. Then the avalanche would come thundering down on him, and Louise would wake him up to stop his screaming.

He watched the Russian officer say something to his wife, a look of astonishment on his face, and then he was holding his arms open, pointing at a wristwatch, and rushing toward Arnie shouting, "Tovarishch! Tovarishch!" Comrade. Comrade.

Podpolkovnik Mikhail Bobrov, military attaché to the Soviet legation in Helsinki, hadn't initially recognized the tall American standing across the room from him because he was in a civilian tuxedo. When he'd last seen the man, he'd been in US Army battle dress.

Upon recognizing Koski, Mikhail was filled with joy, remembering, almost to the point of feeling it all again, the incredible relief that the single vehicle across the river from them was American and not German. For years there had been talk of the Americans opening a second front in Europe, but for years they had done nothing, taking their time in North Africa, then Sicily, then Italy, all the while leaving the Russians to fight around 80 percent of the German army and take the brunt of the casualties. That bitterness had vanished with the elation of finally linking with the Americans. German surrender had to be imminent. He'd let loose firing nearly half a magazine into the air. His men started doing the same, all whooping with joy.

He'd signaled to the two American soldiers about the bridge they'd found intact, just downstream of where they were. He remembered paralleling the two men, he in his American jeep and they in theirs. When they reached the bridge, he pawed through his gear in the back of the jeep and brought out the brandy he'd been saving for months to celebrate victory. He hadn't expected to share it with Americans, but how could he refuse them? They were comrades in arms.

He'd watched the American officer talking on a radio, its antennae waving, thinking to himself the man must be at least a regimental commander. He'd been surprised when he found out that he was only a major on a reconnaissance mission. It seemed the American army had more radios than God himself. And jeeps. And trucks. Did these soldiers not walk?

He'd sent his driver and jeep back to find his division commander and report the good news.

As more Americans arrived at the bridge, they mingled with his own men, opening small cardboard boxes filled with an inconceivable variety of canned food. And American cigarettes! Every box! His men were laughing, lighting up, some two at a time.

Half an hour later, the brandy was gone. He remembered singing "Katyusha," with Koski trying to join in, obviously not knowing the words. Then Koski was singing something about Stalin wasn't Stalin, which made no sense, because how could Stalin not be Stalin? But they both hit their stride with the one about not sitting under an apple tree. He remembered being happily drunk in the back of Koski's jeep, when another jeep pulled up. Its passenger had two stars on his battle helmet.

However, unlike a Russian general, he seemed to be laughing while he was clearly issuing an order. Koski had stood, wavering, making a sloppy salute as the general drove off. Officers and sergeants began shouting, the soldiers all scrambling into various vehicles. Koski nodded at him to get off the jeep. Then, Koski took off his wristwatch and handed it to him like he was bestowing a medal. Without another word, Koski climbed into the jeep with the other soldier and drove away.

Mikhail was waving Koski's watch above his head as he charged across the room.

Louise knew that Arnie hadn't told her everything about his encounter with the big and obviously friendly Russian coming at them holding one arm up and pointing at what looked like a wristwatch. The Russian officer holding Arnie by the shoulders and kissing him on his cheeks, which she knew was embarrassing the hell out of Arnie. She smiled, thinking about how she would kid him about doing his diplomatic duty for the country later that night when *she* was kissing him on his lips.

The elegant Russian woman was slowly walking toward her. Louise struggled with a moment of panic. Did Russian women shake hands? Was she expected to air-kiss her? The briefings hadn't covered that.

She put on her best Delta Gamma smile and the woman smiled back briefly, clearly more reserved than her husband. Holding her drink in her right hand so it would at least make sense she couldn't shake hands if she was supposed to, she said, "Nimeni on Louise Koski," drawing on Beginning Finnish, Lesson One: My name is Louise Koski. She nodded at the two men who were excitedly talking in fluent Finnish. "Mieheni nimi on everstiluutnantti Koski." That had been in Lesson Three: My husband's name is Lieutenant Colonel Koski.

The woman wore an elegant black dress that came nearly to the floor, showing only a glimpse of somewhat clunky high heels. The dress had a white lace collar at the throat that looked to Louise like it was pinned there as an accessory and not part of the dress.

"Yes, my husband also," the woman replied in somewhat easier Finnish, smiling at the two men. "Podpolkovnik Bobrov. Mikhail," she added. She looked back at Louise. "My name Natalya Bobrova." She again smiled briefly, then resumed an interested look but with no smile. "My Finnish not so good. Can read OK, but not talk. My English . . . no English." She stopped there, not even blinking. How could someone so gorgeous be so, so unsmiling? Clearly not Dee-Gee material.

"My Russian not at all," Louise answered in English.

The Russian woman simply looked at her, bringing on an uneasy feeling for Louise. They had been warned to be careful when talking in public, even with people from allied countries like England and France, and it was well-known that the wartime alliance with the Soviet Union was deteriorating, particularly around governing Germany. Even though officially an ally, this woman could be cozying up, seeking information. Maybe she was a spy just posing to be married to the Russian officer. Louise inwardly chided herself for spinning fantasies and forged ahead.

"They meet . . . Enns River in Austria," Louise said in Finnish, unsure she had the tense right. The woman smiled and nodded, but Louise wasn't sure she'd understood her.

Always draw the other person out: her mother's first rule of good conversation. "Other languages?" Louise asked. The woman blinked slowly. Louise took a stab. "Français?" It had been the language of Russian aristocracy before the revolution.

The woman lit up.

Feeling encouraged by Louise, Natalya Bobrova could hardly hold back the rush of French, knowing here was someone with whom she could talk about a passion she'd suppressed for far too long: French literature.

She knew she spoke French with a Russian accent, but she could hold her own with this woman who spoke it with an American accent and looked like some girl in the Coca-Cola ads she'd seen in American magazines in the Soviet legation library.

She quickly sized up Louise. Unstylish forty-millimeter heels. Seams straight. No earrings. Most of the American women she'd met stupidly wore screw-on earrings that they were constantly taking off and on because their ears hurt. It baffled her. Her ears had been pierced since childhood. The woman's dress fit well but was untailored. That seemed odd. She'd assumed that any American woman with diplomatic status would be from the capitalist class and rich enough to have her clothes tailored. Since the dress wasn't tailored, however, she now wondered if the pearls were fake. Not short but not tall. Well maintained. Nails polished. Probably had never worked a day in her life. Still, there was something engaging—*wholesome*—about her.

After a few minutes of conversation Natalya learned that this woman, Louise, had studied French literature at someplace in the middle of America called the University of Oklahoma—openly. She felt a little touch of envy. Natalya's passion for French literature had started with reading French books on her mother's bookshelf before— She stopped herself. After leaving the orphanage, she'd read French literature in secret. If the NKVD had found out, she would have been suspected of being "under foreign influence." The People needed economists. That is what the People paid for, not self-indulgent and polluting foreign studies. That could send her to the gulag—or worse. She was aware of the irony that the first time she'd been able to talk openly about French literature was in a foreign country with an American.

Louise hadn't talked about French literature since college. She glanced away from the Russian woman to see Arnie raising a shot glass of vodka and loudly toasting the Red Army. Clearly the four-drink limit had been forgotten. She wanted to slow him down but knew that would embarrass him. Besides, Arnie was clearly enjoying himself, so why be a wet hen about the drinking.

The two men tossed back their drinks. Immediately one of the waitresses brought them two more.

Louise sighed and gave Natalya a quick smile.

Natalya smiled back. "There will be no stopping them," Natalya said quietly. "He forgets the war by celebrating the comradeship."

"They'll pay tomorrow," Louise said.

"So will we," Natalya answered.

They both laughed, beginning to bond over this all-too-common experience of army wives dealing with bringing their husbands home from war.

They both turned back to look at their husbands when they heard Bobrov shout in English, "To the American Tenth Mountain Division! The second-best ski troops in the world!" Bobrov threw his head back, laughing, holding his glass up for Arnie to touch.

Arnie slowly lowered his own glass, still smiling. Louise knew that smile. It did not indicate happiness.

She quickly translated for Natalya and both looked at each other, both hoping the insult would pass.

"Mikhail fought with our ski troops," Natalya said in French, calling them *chasseurs alpins*, "against the Finnish Fascists in 1939. Then against the German Fascists. He's very proud of them."

Louise couldn't help a slight movement on her face, startled at hearing this woman call Finns Fascists. She instantly regretted her visible reaction. She'd always been terrible at poker. She reminded herself that she had no idea who this Russian woman really was or what her real job was. She did know that she'd already provided the woman with a tell, which she'd clearly read, because she answered Louise's unspoken question. "The Finns stubbornly refused to allow us to provide for our own safety against the Nazis," Natalya said stiffly. "When, they shelled Mainila in November of 1939, we had no choice but to defend ourselves. We, against our own interests, stopped ourselves from taking the whole country. The result of that decision was that they joined the Nazis and invaded us again in 1941."

Louise swallowed her indignation. Telling this woman that the shelling of Mainila was suspected to have been an NKVD operation— and what she thought of the Soviet Union savaging a country one-sixtieth its size—would not help Arnie's cause. There were parts of being a diplomat's wife that were starting to annoy her—like being diplomatic.

Louise regained control, suppressing her reaction to the Russian woman's misunderstanding, or perhaps deliberate distortion of history. "I didn't mean to pass judgment," she said, repressing her desire to counter a lie—and even a little confused about when or even if she should. "It's just that my husband is a Finn." Louise smiled. "We all support our husbands."

Both women turned from each other to again look at Arnie and Mikhail, wanting equally to overcome the sudden tension. The two men seemed to be arguing about something, intensely, but without anger.

"Mikhail said fighting the Finns was hell," Natalya said softly. "Our soldiers were without experienced leaders, food, or winter uniforms."

"I'm sorry. The war was hard on everyone."

"Yes."

Louise tried to think of something neutral to say. "Where did you spend the war when your husband was away?"

Natalya struggled to control her anger, forcing a smile. Was this walking Coca-Cola ad really that naïve, like most Americans? All her rage against the rich American capitalists who'd escaped the horrors of the war came boiling up. She could not help herself. Very slowly she said, "Leningrad."

"Oh." The woman at least had the decency to blush.

"We ate rats." Natalya paused. "Some of us ate each other."

She knew she was now unnecessarily piling on, but it felt so good. It was clear that the American woman was embarrassed. There was half a minute of uncomfortable silence.

Coca-Cola put on a smile and, hesitating only a moment, deftly changed the subject, asking, "Do you have children?" Natalya had to hand it to this woman. This was soldiering on in a vastly different context. But maybe the apparent naïveté was a cover and she was an American agent? She fought down the familiar feeling of not knowing if the person you were talking to was speaking the truth. She now wanted desperately to rescue the struggling conversation that, she had to admit, she'd done her best to make difficult. She wanted someone she could talk to, someone she could trust. She wanted a friend.

"Two," Natalya answered her. "Alina, just three, and Grisha, one and a half."

"Alina, that's a pretty name. And is Grisha a boy or a girl?"

"A boy." Where *was* this Oklahoma place?

"Are they here with you?"

"Yes. I work for the economic section at the temporary legation building on Kalliolinnantie. The legation gives us a young nyanya to look after them," she added.

"Our legation doesn't provide childcare. You're lucky."

"Well," Natalya said, her head cocking sideways as if considering what Louise just said. "I suppose you could say we are lucky." She left it at that. She was sure that the "nyanya," Fanya, worked for the MGB.

Natalya tried to have a good attitude about sharing their flat with Fanya. She knew that the MGB was there to protect the People from internal enemies. Capitalism could not be eradicated without eradicating all counterrevolutionaries who secretly supported it. That's why the People needed an organization like the MGB. So, perhaps some of the men who ran the MGB were overly enthusiastic doing their job, but you wouldn't want a watchdog that didn't scare people, would you? At least, that's what everyone said. Fanya was just a part of how things were.

Natalya, of course, would never express any of these thoughts aloud, not even to Mikhail. Saying nothing is how one survived—how one got good postings outside of Russia.

Louise had, of course, heard of the siege of Leningrad. She knew there had been starvation. But starvation had been an abstract word—until now. She knew the Europeans had it worse in the war. She wasn't naïve. But without American aid they'd all be Nazis now. It seemed to her that there should be at least a little gratitude.

She realized that Natalya had just asked *her* the children question. She recovered. "No, not yet." Was this woman only trying to appear to want to make friends so she could pump her later? She suddenly felt a weary loneliness.

"Will you be working at the legation, then?" Natalya asked, changing the subject quickly.

"No." Louise gave a self-deprecating smile. "Don't speak Finnish. Maybe if we were in Paris. Don't I wish."

"Me, too," Natalya said, showing a pensive mournfulness, which she quickly covered.

Louise was about to ask if Natalya had ever been to Paris but thought better of it, instead saying, "I've never been to Paris."

Natalya smiled. "Nor I." She paused and then said with a bit of a smile, "So, you and I have never been to Paris together."

Louise laughed at the deliberate nonsensical juxtaposition, relaxing with Natalya a little. "It's nice to have *something* in common." A brief smile flickered across Natalya's face. "I've been mostly house hunting," Louise plunged on. "And going to parties." She gestured at the crowd.

"It is part of the job," Natalya said kindly.

"Yes," Louise answered. "Yes, it is. So is finding housing."

"You're having trouble?"

"Quite frankly, yes."

"I guess we are lucky. Our legation supplies housing for us. No searching."

"I wish ours did," Louise replied.

That hung in the air. Clearly Natalya had nothing more to say on the subject. To fill the space, Louise went on. "Once I find housing, I thought I might help out a distant relation of Arnie's who runs an orphanage. There are a lot of orphans. I see them walking on the streets roped together in single file being led to God-knows-where."

"We know about orphans," Natalya said.

Louise caught the sadness in Natalya's voice but couldn't help thinking, *It was you Russians who created all the orphans in Helsinki.* This time the dark thought didn't cause a flicker. She was learning rapidly. "I thought, maybe I could lend a hand. I'm good with organizations." Then she added quickly, "And I love kids." She waited, expecting the then-why-don't-you-have-any question. Louise was thankful Natalya didn't ask it.

This was because, even if Natalya had thought that she would ask the question, she was stopped by the room going quiet.

Louise followed the gaze of those around her to three men entering the large room from an interior open door. Two of the men, big and well-built, flanked the third, a man in his midforties with a receding hairline, wearing rimless pince-nez glasses. He wore the uniform of a marshall of the Soviet Union. But for the military uniform, the man looked to Louise like a college professor or librarian. She glanced at Natalya, who had visibly stiffened. Natalya's eyes were darting ever so slightly, as if looking for somewhere to escape. It hit Louise that they were eyes that had seen much sorrow and not just in Leningrad.

The man raised his hand, in a gesture both of hello and carry on. The buzz in the room slowly restarted. Louise watched Aleksandr Abramov and his wife scurry to meet the man from the far side of the room, followed in a bit statelier manner by Sokolov.

"Who's that?" Louise asked Natalya.

"Lavrentiy Beria," Natalya said quietly. "Head of the MGB."

"Oh." Louise had heard the name.

One of the waitresses was hurrying over to the three men with drinks. They took them. Beria raised his in a greeting to the young woman, smiling. She smiled back a little awkwardly and, almost bowing, quickly backed away. Beria turned to one of the flanking men, said something, and they both laughed. Then, Beria engaged in conversation with Abramov and Sokolov, while Abramov's wife looked on a bit nervously and with a smile that showed no pleasure.

Louise looked to Arnie for a clue. He caught her eye and cocked his head just slightly, shaking it very discretely.

Beria raised his glass again, indicating that the conversation with Abramov was over. He slowly made his way through the crowd, pausing to make a comment to an acquaintance or two. The two bodyguards followed. They were nearing Louise and Natalya, and Natalya moved in much closer to Louise. She started talking animatedly about her love of music in French, her back turned to the small group making its way slowly through the crowd. Louise, facing the group, felt like Beria just briefly sized her up and then moved on to look at others, paying most attention to the young waitresses. The waitresses were clearly avoiding looking at Beria.

Louise was trying to stay in the conversation with Natalya but all the while couldn't help watching Beria's progress through the crowd. She watched him make a slight nod in the direction of the waitress who had initially served them their drinks and, smiling, went to say farewell to Abramov and his wife. He left the room without the bodyguards. The conversation level rose almost instantly.

The two bodyguards were quietly talking with the original waitress. She had a slight but frozen smile on her face. The man escorted her toward a table while whispering something to her. She set down her tray.

Louise watched her being walked from the room between the two large men, her entire body awkwardly stiff. They were then gone.

Louise looked across the room at Arnie again. The Russian officer's face was very close to Arnie's, his drink perilously close to spilling. Louise glanced at Natalya, who was also watching the two men. They both simultaneously averted their gaze and their eyes met. Louise felt that there was someone inside of Natalya looking at her through Natalya's eyes. She wanted the woman inside herself to get to know the woman inside Natalya, but she also knew that it would take considerable time to penetrate beneath their respective roles as wives of intelligence officers. She wondered how it was that a few men in Washington and Moscow could create a world where two women at a party in Helsinki couldn't talk openly to each other.

Arnie and Mikhail had no difficulty talking openly. Up until the crack about the Tenth Mountain being the second-best ski troops in the world, both had felt good remembering their meeting on the Enns.

Arnie, rather clumsily, put his left hand on Mikhail's right, which held the glass.

"I'll not toast to *that*, you Russian son of a bitch," Arnie said in Finnish. He knew that they were playing the good-natured game played by soldiers the world over: putting each other and their units down.

Mikhail instantly raised his glass and shouted, "I'll drink to *that*." He threw down another drink and Arnie followed.

Mikhail immediately shouted something in Russian to one of the waitresses peregrinating the room and within seconds he and Arnie again had full glasses.

"We are, you know," Mikhail said, "the best." He was holding his glass just in front of his chest.

"No, yarntnt," Arnie replied. He shook his head at his slurred speech. "Are not," he repeated distinctly.

The two men looked at each other, professional soldiers sharing mutual respect. They both also knew that a challenge had somehow been issued and challenges among warriors could not be allowed to pass.

"If we were younger, we'd get into a fight over it," Arnie said.

"If we were younger, we wouldn't be here insulting each other."

"I'm not too old to fight, just too old to want to," Arnie said, suddenly serious.

"And I," Mikhail said equally quietly. "Six years fighting the Finns and the Germans is enough for me."

"I would never want to fight you," Arnie said, his Finnish ever so slightly slurred.

"Nor I you," Mikhail repeated.

The two of them stood very close together—in the Russian way, not the American—swaying slightly from the alcohol. Neither spoke. The challenge had been issued, but neither knew how to deal with it.

"Too bad we couldn't just set up a race. We'd beat the pants off you," Arnie said.

Mikhail slowly started to smile. He leaned into Arnie. "But we *can* set up a race."

His bad breath made Arnie pull back slightly. He recovered quickly and leaned back in himself. *Diplomacy in the trenches*, he thought.

Arnie's eyes were drawn to the dark window behind Mikhail. Out there—out there in the dark and in the cold—was where the challenge would be taken up. And settled. He felt a slow awakening of his leg muscles, the familiar feel of adrenaline building before a race.

"You mean the two of us."

"Yes, Comrade. The two of us."

"The loser has to tell the winner that his troops are the best in the world."

"Yes, Comrade. That is what you'll have to do."

Arnie studied Mikhail for a moment. "Ten kilometers. You'll be so far back when I finish, we'll have to send out a search party."

"Hah! You call ten kilometers a race in America? One hundred kilometers."

"What, a *day race*? Fuck that. *Five* hundred kilometers."

Mikhail and Arnie stood there, both a bit blindsided by the escalation.

"You're serious," Mikhail said.

"Yes."

"It would take around ten days."

"Yes."

"My friend," Mikhail said. "I have been in the forests of Northern Finland. In the winter," he added. "The days are cold. The nights are brutal."

"I imagine they are."

"I no longer have a little toe because of frostbite."

"Are you trying to scare me?"

Mikhail smiled, then grew serious. "We would be skiing alone. If one gets into trouble, the other most likely won't know."

Arnie looked over Mikhail's head to the dark window and the beckoning space beyond it. He felt the old excitement and fear.

"Ultimate things," Arnie said softly.

"Yes," Mikhail answered.

The two were silent.

"*Winning* is about the honor of our units," Arnie said. "*Doing it* is about—" He stopped himself. "Don't you miss it? The feeling that what you're doing, right now, really matters?"

"I do miss it," Mikhail said. He looked down at his glass, then back to Arnie. "But it's also about . . . the actual challenge . . . whether we can do it . . . whether we still have"—he was searching for the right word—"the heart."

"Heart," Arnie agreed.

Mikhail raised his glass solemnly in front of Arnie's face. "Five hundred kilometers it is, my friend."

"You're on," Arnie replied.

"To ultimate things," Mikhail said and touched his glass to Arnie's.

"And heart," Arnie replied.

They both tossed down the liquor. Then Mikhail hurled his glass against the wall. Stunned for just a moment, Arnie threw his.

The room had gone silent. Louise and Natalya looked at their husbands, their mouths open.

"What was *that* about?" Louise asked.

"Some sort of wager."

"God. Couldn't they just shake hands?"

"Not Mikhail." Natalya looked at her husband fondly, then turned back to Louise smiling. "Not my Misha."

Louise's attention turned to Natalya's husband, who must have realized that the party might have interpreted the gesture wrongly. He started shouting in Russian, "Comrade, comrade! A toast to our American

allies," looking around and gesturing for one of the waitresses to bring
them another drink.

One of the women plying drinks came up to the two men, clearly
suppressing her own laughter, holding out a silver tray with two more
glasses on it. The buzz in the room slowly resumed.

The two men were now leaning into each other, one hand holding a
vodka shot glass, the other on the other man's shoulder. They were clearly
engaged in some sort of mutual project, one bringing something up, the
other either nodding or shaking his head and countering with something
else. They were also clearly drunk. Just what Louise had feared.

Suddenly, it seemed to her that the room had collapsed to an island
in the sea of alcohol, chatter, and canapés, just the four of them, she
and Natalya and their husbands. She intuited that Natalya felt this as
she did. The two men stood upright. They shook hands solidly, but it
didn't seem like the usual pleased-to-meet-you and goodbye at a party.
Although Arnie and she had been separated for nearly half of their marriage, she was keenly tuned in to his body language. The two held up
their shot glasses and Arnie proposed another toast of some kind and
Natalya's husband repeated it. They threw back another shot. Louise
looked at Natalya. Natalya looked back with her striking almond eyes.
Louise had a vague yet unsettling premonition that with that handshake
and toast, she and this woman before her had been joined in some sort
of shared fate, like lone passengers on a bus with an invisible driver,
hurtling through darkness.

Wednesday, January 1, 1947, 2:00 a.m.
Helsinki Hotel

Louise had held back questioning Arnie until they were alone and walking back to their hotel. Arnie was sobering with the cold.

"What's the story on this Beria guy?" Louise asked. She had her arm wrapped around Arnie's. "Natalya Bobrova was scared when he cruised the room."

"Scared?"

"I mean it, Arnie. Scared."

Arnie took in a deep breath. "She should be." Nothing more was coming.

Louise finally said, "Seriously. Tell me."

"OK," Arnie said. He began as if reciting from some briefing. "Lavrentiy Pavlovich Beria was Stalin's chief of secret police during the war. We believe he was the one who was responsible for the Katyn Forest Massacre. That was around twenty-two thousand Polish military officers and intelligentsia that he and Stalin feared would cause them trouble after the war." He hmphed. "They blamed it on the Germans, and we believed them."

He tightened his coat to his chest, pulling her closer to him.

Arnie continued. "He was also responsible for solving the question of certain ethnic groups that Stalin felt were not compatible with his vision of the Soviet Union. He accused them of collaboration with the Germans, calling them Nazis: Chechens, Crimean Tatars, Pontic Greeks, the Volga Germans, people like that."

"Solving the question?"

"Yeah. He moved them to Siberia and mostly starved them to death. Emptied the Crimea so Stalin could repopulate it with ethnic Russians."

They were silent for several blocks. Then Louise said, "But Natalya's reaction. I mean . . . Yes, that's a bad man, but she seemed, I mean really scared."

"Like I said, she should be. We were briefed on Beria at Strategic Intelligence School. Basically, he's a sexual sadist. He likes teenagers but seems happy with any beautiful woman. Has them delivered. Explains how they and their families will suffer if they refuse. Rapes them. He sometimes plays what he calls the flower game."

"The *flower* game?"

"Has six or seven delivered, strips them naked except for their shoes." He paused. "Anyway, shoes on, they are put in a circle on their knees and elbows, their heads touching. Like a big flower petal. He walks around the circle until he pulls one out by her legs."

"Oh, my God. The cocktail waitress."

"Yeah." He let that hang. "We're told he also offers them flowers afterward, which if they accept, means it was consensual."

"Oh, Arnie." The horror of it hit her like a wave. She felt some combination of nausea and fear moving through her body. They walked on silently—for a long time.

"What if they refuse?" Louise asked.

"Very few would have the courage to refuse Beria." Arnie was momentarily silent. Then, sounding puzzled, he said, "We've been told that he just sends them home in a taxi."

She couldn't stop dwelling on the images of both Natalya and the young waitress, so clearly frightened, and now she understood why. To try and distract herself she asked, "What did they say about Sokolov?"

"Like most of these guys, we don't know much about what they did before the war, but we do know he's a man on the rise. We didn't even have a photograph. This is the first time I've seen his face."

"What does it mean, he's responsible for security?"

"It most certainly doesn't mean guarding the legation from thieves."

Louise gave him an I'm-not-that-naïve look.

"He made a name for himself in the Red Army uncovering traitors and malingerers," Arnie went on. "That's what the NKVD called them. Most of them were tortured and then shot."

Louise took that in. Then she said, "But the Red Army isn't here. I mean, here in Helsinki."

"No. We think this posting to Helsinki is a pretty big promotion for Sokolov. His career during the war was nothing special for the NKVD. They all tortured and executed people. Where he made his career was dismantling German industrial plants and sending them east. He used German prisoners of war as slave labor and didn't mind how many died doing the job." He was quiet for a moment. "Imagine being forced to dismantle your own country." Quietly he added, "That's real defeat."

"Maybe they deserved it," she said.

"Not all deserved it."

She took in the rebuke. "Sorry."

"It's OK. I hated them, too. But with the Soviets now becoming our enemy, the Germans will become allies. They weren't all Nazis."

"Just enough of them."

"That's the point. Dictatorships need just a few ardent supporters. Democracies need everyone. That's harder to do."

Neither said anything for a while.

"And now the Soviets have forced the Finns into making 'reparation payments' for a war the Soviets started. In hard currency and dismantled industrial plant that's being shipped to Russia. I'd guess the latter is why he's here."

"Well, better than shooting kids too frightened to fight."

"If only."

Louise gave him a puzzled look.

"It's true that diplomatic staff don't get shot like Russian soldiers. They just get sent to Lubyanka prison in Moscow where they're tortured until they confess to the crime they're charged with. Then they are shot." He made a wry smile. "Punishing an innocent man is as effective as punishing a guilty one when the goal is scaring people to keep them in line." His eyes narrowed. "And I'd guess Sokolov has a quota for uncovering traitors."

Back in their hotel room, Arnie wanted to immediately go to sleep. Louise managed to get Arnie's tuxedo coat and shoes off before he collapsed backward on their bed. "Oh, no, you don't," Louise said, hiking her dress up. She wriggled her way to an upright position, legs on both sides of him, straining the link between the open-bottom girdle and her stockings. "No sleep until you tell me what you and Colonel Bobrov were talking about."

"Let me *sleeeep*," Arnie begged.

Louise leaned over, her face inches from his. "Talk. I'm serious."

"OK. God." Arnie looked up at her and she sat upright again. "Take off my tie," he said.

She leaned in again. "Not until you talk."

"Aaargh. OK."

Smiling, she began to undo his tie.

"I told you we met on the Enns," Arnie said.

She nodded, working on the unfamiliar bow tie knot.

"He had a very nice brandy. Somehow a bottle of vodka showed up. We celebrated."

"What does that mean?"

"We got drunk." He paused. "Remember I told you I lost my watch?"
She pulled his tie loose and tossed it on the floor.

"Well, I mean he supplied the liquor, so I gave him my watch."

Louise could see his mind going back to the Enns.

She knew that look Arnie had whenever he mentioned even some-thing trivial about combat. The nightmares were worse. She never knew what to do, other than to whisper he was OK and try to soothe him back to sleep. In the morning, she'd strip and wash the sheets, wet from his sweat. She'd asked Arnie several times about his dreams, but he'd replied with, "It was just a nightmare." Sometimes he'd look at her, his eyes darting, and simply turn away. It stabbed her heart at the same time it made her want to scream at him for shutting her out.

She was afraid to ask friends about the nightmares and sweating, fearing Arnie was the only one and he'd look bad. It made her feel iso-lated and alone, which was made worse knowing that the walls of her isolation were self-constructed out of social fear. One time Marge Leflar joked about her husband thrashing in his sleep. She woke him up only to be chewed out because he was about to make a touchdown. They had all laughed. Louise wondered if maybe the touchdown story wasn't true. Maybe Marge had just floated it out there to see if anyone would respond to the clue. No one did, so Marge had shut up—like everyone else.

"Focus," she said, trying to keep him present—and awake.

Arnie became present. "In combat, you have something. It's like a sixth sense. Maybe it's because your life is at stake. The kids could tell whether a new officer was good or bad in ten seconds. So could I. He's a good one."

"I did like his wife. If that's what she really is." She started on his shirt buttons.

Arnie reached up to pull her down. Taking him by both wrists she gently unwound his arms, and he lay on his back. She finished unbuttoning his shirt and started pulling the sleeves off his arms. She rolled him one way and then the other and got the shirt off. Arnie was reviving fast and sat up, pulling off his undershirt.

She gently put her hand on his now-bare chest.

"Not until you tell me what you and that Russian were up to."

Arnie sighed and flopped back down. "We decided to have a ski race."

"A ski race? Where? Why, for crying out loud?"

Arnie didn't answer. This wasn't the first time he'd done something that she couldn't understand and he couldn't explain. She, however, had become good at breaking through his Finnish reticence to talk about anything interior.

"It was that crack about the Tenth Mountain being the second-best ski troops, wasn't it?"

Arnie didn't move or say anything. Then he slowly nodded.

"Pride," she said but not negatively.

He again nodded.

She waited.

"Sometimes, it's all you have to go on," he said quietly. "When the food's gone, the ammunition is low, and no one has slept in days, it's what's at the bottom of the barrel. It's the fumes in the empty gas tank."

"I get that." She rolled off him and looked up at the ceiling. Many of her women friends would make fun of men and their pride. Not her army-wife friends. They knew it was often the only thing that got their husbands back home.

Louise remembered kissing Arnie goodbye when he left Tacoma for Camp Hale, Colorado, to join the newly formed Eighty-Seventh Mountain Infantry Regiment, which grew to become the Tenth Mountain

Division. Louise had chosen to stay at Fort Lewis. Camp Hale was above nine thousand feet in the Colorado Rockies, with the nearest housing in Leadville, a mining town of dubious reputation.

Arnie had been training to fight in the Aleutians and had been bitterly disappointed when he got his orders for the Eighty-Seventh. His objections to the transfer had been denied for "needs of the service." Arnie was one of many Scandinavian and Finnish Americans who knew how to ski and survive in severe cold. He'd been taught to ski by his father who'd grown up on skis in Finland, and Arnie had won several national competitions representing the army before the war, both downhill and cross-country.

"There's no slopes for miles," Louise said. "So, cross-country. But where?"

"Arctic Circle to Kuopio. Five hundred kilometers. Three hundred miles. Choose your own route. No roads allowed. No resupply. No following in the other's tracks. First one to reach Kuopio is the winner. Those are the only rules."

She rolled over on her side and leaned on an elbow facing him. What he'd said scared her. She was fully aware of how many ski troopers had died because of avalanches, falls, and hypothermia—not enemy fire. She knew, however, that an army wife didn't go there. "That's crazy. We haven't even found a place to live yet. I have the Finnish vocabulary of a two-year-old. And you and this Russian are going to . . . what? Just ski off into the sunset?"

"We're not going until February. We figure it'll only take around ten days."

"Ten days!"

"As I said, no roads."

And no telephones, she thought. And out of sight of each other. If Arnie got in trouble . . . She stuffed the thought and said, "How are you going to explain this to Hamilton? If he finds out you're up there on some kind of *Boys' Own* adventure, he could do serious damage on a fitness report."

"We've covered that. We'll both say we're scouting ingress and egress routes. Not mention anything about each other."

"Criminy, Arnie." She rolled on her back and looked at the ceiling. "Can't you just call it off?" she asked.

"It's important to me," he said quietly.

She hesitated, worried about the danger, but she knew if she put her foot down, no matter how Arnie reacted, stay or go, it would severely hurt the relationship.

"I don't like it, but I won't stand in your way."

"Thank you. We already shook hands on it."

"I saw that." She wanted to get off the subject. "So did his wife, Natalya."

"Nice name."

"You like a lot more about her than her name, Arnie Koski."

"Alright. Nice body." He raised his head. "Not as nice as yours." Smiling, she touched his nose.

He flopped back. "Can I go to sleep now?"

"No!" Laughing, she stood and undressed with her back to him, aware that he was watching her. She put on her nightgown and turned around, smiling with anticipation.

"Arrgh, Arnie Koski, you're so frustrating." He'd passed out.

Looking at him, she thought, *Just like a sleeping child.* Someday, maybe. A child that looked like him—or her—or both. Yes, both.

She managed to get the blankets over him and then snuggled in next to him. She knew that he'd heard her objections. She also knew that he'd still do the race. Arnie was good—real good. Dangerous and worrisome as it was, the race also excited her. It could be like their own little Olympics, the United States of America versus Russia!

Wednesday, January 1, 1947, 2:00 a.m.
Natalya and Mikhail's Apartment

Mikhail, used to drinking heavily like most Russian men, recovered quickly. Still, Natalya had to help him out of his uniform. It wasn't the first time. She enjoyed it, jerking his clothes in mock severity. He flopped back on their bed, and she jerked his trousers off.

"You and the American?" she asked, reaching behind to unzip her dress. She kicked her shoes off.

Mikhail held up the arm with the wristwatch.

"*He's* the one who gave you the watch?"

Mikhail dropped his arm back down and nodded. "Good comrade," he mumbled.

Natalya stood still, the top of the dress around her hips, showing the lacey bodice of her one good slip. She looked meaningfully at the bedroom wall that separated their bedroom from Fanya's. The legation had put the nyanya in the room adjoining their bedroom. Natalya had found a stethoscope hidden in the girl's clothing. She said a bit louder, "You know you don't mean that. He's a spy, pretending to be your comrade to get into your confidence. The Americans are trying to stop us from securing safety for our borders." She dropped to a whisper, pleading, "Misha." She glanced at the wall again.

Mikhail grunted, with his own glance at the wall, acknowledging her. "I meant during the war," he said at normal volume. "When I met him, the Americans were helping us defeat the Fascists." Now he looked up at the ceiling, rolling his eyes. "But you're right. Now, we must be on our guard. Fascism was a common enemy, but the next enemy of the revolution is capitalism, as it was before the Great Patriotic War."

"It was so clever of you, getting that American drunk to get information," Natalya chimed in.

"He spilled a lot, too. One great American weakness is they don't hold their liquor like men. I'll put it in a report tomorrow."

Natalya was wriggling out of the dress, nodding approval. She put her finger to her lips and walked closer to him. She seductively started removing her slip. Mikhail sat up on his elbows. She'd been raised as a good Russian woman. She knew how to please a man. And that pleased her.

Afterward, both smoking cigarettes in the dark, she turned her head to whisper in his ear. "So, what did you and the American really talk about?"

"We're going to have a race," Mikhail whispered. "He's apparently an exceptionally good skier. One hundred percent Finnish stock. Fought the Fascists in the Italian mountains."

"A race? Why?"

"For fun."

"Fun? What? You want to relive the 1939 Finnish campaign?" Mikhail had told her about Russian boys frozen into awkward shapes and she'd seen the missing little toe on his right foot, amputated for gangrene resulting from frostbite.

"You know that's not true. You know better."

Natalya looked down. "I'm sorry. I know that." Of the many nightmares from which she'd shaken Mikhail awake, a large number were from his first combat experiences with the elite Fifty-Fourth Mountain Rifle Division in the 1939 defense of Leningrad and the vital

Leningrad-Murmansk rail line. "Still," she said, quiet for a moment. "It was that toast of yours to the second-best ski troops, wasn't it?"

"Mmmh."

"He took umbrage, didn't he?"

"Mmmh."

"Mikhail . . ."

"To see who's best. We'll each represent our troops."

"Mikhail."

She kissed him and then mischievously parted his lips with her fingers. "Talk."

"Alright, alright." He pulled her hand from his mouth. "It's to see if I still have it in me."

"Have what in you?"

His voice changed. "Grit."

Natalya then realized this was something her husband had to do. Was going to do, no matter what. She felt just the slightest chill of fear.

"When?"

"In February. We'll start at the Arctic Circle up by Rovaniemi. Five hundred kilometers. No roads allowed. Choose our own course. First one to Kuopio wins."

The fear grew. "Wins? What will you win?"

After a moment he answered, "Self-respect. I get so little of it these days."

She rolled over and stubbed out her cigarette. Leaning in close to his face, she kissed him, stroking his hair and whispering, "I know that you do this job for us. I know you don't like it. I know. And I love you for it." She put her hand on his cheek. "Would it be allowed?"

"We've agreed to talk to no one about it. Just between us. Two soldiers. No one will know. I'll say that I'm going up north to do something like identifying bridges, estimating road carrying capacity, whatever. I'm given a lot of freedom as long as I stay in Finland."

"They always find out."

"*They* won't bother. They hate the cold. It's just the two of us. He's a professional. He understands and he won't say anything."

"What if you lose and they find out? You're a Hero of the Soviet Union. It'll embarrass the Party. *They've* shot people for less."

"It's just a race between two soldiers." He sighed, exhaling smoke. "Can people do nothing without it being political?"

"You know that everything is political."

"Even this?" He was gently moving his hands between her thighs. Her normal reaction would be to murmur softly and open to him. This time she did neither.

Moving on top of her, looking at her face, a bit discomfited, he smiled reassuringly at her. "I won't lose."

Natalya put both hands on his cheeks. "Don't do it."

He shook his head slowly, gently taking her hands from his face, and rolled off her. "It's too late," he said. "We broke glasses and shook on it."

She flopped onto her side and stared into the dark.

Wednesday, January 1, 1947
Helsinki Harbor

The legation was closed for New Year's Day, so Louise and Arnie slept in until sunrise, around nine thirty. Arnie was badly hungover, but Louise managed to get several glasses of water and some aspirin into him. It was too late for the hotel breakfast, so she talked him into walking down by the waterfront to see if they could find some coffee.

Louise immediately felt the cold wind, as she'd felt it every day since they'd arrived. The temperature wasn't much different than at home, around freezing all the time, but the darkness . . . In Oklahoma, skies were clear over half the time even in the dead of winter, and the sun rose when it was supposed to instead of nearly midmorning.

Four- or five-storied old brick buildings, ranging from traditional red to lighter shades of ochre and cream, fronted on a wide street and wharf area that gave the impression of a large open plaza. A huge domed church rose from behind the front buildings, dominating the scene. The whole setting was one of austere utility, the antithesis of what Louise imagined a Mediterranean waterfront would look like.

Everything was closed, so they couldn't even find a cup of tea. Walking in the cold air, however, looking at the small freighters and different varieties of fishing boats, Arnie soon revived.

They wandered close to Kaarina's neighborhood and Louise said, "Why don't we wish Kaarina and Pietari a happy new year?"

When they got to Kaarina's house, however, no one was home.

"She's probably at the orphanage," Arnie said.

"Oh, Arnie, let's go visit her. She's family and we should show an interest."

His nonverbal response wasn't enthusiastic.

"She told me the address," Louise said. "She walks there, so it can't be far."

Arnie grunted.

"She seemed very keen to have us visit."

Arnie sighed. He nodded his head sideways as in "you lead the way."

After only a couple of false turns in some narrow backstreets, they came upon what looked like an abandoned estate with an old mansion set behind a wrought iron fence on good-sized grounds. Coming from behind the building, out of their sight, was the sound of children—lots of children. It reminded Louise of the noise of her grade school playground in Edmond. It also reminded her how quiet—how empty—their home felt when Arnie was away. She linked arms with Arnie as they walked around the fenced grounds to the back side, as if his solidity could somehow fill the void.

There must have been a hundred children, most of them under ten, tearing around some hastily built wooden playground equipment. Several of the children were sitting next to the wall of the building, rocking themselves, staring at nothing, some hugging themselves, some with their thumbs in their mouths. This was no grade school playground.

Two little girls sat cross-legged across from each other. One, her face horribly disfigured from burns, was holding a primitive rag doll. The other girl had one hand on her knee, as if comforting or reassuring her.

"Oh, Arnie," Louise gasped. Both girls had been blinded. She involuntarily put her hands to her mouth.

"War," Arnie said quietly.

They silently watched the children for a few minutes. Then they saw Kaarina approaching them from inside the fence. She was wearing a gray wool skirt and a beige cardigan sweater draped over another sweater of coarser green wool. She had a wool scarf tied over her hair, which was set in a bun.

A child ran up to her. Kaarina knelt, said something, and pointed to one of the play structures. She gently shooed the child along and started back toward Arnie and Louise.

"Päivää," she said, not formal, like *hyvää päivää*, which meant "good day," but more formal than *hei*, which was like saying hi in English. Kaarina was always dignified.

Two boys, both around eight, suddenly started screaming at each other. There was a flurry of swift punches, thrown wildly and harmlessly because of their age. Kaarina started running for the fight. One boy ran, leaving the other with a look of smug triumph. The boy who ran, however, had run to an empty flower bed where a large wooden stake was set in the ground. He jerked it loose and came screaming at the other boy, flailing at him, striking a severe blow across the boy's eyes. The boy shielded his face and head and the boy with the stake went in for the kill. He was stopped by Kaarina, who took several blows herself before she wrestled the stake from the furious boy. She then got him under control by grabbing his shoulders. She said something sharply to the boy in Finnish and slapped him. The boy screamed something at her and ran off.

Louise was stunned by the violence.

"War," Arnie said again.

Watching the small child running away from them, Louise noticed how narrow his shoulders were, how thin his arms. She suddenly wanted to hold him. She looked at Arnie. "Oh, Arnie," she said. "It's all so heartbreaking. And brutal."

Kaarina, too, was watching the boy run away. She turned to look at Arnie and Louise, her face sad. "Welcome to my world," she said. Then, almost apologetically she added, "He'll have to be punished."

"Punish him? Why?" The look from Arnie immediately signaled to Louise that she'd spoken out of turn.

Kaarina's face was impassive, but her eyes drilled into Louise. "For striking the other boy with the stick."

"But they were both fighting . . ." Louise trailed off, feeling Arnie softly grip her elbow. "I mean, maybe both—"

"It's for his own good."

It was quite clear that Kaarina would tolerate no one interfering in how she ran the orphanage.

"Of course," Louise said. Realizing now was not the time to talk about child-rearing, Louise asked, "Are you by yourself?"

Kaarina softened, apparently also wanting to get out of the conflict. "No." Kaarina smiled. "Sometimes, like today, it feels like it, but no. There are five of us, one at home for a full day off, four here four days in a row, one inside, one outside. That's me today. We do twelve-hour shifts and rotate nights."

"Criminy."

"What is that word?" Kaarina asked pleasantly.

"Uh. It means . . . uh—"

"It's slang," Arnie broke in. "A polite way of saying 'Jesus Christ.'"

Kaarina laughed. "Here, we evoke the name of the devil, Satan," she said. "Perhaps a fundamental difference between our countries? The optimists and the pessimists?"

"Perhaps," Arnie said. "But pessimists don't leave everything behind and sail off to an unknown new world."

Kaarina smiled. "True, but maybe if you're pessimistic enough, you sail off because the future holds nothing for you at home."

Arnie simply nodded at this.

Then Kaarina asked, "Would you like to see the orphanage?"

Louise looked up at Arnie. Arnie smiled his agreement.

"Yes," Louise said. "Yes, we would like that."

Kaarina introduced them to her fellow staffer, then took them to a dormitory room stuffed with small beds, all just far enough apart for an adult to squeeze by. One little girl was under one of the beds, her thumb in her mouth. Another was sitting upright, holding her stomach, rocking back and forth. She made no response to Louise's attempt to talk to her. One girl, around five or six, was on a low makeshift gurney of wood and what looked like old tricycle wheels, being noisily pushed down the hallway by two other girls. All three stopped and stared at Louise. At a word from Kaarina, most likely about not staring, they ran down the hallway, giggling. The one on the gurney didn't have any legs.

Kaarina asked them into her office for tea after the tour. Louise's hand shook as she put the cup to her lips. She quickly put it on her lap, helping steady it. She looked at Arnie, steadier, but somber.

"You do all this with just five of you?" Louise asked, finally able to get the cup back up to her mouth.

"Well, depends on whether one calls what is happening here *doing*. We feel overwhelmed." She paused. "You see, there just isn't enough money for more staff."

"But, surely," Louise said, "there must be government funds, charities. I mean—"

Arnie had gently put his hand on her thigh.

"It's OK, Arnie," Kaarina said. She turned to Louise. "It's in large part because of the reparation payments to the Soviets."

"I'd forgotten," Louise said quietly.

"The economy is just starting again. That means less taxes for things like orphanages and even less charity money. Things are so tight, it's even hard to get volunteers." She sighed and her shoulders sagged briefly. "Still, they're all fed and sleep warm."

"Yes. Thank the Lord," Louise said.

Kaarina gave her and then Arnie a look, saying nothing. Louise could see that Kaarina didn't attribute the food and beds to God.

Without thinking, Louise asked, "How can we help?"

Kaarina thought a moment. "Unfortunately, you're not rich?" she said with a slight smile.

Louise and Arnie both smiled, ruefully acknowledging this.

Almost absently and to no one in particular she said, "We do need money." She turned to Louise. "We also need bodies. Perhaps, after you've gotten settled of course, you might come by and take some of the children during the day. Until your Finnish improves . . ." She trailed off. It was clear she was trying to come up with something. "Maybe bring needles and thread, some bright cloth, and help the girls sew something?"

Louise grimaced. "I don't sew so well."

"Oh." It was said with a bit of surprise.

"I mean by hand," Louise said quickly. "If there were a sewing machine, maybe."

"Just come and spend time," Kaarina said, nodding and smiling. "You'll figure something. They really aren't demanding."

"What about finding families in America?" Louise asked. "I could help with that. I used to volunteer at an orphanage run by our church. It was where I first got really interested in early childhood education."

"You're a teacher?" Kaarina asked.

"Well, not anymore. It's being in the army." She shrugged, a little apologetically. "I do miss it."

"Of course. Working with children." Kaarina seemed to search for something to say. "What was the name of your orphanage?"

"It's called the Wichita Orphan Home and Manual Labor School."

"Manual Labor School?"

Louise suddenly felt defensive. She'd never really thought about the name of the church's orphanage. "The children need to become independent."

"But why *manual labor*?"

"It's an Indian school," Arnie broke in. "They don't like going to school, so it's really their best shot."

"But surely, there are schools for diesel mechanics, secretaries—"

"The children were mostly very young," Louise said quickly. "Those schools could come when they get older."

"Mmhh," Kaarina said. There was an awkward silence. "Well, no matter." Kaarina smiled. "The simple truth is that we can always use another pair of hands."

Louise nodded. "I'll come by. Whenever I can."

"Wonderful. Whenever you want." Kaarina seemed to hesitate. Then she said, "Would there be any chance of some coffee from the legation?"

Arnie and Louise were quiet all the way back to the hotel. Once in their room, Louise could hold on no longer. Arnie held her until she stopped sobbing.

"Arnie," she said, speaking into his chest. "We have to do something."

"Sure. But what? It's like this all over Europe."

"Yes, but we're here!" She pushed back away from him. Her own intensity surprised her.

Arnie could only blink.

"Oh, Arnie. Can't you get money from State? They're throwing money at Germany."

"Yes, but—"

"But nothing. They were the ones who made the orphans."

"You know it was the Russians."

"Yes, I know it was the Russians. Same thing. Bad actors. Why are we helping the Germans and not the Finns, who didn't do anything to us?"

"*We are* helping the Finns. We're allowing dollar loans. We're the big brother the little brother can call on if the fight gets too tough. You think Stalin settled for an unoccupied Finland because he was nice?"

"Phwfft. He settled because he didn't want another bloody nose."

Arnie was stopped for a moment. "OK, you're right."

"My favorite words."

"But *right now,* he's being careful because of us." Arnie paused. "All that is big-picture international relations. I've got a big enough job, right here, now. I *need* you."

"To go to parties," she said a little sullenly.

"Don't sell yourself short. It's what diplomats *do*. It's called building relationships. Real work gets done at parties and real information gets passed."

"I know." Louise sighed. "It's just so . . . so indirect."

Arnie pulled her back in to him. "Honestly, Louise. I know how much you loved working with children. Just remember we're here to do a job. As long as you still have time to do the job, I'm fine with you getting involved in Kaarina's orphanage. But don't disappear on me. You know how bad I am at parties."

"Don't I," she said. "That afternoon your friend brought you with him from Fort Sill, I think you said three words."

"That's because you said three thousand."

"Not true." She paused. "Well, maybe." She had started circling one of his buttons with her forefinger. "But you were *so* exciting."

Arnie laughed. He knew full well her first impression of him. "I know, like watching paint dry."

"Oh, so much more. Like watching *mud puddles* dry."

He laughed again. "It's not just parties," he said. "Remember, I need you to grease the social skids, make friends with the wives in the community. It's important, and it's something I can't do, for obvious reasons."

"You *would* look pretty silly asking Natalya Bobrova to tea," Louise said. "OK. I get it." She sighed. "It's just that I want to do *something*. Something *more*. More direct." She sighed and then said very softly, "Maybe if we had children, I'd feel differently." She looked up at Arnie. "Maybe help the children. Be around the children."

Arnie gently hugged her, stroking her hair.

Louise brought up the orphanage again during dinner in the hotel basement.

"Louise, truly, I'd like to help them, but I just don't think the army or the State Department want their military attaché in the orphan business."

"Get honest. You don't want *me* in the orphan business."

"OK. You're right."

"Didn't feel so good when you said it this time."

Arnie chuckled. "You're right. You're right. You're right."

She had to smile. "OK. Of course, you want me home. *I* want to be home. But not if I'm just sitting around planning cocktail parties." She opened her hands to him above her plate. "We don't have any kids now. I can do parties with my eyes shut. Those orphans of Kaarina's need . . . They need mothers." Her voice dropped to a whisper. "And I guess I need to be one."

"Oh, Louise." Arnie took her hands in his and pulled them toward him. Reaching across his plate he kissed them. "I didn't know what it meant for you. Do it. Just don't leave me high and dry."

They looked at each other across the table. Then Louise said, smiling and pulling her hands back, "I'll be at every party."

They were silent for a while, then, shifting the mood, Arnie asked, "But what will you do for them? We're not rich. You don't speak Finnish."

"And I can't sew," she chimed in, making Arnie chuckle.

"They need money," she said seriously. "They need someone who is good at raising it. I spent a lot of my time as chapter president chasing rich alumni. And I was pretty darned good at it."

"I'll bet you were." It was a genuine compliment and it felt good to be seen. "But how will you go about it?"

"Aren't there State Department funds for war relief?" Louise asked.

"I don't think so. Technically, we're still at war with Finland until the treaty gets signed."

"God, Arnie. How long is that going to take? The war was over nearly two years ago. Fat-assed diplomats in Paris waiting for just the right word on some piece of paper while Kaarina and those children"—she straightened back in her chair—"they need money. I can get money."

"Like I just asked you, how?"

"I don't know. Yet." She was silent a moment. "I'll call Max Hamilton and ask him. He told me once to let him know if I needed anything. I'll see if he meant it! Do you think he'll see me?"

"Sure, he will. He's in love with you."

She rolled her eyes.

"But," Arnie went on, "he won't give you any money."

She knew she had Arnie's blessing. She also knew she was on her own.

Friday, January 3, 1947
Max Hamilton's Office,
American Legation

L ouise had called Hamilton's office first thing Thursday morning and got herself on his calendar Friday afternoon, telling his secretary, Helmi, that it would only be fifteen minutes. After the dinner with Max Hamilton and his wife, Louise had spoken several times more with Hamilton at one of the many Christmas parties and was now on a first-name basis. She found herself increasingly more relaxed with him and appreciating his old-fashioned politeness and good manners.

Her father had taught her *about* business, but her mother had taught her about *doing* business. The more pulled together she looked, the more she was taken seriously. The problem was her more pulled-together clothes were either at some army warehouse in God-knows-where or on the Atlantic Ocean. On Friday morning, to her normal street outfit she'd added a simple nylon chiffon scarf she'd found in a small women's retail store, surprisingly with a Sears and Roebuck label, and she applied some of her precious red lipstick. So far, she'd found no replacement in all of Helsinki. In fact, she'd seen none on Finnish women and wondered if maybe they didn't wear makeup.

When she was ushered into Hamilton's office, he was as cordial and gracious as he'd been before, as she expected. He was, after all, a diplomat. But he was also warm and welcoming, which she hadn't expected.

She smiled through the polite questions of health and finding housing, waiting until he finally asked, "So, Louise, how can I help you?"

Then *he* waited.

Louise then launched into the plight of the orphans. When she finished, Hamilton walked over to the window. He looked out at the gray sky in the gray streets for some time.

"Louise," he said, turning to face her. "The war was terrible. More horrible than most Americans can ever imagine. I've seen some of those children, and I saw too many of them in France in the last war."

Her hopes were rising.

"I know I have the seemingly impressive title of envoy extraordinary and minister plenipotentiary." He chuckled. "That is a very traditional title, carefully constructed to signal just what authority I have. And don't have." He paused. "Because I am not an ambassador, I do not have the authority to direct funds to private charities, no matter how worthy the cause."

"But surely there must be *some* money. Criminy, with what we spend on defense and—"

"Louise," he interrupted gently. "Every penny is budgeted and publicly accounted for. I do not run a spy agency like the OSS that can keep expenses secret."

She couldn't hide her disappointment. "But, Max, we spend *millions* on foreign aid! Surely . . ."

Hamilton cocked his head sideways at that. "Louise," he said gently. "We, in the field, *distribute* foreign aid. We don't decide who gets it."

She took that in. Of course. Bureaucracies.

"Maybe you could raise the money privately," Hamilton suggested, "some sort of fund drive or raffle."

Louise nearly blurted out, raffle what? They didn't have enough money to buy anything to raffle. She held her tongue. He was trying to help.

"I would be happy to make a personal donation," Hamilton con-tinued, "contribute some of my own money," obviously trying to soften the blow. "And perhaps some of the others on staff might be willing. You have my permission to ask them."

"Thank you. That's very kind." Louise thought a moment. "Just out of curiosity, what do you have authority to *distribute* funds to?"

Hamilton chuckled. "Almost anything that looks like it's keeping Finland on our side but doesn't make the Russians mad."

"You mean something like what we're doing in Germany." She was thinking rapidly. "Like reconstruction."

He nodded. "Something like that."

"I'll try and think of something."

"Do that. I'll always be happy to see what you come up with. Albeit," he sighed, "I can't promise anything, even if I am a plenipotentate." Smiling, he stood and held out his hand.

Walking back to the hotel, Louise felt as somber as the streets. She knew that whatever she came up with must be something Hamilton could put into a letter or budget document. Hamilton had said that the Department of State's primary mission was to keep Finland in the camp of the democracies. Surely, helping a Finnish orphanage would qualify. She'd taken civics in school, but civics never said a word about how things actually worked in politics—things like budgets. At the base of it all was money. An image of a cartoon politician with a string tie and potbelly rose in her mind. That person wouldn't be motivated by sympathy for foreign orphans who couldn't vote she thought wryly. If she could only think of something that a politician or bureaucrat could use to make themselves look good. Something. The germ of an idea was starting to form.

By the time she reached her room, there was a spring in her step. She'd come up with the idea of a joint American and Soviet effort that could fit under the general umbrella of "war reconstruction." She knew a large percentage of Americans still thought of the Russians as friends. They referred to Stalin as Uncle Joe. It made Arnie furious, but that was political reality. The angle could be continuing to work as allies, just like in the war, but now for peace. What better than a project like caring for the orphans of our common enemy? An act of generous forgiveness. She could write a letter—no, Hamilton could write a letter to some bureaucrat with a green eyeshade whom she imagined sitting in Washington with a big rubber stamp—a letter that could extol the twin virtues of greatly furthering relations with Finland *and* the Soviet Union. Before that letter from Hamilton could be written, however, she needed the project to be a joint project. She needed help to firm up the Soviet side—and she already had the person in mind.

She wrote a note to Natalya Bobrova that evening, saying how much she'd enjoyed meeting someone her own age at the legation party, someone with whom she could talk about French literature. She ended it asking if Natalya and Mikhail might be attending the performance by the Liberation String Quartet at the French embassy Wednesday evening. Perhaps they could sit together. She dropped the letter off at the Russian legation first thing the next morning.

Wednesday, January 8, 1947
Cultural Event, French Legation

When Arnie got back to the room from work on the next Wednesday, he handed her a note with a hammer and sickle on the letterhead. "What's this?" he asked.

She took it, a bit surprised. Mikhail had answered in Finnish the invitation she'd written to Natalya in French. She was also surprised by the poor quality of the paper. "I asked Natalya if she and Mikhail would like to join us for the French string quartet performance. That's all. I thought I was supposed to facilitate these kinds of social relations."

Arnie took the note back, sighing. "Louise. *Everything* is read by the MGB."

"So? I knew that."

"They don't like notes being passed around in languages they don't understand. That's why Mikhail wrote back, to *me*, in Finnish."

"Good gracious, Arnie! The note is harmless. I asked if they'd like to listen to some music."

"And some MGB spook will be wondering why the wife of the American attaché would be trying to make friends with the wife of the Soviet attaché in a language he doesn't understand. Don't you think it would look a little suspicious?"

"Everything looks suspicious to them."

"Louise," Arnie said very evenly. "Yes. But in America, suspicious is something you investigate. In Russia, suspicious is a crime. Think about the Bobrovs."

She felt a slight chill in her spine. After a pause, she mumbled, "That's ridiculous."

"To an American."

The household goods finally arrived on Tuesday. The problem was they still hadn't found a place to live, so Louise asked Hamilton if Pulkkinen could help her pick up the crates.

Pulkkinen knew of a warehouse by the docks where they could store things until she found an apartment. After a couple of trips with the wooden crates roped to the top of the Fleetmaster, he helped Louise open them with the car's tire jack. They went through four before finding her dresses.

"On our next move," Louise said to Pulkkinen, "I'll be sure to label the crates, not just the boxes inside them."

Pulkkinen just blinked.

"Pulkkinen, I'm making a joke."

"I know."

She vowed she'd break through that reserve. She pulled out a dress and, holding it to her breast with one hand and against her stomach with the other, she said, "I just love this one." She twirled around, letting it flow out. Then, moving with it as if with a dance partner, she asked, "What do you think?"

"It looks good."

"You're as bad as my husband." She flopped the top of the dress down. "You Finns have one word that covers anything complimentary: hyvää." She began folding the dress.

Pulkkinen smiled. "Forgive my reticence."

She remarked to herself his use of the word "reticence." "Where did you learn to speak English so well?" She'd asked the question in the same kidding vein, but for some reason Pulkkinen's face flickered with some sort of reaction, which he quickly tried to hide.

"In school," he said.

"Pretty good school," Louise said, returning to pick through the clothing. She pulled out one of her dresses that was a favorite of Arnie's and two of her favorite slips, adding them to the small pile on the floor. Then she picked out some clothes for Arnie.

That evening, she came out of the bathroom wearing the dress Arnie liked. "You still like it?" She gave a twirl, causing it to float up just a bit above her knees, showing the lace on the slip's hem.

"It looks good."

"You Finns. That's exactly what Pulkkinen said when I showed it to him this afternoon."

"What can I say. Maybe it's genetic."

She fluffed the skirt to make it hang better. "He used the word 'reticence' today. When I asked him where he learned such good English, he, I don't know, he reacted somehow, like it flustered him. I mean . . . I don't know."

"Big word for a driver," Arnie said.

"That's what I thought."

Despite having minored in French, the closest Louise had ever gotten to France was with Arnie at the French legation's Christmas party. Then, Christmas decorations had overpowered everything. Now, with the holiday decorations gone, she saw that there had been an underlying elegance that now was revealed: the curtains, the style and quality of the furniture, the style and quality of the clothes. It was as if someone tried to bring a little Paris north with them and had done a rather good job of it. There were long tables covered with heavy white tablecloths. Waiters stood by, pouring French wine. There were trays of baguettes with crusts of golden brown, as if they'd been baked in Riviera sunshine, laid out next to an enormous variety of French cheeses. Dozens of silver trays held beautifully presented canapés made of salmon, quail eggs, and olives of various sizes, unlike the plain and uniform black ones they got in cans from California back home. She tasted a large green one, surprised by the firmness of its texture and then additionally surprised to find that it had a pit in it. That was also unlike the olives back home.

Louise was taking it all in and soaking it all up. This was as close to real France as she'd ever been. Even in high school, with her one year of high school French from Madame Jones, who spoke French with just as broad an Oklahoma accent as she did English, Louise had dreamed about Paris. It had taken the whole first quarter at OU to stop pronouncing words like "*fenêtre*" like "fe-netter." Madame Jones said things like "winder" for "window," so she was at least consistent.

Louise's dreams of going to Paris had, however, been modified after marrying Arnie to going there with him someday on an extended leave. Then the dreams were shattered by the war.

She and Arnie moved into the flow and chatter of the crowd, sticking close to each other, smiling and nodding. It felt like trying to enter a ballroom floor to join a rapidly circling crowd of waltzers.

She spotted Mikhail in his uniform standing with Natalya against the wall just to the right of the door that led into the even larger room where the quartet would be playing. Natalya was in the same long black dress she had worn to the New Year's Eve party, only the lace collar was gone. She wore no jewelry other than simple silver hoop earrings. Louise could see that Natalya's dress would do for a formal occasion or a less formal cultural affair. Clearly Natalya had to make do on a limited wardrobe just like she did. But then, Natalya could have worn a housecoat and still looked elegant.

Making their way to Natalya and Mikhail through the crowd, Louise began to understand what her mother had referred to as breeding. The women in this room, she realized, had probably worn expensive clothes since they were in diapers. She felt like a farm horse in a pasture of thoroughbreds. She smiled at a memory from one of the earlier holiday parties. An Englishwoman with a tony accent had told Louise that to most Europeans, Russians and Americans seemed quite alike. Both were the outgrowths of frontier cultures, warlike people who'd expanded across entire continents, crushing all before them, who didn't know when to stop wearing white in the fall. With an inward chuckle, she had to admit that she was beginning to see the woman's point.

She smiled brightly at Natalya, trying to think of an appropriate greeting that would draw her out. To her relief, Natalya smiled back. Then Natalya's smile faded, replaced by her placid and nearly expressionless face, as if she were wearing a mask. Arnie's cautioning about the note came back to her. Of course, no one read other people's mail in Oklahoma. The right to privacy was inviolable. She wondered what it must be like to live without it.

She was suddenly aware of how little she'd appreciated the birthrights, far beyond material wealth, being American granted. Arnie had fought for those birthrights, and a lot of their friends had died so others could live in freedom with their benefits. Then she was surprised by a feeling of gratitude. She looked up at Arnie's face, which was animated by whatever he and Colonel Bobrov were talking about in Finnish. Arnie glanced down at her, giving her a puzzled look. She blinked her wordless thanks. Clearly mystified, Arnie smiled, put his hand on her lower back, and rubbed her with a tiny circular motion, just above her rear. Then he resumed his conversation.

Louise glanced at Natalya. A softening of Natalya's eyes showed that she'd taken note of the brief display of tenderness. The mask, however, remained. Louise now knew that there was a friend in there behind that mask. But how to get to her?

Louise started in French with the usual warm-ups: how were the children, the weather, has Natalya been to the fish market on whatever street. The conversation between the two women seemed to have empty spaces, moments when people were thinking what to say, particularly Natalya. Then it hit Louise. Natalya was shy! How could someone so beautiful be shy? Maybe say something about the music.

"I read somewhere, once, that the Debussy quartet they're playing tonight is his only one," she led off in French. "It's supposed to be quite"—she searched for words—"unclassical." Could she be any more inarticulate she thought.

"Yes," Natalya said. Her smile was gracious, a welcome relief. "It is supposed to have been highly influenced by Nadezhda von Meck."

Louise couldn't help a puzzled look.

"Tchaikovsky's patroness."

"I love Tchaikovsky," Louise said, then paused. "I was a tin soldier in *The Nutcracker* when I was eight." She rolled her eyes in self-deprecation.

Natalya smiled, saying nothing, but Louise could see she was holding something back.

"What? Come on."

Natalya now blushed. "I was the Sugar Plum Fairy."

They both laughed. The ice was broken.

Wednesday, January 8, 1947
Streets of Helsinki

The concert ended at nine thirty. Louise suggested that since the night was still young, they all walk back to their living accommodations together. She had a brief nervous moment when Natalya said something in Russian to Mikhail, her tone of voice indicating that she wasn't sure. Of course, the children, Louise thought. She sighed inwardly in relief when it became clear that Mikhail and Natalya would join them. It had been the whole reason for inviting them to the concert in the first place.

The night was crisp, cold, and clear. "The Liberation Quartet was very good," Louise said.

"I like string quartets," Natalya said. "They're so uncluttered, like good poetry. Following any more than four parts is beyond me anyway."

"You can follow all four parts?"

Natalya nodded shyly, then looked down, saying nothing.

Arnie and Mikhail were walking well ahead of them.

Natalya nodded toward the two men's backs. Louise caught her drift immediately. "Maybe it's because their legs are longer," she said.

"It's because when they start talking about the army, they forget we're here."

Louise laughed. "We do seem to have a lot in common."

They walked silently for a bit, then Louise asked, a little hesitantly, "Did you notice how elegant all the French women looked tonight? For a simple concert."

"I did."

"When I get around French women, like tonight, I feel, I don't know, dowdy."

"Inelegant," Natalya said.

"Gauche."

"Not that far."

"What is it about them?" Louise asked.

"Raised with it. Russian aristocrats were like that," Natalya said wistfully. Then her eyes flicked, almost imperceptibly, but Louise caught the movement. Natalya abruptly changed her tone of voice, saying a little more loudly, "Of course, that was before the revolution. They were selfish, ignorant, and self-indulgent people."

"I don't know, Natalya. I mean, think of all your great writers and musicians. Most of them were aristocrats."

"Because no one else had the time or money. That's why these French women look as they do. They can buy quality." She briefly looked down on her dress. "Everything. Good wool, fine cotton, silk."

"And they all travel with tailors," Louise added.

Natalya chuckled, about to make a retort, but she had clearly stopped herself.

"What?" Louise asked. "Come on. Spill it."

"It's an old saying. A French woman has a small closet full of expensive clothes. An American woman has a large closet full of cheap clothes. And a Russian woman"—she paused—"a small closet half-full of cheap clothes."

Louise laughed. It surprised her how much she liked this woman. She'd expected not to like Communists. She didn't expect one to be like Natalya. "I didn't think Communists had a sense of humor."

As soon as it came out, Louise regretted it. A cloud had passed over Natalya's face.

"Maybe you're right, but Russians do," Natalya said.

"Of course. I didn't mean to . . ." *How to get out of this one*, Louise thought. "I mean you're absolutely right about the clothes. When I was a girl, my mother made all our clothes. Now the clothes just seem to pour out of factories."

"Yes," Natalya said. "Your country is still in the capitalist stage."

Louise felt a bit affronted. "What do you mean by that?"

"No, please don't misunderstand. It's nobody's fault. It's just that the world develops in fits and starts. I just meant, if America had already thrown off its capitalistic yoke, there would be none of the tension between us. I mean our countries."

"I don't feel like I'm under some capitalist yoke."

"That's because you are from the capitalist class."

"My father ran a lumberyard!"

Louise stopped walking. This was not going as she'd hoped. Natalya also stopped, her breath now hanging in front of her face in an icy cloud.

"I just want to be friends," Louise said.

"My Russian emotional temperament," Natalya said. "Tension between our countries doesn't mean there has to be tension between us." She looked up the dark street at Mikhail and Arnie leaning in to hear each other, huddled against the cold. "Our countries could very well be at war in the near future," Natalya said softly. "Those two could soon be trying to kill each other."

Louise saw that Mikhail and Arnie had stopped at a street corner under a dim light. Arnie was shading his eyes, trying to see into the darkness better. When he was sure he'd caught their attention, he pointed up a small street.

"I need to confess something," Louise said as she and Natalya were joining Arnie and Mikhail. "I asked Arnie to take a certain route back to our quarters. I was going to make it look accidental."

Natalya gave her a puzzled look.

"I need help. That is, I want help. There is an orphanage up that street. Arnie's cousin runs it."

Natalya stiffened just slightly. "I've seen too many orphanages." She went quiet. "One too many."

"You were orphaned? I'm so sorry. In the First World War?"

"No. My parents were . . ." Natalya stopped. "Died," she continued.

"Oh, Natalya. I didn't mean to bring up bad memories."

Natalya's face had returned to its usual cool mask. After a moment she shrugged and said, "You couldn't have known."

"No. Maybe it's more of a reason for you to see this one."

"They're all the same." She looked at Louise suspiciously, then said, "And why do you care?"

There are always these moments in a new friendship where a decision about how much to reveal must be made. The fear is that revealing too much might end the budding relationship. The reality is that not revealing what truly matters will ensure that the relationship remains superficial.

Louise plunged. "I suppose it's because we've been trying for years to have children and . . ." She still did not know how deep to go with this. "It just hasn't worked out."

Louise broke eye contact. "It's just, I suppose, being around children is . . . I don't know."

"Comforting?" Natalya asked.

Louise shrugged slightly but didn't answer.

"Encouraging."

Louise nodded.

"OK," Natalya said. "Let's go."

* * *

The two women walked side by side for a block or so, saying nothing. Louise felt a kinship with this new friend and somehow knew Natalya felt the same.

"The children here do need help," Louise finally said.

"What could *we* do?"

She'd said *we*. Louise homed in. "I don't know. Yet. All I know is that I'd like to help. I don't know for sure if Arnie wants me to. I don't even know if it's something that's allowed for the wives of diplomats. But I think you and me together, sort of a joint project, *that* sounds very diplomatic."

Natalya chuckled. "Comrades. Arm in arm," she said sarcastically.

"Hamilton, that's Arnie's boss. Well, not his army boss. Anyway, it gets way easier to get permission if you'd be part of it." She looked to see how this was all being received. "Natalya, we could do so much good for them, those orphans. I just know we could."

Natalya's eyes seemed to soften.

"Another confession. I already told Arnie's cousin we'd stop by tomorrow afternoon. I was so sure you'd want to help once you saw the place tonight."

"Do you have any more to confess?"

"Well, I'll confess to even juicer stuff if you'll come tomorrow."

"I'm not sure your husband would like it." The tone had lightened.

"Not *that* kind of juicier."

Mikhail and Arnie were heading up the street toward the orphanage. Natalya gave Louise a look, then followed them, leaving Louise to catch up, but hopeful.

The four hesitated before the orphanage's head-high wrought iron gate. It was unlocked, and Arnie pushed it open. The others followed him inside the grounds. The large stone building stood silent and dark in the quiet playground. Louise saw Natalya move in closer to Mikhail. They stood there silently watching the darkened building. She whispered something to him and he put his arm around her and kissed her hair.

After about half a minute, Natalya turned to Louise. "It brings back memories. Not all good."

Louise nodded and waited, giving Natalya some time. Then she said, "Maybe we can help these kids have fewer bad memories."

Natalya's face was working. "Yes. Fewer bad memories."

It took Louise aback to see tears forming. She hesitated, then said softly, "Can you say?"

Natalya shook her head, no. Louise waited. "It was . . . with so many children you'd think . . . I was kind of alone."

"Alone? Why would you be alone?"

"My background. Hard to explain. My mother and father were . . . not desirable."

"Not desirable," Louise said flatly.

"Dah."

Louise saw another crossroads had been reached. She tried to think of saying what she wanted to say without it sounding maudlin or presumptuous. She nodded toward Mikhail and Arnie, both still deep in conversation.

"I told Arnie's cousin we'd come after work tomorrow," Louise said. "Please come. Just for half an hour. I'll meet you here. I have this idea about a joint American-Soviet orphan project. It can make good publicity for our Department of State and any politician who gets behind it. I would think it could be the same on your end." She stopped there, hoping she'd made the project just enticing enough for Natalya to at least explore the idea.

Natalya said something to Mikhail in Russian and Mikhail answered her quietly and seriously. She turned to Louise. "Dah. OK. Half an hour after work."

Thursday, January 9, 1947
The Orphanage and Apartments

The next day, Louise was waiting just outside the orphanage gate in the late-afternoon darkness. The darkness hid the overcast sky, but she still felt its presence, like she was constantly ducking beneath a low roof. When she saw Natalya walking toward her with her dancer's posture and movement, she consciously straightened her shoulders and tucked her chin. She still didn't know how to greet her, but Natalya solved the problem by moving her cheeks quickly to Louise's right and left in a quick air-kiss.

"I only have half an hour," Natalya said. "My children."

"Of course. No more time than that."

Louise led her to the old mansion's ornately carved front door. She rang the brass bell that was attached above it with a leather string hanging from a clapper. Within a minute, Kaarina Varila peered through a small opening. Flickering light, perhaps from a lamp or candle Kaarina was holding, lit Louise's face and Kaarina smiled warmly upon recognizing her.

When they were inside, in her halting Finnish, Louise introduced Natalya.

The smile froze. "Hyvää iltaa," Kaarina said. It was a very formal—and cold—good evening. Natalya responded equally formally. There was an awkward silence.

Kaarina turned to Louise. "I'm guessing she only speaks Russian, like the rest of them."

Louise put on a smile she wasn't feeling. She hadn't expected Kaarina to react to Natalya as she did. It wasn't as if Natalya had bombed Finland. "She, I think, reads Finnish enough for her job at the Soviet legation but can't speak it." She tried a joke. "I mean who can?" Kaarina didn't respond to the joke. "She speaks French. Really well. We speak French to each other," Louise added.

Natalya had gone into Russian stony face.

Louise started scrambling to somehow reduce the tension, fill the empty space with some words. "We're both here to help. Just wanted to stop by to see the place. See if there's something we could do."

Kaarina still said nothing.

This irritated Louise, as if Kaarina were disregarding their offer to help, and she was being unfair to Natalya. Louise didn't hide her annoyance when she said, "She's just here to help, too. The children don't know a Russian from a . . . from a Martian." She paused. "She was raised in an orphanage herself."

Kaarina softened a little. "Orphanages at their best are bad experiences. Was it the first war?"

"No. She said it wasn't. She said her parents were undesirable to the state."

Kaarina looked back at Natalya. "Well, she may not be all bad."

Louise looked at Kaarina for a moment to make sure she was on solid ground, then turned to Natalya and said in French, "She asked if we want to see the orphanage."

"How kind," she said with just a hint of sarcasm. "Not exactly a warm welcome."

Louise let it drop. Kaarina was already walking into a large room that decades ago may have served as a small ballroom. It was bedlam, children running, some girls jumping rope, two boys kicking a small pillow bound tightly with a thin rope that served as a soccer ball.

"Looks like you could use help supervising the play," Louise said with a smile.

"We could," Kaarina answered. "We also need help washing pots, washing clothes, cleaning floors, cleaning toilets." She looked at Louise. "I don't suppose either of you would be interested."

"Whatever is needed. Really."

Kaarina studied the two of them, probably wondering if Louise was being genuine. "What we really need," she said, "is help with clothes and good food. Things that take money."

"That's exactly how I was hoping we could help," Louise blurted out. "That's why I brought Natalya into this." She turned to include Natalya in the conversation. "With a joint Soviet-US project, there's a chance that the legation could find some money."

"A fat chance," Kaarina said.

"No. Really. I talked with Mr. Hamilton, the chief of station."

Natalya was looking to Louise to translate. "Talking about how we can help," Louise said to her in French.

"I thought I heard the word 'money,'" Natalya answered, saying "money" in English.

"You did. I think we can help."

The shrug followed.

They followed Kaarina into a large, dimly lit room. It was filled with four rows of about fifteen cots each, all spare, plain, now empty, made up with varying degrees of success, obviously by the girls themselves. About five of the beds had a ragged stuffed animal on the pillow. One had a doll, carefully laid beneath a tiny, crocheted blanket.

"This is the girls' room," Kaarina said in English. Louise translated. Natalya nodded, licking her lower lip pensively. She put her hand on the tiny blanket for a moment, then quickly pulled it back. She was trying to smile, but her lip was quivering. Louise reached out and touched her. But it was as if Louise weren't there. Natalya had withdrawn to some inner world.

Kaarina cleared her throat, wanting to move on, and Louise followed her. Louise turned back to look at Natalya, who seemed to return to the present, aware that Louise and Kaarina were waiting on her. She rejoined them. They entered another large room.

"This is where the boys sleep," Kaarina said. It was sparer and plainer than the girls' room. The beds were made but clearly to a different standard and level of success. There were no toys and no stuffed animals. A lone little boy lay on one of the beds, staring up at the ceiling. He didn't respond to Louise's attempts to connect.

Louise and Natalya looked at each other, Louise hopeful and questioning, Natalya expressionless, her face a mask.

Kaarina led them down another hallway, her and Louise together, Natalya lagging behind. "Your Russian *comrade* doesn't seem all that happy about being here," Kaarina said to Louise in a near whisper. They both looked back to see where Natalya was. She had turned around and stopped, holding her arms around her chest, looking at the girls' sleeping room.

Natalya took the long way home, smoking three cigarettes to calm herself. As soon as she got home, she lit another cigarette and began making dinner. Fanya, a slightly plump girl of about eighteen with dark hair that had been rolled on top and hung to her shoulders helped Natalya feed the children, a cigarette dangling from her mouth, the smoke making her squint. The routine of feeding her children slowly calmed Natalya, nourishing through them the unfed child she'd been.

Mikhail got home around seven and rolled around on the floor with the children, laughing, letting them climb over him. Natalya watched, loving them all, remembering her own father.

She broke the spell to call Mikhail to the table for their own dinner. As the two of them ate, Fanya got the children ready for bed. Then, Natalya finished putting the children to bed, reading aloud to them until they fell asleep. She returned to the kitchen to wash the dishes, while Mikhail worked at the kitchen table, his usual evening activity.

Natalya returned to the small living room to find Fanya on the couch looking at an interior page of *Helsingin Sanomat*.

"I didn't know you read Finnish," Natalya said. She was pretty sure that Fanya did *not* read Finnish. She guessed that the girl was looking at the photographs of the latest fashions from New York, London, and Paris in the women's section.

She knew that the Party would condemn high fashion as decadent. She knew she should as well but couldn't quite bring herself to it. She scoffed inwardly at the pull of the beautiful clothes, telling herself that it hardly made any difference, since it was impossible to buy high fashion—or even a foreign-made dress—in Russia anyway. And, of course, haute couture fashion was ridiculously out of reach for almost all women even in the capitalist countries. Fashion was used to keep workingwomen from recognizing their servitude by entertaining them with dreams of the plausible impossible. Hah. And Marx said religion was the opiate of the masses. But then, she thought, how was it different than any other form of entertainment—or beauty? Were music and plays decadent? She pushed the lure of beautiful clothes away from her mind. It was silly, unreal, and definitely counterrevolutionary longing.

After about half an hour, Fanya went to her room. Natalya sat down where she'd been and pulled out the style section for herself. She touched one of the photographs, as if trying to feel the texture of the dress.

Mikhail moved behind the couch, looking over her shoulder, gently twirling a strand of her hair with his forefinger. "Too bad I'm not the attaché in Paris, Natashenka," he said softly.

"Or London," she said, reaching for his hand without looking at him and pulling it down to kiss it. He kissed her ear.

She glanced at Fanya's door. Bringing his hand to her cheek and nuzzling it, she whispered, "It would take far more than being a Hero of the Soviet Union."

He whispered back, "I'd have to kiss so much ass, you'd have to chisel the brown off my nose."

She pushed his hand away giving him an impish smile and going loud again said, "Wouldn't it be wonderful if we could help our Mother Russia and the Party in one of the big embassies in the heart of our enemies?"

"Maybe, someday," Mikhail said aloud, "if we do well here."

Natalya glanced at their own bedroom door. She touched his lips with her forefinger. "I'm so sleepy," she said. "Having to be with that shallow American woman after work just so you can get closer to her husband. The things I'll do to get you to Paris." She was pulling him by both his hands toward the bedroom as she was talking.

When they got into the bedroom, Mikhail closed the door and they both begin undressing, she, slowly and deliberately, he a little more hurriedly. She dropped her shoes without using her hands and unbuttoned her dress. She let it puddle at her feet, revealing the silk slip Mikhail had looted for her from a wealthy German manor house. He was standing very still, watching her. One of the many things she loved about her husband was that he was totally unabashed about having an erection.

When they finished, she snuggled her cheek into his chest.

He whispered in her ear, "So what did you and Mrs. Koski talk about?"

Natalya didn't answer, looking up at the ceiling, images of her old orphanage flooding in. Those long, frightening nights, still trying to believe that somehow, somewhere, one or both of her parents had lived. The meanness of so many of the other girls. The cold institutional hallways. The cold beds. The cold. The barely adequate food. The unfairness. The loneliness.

"I told you what she said that night we first saw the orphanage," she whispered, still looking at the ceiling. "Even if it's just to make fewer bad memories."

"Is it something you want to do? Help at the orphanage? I know it can't be easy for you."

She twisted to look at him, whispering just inches from his face. "Oh, Misha. If I can just make fewer bad memories for just one of those little people. Just one of them."

Mikhail let her snuggle into his chest, gently stroking her hair. She knew he had no real idea of what life had been like in the orphanage. How could he? His own childhood had been nothing like hers. Both parents worked for the Kharkiv Locomotive Factory, which built tractors and tanks. They were solidly industrial working class in a favored ministry. That had gotten Mikhail out of the Ukraine and into Moscow Military School, the first step to becoming an officer.

"So, are you going to help then?" he asked again.

The twinge of fear—or guilt—rose from somewhere primitive, as it did so often. It was a simple question, but would she be allowed? What if it would be seen as fraternizing? What if she said the wrong thing? Could Mikhail turn her in? She fought it down as she had so many times before. She knew these fears were irrational, especially about Mikhail. But these reactions just went off, like saliva in Pavlov's dog. She'd been conditioned and she couldn't stop the reactions. She could only live with them and try not to let them run her life. She knew Mikhail loved her, would never betray her, but then—back came another dark thought and again she had to take a deep breath to keep it in its place. Her father had loved her mother and he had disappeared one night, leaving her mother behind. Then, two weeks later they came for her. Did her mother betray her father to the NKVD? Did he betray her under torture? In the end, it made no difference. Her parents had only survived as long as they had because her father had fought for the Bolsheviks in the civil war. Their aristocratic backgrounds eventually doomed them, no matter what their politics. She steeled herself to talk honestly with her husband. In the Soviet Union, every confidence with someone you loved was an act of political courage.

Finally forcing the dark thoughts back down, Natalya said, "Mrs. Koski, Louise, wants me to help her raise money for the orphanage. Some sort of joint American-Soviet effort."

"Hmm. Sokolov would love that. Gets you close to Koski's wife, would help Sokolov identify the leanings of important donors."

"I don't want to work for Oleg Sokolov." She shuddered slightly. "The NKVD gives me the creeps."

"MGB," he corrected her. "Whole new postwar reorganization."

"Same horror," she whispered. "I do *not* want to work for Sokolov."

"Everyone works for *a* Sokolov, just not this particular one."

"He looks at me . . . you know . . . it's creepy."

"Everyone looks at you."

"I know." She said it as if acknowledging the weather. "But not that way. He's like a hungry dog looking at a steak. And I'm the steak. Creepy."

They were both quiet.

Snuggled up against Mikhail's warm back and legs, she remembered Mikhail whispering to her one night about Stalin's purges early in Mikhail's career and how he had survived them by staying, as he put it, off the skyline. That tactic had gotten him a battalion command. Then came the Hero of the Soviet Union action that nearly killed him. That got him the division chief of intelligence job, which then led to the privileged post he now held—along with free bus transportation and an additional forty-five square meters in living space at a reduced rent if they were still in Russia she thought scoffingly. Six years of hell for an additional forty-five square meters of Communist heaven.

Mikhail had told her about the hundreds of thousands of murders in the late 1930s that the government was keeping secret. It couldn't be hidden from the army because the empty billets were there nearly every morning. Every Russian officer who survived knew full well how many did not. None of the soldiers, including Mikhail, were about to say a word about it in public. In private, however, he talked. She almost wished he hadn't. It was just one more secret to keep quiet or lie about, one more added weight to the burden of constantly guarding her thoughts, lest they both get marked as counterrevolutionaries or enemies of the People.

In public, even at the dinner table, she never knew if what Mikhail was saying was true or false until she could get him alone. She just smiled and kept quiet. Only at night, only in their bed, not even in their bedroom, when they could whisper in each other's ear, could they speak the truth. Even then, knowing that he wanted to protect her, she couldn't be certain.

What good was knowing the truth, anyway? How did it help her—or her family—learning from Mikhail that Stalin had executed tens of thousands of innocent people and sent several million more to starve and die in the gulag? How did it do any good to hear Mikhail whisper a name like Beria? Beria, who enjoyed gruesomely imaginative ways of inflicting pain. Beria, who picked out the prettiest girls. Natalya had known two of those girls—one who came back and one who didn't. Such truth she did not want to know—and if she did, how would that help her here and now?

* * *

Returning to the present, she whispered in Mikhail's ear, "Louise asked me for tea tomorrow afternoon."

"It's up to you, of course," Mikhail said, squirming around to face her. "But seriously, consider working with her. You want to help orphans. And it would look good. Might even help get us to Paris."

She made a fist and gently bumped his shoulder. "I don't want to spy on her." She was quiet for a moment. "I like her, Misha, but our countries are becoming enemies."

Mikhail reached for the pack of Camels on the bedside table. He'd pulled out one of his Balomorkanals that night they'd all visited the orphanage and Arnie Koski had wrinkled his nose and offered him one of his Camels. Seeing how much Mikhail enjoyed it, Arnie then gave him the rest of the pack, joking about seeing some of Mikhail's soldiers on the Enns with two in their mouth at the same time. A good memory. There were a few. He lit a Camel and blew the smoke carefully into the darkness, savoring the milder flavor. He and Natalya had agreed to only smoke them after making love. They'd leave the Balomorkanals out in the living room, not caring if Fanya snuck a few of those. "I have the same sadness," he said. "I like both of them."

Mikhail made a smoke ring, but in the dark could not see if he'd been successful. "And you're right. Our countries are becoming enemies. I miss the clarity of the Great Patriotic War."

"I miss nothing of it."

"No, I suppose not." He formed another smoke ring. "We soldiers, at least, were defending those we love against enemies we knew."

"Defending against who? Other soldiers who were defending the ones *they* love from soldiers like you?"

"You're trying to make war look absurd with an old argument," he said. "I agree. If everyone were motivated like the soldiers doing the actual fighting, war *would* be absurd. But you're confusing what motivates soldiers from what motivates politicians." He inhaled slowly, held the smoke in, then let it out. "Maybe, now that the war is over, I should get out of the army."

"Misha, you love the army. And you love your country."

"Unfortunately, the army doesn't report to my country," Mikhail replied. "It serves the Union of Soviet Socialist Republics, and it reports to Stalin."

"And Arnie Koski reports to Harry Truman. What's the difference?"

"Well, I suppose it's that Truman reports to the capitalists who paid for his elections."

She giggled. "Well, at least Comrade Stalin is his own man."

He laughed and gently kissed her. "Making jokes about Stalin," he whispered, "can get us both to Siberia."

He stubbed out his cigarette and rolled over to sit on top of her, her narrow waist between his knees. Natalya began stroking his hips, very slowly.

"You think Colonel and Mrs. Koski have talks like this?" she whispered.

"Probably," he answered. He leaned close to her ear. "Only they probably don't have to whisper."

She pulled his head in and kissed him. Then she opened to him again.

Louise and Arnie weren't talking; they were trying to make a baby. When they'd finished, Louise put her legs up on the headboard. Arnie, sitting next to her legs, his back against the headboard, looked down on Louise's smiling face.

"This time, for sure," she said.

He smiled gently. "It's OK, Lulu Moppet. It's OK if we never have kids."

"OK for you, maybe." She wiggled her hips as if it would help the sperm along.

After a brief silence, Arnie asked, "So did you have a success with Natalya Bobrov?"

"Russian women add an *a* to their names," Louise said.

"Bobrov*a*. So, did you get anywhere?"

"I don't know. She's good at hiding."

"It's how Russians survive."

"My idea is to get her to go with me to her legation. We take at face value that it's the way our governments say it is: that we're still allies." She scooted her rear end closer to the headboard. "We're still allies, right?"

She felt that Arnie was angry. He never showed it, but she never missed it, either. "What?" she asked.

"Officially," he answered. "Unofficially . . ." He moved to sitting on the side of the bed, his back to her. "Don't go see Abramov."

She lowered her legs from the headboard and moved to talk over his shoulder. "Don't be worried. I know we are falling out with the Russians, but for right now, all we need is *officially*, not actually. My plan is for Natalya and me to see Abramov together. Natalya can get us ten or fifteen minutes, because she works for someone who reports directly to him."

"I don't know," he said to the wall.

"Arnie. What's the risk? Think of the children."

He seemed to take that in, thinking about the pros and cons. "So, what's the pitch?" he asked.

"I'm having coffee with her tomorrow. Or at least tea. I want the two of us to ask Abramov if he'll help fund my idea of a joint Soviet-American goodwill project to help Finnish orphans."

"Good luck with that," Arnie said sarcastically.

"Oh, don't be so pessimistic. They like good publicity as much as anyone. And I'll charm the pants off him."

He didn't reply.

She simply wasn't going to be dissuaded by his natural Finnish pessimism. However, maybe she shouldn't have mentioned charming Abramov's pants off him.

Then Arnie asked, "Where are you meeting Natalya? It's important." So, it wasn't Abramov he was worried about.

"I suggested that little tea shop we like, but she insisted on tea at the Soviet legation."

"She's no fool."

"No, she most certainly isn't."

"Be careful with her. They'll be asking her to report everything."

It stopped her for a moment. Of course, it was possible. But no, surely not Natalya.

"Oh, Arnie. I'll be careful. Relax."

Friday, January 10, 1947
Soviet Legation and Natalya's Flat

E
ven though Louise had been an army wife for years, she could never get used to armed guards. To be more precise, it wasn't the guards, who were usually teenagers. It was the weapons. There is some latent violence in a loaded weapon that made her vaguely fearful. That feeling was exacerbated considerably when she presented her identification to one of the two guards who stood on either side of the Soviet legation front door. They were armed with what Louise called machineguns.

One of them disappeared inside. A few minutes later he returned, with Natalya just behind him. There was again the brief awkwardness of being air-kissed on both sides of her head, Louise pretending to be an old hand at it, and Natalya led her into a rather cozy wood-paneled room, settling them both into large armchairs. An older Finnish woman dressed in a practical maid's uniform served them tea.

They were just beginning to loosen up, both enjoying speaking French, the talk turning from formalities to pleasantries and finally to a discussion of the project, when a woman came into the room, a bit flustered. She leaned and whispered into Natalya's ears. Natalya stood and the woman left.

"I'm so sorry," Natalya said to Louise. "Fanya, our nyanya, is outside with both Alina and Grisha. Alina is throwing up."

Louise stood as Natalya gathered herself together. "Please," Natalya said, "you must finish your tea."

"I wouldn't think of it," Louise said. Natalya was already moving. Louise grabbed her coat, which was hanging on a coat tree near the door, and hurried out behind Natalya.

Out on the street a very distressed little girl of about three, with nearly white-blond hair, was crying. The front of her coat was spattered with vomit, so the vomiting had been since she'd been dressed to go outside. This must be Alina, Louise thought. Both guards were flustered. A little boy, equally towheaded, was staring at their machineguns, Grisha. A somewhat plump girl of around eighteen, presumably Fanya, was holding their hands, clearly at the end of her rope.

Natalya knelt down in front of Alina, wiped her mouth with her hand, wiped her hand on Alina's coat, and hugged her.

"I'm so sorry," Natalya said again to Louise.

Fanya lit a cigarette, blowing out smoke with relief.

"It's OK. Can I help?" Louise asked.

"No. Please don't bother. It's just an upset stomach." Just as Natalya said that, little Alina doubled over and began heaving.

"That's more than 'just an upset stomach,'" Louise said. "I'll help you take them home."

Natalya gave Louise a look of thanks, and the entourage headed for Natalya's flat. Just before they reached it, Grisha threw up.

Natalya was clearly at odds with whether to let go of Alina to help Grisha. Fanya was standing by, her cigarette almost finished. Louise stepped in and took Alina, leaving Natalya to tend to Grisha.

They got the children up to the flat.

"Is there a doctor?" Louise asked.

Natalya shrugged. "There's a nurse at the legation. How to reach her? No telephone." She felt both children's foreheads. Apparently, there was no serious fever.

Little Grisha heaved up another load. He let out a wail. It clearly hurt. Natalya started taking off his clothes. She looked at Louise. "What can we do?"

Louise simply said, "I know." She headed for the door. "I'll be right back."

She'd just gotten the children in bed when Louise returned. She had a small bottle with her. Natalya looked up at Louise questioningly.

"Coca-Cola syrup," Louise said. "It helps nausea. I brought it with me on the boat because I get seasick sometimes."

Natalya couldn't help a smile. Coca-Cola. She was really beginning to like this woman.

Saturday, January 11, 1947
Dinner at the Bobrovs'

Tea with Natalya on Friday went better than Louise had hoped. Natalya agreed to try to arrange a meeting with Abramov, the head of the Soviet legation.

The next day, Louise got a note from Natalya saying the meeting was set for Monday, the thirteenth, just before lunch. Along with the note was a dinner invitation, just the four of them at Natalya and Mikhail's flat.

It was dark when Louise and Arnie arrived at the Bobrovs' four-story stone building. She'd wanted to bring flowers or maybe some chocolates as a gift but had found neither. She had, however, gotten a can of Nescafé, which had been common fare for US troops during the war.

Inside the large double doors was a small reception area. Louise was surprised to find a male concierge sitting behind a counter. The buildings she'd been looking at didn't have one. She'd already been a bit envious of Natalya after she told Louise that she lived there for free, along with other Soviet legation staff and families. Now it seemed the Soviet legation even provided its families with free security. And here she was having to find a place for her and Arnie to live with virtually no help from the American legation.

The concierge, a humorless man in a cheap blue suit, politely but firmly asked her to sign in to a logbook stating who she was visiting and why.

Mikhail greeted them at the door to their flat. The air of the flat smelled of cigarette smoke, acrider and harsher than what Louise was used to. The living room was small, giving the sense of being overheated.

Natalya stood directly behind Mikhail, holding Grisha, while Mikhail helped the Koskis take off their heavy coats. Alina was peeking out shyly from behind Natalya. She had her hair in a long plait and Natalya had placed a purple bow just above her left ear.

Louise's heart melted.

She presented Natalya with the coffee, which seemed to genuinely thrill her, and knelt down to look Alina in the eye. She was still peeking out from behind Natalya and had followed her as Natalya placed the tin of Nescafé on a coffee table next to two partially smoked cigarettes still burning in an ashtray. Both had small cardboard tubes like little throwaway cigarette holders attached to the part with cigarette paper and tobacco. Both tubes had been crushed flat, probably to make the cigarette easier to hold.

"Do you remember me?" Louise asked the little girl in English. "Are you feeling better?" She was aware of Arnie bending over behind her back, coming down partially to Alina's level. Alina stared at them, obviously not understanding.

"She is much better," Natalya said in French. She bent down and said, "Alina," followed by Russian. Alina, in a long nightgown, made a quick curtsy, then looked up at her mother to make sure she'd done alright. Natalya beamed. "And Grisha. Show the Koskis how you are standing." She put Grisha on his feet and he stood there, only wobbling slightly.

Louise clapped her hands. "Oh, can I hold him?" she asked in French. Natalya looked with an exaggerated question on her face at Grisha, who looked a bit puzzled. She picked him up and handed him to Louise. Louise had to steady herself because of the little boy's muscular weight. "Wow, what a sturdy little man," she said. She turned to show the little boy to Arnie, who had resumed standing next to an obviously proud Mikhail.

Louise felt a little hand touching her knee and looked down at Alina, who was unhappy about her little brother getting all the attention.

Natalya said something sharp to Alina in Russian. Then to Louise, "I apologize. We are too indulgent with our children. They see so little of us during the day," she went on.

Louise leaned down toward Alina, finding she had to squat slightly to keep her balance with Grisha. "Are you spoiled?" she asked in English. Alina looked at her wide-eyed, obviously not understanding. "I would spoil you. I would spoil you rotten," Louise said.

She looked up at Natalya. "They are beautiful," she said. "You must be so proud." She turned again, bouncing Grisha slightly. Grisha was looking at his father, turning his head as Louise turned. She saw Arnie looking at her, his mouth smiling, his eyes sad. He knew. He knew how she longed.

Natalya gathered Alina in closer to her and Louise stood. It was then that Louise noticed Fanya who was watching the entire scene from the kitchen doorway. Natalya introduced her to Arnie as their "au pair." Fanya held her hand out, trying to be an adult, saying something in Russian. Then, she and Natalya went with the children to their bedroom while Mikhail served vodka "to warm up," as he put it. Natalya had put out some pickled herring and beets to go with the vodka and Louise nibbled at them, politely pretending to listen, trying to pick out words as Arnie and Mikhail spoke in Finnish, with Arnie occasionally trying to bring her in. She was relieved when Natalya finally reappeared, leaving Fanya with the children.

She sat down next to Louise and reached for the glass of vodka that had been waiting there for her. She took a good-sized drink and settled back into the couch. "You don't know how I needed that."

"Oh, Natalya," Louise said. "You don't mean that."

"Well, not really, but sometimes I could happily feed them to the lions. You have no idea."

Although she knew Natalya didn't mean anything by it, Louise felt a sudden cloud pass over her.

Natalya sensed the mood shift. She touched Louise's hand and very warmly and softly said, "Someday you will have an idea. I'm sure of it."

Louise could only nod.

For dinner, Natalya had cooked a large lake whitefish, which she served nicely displayed. Mikhail did the honors of carving and serving. It would have been totally enjoyable but for the odd presence of Fanya, who'd joined them at the table and spoke only Russian—or said she did. She just sat solemnly silent through the entire meal. Initially, Arnie tried to include Natalya, who spoke a rudimentary English, but Mikhail's English was virtually nonexistent, so Arnie kept lapsing into their common and fluent language, Finnish. This tended to leave Natalya and Louise speaking French and the conversation neatly divided by gender. Fanya helped clear the table and excused herself.

After the dishes had been cleared, more vodka was served. It was likely the vodka that led to the heated discussion between Louise and Natalya of the recent war in Europe. It was the first time that Louise heard directly that the Russians weren't pleased with the American effort.

"We sent you unimaginable amounts of trucks, gasoline, food," she said to Natalya, somewhat affronted.

"Yes, my new American friend," Natalya said. She slowly tapped ash from her cigarette into an ashtray that was sitting in the center of the table. "After 1943, when you were sure we would win. As Comrade Stalin said, your money, our blood."

Trying to remain in diplomatic mode, Louise translated what she said, as calmly as possible, to Arnie, appealing silently for some help with a look.

Arnie explained in simple Finnish that he thought Natalya could understand, occasionally asking Louise to translate something into French. The gist of it was that America was completely unprepared for the war, its army about the size of Bulgaria's when the war started. The United States simply couldn't open a second front against Germany until June of 1944, when they did so with the largest and most complex military operation in history, the Normandy invasion. This forced the Germans to fight on two fronts, hastening the Red Army's entry into Berlin.

After Arnie finished, Natalya put her silverware down and in her quiet but totally commanding way, said, "Too little, too late," in plain English. The expression was obviously familiar.

Louise had no answer, but her mouth was slightly open. Mikhail inquired in Finnish and Arnie answered him. Then Mikhail said something to Natalya in Russian and Natalya answered him, heatedly emphasizing her points with her fingers, as if counting.

Mikhail smiled at Arnie and Louise, then said something to Arnie in Finnish.

"What did he say?" Louise asked.

He apologized for Natalya's anger, then added, "We, of course, see things differently."

Louise replied, "Of course."

Arnie's tone changed. "I think we should get out of this conversation."

Louise smiled broadly at Mikhail, raised her vodka glass to him, and said, "To the Red Army."

He understood that. Glasses were raised, clinked, and Natalya, also a bit flustered, picked up a tray already set with four coffee cups and shooed the men into the living room.

This proved to start the best part of the whole night. Louise and Natalya stayed in the kitchen and had two coffees, both mixed with vodka. While their husbands talked in a foreign language in the other room, the two women found themselves absorbed in each other, finding out about their childhoods, their time at university, how they met their husbands.

On their way back to the hotel, Louise said, "I really like Natalya." After a while she asked, "No one at home ever talks about the Russians. It's like we won the war all by ourselves"—she smiled—"along with a little help from Winston Churchill. How bad was it for them?"

"No one knows for sure, but civilian and military deaths, over twenty million, close to ten million killed in action. We lost about four hundred thousand," Arnie said grimly. "Pacific *and* European theaters. That's twenty-five Russians for every one American."

"Oh," Louise said. "I see."

Monday, January 13, 1947
Lunch at the Soviet Legation

Louise's high hopes for getting money out of the meeting on Monday with the Soviet envoy were dashed.

First, she'd overestimated her ability to pitch ideas when there was no shared language, which also prevented her from turning on her usual charm. Louise had to rely on Natalya to do all the talking, while she sat there smiling like an idiot with no idea whether Natalya was making a good pitch or not. Second, she never for a moment thought that Oleg Sokolov would be there. When Natalya told her that they had a meeting with Envoy Abramov, Louise assumed they'd been invited to talk with the top man. Indeed, they did do all their talking with Abramov while Sokolov sat quietly, occasionally smiling and nodding but saying nothing. However, watching Abramov's body language and his occasional glances at Sokolov for approval, Louise realized she'd been naïve about who really held the power. It was the secret police.

Envoy and Minister Plenipotentiary Abramov only took ten minutes to say he did not have any authority to be involved in a foreign private charity.

When Natalya relayed this answer to Louise, her first response was, "Well, there are some things our legations have in common." She immediately followed with, "Tell him that he's missing the point. We want to make it an official joint Soviet-US project. It's not private charity.

It's . . ." She searched for a word. "It's like foreign relations. It would be good publicity for both countries."

"I think it best not to tell the envoy he's missing the point," Natalya said quickly. She turned, smiling, to Sokolov and Abramov. Louise couldn't understand her words, but the meaning was clear: we are so grateful you spent time with us.

Natalya gave Louise a look that said, "I'm sorry," and then she rose from her chair. Sokolov and Abramov rose as well. The two men gave a quick nod and Natalya smiled and bobbed her head down. She looked at Louise as she turned toward the door. Louise couldn't remember the protocol lessons, so she shook hands and did a very shallow knee bend, then felt foolish. She should have asked Arnie before the meeting. Damn. It was so much easier in Oklahoma.

Giving the two men her best and brightest Delta Gamma smile, she said, "Bol'shoye spasibo vam," as she'd learned from Arnie the night before. She turned to follow Natalya.

Then Sokolov said in English, "Please, one moment."

She'd forgotten that he'd spoken English at the New Year's Eve party. She smiled at him. "Mr. Sokolov?"

"Perhaps you ladies would like lunch?"

He turned to Natalya and presumably asked the same thing in Russian. Louise was certain only that she caught the briefest flicker of fear on Natalya's face before she broke into a beautiful smile. *As if she'd just been made Queen for a Day*, Louise thought a little darkly.

"He wants to take us to lunch in the legation dining room," Natalya said to her quietly in French. "Only the big bonnets eat there." She said the latter phrase almost deferentially.

Louise stopped herself from a quip about the classless society. Instead, she turned on "you're doing fine Oklahoma" in her head and, beaming at Sokolov, said, "We'd love to."

If it was awkward in Abramov's office, it was more so at lunch. Sokolov knew he was charming. Louise felt charmed and flattered. At the same time, however, she knew that Sokolov knew he was charming her. So, it felt somewhat like being in a play. She wondered if all diplomatic conversations were like this. It also occurred to her that maybe all the talk about Sokolov just wasn't true. It didn't jibe with this rather charming man talking to her over a perfectly nice lunch. Maybe it was all rumor. He could even encourage it, because it would make people afraid of him, a common strategy for gaining power.

She would normally have looked to Natalya for some insight on how to read this man. She needed her interpretation not just of the language but of the meaning behind the words. The problem was, because only Sokolov spoke Russian and English, he controlled the conversation, talking to Natalya in Russian and to her in English, isolating Louise from comparing notes with Natalya in French, which would have looked disrespectful at best, but, remembering Arnie's reaction to her note to Natalya in French, suspicious, perhaps even dangerous for Natalya.

For Natalya, lunch was like sharing food with a rattlesnake. The food was of course excellent. The bosses ate well—and drank better. There were items on the menu that Natalya had only heard of but never seen, and Sokolov generously urged her and Louise to order anything they wanted. She hesitated, feeling a little guilty. Mikhail, who had access to such information, had told her several weeks earlier that tens of thousands, including children, were at this moment dying from starvation in the Ukraine. Mikhail explained it as a necessary cost of establishing Communist governments in Eastern Europe. Large quantities of grain were being sent from the Ukraine to keep Eastern Europeans from starving, lest they turn to the capitalists for help. A revolt in one of the recently occupied European countries would put a large hole in the buffer zone Comrade Stalin was building to protect Russia from the Western capitalist imperialists. So, Ukrainians starved. Comrade Stalin was cruel—she knew that—but he was no fool. Better some Ukrainian kulaks lose a little weight than lose another twenty million Russians to invasion from the West. Cruel times require cruel leaders. She pushed down a niggling thought that perhaps cruel leaders create cruel times.

She looked at the enticing menu items before her. Obviously, the food was already here. It couldn't go to the Ukraine anyway. So, bosses ate better than the bossed. So what? She didn't want to think on it any further. She'd always been told that the Party was there to make sure that everything was shared equally. Well, certainly it was true in Russia. But she'd never been to a boss's lunchroom in Russia.

She ordered as many unfamiliar menu items as she could without making herself look ridiculous.

Natalya could see that Louise was getting more giggly than usual, laughing at Sokolov's quips. Natalya was uncertain which of the two women he was playing to more. Probably both. Louise, bless her Oklahoma heart, was as wholesome, lovely, and innocent as Cosette in *Les Misérables*. She had long known that such innocence attracted men of power like Sokolov, who were far from innocent and seldom dealt with innocent people. She was also painfully aware of another difference between her and Louise. If she were to somehow anger or alienate Sokolov by rejecting him, for example, which she certainly would, he could seriously hurt her husband. If Sokolov made a play for her, it would only be an exercise in power, something that he probably did frequently and presented no challenge. Louise was under no such threat. If, however, he managed to seduce Louise, he'd brag about it for years.

The food was wonderful and eating it a rare opportunity, but Natalya felt a whisper of fear, as if she were hearing the quiet warning rattle of a pit viper. If she reached for a kotlety would the snake strike her hand?

* * *

Between the main course and dessert, Natalya managed to find some private time in the ladies' room with Louise, who immediately asked her, "Why do you think he invited us lunch?"

"He's just being polite," she answered, annoyed at Louise's impulsiveness. She rolled her eyes up at the ceiling. Louise looked puzzled for just a moment, then caught on.

Louise had been taught by both her mother and father to never accept a low-level no. By that they meant if some bureaucrat turned you down, you somehow got an appointment with the next bureaucratic level up and asked for the same favor. She'd further learned from Arnie that the indirect approach usually yielded more satisfactory battlefield results and with lower casualties than a direct assault. Having just before lunch perceived who really called the shots at the Russian legation in Helsinki, she'd decided to take up the cause of the orphanage with Sokolov directly. At lunch, she'd spent most of the time, up to now, softening him up. Now, however, over tea and dessert, it was time for the request.

She studied Sokolov as he studied the breasts of the young woman pouring the tea. His thick, dark hair was combed straight back, giving him a bohemian air. He had classic Slavic high cheekbones. On Natalya, they made her exotically beautiful. On Sokolov, they seemed to set his eyes back behind them, giving the impression that he was looking at you secretly.

The young woman finished serving the tea. Sokolov turned his attention back to Louise, without acknowledging the server at all. Louise felt that excitement of mutual attraction mixed with a little danger.

Careful, Louise, she thought to herself. She'd spent most of the war years with lonely women, all of whom are vulnerable to what she was feeling now, the titillation of being desired, even though she knew that she'd never cheat on Arnie. Even more pleasing, however, was being more desired than Natalya. Back then, it was just other lonely wives. Here, it was Natalya, more beautiful and sophisticated and probably more intelligent than any of them, including her.

She saw Natalya take a sip of her tea and look at her over the top of her cup. Louise could tell that Natalya knew what was going on.

She took a sip of her own tea and lowered it just enough for Sokolov to see her smile. "I haven't had such good tea since, well"—she laughed— "I've never had such good tea."

"Yes. Russia is known for it."

"We Americans always think of the English."

"They do have good tea. I was there in 1936."

"So, that's why your English is so good," Louise gushed.

Sokolov smiled. Bingo.

"Mr. Sokolov—" Louise began.

"Please. Olezka."

"Olezka," she said, putting just the right amount of warmth into it. "I am not a diplomat."

He nodded—of course. He waited to see where she was going.

"I come from a place called Oklahoma, where we speak plainly."

"That sounds like a very nice sort of place."

"It is."

"You wish to speak plainly?"

Louise launched. "You were in the meeting with Envoy Abramov." She smiled ruefully. "You know that it sort of flopped."

"What is *flopped*?"

"Like a person flopped back on a bed." She mimed it throwing her arms back. "Collapsed."

"Yes. It flopped." He paused just a bit and Louise tilted her head, encouraging him to continue. "He cannot find a way to give you money." Then he stopped.

Louise knew he was waiting for her to move. So, she did.

"Natalya and I, as we explained, think a joint American-Soviet effort to help the orphans would look very good in these tense times."

"Look good where?"

"With a little push, we could have it in newspapers and radio all over the world. Right now, the news is about nothing but tensions. Maybe it's time for some positive publicity."

"Publicity. Is that an American word for propaganda?"

Was he being serious or making a joke? "Let's just say it means doing a good job and letting people know about it."

Sokolov shrugged and made as if thinking it over. "It would, of course, have to be reviewed."

"Of course. Of course. We'd do nothing like that without you having a look at it." She leaned across the table toward him. "Can you help us? Just a little seed money. We can do the rest."

He smiled. "Perhaps." He shrugged again. "But, money is difficult."

"I know that. But surely, it is a cause that the Soviet legation would love to be part of. It would help people understand just how generous and kind the Soviet Union really is." She knew someone as sophisticated as Sokolov knew that they both knew the Soviet Union was neither generous nor kind, but publicity countering that fact was a good thing. "And Natalya would really like to help," she continued. "You know she is an orphan."

Hearing her name mentioned, Natalya turned toward Louise. "Natalya, tell him how you lost your parents."

"No need," she said. "He knows already. It's what he does."

"Oh."

"It is usual."

Sokolov was sipping his tea. He put down the cup and spoke to Natalya in Russian.

Natalya turned to Louise and said in French, "Whatever you said, he says he's not opposed in principle. He, however, wants to know if we have a specific number in mind. Do we?"

Louise turned to Sokolov. She had worked this out before the meeting with Abramov, but they'd been dismissed before she could say it. She gave him the number.

There was no reaction at all. He simply blinked. Then he said, in English, "You understand, of course, that a joint effort would require joint funding." He let that hang in the air.

Louise blanched inwardly but kept her positive face on. Did Sokolov somehow know that Hamilton had already turned her down? Could she make some headway with Hamilton if he knew—or more precisely if his masters back in Washington knew—that the funds would be matched by the Soviet legation?

"Of course," she replied. "Max Hamilton has already assured us of his support." She remembered arguing with her mother when she was in high school that all lies were bad. How could society function, she'd asked, if no one knew who was telling the truth and when? Her mother had actually taken her hand—something she rarely did—and looking into her eyes said, "You're too young to understand white lies. They can be used honorably, but only by mature people." She hoped the current lie and her level of maturity were the case. As soon as she told Sokolov that she had Hamilton's support, implying that the money was guaranteed, she'd felt that same feeling she got climbing the back side of Suicide Rock at Wolfarth Lake, emerging from the cottonwoods out onto the open space next to the cliff's edge to look down at her friends, all looking up at her and all wondering—including her—whether she would have the courage to jump.

Sokolov looked at her. He seemed to be studying her eyes. She felt like she was falling down the face of the cliff. It was too late now. The money would have to be found.

Sokolov said, "OK. I will see what can be done."

Victory.

Sokolov spoke rapidly to Natalya, who nodded and smiled. "I have told Natalya there is no problem," he said to Louise.

"I am so grateful."

"So, that is behind us." He smiled. "I understand your search for housing is not going well."

"How do you know that?"

"Please, Mrs. Koski, shall we say I heard it . . . how do you say it . . . through the grapevine." He smiled, but it was like someone knowing a secret.

She felt a chill. "Well, the grapevine has it right. I'm going crazy in that hotel of ours. We've been there over a month."

"Finding suitable accommodations is always difficult," he said evenly.

Louise nodded, smiling, wishing he were a little more sympathetic.

"And now"—Sokolov looked at his watch—"I am so sorry, but I have a meeting to attend in just a few minutes. It has been a pleasure meeting you." He turned to Natalya. "Both of you." He turned back to Louise. "Perhaps we could meet again, to let me know how your search is going."

"Of course." He then said something in Russian to Natalya, who bobbed a quick nod of her head. "Mrs. Koski," he said as a farewell. He raised his hand with one finger in the air. A young man appeared from somewhere, clearly there to escort the two women out.

After the two women left, Sokolov put his elbows on the desk back in his office and cradled his face in his hands, overcome with longing. He could have wept for the feeling of loss, watching these two women during lunch, but he'd gone beyond weeping years ago. Last time he'd wept was for the death of his wife and two young daughters. He had been stationed on the Polish border when the German onslaught came. His wife and family had been at her parents' house in Ukraine. He had not heard from them since. He'd searched for them for a year, but by June of 1942 there was still no trace of them, and he knew there never would be.

On that June day, he'd wept. Since then, he pursued his job of keeping his country and the Party safe from threats with grim determination. He'd tortured German prisoners and any German or German sympathizer he thought might have information that would help them destroy their German enemy. He'd tortured fellow Russians to make sure they *weren't* enemies. He sent them all to their deaths, to make sure others would not become enemies if they were thinking about it. But that suspicion, that some might be *thinking about* betraying the Party, was shared by many—and that became an additional and frightening motivation all its own. The closer they got to Berlin and the end of the war, the more the motivation of uncovering the Party's enemies faded and the motive of uncovering those who might be thinking about becoming the Party's enemies grew—and became primary. He had to constantly prove his loyalty. So, he grimly set himself a goal of a certain number of arrests and convictions each month. It was the only way to assure that some other NKVD officer wouldn't accuse *him* of being an enemy. If some innocent suffered from torture or was wrongly executed—well, many innocents suffered from combat, from wounds, lost their lives—all in defense of the ideal that kept him from suicide, the preservation of the revolution, the Party, and deepest of all, Mother Russia.

He'd lived through years of brutal war, witnessing atrocities and the results of atrocities committed by both sides. He'd seen the pathetic scraps of the barely human survivors of three German concentration camps. He'd watched weeping Russian prisoners, liberated at last from their slave labor in prisoner of war camps, men whom he had to torture to be sure they were still loyal, most of whom were sent to the gulag just to be sure. For Sokolov, the systematic raping of German women and the brutal employment of German prisoners as slave labor was a just—and lenient—punishment for being Fascist supporters of the regime that had killed over twenty million of his people and his own family. He'd lived all of this since that last day of tears in June 1942 and it had put Sokolov far beyond weeping.

Yet, these two women, eager to do good, the one as striking and exotic as any heroine that Modest Mussorgsky could have dreamed into existence, the other, the kind of woman in whose lap you'd like to place your head, staring up at a clear summer sky after sharing a picnic, filled him with longing so terrible he wasn't sure he could ever raise his head from his hands and look at his world. That longing was of course tinged with the excitement of sex, but he knew the longing was for something to fill the dark hole of despair that lay beneath the thin ice upon which he skated. Both women were married to blind, self-righteous soldiers who didn't deserve them. People like him did the hard, dirty work that kept the state safe, only to have people like Bobrov look down on them. As if the army didn't do more raping than the NKVD, as if killing an enemy of the state when you are both in uniform is somehow morally superior to killing an enemy of the state when neither of you is in uniform.

And the two women gave themselves to *them* and not to him.

He nearly hurled himself up from his desk, tearing himself from the emptiness and, yes, self-pity. He laughed at himself, derisively and out loud. He went to stand before the window, staring into the gloom. He imagined the land beyond the buildings, much like the land of his home south of Moscow, gently undulating to outright flat, the altitude never varying by much more than a hundred meters. There were lots of lakes outside Helsinki. He remembered the lake just south of the village. He and his friends used to swim in it on hot summer days. They skated on it in winter. When he last saw it, three burned tanks, one German and two Russian, littered the shore.

He looked back at his desktop. It had the usual files, compilations of activities that could be seen as detrimental to the state. He'd have to uncover some threat soon, or he'd come under suspicion. It was the constant pressure of the job. It occurred to him that he should start documenting visits between Natalya Bobrova and Louise Koski. They could easily be made to look suspicious. He didn't like the idea. He liked both of them and both seemed to be decent, albeit the American seemed somewhat innocent. Then, he thought, maybe the innocence was a cover. He sighed, knowing he'd have to document visits, just in case one or both of the women came under suspicion. If he didn't show that he had suspected them, then he would himself come under suspicion.

He slumped back down in his chair and picked a file at random. He didn't open it.

Friday, January 17, 1947
Natalya's Flat

Because it was Fanya's normal evening off, Natalya had asked if Louise could come to her flat on Friday night to continue planning the joint venture.

When Louise got to Natalya's apartment, she was surprised to find Fanya still there.

As Natalya took her coat, Louise said, "I thought it was Fanya's evening off?"

"It is," Natalya said. She glanced into the living room where Fanya was sitting in an armchair, reading. "She knew you were coming."

"Well, that's flattering."

"Don't flatter yourself," she said softly. She led Louise into the living room. Fanya stood politely, nodded, and sat back down without smiling or saying anything beyond hello. She returned to her reading.

Louise gave Natalya a look, but Natalya shrugged as if nothing were unusual.

Alina and Grisha were both on the floor at Fanya's feet, playing with pots and pans. There was a little stuffed giraffe on wheels and a ragdoll abandoned on the floor next to the couch.

Louise squatted, pulling her skirt tight across her thighs. "Hello Grisha. Hello Alina," she said, smiling warmly. She quickly modified her American hello to *privet*.

Grisha looked at his beaming mother. Natalya encouraged him with a nod and a smile. She turned to Louise. "He doesn't talk much, yet." Alina had been silently looking at Louise, as if still trying to figure out if Louise were safe or not. She had her mother's incredible eyes.

"Oh my," Louise said to her in French. "You are going to be a heartbreaker." Alina, not understanding, looked over at her mother.

Natalya laughed. "Very likely, including her own in the process."

Louise looked up at Natalya. She wondered if perhaps Natalya had a heartbreak of her own when she was younger. She wanted to ask but thought it might be too personal. Instead, she asked where Mikhail was.

"Working. Always working."

"What's he working on?"

The look Natalya gave her made her wish she hadn't asked that.

"I'm so sorry. I don't mean to pry. I'm just . . . Oh, hell. I *goofed*." She used the English word, as she didn't have one in French.

Natalya smiled. "*Goofed*?"

"Made a stupid mistake." She then quickly added, "Unintentional."

"Aren't all mistakes unintentional?"

"I suppose they are," Louise said. It sounded so dumb.

Was Natalya sparring with her? Why? She just wanted to be friends. She knew that Natalya wanted the same. She suddenly envied her friends whose husbands had been given regular military assignments in Germany or Japan, where they didn't have to walk on these eggshells of diplomacy.

Natalya was looking at her it seemed a little sadly, with those luminous café au lait eyes of hers.

To do something to fill the uncomfortable silence, Louise arranged herself to sit on her bottom a little closer to the children, her legs crossed. She held her arms out to both. Grisha looked at his mother, and seeing that she was smiling and nodding encouragement, crawled over to Louise, who quickly scooped him up and settled him on her lap. Alina, not to be outdone, quickly crawled onto her lap next to him. She had them both, now, hugged together. She took in a deep breath, smelling their hair.

Alina broke Louise's hug and crawled over to where Fanya was sitting on the couch. She started banging a pot with a spoon. Fanya ignored her. Natalya moved to sit on the sofa next to Fanya and leaned down to engage with Alina. Fanya just kept reading.

Wondering what kind of nanny this Fanya girl was, Louise began playing a finger-pulling game with Grisha.

After a few minutes, Natalya rose to her feet. "I think it's time to put them to bed."

"Can I help? Please say yes."

Natalya chuckled.

"What?" Louise asked.

"I'd forgotten that washing my children is a joy not a chore. It's all too easy to do." She paused. "Forget. Not the chore."

Natalya got the two children bathed and ready for bed while Louise tagged along, enjoying watching Natalya, occasionally pitching in where she could. At one point Louise asked, "Doesn't Fanya help you put them to bed?"

"I told you. It's her evening off."

"Oh." Louise took this in. "But why—"

Louise was cut off by Natalya flicking her hand up, where Fanya couldn't see it, in the universal sign for stop. This young, somewhat awkward and plump nanny frightened Natalya, in her own home.

They finished settling the children and sat at the kitchen table to plan. Natalya had brought out a bottle of vodka and English Orange Squash. Louise was at first horrified, but wanting to be polite, accepted the drink. Natalya seemed to be very proud of being able to offer the cocktail.

"Do you have a name for this?" Louise asked.

Expecting something in Russian, she was surprised when Natalya, expressing her own surprise, said, "It's a *screwdriver*. You don't know it? I understand your pilots invented it during the war."

Louise shrugged, a no. "Well, my husband always said that the Army Air Corps is wonderfully inventive when it comes to, uh, creature comforts."

Several screwdrivers later, the plan, mostly about finding money, was done, despite the two women increasingly giggling like schoolgirls. Natalya, who'd been in Helsinki a few months longer than Louise, added considerably to the plan. Because a sizable number of older Finns spoke Russian, a remnant of Russification before Finland gained independence thirty years earlier, Natalya would take on most of the Finnish fundraising possibilities, while Louise would focus on the Western European expat community, most of whom spoke English.

When it was clear that the planning was over, her inhibitions gone with the last screwdriver, Louise said, "So. You had a heartbreak, didn't you. Come on. Tell me."

Natalya, pressing her lips together and repressing a smile, shook her head.

"Come on," Louise wheedled.

"OK," Natalya said.

Louise sat back down.

"When I was sixteen, I spent a summer, like many students, working on a collective farm. Potatoes! I still can't eat them."

Louise encouraged her nonverbally.

"He was funny. Intelligent."

"And?"

"Yes. He was good-looking." Natalya seemed to be looking at the memory. "Thick blond hair. Those kind of arms and shoulders that make you feel safe."

"So! You kissed him."

"I did. My first."

"And . . ."

"And what?"

"What happened to him?"

She hesitated. "They came and got him," she said softly.

Louise blinked. "Who came?"

Natalya looked at Louise with incredulity, which she quickly covered. She nodded toward the living room where Fanya was sitting.

"But what for? I mean, there must have been some charge."

"Only if there is a trial. There was none."

"You never heard from him?"

Natalya shook her head, her lips pursed.

"You must have been heartbroken."

"I don't think you have any idea," Natalya said.

Louise could only stay silent, overwhelmed by the sudden understanding of what it must be like to live in a world where "they" could come any time and take away your first love.

"Yes. I was heartbroken," Natalya said, breaking the silence. "But whether in love or life in general, any Russian over the age of three has been heartbroken."

As Natalya was escorting Louise down to the front door, they were alone for a moment on the stairs. Still a bit inebriated, Louise plunged in with the question that had been on her mind the whole evening. "Fanya doesn't speak French, does she? Why were you shushing me?" Natalya, too, had a bit too much to drink. In a low, patient voice she explained,

"No. I don't think she speaks French. But we can't be sure, so we have to be careful." She shrugged. "She doesn't need to. Not her job."

"So, what is her job exactly? Her other job," Louise clarified.

With a wistful smile Natalya said, "She keeps track of our conversations with visitors. It is usual."

"Usual?"

"Yes. The revolution is still new. It is important that opposition to the revolution be uncovered."

"You can't believe that."

"Louise," Natalya said slowly and carefully, "we believe what we must."

Saturday, January 18, 1947
Louise and Arnie's New Flat

T he next day, Saturday, a message was brought up to Louise and Arnie's room. Arnie was working sixty-hour weeks, so he wasn't there. Louise tipped the messenger and quickly opened the envelope. It was a message from Natalya. She knew of a couple vacating their apartment.

She held the note against her chest, doing a little dance, thinking how nice it was to have a new friend who was looking out for her and Arnie.

She ran down the stairs to the lobby to call Natalya at work, as she'd requested in the note.

An hour later, she met Natalya in the small hotel lobby. Natalya was bundled in a thick overcoat and smoking, her cheeks flushed from the cold. She'd obviously walked from her work.

"Oh, Natalya," Louise nearly squealed. "I cannot tell you how much this means to us. You're a miracle worker. We're so grateful. Thank you."

"First, let's see if you like it," Natalya replied. She smiled a bit shyly in the face of Louise's effusive praise.

"How ever did you find out? Does anyone else know?"

"I have a friend who processes all the routine personnel paperwork. She got wind of a transfer." She smiled shyly again, looking briefly at the floor instead of at Louise. "She told me, and I asked her if she'd keep it to herself for a day or two." She gave a little chuckle. "You know, knowledge is power."

Louise wasn't sure Natalya was referring to her friend or herself. She didn't really care.

"Can we see it now?" Louise asked.

Natalya nodded, smiling.

The two hooked elbows as they walked along the icy sidewalk. Louise hadn't linked elbows with anyone except Arnie since she was in junior high school. It felt good. It was accepted here.

Twenty minutes later, they arrived in front of a beautiful old stone apartment building. Natalya opened the large ornate door and ushered Louise into a small reception area with two stuffed chairs, a side table between them with the ubiquitous ashtray. Waiting for the elevator to come down to their level, she whispered, "My friend told me they're moving tomorrow. A sudden transfer back to Moscow. I think we know about it almost as soon as they did." She smiled conspiratorially. Louise smiled back.

Arriving on the fourth floor, the highest, the elevator opened onto the center of a hallway with bare walls. Two apartments on the left and two on the right stood opposite each other. Louise knew that meant they would have a corner apartment if they got it. She waited eagerly while Natalya knocked. A woman opened the apartment door and, looking at the floor, let Natalya and Louise in. It seemed to Louise that they were expected. But, of course, Natalya—or maybe this friend in the office—could have told her. It was clear the occupants were leaving; there were crates and cardboard boxes everywhere.

Natalya was speaking Russian with the woman. The woman looked down, avoiding Natalya's eyes, and mumbled something. Quickly looking at Louise, she got a coat and scarf and left.

"She needn't go," Louise said.

"You need to have some time with the place alone," Natalya said. "She'll be fine."

Louise was walking around, looking out the windows. She could see the harbor.

"Who lives in the building?"

"Mostly Control Commission families. We had two legation families here. This one is returning to Moscow."

"Didn't seem like they got much time."

"It's usual," Natalya said quietly.

Louise inspected the bathroom. When she came back, Natalya gave her a questioning look.

"I love it," she said. "I don't know how I can ever—"

Natalya stopped her. "It is what friends do."

Louise nodded, grateful, both for the information on the apartment and for the fact that Natalya had called her a friend.

"Of course, I want Arnie to see it." She knew it was a formality. As a good army wife, selecting the apartment was her job. Arnie wouldn't care as long as she liked it.

"Of course."

"Can I bring him here tonight?"

Natalya gave that all-expressive shrug. "Why not. They're leaving tomorrow. Everything mostly packed up. The usual routine is for them to stay temporarily at the legation. So, it'll be empty by the time Arnie gets off work."

"Oh, I *love* it."

Louise made another quick tour. To heck with Arnie. He'd love it if she loved it. And she loved it. "We'll take it. What do we need to do?"

"You'll need to talk to the building manager. She'll have the lease and the keys." Natalya handed Louise a piece of paper with a Finnish name and phone number on it. "My friend has the names of everyone's building manager." Again, the shrug. "It's part of her job."

*　*　*

Louise wasted no time contacting the manager. When Arnie got home that night, she rushed him over to the apartment. The packing boxes were gone. The apartment was empty, the living room lit by a single-bulb overhead light.

Arnie made a quick tour, looking out all the windows. He never even went into the bathroom. "Looks OK to me," he said. "Is there a lease?"

Louise proudly pulled the lease from her purse. "Six months minimum, a year if we want to lock in the price longer."

Arnie smiled, shaking his head in appreciation. "You are a treasure."

She beamed as he looked over the lease. It was written in Finnish. When he got to the last page, he smiled. "It looks like we've already agreed to a year."

Louise looked closely at his face to read his mood.

"You want to celebrate?" Arnie asked.

Louise clapped her hands before hugging him.

Hamilton OK'd Pulkkinen to help Louise move on Monday afternoon, as Arnie was scheduled at Finnish army headquarters for the whole day. Pulkkinen was his usual helpful, stolid self. When the last crate had been deposited in the new apartment, Louise offered him a cup of coffee, a perk of being with the American legation, made on their new stove. Not only was it a gesture of thanks, but she was determined to find out more about him.

She sat a mug down in front of him, poured herself a mug and sat opposite.

"So, *Pulk*kinen. I don't even know your first name."

"Toivo."

"Does that mean anything in English?"

"Hope."

Luckily, she'd had a lot of experience starting conversations with Arnie's relatives. Getting to answers that had more than one word took time.

"Where did you grow up?"

"Kaustinen."

"Where's that?"

Pulkkinen blinked. Then he said, "Up north."

Two words.

"Up north?" She left the question dangling.

"Near Kokkola."

"That's where Arnie's family is from!"

"I know."

"You know?"

Again, there was this slight hesitancy, just as when he'd used the word "reticence," as if he'd let something go that he shouldn't have. He quickly added, "We drivers are briefed."

When Arnie got back from work at eight o'clock that night, the apartment was strewn with ripped-open packing crates from America. Louise was exhausted. Still, she had managed to go down to the harbor to get a fish, which she fried on the tiny electric stove. It was their first meal at home since they left America.

Later, in their familiar bedding, they made love for the first time in their new home.

Arnie was nearly asleep when Louise pulled her legs off the wall behind the bed. There was no headboard.

"Do you think Pulkkinen's a spy?"

"Yes."

She scooted her back against the wall.

"You do?"

"Yes. We just don't know who for."

"Arnie!" She shook his shoulder slightly. "Talk."

"He's young. Maybe his first assignment. Makes mistakes."

"He doesn't seem like a Communist."

"What does a Communist *seem* like, Louise?"

"Oh, you know. Sort of shifty."

"Shifty." Arnie looked at her a bit incredulously. "Louise, my grand-mother, Aino, is a Communist."

"Oh. Yeah. I keep forgetting."

"Because she's not shifty."

She was momentarily stopped. Still, the thought of Pulkkinen being a real spy was exciting.

"So, do you think he works for the Russians?"

"As I said, it's a good possibility."

"There are others?"

"The Valpo, short for Valtiollinen poliisi, Finnish secret police. Their upper ranks are riddled with Russian sympathizers." He paused. "Could be the English."

"Arnie! The English?"

"We spy on them."

"We do? But Arnie, they're our allies!"

"So were the Russians."

"Oh, Arnie. Really?" She was leaning on an elbow, looking at him directly.

"Really," Arnie said, but there was a hint of a smile.

"You're just kidding me."

"OK. It's unlikely he works for the Brits. Besides, they probably wouldn't have the budget."

"Whew. It's bad enough not knowing who's who around here."

She lapsed into silence. Then, before he could fall asleep, she asked, "What do you think?"

"About?"

"About the apartment?" she moaned.

"It's great. I love it."

"Good. Me, too."

"How ever did you find it?"

"Natalya heard about it and sent me a message."

Arnie stiffened. He turned to her, totally awake. "Natalya? How did she learn about it?"

"She has a friend who works in personnel."

"A friend," Arnie said flatly.

"She sees all the paperwork about a lot of things, like who's getting transferred."

Arnie pulled her ear in next to his lips—a bit roughly she thought—and whispered, "Are you nuts?"

For a moment, she was stunned by his reaction. Then, her stomach dropped. Fear-tinged suspicion flooded her with thoughts. Why had that woman been expecting them and so, so compliant? In retrospect, it seemed like she'd sort of been a little frightened. Of Natalya? No, impossible. But maybe not. Louise realized that she still barely knew Natalya. She felt a little dizzy. Her intuition said Natalya was a friend, but could she trust her intuition in a world filled with disinformation and deceit?

Arnie put his forefinger to his lips. "That's so nice of her," he said aloud. "I think maybe you've found a friend."

He got out of bed and began looking around the room, naked. He was on his knees by the steam radiator beneath the window when he suddenly rose, pointing down at the floor. He motioned for her to come over. He put his finger on what looked like a floor bolt and pointed a finger at her to wait.

He went to the dresser, took one of his business cards, went back and slid the card between the bolt head and the floor. It was clearly fake.

He gave her a fierce look. She put her hands to her cheeks, mouthing, "I'm so sorry."

Arnie motioned her back to the bed, then in a normal voice, said, "How about something to eat? You know how I am after . . . You know." His eyes were shooting lightning.

She recovered enough to say, "OK. How about some eggs?"

She scrambled some eggs and made toast in the small electric oven, saying nothing. She felt stupid. She wondered if there was any way of getting out of the lease.

She put the eggs in front of him and sat down. After several bites, he began writing on the margins of the newspaper that was on the table. He pushed it across to her.

There are probably others, his note read.

She wrote, *Do you want to get out of the lease? I'm so sorry.*

Arnie wrote on the paper again. *You should be.*

He let that sink in, then he wrote, *Could use to send false information.*

Louise reached across the table to touch his hand, again mouthing, "I'm so sorry."

He pulled his hand away.

She wanted to be swallowed by some large animal.

Monday, January 20, 1947
Soviet Legation

On Monday morning, Julia, Sokolov's secretary, stopped in front of Natalya's desk. "Comrade Sokolov would like to see you."

Natalya's stomach fell, but she put on a bright smile. "Now?"

"He said at your convenience."

Natalya stood, patted her hair, and straightened her skirt. Julia was already walking away. At your convenience meant now.

When Julia ushered her into Sokolov's office, Sokolov was going through what looked to Natalya like a personnel file. "Comrade Bobrova to see you," Julia said and left, leaving Natalya standing there. Sokolov looked up without smiling. With a quick gesture, he indicated that she should sit. Then he continued going through the file.

Natalya sat down and waited, her hands on her lap.

Sokolov closed the file and casually moved it closer to where Natalya could see it. "Your husband has a remarkable war record," he said, smiling. "We don't see many Heroes of the Soviet Union."

Again, the small dropping sensation of fear. They'd been in Helsinki several months, so Sokolov wasn't just looking at the file to get acquainted.

She smiled brightly and said, "Yes. I am very proud of him."

"As you should be," he said. He smiled back, but it reminded Natalya of the way Galena Semyonova, who bullied her at school, used to smile when she collected the weekly kopeks Natalya had to pay to keep Galena quiet about her aristocratic parents.

"I see that he fraternized with American troops during the war."

The fear grew. He, of course, had met Colonel Koski in Austria. But that wasn't fraternization. Was it?

"He did link up with American troops, our allies, when the Red Army was surrounding the Germans," she said carefully. "It is not a secret that he met Lieutenant Colonel Koski."

"And they got drunk."

What to say to that? Every combat soldier in the Red Army got one hundred grams of vodka a day. If they'd distinguished themselves, they got two hundred. Half the male population had been in the Red Army and half of them got through the war courtesy of the green snake: vodka. "Would two soldiers not celebrate our victory over Fascism?" she asked innocently.

Sokolov actually chuckled. "Oh, you're good," he said. He then flipped some pages. Looking up again, he said, "Louise Koski was at your flat from around seven until nine Friday night."

Again, the lurch. "Yes, Comrade Sokolov. We were working on the joint orphan project."

Sokolov leaned back in his chair. "Yes, yes," he said. "Of course." He said it as if he'd somehow been reminded of the project. She knew full well that Fanya had informed Sokolov of everything.

"We're making good progress," she said.

"Good. I'm so glad to hear it. We care about the Finnish orphans, of course, even when we have so many of our own children orphaned. We are all in this together after all. There are just orphans, children, not Russian, not Finnish. Children know nothing of national borders. Nor will they ever once capitalism withers away," he added quickly.

Natalya smiled. She knew Sokolov was spouting just one of many Party clichés. He was signaling the tone for what would be coming next.

She knew how she must respond. "I am so happy that you've given me an opportunity to make such a vital contribution."

Sokolov smiled. Then he leaned forward. She knew that he knew that she knew how to play. That was part of the privileged life.

"Comrade Bobrova," he said. "You and your husband have excellent records. You have both been good and loyal comrades, and we have no problem commending you to your superiors." He gave only a quick glance at the files. She knew what was coming next—and it came. "I would like you to do us a favor though."

"Of course, anything."

He made a slight frown, as if thinking, to make what he was about to say sound like he hadn't thought about it until just this moment. She also knew that he knew that she knew. It was the game. Everyone played. "This Louise Koski . . ." he began slowly.

Natalya nodded, expectantly.

"She is, how should I say it, unguarded?"

Natalya nodded, joining the conspiracy. She knew he was about to ask her to pump Louise for information. She'd feared the possibility ever since they'd had lunch. *Unguarded*, she thought with a slight smile. Comrade Sokolov was mistaking naïveté for stupidity. It was a common mistake made by powerful men, particularly when it came to women. Yes, Louise Koski was naïve, Natalya thought, but the longer she knew her, the more she realized Louise was far from stupid or a pushover. Quite the opposite. "What would you like me to learn, Comrade?" Play the game.

"Woman stuff. You know. Talk about husbands. What they like. What they don't like." He paused. "Weaknesses."

She nodded.

"Is Colonel Koski more Finnish than American? Or the other way around?" He slowly shook his head. "It's a problem we don't share. If you're a Russian, you're a Russian. We have no such thing as they do like Japanese Americans or German Americans."

"Is that it, Comrade Sokolov? Stuff wives know?"

"Mostly." He pursed his lips, again pretending he was thinking. "What is he working on? Who have they seen socially? What does he complain about? Legation gossip. Who is new? Who is in favor?" He paused, then making it clear how important it was, said, "We want to know if they're really married. She could be an agent using the cover of a naïve American wife to get closer to other wives." He looked at her with those oddly dead eyes. "Wives like you."

The small stomach lurch was her signal that she was on dangerous grounds. She was frightened. She dared not show it. To do so would not only make her look weak but also that she'd been taken in and was therefore a security risk herself.

"Of course, Comrade Sokolov. I've been fully aware of that possibility. This whole American-Soviet orphanage project always did seem a bit contrived." She observed herself saying that, but in her heart, she couldn't believe Louise was a spy. But then, a good spy would want her to believe that.

Sokolov made a noncommittal grunt and began tidying the files on his desk. Natalya understood this was her cue to leave. As she was getting to her feet, he said, "Perhaps it will be best if you kept this talk between us," he said.

"Of course."

"That includes telling your husband."

She gulped inwardly. "Of course."

"I'll make sure there's no problem with your work commitments in the economics section."

"Thank you, that's very kind."

Natalya was now frowning, thinking hard. "But when women talk about their husbands," she said, "they share information. Otherwise, there's no trust. What should I share?"

Sokolov chuckled. "My dear Natalya." She noticed he'd dropped the Comrade Bobrova. "Make things up."

Natalya went back to her desk somewhat relieved. Because one could be accused of anything, one never knew why they were being summoned. She knew that she should feel proud that she could help the Party. It was a good thing that she'd been asked to help. She, however, couldn't shake feeling guilty about informing on Louise, whom she was starting to see as a friend. That had engendered mixed feelings when Julia, Sokolov's secretary, gave her the information about the flat coming vacant. But that was life she thought. After all, we aren't children. The more troubling issue was whether or not to go against Sokolov's order and tell Mikhail. The old nagging question of who had informed on her father, or if he had informed on her mother—or someone on both—rose again. She fought it back down. Surely, Mikhail should know what she was doing, but she was horrified that the thought had risen unbidden that Mikhail might inform on her if she went against Sokolov.

Monday Evening, January 20, 1947
Koski Apartment

Louise had taken considerable time to find salmon, Arnie's favorite. She managed to buy a landlocked species that had been caught in one of the large lakes. It was smaller than the Chinook salmon Arnie raved about from his childhood, but it had the same flavorful deep pink meat.

When Arnie got home, the table was set, and the apartment filled with the warmth and aroma of a good dinner.

Arnie hung his heavy coat in the closet and came into the small kitchen. He leaned against the doorjamb, watching Louise put the final touches on two plates. She looked at him and smiled.

"Wow, salmon," he said brightly. Then he mouthed, "I'm not mad at you," silently adding, "anymore."

She grimaced, and mouthed back, "I know you were angry."

He slowly nodded.

He walked over and kissed her. He stuck his finger into some of the hot juice from the salmon and quickly pulled it back, reflexively putting it in his mouth.

"Serves you right," she said. However, there was a bit of an edge to it, not her usual banter about Arnie tasting her cooking before she served it, which was an ongoing but pleasant battle. "It's what it feels like when you stick your fingers into something that someone should have told you was hot."

She watched Arnie take that in, aware that the snippy remark about getting fingers burned was motivated by feeling a little stupid.

She finished frying the salmon and when they sat down to eat, she asked, "Did you talk to Hamilton?"

Arnie mouthed, "Careful," and pointed to where they'd found the bug. "About the orphanage project?" he asked.

"Yes." Louise was making a face, nodding understanding.

"Yes," Arnie replied.

There was the usual pause.

"Yes, what?"

"Yes, I did."

"Oh, Arnie, my God, what did he say?" Then, she saw that he was grinning. "Damn you, Arnie Koski."

They both laughed.

"He likes the idea," Arnie said aloud. He had risen and was walking toward the kitchen counter as he talked. There he found some paper and started writing on it. "He said we need to do everything we can to get Finnish voters favorable to governments favorable to us." He sat down and showed her the note. *We'll leave it in. Can pass false information.*

She mouthed, "No." Grabbing the pencil and paper, she wrote, *We'll be prisoners in our own house!!!* while saying aloud, "Oh, that's great news."

Arnie rolled his eyes and wrote, *How bad can whispering in bed be?*

Louise shook her head but was smiling. "How do you like Finnish salmon?" she asked, while writing down, *Is this what you call diplomatic language?*

Arnie tucked into the salmon, grunting approval, and said, "It's really good. Maybe less fat than Chinook, but really tasty."

And with that conversation began what for Arnie and Louise would be communicating in the equivalent of a second language. Free and easy discourse was the first casualty of the loss of privacy.

Week of January 20–26, 1947
Helsinki

In addition to dividing the money search along political as well as language lines, as they'd done previously, Louise and Natalya also decided that Natalya would take the organizations that were either dominated by or sympathetic to the Communist Party, while Louise would focus on those organizations and people who remained in the free-market capitalist camp, or more simply put: pro-Russian or pro-American. One obvious strategy would be to push the position that there were no Communist or capitalist orphans. They both agreed, however, that a key tactic would be to have the two camps competing for who was the more generous. They carefully constructed talking points to make it understood that there would be good publicity about an organization's generosity, but the publicity would apply to others as well.

Despite their careful planning, it didn't go well. Organizations and individuals both were nearly flat broke from years of war. Several people joked, saying they wished that they had foreigners looking for money for them. Natalya got some small donations from left-leaning labor organizations—even a little from the SKP, the Suomen Kommunistinen Puolue, the Communist Party of Finland, made legal as part of the 1944 Moscow Armistice. The Party was a powerful force. Its front organization, the Finnish People's Democratic League, held roughly a quarter of the parliamentary seats. Louise managed a little here and there from bank managers, owners of small businesses, and even some from larger Finnish corporations. The total, however, fell far short of their goals.

Sometimes the two women solicited together, trying to communicate unity, only to be disappointed together. They would find solace in a small café they'd discovered by accident near the harbor, which was also within walking distance of their apartments. Both had walked by the place often before they knew it was a café. Typical of the Finns, the exterior of the café gave the distinct impression that whatever was behind the door wasn't open for business. Clearly, the same signal wasn't sent to the Finns, as they found many inside, talking with polite dignity, obviously enjoying themselves. As Louise once joked with Natalya, "What would you expect from people whose front doors open on their backyards?"

Even though their French was fluent, it wasn't native to either, making conversations sometime less flowing than they both wanted. French slang wasn't taught at the University of Oklahoma. Nor could it be learned from the somewhat suspect grammar books and dictionaries found by Natalya. Still, they "gabbed," as Louise labeled it, using the American slang that Louise was somewhat proudly teaching Natalya, who found herself picking it up easily.

Louise talked freely about everything, making Natalya think her job for Sokolov was almost too easy. Was America really this open and unguarded? Or just this Oklahoma place that Louise seemed to both love and make fun of simultaneously? Or was Louise acting?

She shoved the suspicion down, mainly because to talk so freely was so pleasant. In the tea shop, away from Fanya and the watcher in the foyer, Natalya shared about her life before Helsinki, school days, family, hopes for the future. Increasingly, they talked about their husbands, whom they both loved deeply, had worried about for so long—and still worried about. She found herself liking Louise more and more, which made her feel increasingly guilty about collecting information for Sokolov.

Still, Natalya did her job, dribbling out something personal about her and Mikhail or something harmless about Mikhail's work, just enough to keep conversation flowing in a direction that would enable her to report something useful to Sokolov. Her guilt would be amplified when she got five times the information back from Louise.

Natalya dutifully reported almost everything to Sokolov—almost. There was a line she wouldn't cross.

"Does he drink?"

"Well, certainly at parties."

"What about at home?"

"I don't know."

"Find out. How much. Is it a weakness. Is it a problem."

"You mean is he an alcoholic?"

"Yes."

"I think it's more like he's a teenager who just doesn't handle alcohol well. I really don't know what his drinking habits are."

"Find out. Ask his wife," Sokolov said, as if talking to a five-year-old. "That *is* what we're doing here. No?"

"Yes. Of course."

"Is Louise happy with the marriage?" Sokolov's tone had become more businesslike.

"Very."

"How do you know?"

"Whenever she complains about Arnie, she does it with love. You can tell."

"You think that's possible? To complain to someone else about someone you love?"

"Do you want my opinion about marital love or information?" *Careful*, Natalya thought. That tongue of yours has no place in front of the MGB.

Luckily, Sokolov smiled at the sharp rejoinder. "Both," he said. "But for now, information. What does she complain about? Push her on this."

So, the sparring with Sokolov would go. Sometimes deadly serious, sometimes with banter. Sometimes in the morning. Sometimes when she should have been returning home. She lived with the anxiety of never knowing when she'd be called in to report, so she always had to have a summary ready to go. She also didn't know for certain if Sokolov had Louise's apartment bugged. She assumed that he did, but if she asked, it would make him aware that she was suspicious that the apartment was bugged and was therefore tailoring her report to match what she thought Arnie and Louise were saying that Sokolov had already overheard. Better not to ask but rather assume Sokolov would rely on more than one source of information. If ever she had time alone in Louise's apartment, she must be sure to ask questions that would indicate to Sokolov that she was making a best effort. On the other hand, maybe it would be better to never go to Louise's apartment. All these thoughts were crowding the back of her mind while she was answering Sokolov's questions. Walking into Sokolov's office felt like mounting a balancing beam set above spikes.

For Louise, the frustration of pounding the streets for so little money was offset by the closeness she was developing with Natalya. She had never known a foreigner before, nor had she been close to a woman as intelligent and well educated as Natalya, who seemed far more sophisticated than she, even though this was Natalya's first time out of her native country as well. Louise had always been a bit intimidated by elegant, beautiful women—and Natalya was most certainly the most elegant, beautiful woman Louise had ever known—but that hadn't been much of a problem in Oklahoma. There, it seemed like her mother's friends went out of their way to tone themselves down. Fancy clothes were for "rich people," and bright colors were for children or foreigners. Ideas were for "intellectuals," a somewhat suspect category of women who seemed to inhabit New York City and Paris.

Her sorority sisters had all exuded a cultivated wholesomeness—fresh and clean, no frills—unconsciously reflecting the views of their mothers. She herself had taken on the same persona. She knew that she was Ivory soap, while Natalya was musky perfume, even though she didn't wear any.

Louise also liked Natalya because she seemed genuinely interested in her and in what her and Arnie's life was like. It was a pleasure telling her about their lives, sharing the wealth in a way, but she was always a bit self-conscious about looking like she was bragging. The facts were that she and Arnie had grown up safe and secure, with good parents. She was proud of being an American and wanted to share with Natalya all that was great and lovely about her country. She just felt sad that Natalya's life hadn't been as blessed.

Monday, January 27, 1947
The Orphanage, Natalya's Flat

On Monday afternoon, after a week of soliciting, Louise, Natalya, and Kaarina Varila met at the orphanage. Kaarina was effusive with her thanks to Louise and a bit more polite to Natalya. All three, however, were disappointed in the results. The money was a trickle; the need a vast inland sea. Louise felt she was failing. Everyone was a little frustrated. The three of them, however, dutifully started writing thank-you notes. Kaarina wanted each note to be personal. She wrote them out by hand—and if French, or Russian were needed, Louise or Natalya would write the note. Kaarina would copy it in her own handwriting before signing. Kaarina felt it was important that the person who was using the money do the thanks—and show how the money was used.

After several thank-you notes, Louise had to ask, "Kaarina, I don't see any of the money being applied to things like books or even toys. When I was teaching first grade—"

Kaarina interrupted her. "I don't need to hear about how you taught school in America."

"I didn't mean to compare." Louise was a bit put off. "It's just that these children probably haven't been in school, some for several years."

"We have a perfectly good education system in Finland. I think what the orphanage needs right now is clothing, blankets, and kitchen tools."

"Well, sure, but *are* the children going to school?"

"Not yet."

"But won't they be behind?"

"Is this your famous Dr. Spock speaking?"

"Come on, Kaarina. This is just basic, you know, education. I was teaching back in America—"

"Back in America, back in America. You are in Finland and the children need many things more than books." She paused. "And toys."

"Louise," Natalya gently interrupted. "Que se passe-t-il?"

Louise replied in French. "It's about where the money is being spent."

"Perhaps we should let Kaarina decide that."

"I didn't tell her or decide anything," Louise answered, aware that she was sounding peevish. Louise knew she had her dander up. It was always the same. Basic needs never included the basic need of every society on earth: to teach the children how to *think*.

She expressed this opinion to Kaarina. Kaarina expressed her own opinion back. This was repeated. Then Louise lost her temper.

"Need I remind you that who pays the piper calls the tune?" Louisa said.

That hung in the air. She wished she hadn't blurted it out.

Natalya cleared her throat. "Qu'est-ce que c'est?" she asked.

"Rien," Louise spit back.

Kaarina had both hands on the table in front of her, her shoulders raised, the way animals make themselves look big before they fight.

"You Americans, with your money," she said. "Too bad you don't have an education system that can teach you how not to throw it around so stupidly."

"Kaarina," Natalya said.

Kaarina turned on her. "And I don't need to hear from any Russians."

Natalya held up a palm in surrender. She sat back in her chair, leaving the field.

Kaarina turned to Louise. "You don't seem to understand. Finns don't dance to anyone's tune but their own."

"Which could explain why you're in the pickle you're in right now," Louise retorted.

Kaarina and Louise looked at each other. Louise realized that Kaarina's pride would not allow her to speak first. She swallowed her own. "Of course, you're the one who decides how best to spend this money." She saw Kaarina's chin rise almost imperceptibly in victory. She realized she'd just learned one of the basic rules of good diplomacy—and it was a very hard one to follow.

Natalya and Louise left the orphanage together in the dark around dinnertime, both clutching their coat buttons against the constant wind. Louise exhaled, somewhat dramatically, her breath forming a visible cloud lit by the faint streetlights. "That was a little rocky," she said. She translated the argument for Natalya.

"Everyone is a bit frustrated that the money isn't coming in as we'd hoped," Natalya said.

"Yeah. I suppose so. In any case, we've got to come up with something better."

"Sure, but what?"

Louise brightened. "Come over to my place," she said. "I have a bottle of tax-free bourbon. Enough of that and who knows what we'll come up with. Besides, after what just happened, I need a drink."

"What is this bourbon?"

"Sort of like vodka made out of corn."

Natalya grimaced. Then she said, a little apologetically, "Perhaps it would be best if you came to our place."

"You don't want to try bourbon?"

"No, it's not that." She hesitated. "We find it more," she hesitated, "*comfortable* if we entertain in our own homes. Why don't *you* come for tea?"

Louis shrugged. "OK."

* * *

Fanya had already fed the children. Mikhail was still at work. After a brief reunion with Alina and Grisha, Natalya went to the kitchen to start making the tea, followed closely by Alina, hanging on to her skirt. Grisha, who'd been standing with one hand on the coffee table, started after his sister, cruising with one hand still on the table. Finding that too slow, he dropped to the floor and crawled rapidly into the kitchen. Fanya got up to go after the children, but Louise got there first. She swung Grisha up to her face, surprised again at how sturdy—and heavy—the little boy was. She pulled him in close to her feeling his heat.

Natalya came out with a plate of small boat-shaped stuffed buns and a pot of tea, followed by Alina, who stood just past the kitchen door watching Louise and her little brother. Louise quickly realized it must look a bit odd and loosened her hug on Grisha. Natalya set the teapot and buns on the table and gave Louise an understanding smile before she returned to the kitchen. Alina remained at the doorway, saying nothing. Louise sat down with Grisha on her lap and played with his hands while the tea steeped. Natalya returned, poured a cup of tea for Louise, and then picked up Grisha from Louise's lap. Pointing at the buns with her chin, she said, "Eat. Please."

Louise took one and found it filled with a surprisingly sweet cherry, not quite pudding and not quite jam. "What is this?" she asked. "It's delicious."

"Pirozhki, filled with cherry varenye."

"Oh, my God in heaven," Louise said with her mouth full.

Natalya smiled with pleasure.

Louise helped Natalya put the children to bed and the two of them returned to the kitchen. The teapot was empty and the pirozhki gone.

Louise looked at the empty vessels a bit despondently. Natalya, however, smiled. She peeked into the living room to see that Fanya had retired to her bedroom and walked over to a cupboard. Reaching high, she pulled down an opened bottle of vodka. With a smile she placed a bottle of soda water and two glasses beside it on the table. Then, she went to the small icebox and put out a plate of pickles and tiny fish that Louise couldn't identify.

The vodka soon had the two women talking more deeply. When they'd all been together with their husbands, they'd talked briefly about what they did before the war, but it had stayed mostly at a surface level. Now came more details and tentative disclosures that bloomed into deeper, more personal stories. Both women tried hard to be honest, but Louise thought Natalya was holding back and asking Louise to reveal more about herself than Natalya did. Louise thought it must be because of the in-and-out presence of Fanya.

Natalya couldn't help noticing that Louise dropped comments about a life that would be unlikely for any but the highest government officials, yet Louise's father didn't even have a government position. Louise's family seemed to have a car of their own. She even said that she had her own bedroom! And her mother had time to play cards and drive the car, all by herself, to a larger city where she bought clothes and other things. And they had three dogs. Three.

When Louise once let it drop that all her friends had similar situations to her own, Natalya didn't believe this for a moment but decided to be kind and let Louise go on. Any friend was going to have a few flaws—and it looked like Louise's was exaggerating about how good her childhood was. Natalya decided that she wouldn't even bother reporting it to Sokolov.

Louise did mention something she called the Depression, which was a time when her family didn't buy new shoes before school, as they usually did, and she went to work for her father in the family lumber business, because her father had laid off two of his workers. Natalya knew that one of the many flaws of the capitalist system was its horrible business cycles—which Soviet planning had eliminated. Louise talked about the Depression as if it were a major catastrophe. To Natalya, who'd lived through the famine of 1932–33 that killed six or eight million mostly Ukrainians, what Louise described was a bump on the road.

Mikhail walked in, his broad face opening in a smile when he saw Louise. He bowed slightly to her. Natalya rose to kiss him. He was unable to say anything in English other than, "Hello. Good day." He said something in Russian to Natalya, made a slight bow again, then disappeared into the children's bedroom.

"Misha says to please forgive him. General Kristall is visiting from Moscow. There is no escape." Natalya chuckled. "He is Misha's boss's boss. That's not his real name. Kristall is shorthand for Moscow State Wine Warehouse Number One. They make that vodka you are drinking, not wine. Misha will not get home until morning." She smiled. "Tomorrow he is going to have a very bad head."

"We have generals like that. There's a lot of drinking in our army, too."

"All armies have generals like that," Natalya said. "But I think 'a lot of drinking' means something different to a Russian than to an American." Smiling, Natalya then asked, "Does your Arnie drink?" Louise thought it was a bit forward but reminded herself that what was private in some cultures might not be in others.

"Hardly at all. The New Year's Eve party was an exception," she added hastily. "His mother told all her children not to drink anything at all. She says it's a particular Finnish weakness."

"So," Natalya said, "has Arnie shown any signs of this," she emphasized the word slightly, "weakness?"

"No, no," Louise replied. She wondered why Natalya would even ask such a thing. It made her feel uneasy. Natalya seemed reticent about revealing her own private life but had no trouble asking sometimes pointed questions about Louise and Arnie's. Had she known about the bug? But she didn't *want* to feel suspicious about Natalya. She remembered her own mother telling her more than once that if you want to have friends, you can't want ones without flaws. Such people didn't exist. But spying on a friend was more than a flaw. She couldn't just ask Natalya, because if she was spying on Louise, she'd say no. If she wasn't spying, she'd also say no. It was obvious that trust couldn't be based on words.

Mikhail came out of the children's room and disappeared into what might have been another bedroom. He emerged with a pair of skis. Louise lit up. "Oh, you guys," she said in English. She switched to French and started talking to Natalya. "This ski race they've concocted . . ." She didn't finish.

Natalya had put her hand on Louise's arm, shaking her head just slightly. She nodded sideways toward the closed door to Fanya's bedroom.

Louise quickly recovered. "Is Mikhail going skiing someplace?"

"Part of Mikhail's job is to go north to check on bridge widths, road surface conditions, that sort of thing. For tanks," Natalya said. "He's taking his skis in case he needs them." She laughed. "He knows he won't want to work on them tomorrow after a night with General Kristall."

Louise laughed, joining Natalya's small conspiracy, but she caught a glimmer of Natalya's fear. She was so grateful that in America you could say anything you wanted without fear of reprisal. You could rely on the government and the press to always tell the truth. In America, a fact was a fact. Period.

Wednesday, January 29, 1947
Helsinki Train Station

On Wednesday morning, Louise walked Arnie to the train station where he would take the train to Rovaniemi, a town almost exactly on the Arctic Circle, just fifty miles from Sweden and one hundred miles from Russia. Rovaniemi had been leveled by fire caused by the explosion of a German ammunition train during the fighting between Finland and Germany in the fall of 1944. Ironically, the ammunition train had been blown up by Finnish commandos harassing the retreating Germans. Just months before this, those same commandos had been fighting alongside those Germans to keep the Soviet Union out of Finland. One of the demands of the 1944 peace settlement was that Finland force all German troops out of Finland. That meant fighting those who just weeks earlier had been comrades in arms. This was harder on soldiers than it was on politicians.

The locomotive was nearly hidden in the steam condensing in the freezing air. Louise hunched into Arnie, trying to extract as much heat from him as she could through the coarse wool of his cross-country skiing outfit. His skis and pack lay at their feet.

She heard what she assumed was the "all aboard" in Finnish. Arnie, as usual eager to get going, reached for his pack. She helped him get it on his back, trying to contain the niggling worry that this might be the last time she touched him, marveling that he was intending to carry it over three hundred miles. She could barely hold it up as he struggled into the straps.

He bounced the pack up and down, settling it, and turned to her. "Send out the search parties if we don't get to Kuopio by Wednesday, the twelfth."

"Don't even think it," she said seriously.

"We'll get there on Monday." He looked skyward. "Given no major weather glitches."

"And you'll get there *first*," she said. She turned her head up for a kiss. He awkwardly hugged her and gave her a quick kiss. She couldn't hug him back because of the pack, so contented herself with one last feel of his shoulders.

He began to reach down for his skis, but she stopped him. "One more, for the winner." She knew he was uncomfortable kissing in public but had fun teasing him. She also knew he wouldn't resist. This time she held the back of his head, pulling him in, holding him to her. The last time they'd kissed at a train station like this was in Tacoma, Washington, when he'd shipped out for Europe after a brief leave. She'd been afraid it would be their last.

The whistle blew and Arnie broke off.

She watched his back as he made his way down the platform, remembering the first time she'd said goodbye to him at the train station in Norman, Oklahoma. They'd met her sophomore year on October 24, 1936, the weekend of the big game against the Sooners' traditional rival, eighth-ranked Nebraska. Her date had gotten the flu. A sorority sister rescued her by getting her boyfriend, who as at Fort Sill, to bring a friend. That was Arnie.

It was clear from the first minute that this lean man, with dark hair she wanted to get her fingers into, wasn't much good at chitchat. By the end of the weekend, however, it was clear that he was good at deep conversation, with just enough words. When she and her girlfriend put their two soldiers on the train, she'd stood watching it disappear until her girlfriend had taken her arm and said, "We can't wait for them on the platform."

Arnie hitchhiked to Norman every time he got leave, saving the train fare. But their yearlong college idyll was shattered in March of 1938, when the army promoted Arnie to first lieutenant and transferred him to Fort Lewis, Washington.

Louise graduated in June 1939 and took a job teaching first grade at Lincoln Grade School in Tulsa. When Arnie asked her to come out West over the Christmas break, Louise took the train to Tacoma, against her parents' wishes.

She smiled at the memory of *that* parting.

Now, bouncing up and down against the cold, clutching the front of her coat, she was once again watching Arnie board a train. "Go Arnie! Go America!" she shouted.

He turned back, rolled his eyes, and disappeared.

She whispered, "Go with God."

The train pulled out, steam venting from the pistons. She watched until the smoke from the boiler thinned to invisibility. Then she turned to begin the walk back to the empty apartment, feeling very much alone.

As she left the station, the tears started, laying small wet tracks that froze on her face. Her period had come that morning. Passersby would think she was mourning the departure of a loved one. She wondered how often she herself had mistaken the true cause of a woman's tears.

Thursday, January 30, 1947
Bobrov Flat

Mikhail left the next day to avoid being seen with Arnie. Both men knew their cover stories were good. They had also agreed, however, not to be seen leaving together and to keep their itineraries vague.

To make sure no attention was drawn to Mikhail leaving, Natalya decided to say goodbye at their flat. She was filled with worry. First there was the fear that the MGB would find out that Mikhail had lied about his reason for going north. They always found out. That's why trying to hide something was never as good a strategy as trying to show a positive Socialist motive for doing it. She'd made sure that Fanya overheard her talking to Mikhail about his upcoming visit to an armored training regiment, around a hundred kilometers north of Helsinki. Fanya would, of course, relay that information to the MGB, probably a direct report to Sokolov. The MGB would figure the training-regiment story was Natalya covering for Mikhail. Mikhail, of course, would want to cover his "true" reason for going north, which was reconnoitering roads, bridges, and possible airfields. This was because, Natalya was certain, Mikhail's story about going north to reconnoiter invasion paths would already have been reported to the MGB through their spies in the GRU, army intelligence. Having Fanya report a "false" story would probably satisfy the MGB that Mikhail was indeed going north to do legitimate military intelligence. *That,* however, was the actual lie. She shrugged off the Russian dolls within Russian dolls web of lies and explanations. It was what one did. It was the way life worked.

What she feared more than Mikhail's race being found out were winter conditions in Finland. Mikhail's missing little toe attested to them. Even though Mikhail drank and smoked as much as he had during the war, he was now older and in a sedentary job, but he still believed he was in his twenties. She knew the rules meant that Mikhail would ski alone. If something went wrong, he would die alone.

Added to that fear was that of the race becoming public. The MGB would then know for certain that Mikhail had lied about why he went north. The government could lie. It was for the good of the People. People, however, could not lie. That was bad for the government. Mikhail would have to be punished. In addition to that, if Mikhail lost in public, the capitalist Finnish press would make a very big deal about a Hero of the Soviet Union losing to an American. The Party and the state would be embarrassed. That would be worse than being lied to.

Damn Misha's uninhibited spontaneity, even fearlessness. Those were things she loved about him. They could also destroy their lives.

Natalya put her hands around the back of Mikhail's head, feeling his thick hair, the strength of his neck muscles. "Misha," Natalya said, pulling him closer so her eyes looked directly into his, "don't go."

He held her close. Looking beyond her head into the future, he said, "Don't worry, Natashenka. Don't worry." He gently pushed her back. "Hey, think of it like the Olympics."

"We don't participate in the Olympics for good reasons. We never lose that way."

"Well, we should participate in the future. We need to show how a Socialist people are a better people. In every field."

She nearly hissed, whispering, "Misha, stop that nonsense. We could lose you."

He began collecting his gear, now a little annoyed. "It's just a ski race for heaven sakes." He smiled that cocky smile, another damnable reason she was attracted to him. "And I'll win."

She gave him a long kiss at the door, feeling the pressure on her lips, trying to lock it into her memory. Neither could stand parting without some sign of the deeper bond.

Mikhail disappeared down the stairwell and she turned inside. Fanya was sitting on the couch in the living room. She looked up at Natalya and smiled. Natalya wanted to scream at her and slap her supercilious face, but she stuffed her anger down with her fear. Mikhail would be alright. He always came through.

Friday, January 31, 1947
Rovaniemi, Finland

Arnie and Mikhail had chosen Rovaniemi to start their race because it provided a good cover story for their absence from Helsinki. Rovaniemi was a road and rail hub that sat on a direct invasion path from Russia to both Sweden and Norway. Conversely, it sat on the direct invasion path from Sweden and Norway *to* Russia. Any military plans would have to include intelligence such as the location of key bridges and their load limits, the location of existing airfields and types of aircraft they could accommodate, as well as a thorough reconnaissance of possible escape routes for downed pilots. It made perfect sense to everyone in the Soviet legation and the American legation that their military attachés would want to go there with his skis.

The Germans had encouraged the fire started by the Finnish commandos blowing up the ammunition train. They let the fire burn Rovaniemi to the ground in retaliation for Finland changing sides and joining the Russians. Most Rovaniemi had been made of wood. Now although the streets had been cleared of rubble, the town was still a charred ruin. Isolated stone and brick chimneys rising from the ashes like gaunt gravestones. Scraps of clothing, frozen solid, peeked out amid charred wood and crusted snow, along with an occasional broken kitchen utensil or bowl. Anything useful had been gleaned long ago by the townspeople, most of whom had fled to Sweden just before the town was turned to ash, an arduous journey during which 279 died. Another 200 died when they tried to return—from land mines left by the Germans. Many people lived in cellars. Arnie couldn't help but feel proud of his Finnish heritage, because it was clear that these indomitable Finns had returned to Rovaniemi to rebuild it.

He spent Friday carefully watching for unexploded land mines and mapping roads, noting which were wide enough for armor to get through. He skied out to the frozen-over local reservoir and estimated how many soldiers it could supply with water and for how long. For damned sure, he thought, the Russians had been crazy to think they could use armor up here. The landscape was covered in streams, lakes, and bogs and looked like a roller coaster. All attacks—and all supplies—would have to move on one of the very rare roads. Supply lines would be stretched back for miles, totally vulnerable to air strikes—or the circular attacks of infantry moving through the woods on skis, precisely what the Finns had done to the Russians in 1939.

He was already organizing his assessment in his head when he checked in with the local police. He told them his real name, the scouting mission he was on, and that he would be around a night or two, then move on. He was reassured that they were firmly in the anti-Communist camp, unlike the Valpo, and maybe, Pulkkinen. After Louise's remark about Pulkkinen's English, he'd dug into everything they had on him and had pretty much convinced himself that Pulkkinen worked for the Valpo, not the MGB. What he wasn't sure of was whether Pulkkinen was a Communist, like too many of his bosses.

Although Arnie had truthfully identified himself to the local police, he still registered under an assumed name at the bed and breakfast, posing as a returning expatriate Finn searching for family members after the war. This was to assure the local police that he was trying to hide secret work from the locals but had let the police in on the secret, flattering them. He assumed Mikhail, who was due to arrive on the evening train, had done something similar. It was kind of fun, all this cloak-and-dagger deception.

For Friday night, they'd chosen to stay in the same house on the outskirts of town, knowing it had only one room to rent. They both had a great time feigning reluctance to share the room when they arrived simultaneously "by coincidence." Arnie used the same cover as the night before and Mikhail played a jolly apparatchik from the Allied Control Commission who was scouting the countryside for more of the vast amounts of matériel that were being shipped to Russia as part of Finland's reparation payments. The woman letting out the room had made it clear, albeit politely, that she didn't like Russians. When they were in the room, Mikhail commented on it.

"You're gutting the place and they're broke," Arnie said.

"My dear comrade American," Mikhail said. He had undressed to his long johns and was carefully laying out the clothes he'd put on in just a few hours. They'd agreed to leave at three thirty in the morning. "The Finns are lucky to remain unoccupied by the Red Army."

"Because they would fight you to a standstill, like they did in thirty-nine."

"That, like most mythology, is based on only a partial truth. They sued for peace because we were about to crush them."

"So why didn't you?"

"I think because Stalin didn't want to pay the enormous cost in lives"—he gave a knowing nod to Arnie—"notwithstanding the prevalent, and very mistaken, American myth of butchering our own soldiers. We could have crushed the Finns in 1944, but we probably would have lost thousands doing it. It is much better to have left Finland unoccupied but with very clear instructions to keep clear of the West, which means no American forces on Finnish soil. You see, we're not afraid of the Finns. There are less than four million of them. What we're afraid of is Finland allying with some country that has a lot of people and therefore could launch an army from Finland and be in Leningrad in hours. We're OK with Finland being nonaligned, as long as there's no foreign army in Finland threatening us as you do with your army in Germany. Norway is very unlikely to allow American troops there, despite them being firmly in the capitalist camp. And Sweden," he grimaced, "they claimed neutrality but basically collaborated with the Nazis, primarily selling them high-quality steel. You'll get little comfort from them. So, we keep you out of Finland and Scandinavia by virtue of your own ideals about never violating a country's neutrality. Sort of ironic, don't you think?" He chuckled. "There is also another irony, which I don't think many of you Americans are in on."

Arnie gave him a questioning look.

"Business, my friend. American capitalists will not loan money to any country under Soviet control. But they will loan money to Finland. So, the loans come in from America. Those loans, in hard currency dollars, help Finland make the reparation payments we forced on them in the 1944 treaty. Thus, American capital helps rebuild the Soviet economy. How's that for a joke?" He laughed. "Had Comrade Stalin been born in New York, he would have been a Wall Street millionaire."

Arnie went along with the joke. He had to own that it had never occurred to him just how clever the Soviets had been about neutralizing Finland. Then he sobered. "But if America and the Soviet Union go to war, would you violate Finnish territory to attack Norway?"

"Of course. First, we have not stupidly tied our own hands with a declared stance about honoring the 1944 Moscow Armistice. Agreements that don't work for both sides should be torn up. Second, Finland was part of Russia until the revolution. We'd have every moral right to cross into Russian territory."

What Mikhail was laying out for him gave Arnie a sense of foreboding. "Is this really accepted policy? At the highest level?"

"Yes."

Arnie took it in. "You really think that way?"

"No." Mikhail laughed again. "As a political person, I can see it is a useful excuse. The real reason we would violate Finish neutrality, or anyone's sovereignty, or any part of international law, is that we will do absolutely anything to avoid a war on Russian soil again. *Anything*, my friend."

"We don't want to invade you."

"Just drop atomic bombs on us."

Neither said anything for some time.

Mikhail spoke first. "We are falling into the antagonistic paranoia of our masters. I often think of our meeting on the Enns."

"Me too."

"A good feeling."

"It was a good time. The war was nearly over, and we'd won."

"Do you miss it?" Mikhail asked.

Arnie paused. It didn't seem right to say he missed something so horrible. He knew Mikhail had probably seen more fighting than he had, so would understand what he was about to say. Now was no time to be dishonest. It might be the last time they could speak from their hearts, given the way "their masters," as Mikhail put it, were heading. "I feel terribly sad. All those dead kids. Dead friends." He took in a breath. "But I saw Buchenwald."

"And I, Auschwitz."

"Worth fighting for," Arnie said. Mikhail simply nodded.

After some silence, Arnie said, "But we were no angels."

"You weren't."

"I meant we, as in both our countries."

"I meant you, as in America. Who firebombed Hamburg, mostly women and children?"

"At least we didn't rape our way to Berlin."

"You never got to Berlin. You hung back while we did the dirty work."

"There. You said it: dirty work."

"Phhww. Who firebombed Dresden?" Mikhail asked.

"The British. And who murdered over twenty thousand Polish officers and intellectuals in the Katyn Forest and blamed it on the Germans?"

"And who firebombed Tokyo and leveled Hiroshima and Nagasaki with atom bombs. Again, mostly women and children?"

With the dark humor of the frontline soldier Arnie said, "Yeah, can't make an omelet without breaking an egg."

Mikhail immediately laughed, ending the threat of a fight, but he chose to reply seriously. "We broke a lot of eggs, Comrade."

Again, there was silence.

"You didn't answer my question," Mikhail said.

"I've never felt so alive."

Mikhail nodded. "We truly do understand each other."

They rolled out their maps. Arnie had one from the Finnish Army and Mikhail had one from the Red Army. Both men were good at reading topographic maps, having done it many times a day for most of the war. They'd both already worked out their general race route, which they now compared. They'd agreed back in Helsinki that each would choose his own way, but they knew they'd likely often see each other if the race was close. This was because terrain and conditions would force the same choice of route on both of them. Since they'd agreed to not use roads—and there were few roads this far north anyway—that meant using the frozen rivers and lakes as much as possible.

"One last thing we've never discussed," Mikhail said. "We both know that we've been sitting on our asses for over a year."

"And?" Arnie asked cautiously.

Mikhail dug into his pack and pulled up a round cylinder with German writing on it. He held it in front of Arnie.

Arnie smiled. "Pervitin," he said. "The Germans ate it like popcorn."

"Yes," Mikhail said. He waited a moment then gestured, curling his fingers. "Come on."

Arnie smiled and dug into his own pack. He pulled out a box of Benzedrine tablets.

"Bennies," Mikhail said.

"Pep pills."

"Tanker chocolate."

They both laughed, but the question still was not answered. Finally, Arnie said, "Let's agree that five milligrams of Benzedrine is about the same as three milligrams of Pervitin. OK?"

Mikhail nodded agreement. Thinking a moment, he said, "How about you take nine pills and I'll take fifteen? That's about one a day for you, if you chose to use them that way."

They agreed, counted out their pills, and threw the rest away.

They decided to head east from Rovaniemi on the ice of the Kemijoki River. Because of the narrowness, this would pretty much keep each in sight of the other since they would be moving at about the same pace, conserving energy for the days ahead. Later that day, they'd turn south to the Näskänselkä-Isoselkä lake system, east of Ranua. This is where they'd split and truly begin racing, Mikhail on the east side and Arnie on the west. From there, they'd ski south on the Pudasjärvi waterways, then overland to the Oulunjärvi lake system, then due south again on the Kallavesi lake system to Kuopio. Five hundred kilometers—three hundred miles.

Saturday, February 1, 1947
Outskirts of Rovaniemi
Race Day 1

When they left the warm house six hours later, the cold struck hard and fast—as did the beauty. The northern lights were dancing, displaying moving curtains of green. The snow, even at night, was brilliant in the light of the waxing half-moon.

Arnie had a tiny thermometer attached to a piece of wood, a souvenir from the ski resort on Mount Rainier. He could barely see the small column of mercury it was so short—probably around ten degrees below zero Fahrenheit. There was no wind. There was a stillness that made both men unwilling to break the silence.

They'd agreed to start at 0400. Mikhail lifted the watch Arnie had given to him. Arnie followed suit.

"One minute," Arnie said, watching the second hand, his heart rate already up. "Thirty seconds," he said.

Mikhail was showing his own excitement, moving his skis back and forth. "I'll be waiting for you in Kuopio."

Arnie flipped him the bird and laughed because his middle finger was covered by his mitten. He gestured with the whole mitten and Mikhail laughed, getting the message. Arnie started counting down, "Neljä, kolme, kaksi, yksi. Mene!"

They both set off, moving together, in a steady, kilometer-eating pace.

Sunday, February 2, 1947
The Kemijoki
Race Day 2

By Sunday, they'd lost sight of each other. Both had veered off from the Kemijoki river and were traveling overland, their speed slowed greatly because they were now navigating forest and no longer on river ice. At the top of a small rise, Arnie caught sight of Mikhail in a shallow valley to his west. They were about even. He'd worried that he'd slept too long, burrowed into a snow hole he'd dug with his small folding shovel, but apparently he hadn't.

He checked his little thermometer. The temperature was hovering around zero in the daytime. The major problem wasn't the terrain—problem enough—but the constant fight to keep sweat and condensation from freezing on the inside of his clothes, robbing him of energy, possibly pushing him unknowingly into hypothermia. While still moving, he tore the wrapper from a K-ration bar and ate it followed by a chunk of dried reindeer meat.

Sunday, February 2, 1947
Helsinki

While falling asleep Saturday night—at the same time Arnie was digging his snow hole—something Max Hamilton said when she'd gone to him for help was niggling at Louise—something about a fundraiser or raffle. She'd rejected it out of hand because she could think of no gimmick or major prize to motivate people to buy raffle tickets. What about other ways to raise money—like a bake sale? She laughed at herself. She could just see Natalya at a bake sale. What had worked back home? There were different kinds of raffles. What about those fundraisers where people tried to guess the number of marbles in a jar? Or like at the lumberyard when everyone tried to guess the point spread of the Nebraska-Oklahoma game. A point spread in a big game—what about the time difference in a race—Arnie and Mikhail's race!

She sat up in her bed, sleep banished. The orphanage could sell tickets, call it a raffle. The buyers would guess the difference in time between Mikhail and Arnie. The person guessing closest to the time difference would win a prize. And the prize could come from a portion of the money generated by the ticket sales. Self-funding!

She was so excited about the idea that the first thing Sunday morning she composed a press release and spent the rest of the morning pounding out several carbon copies on the little Raleigh portable typewriter that she'd had since college. She realized that she would have to get the press release to the papers by evening if she was going to make the morning editions.

She finished the press releases and was over at Kaarina's flat just before noon. She needed her to translate the release into Finnish, and she was also eager to show Kaarina what she'd come up with to help the orphanage.

Louise had expected it might take a little salesmanship to get Kaarina on board, knowing the whole concept would probably be foreign to her, and perhaps seem a bit crass. Enthusiastic salesmanship, however, was Louise's forte, and in the face of the failures of the door-to-door donation effort, surely Kaarina would see the raffle would be a far better money raiser.

She delivered her very optimistic, well-thought-out pitch, then handed Kaarina the press release, asking her to translate it into Finnish.

Kaarina read it. When she finished, she looked up and Louise detected a fleeting furtive look, quickly repressed. "Has Natalya seen this?"

"Not yet. I'll take it over to her this afternoon before we go to the papers with any changes she might want."

That elicited a mild grunt, quickly followed by another question on the old topic. "What makes you think this will work?"

"It's done all the time, in America."

Kaarina looked again at the press release in her hand. "This isn't America," she murmured. "What if we don't sell enough tickets to cover the prize money?"

Typical Finnish pessimism, Louise thought. "I can make up the difference. Arnie won't mind. But I think we won't have to worry about that."

Kaarina nodded. "How do we sell the tickets?"

It stopped Louise for a moment. Then she said, "Through the newspaper stands. Use the same distribution as the papers, they sell the tickets and collect the money. They can claim it's their contribution to the charity drive."

Kaarina took that in.

"We can make a lot of money for the orphanage," Louise said. Money always worked with Arnie's relatives.

Kaarina was showing a hint of a smile. "And we put this in the newspapers, and . . . " she paused. "This could generate a lot of excitement." She smiled more broadly. "And some good money."

"Yes. Exactly."

"Maybe we need some time to get ready for this, what do you call it, raffle, before we take it to the newspapers."

Louise grew urgent. "We can do all the tickets this afternoon. But, if we don't get this to the papers by this evening, we'll miss the Monday morning editions." Knowing Kaarina had bought the concept, Louise focused on the need for speed. "There are only so many days left in the race. We can't waste a single one of them."

"What must we do then?"

"We just need to print tickets. Do you have a mimeograph machine?"

"No. But the church has one."

"Do they have a typewriter that can cut a stencil for it?"

"Why would they have a machine without being able to cut a stencil?"

Louise fought her annoyance at being treated like an ignorant child. "Can we go to the church now?"

Kaarina went to get her coat.

The rest of the day was a blur of securing the use of the mimeograph machine, designing and making the stencil, cranking out several hundred sheets printed with multiple raffle tickets, then cutting them out and numbering them. Even Kaarina was uncharacteristically enthusiastic, joining in designing the tickets and flyers. While Louise was cranking out pages of tickets and cutting them with scissors, Kaarina translated Louise's press release into Finnish. Everything was ready to go just before dark.

"I'm taking the press release over to Natalya now," Louise said. She was putting on her coat and mittens as she spoke.

"Do we have to?" Kaarina asked. "What if changes make us miss some deadline?"

"It's a joint US–Soviet Union project," Louise said. "We need to loop her in. At the very least, just to be courteous. I don't think she'll change much, if anything."

Kaarina shrugged at this. "I suppose so. But you yourself said we can't lose a single day."

Now instead of having to drag Kaarina along, she was having to slow her down. "Don't worry," Louise said, pulling her wool cap down over her hair. "Just wait here. I'll get right back if we need to change anything. Then we can go to the papers together. I've done this lots of times. We just need to get there two or three hours before press time." Louise smiled excitedly at Kaarina. "We're going to make a lot of money when we sell all those tickets."

Kaarina looked at her and solemnly said, "Yoh, I think we will. I'll make more tickets while you're gone. Make even more money."

Louise smiled broadly. Kaarina had clearly been sold on the idea.

Louise hurried over to Natalya's flat, full of energy. After signing in with the man at the desk, she nearly bounded up the stairs to Natalya's floor.

A puzzled Natalya opened the door. "Louise. What are you doing here?"

"I've got this fabulous idea for raising money for the orphanage." She nearly waved the press release in Natalya's face. "I've got to talk to you about it."

Looking puzzled, Natalya ushered her in.

"Kaarina and I have been working all afternoon making tickets," Louise said, taking off her coat. "This has to get to the papers tonight, so the article will come out first thing tomorrow."

"Tickets?" Natalya asked. "Slow down." She took Louise's coat, hat, and mittens. Then nodding at the paper in Louise's hands, she said, "And, what is this?"

"It's a money maker, that's what it is. We're going to have a raffle," she said, proudly.

"What is a raffle?" Natalya asked.

"You have a really great prize. Then you print tickets with numbers on them with stubs that have the same numbers. You sell the tickets, each one for just a small amount of money. But people can buy as many as they want, making their odds of winning better. Sometimes you just put all the tickets into a big container and draw one out, but sometimes you have a guessing contest and people write their answers to the contest on the tickets and they can win that way."

Natalya nodded, keeping silent.

"But to really raise money, you need to sell a lot of tickets, and to do that you need some sort of publicity idea that can be advertised, like in the papers."

"And, what's our prize? And how do we pay for it?"

"That's what's so great about my idea. We sell the tickets and use some of that money as the prize. The orphanage doesn't have to put up any money ahead of time."

Natalya looked skeptical.

"It's done all the time in America," Louise said.

"It kind of sounds like something for nothing."

"That's why it's so great!"

Natalya took this in. "So, what is the publicity idea?"

"With every ticket you buy, you guess the time difference between Arnie and Mikhail. Think of it." Louise was talking fast in her excitement. "Two war heroes, friends and allies, making money for a joint Soviet-American orphanage project. Every day the papers can run stories about who's ahead and by how much time whenever anyone catches sight of them."

Natalya gasped. "No. You must not." Her hands had gone to her face, covering her mouth, her eyes wide with shock. "Has anyone seen this?"

Louise was stunned by the reaction. Her excitement quickly devolved into an uneasy feeling she'd done something wrong. "Only Kaarina," she answered. "Why? What's wrong?"

Natalya shook her head in disbelief, then, as if talking to a child, she said, "Misha is a Hero of the Soviet Union. What do you think Comrade Stalin or Comrade Beria will think if a Hero of the Soviet Union is beaten by a degenerate, soft capitalist American?"

"You know Arnie isn't . . . "

Natalya cut her off. "Of course, I know Arnie isn't. But that is the image our government wants our people and particularly our new allies in Eastern Europe to believe. You send that, that . . ." She pointed her finger at the press release as if accusing it, accusing Louise. "'Publicity' to Finnish newspapers and it won't be a race between Arnie and Misha, it will be a race between my country and the capitalist West. Even the pro-Soviet papers will portray it that way."

"So," Louise almost said, "so what," but checked herself. She was aware that Natalya wasn't just upset, she was frightened.

"If Misha loses—in front of the whole world," Natalya's voice had become soft with fear, "*Stalin* will be humiliated. At best, Misha will be tortured and sent to the gulag for collaborating with your husband and any number of other offenses. More likely, they'll kill him—after they torture him." She let that sink in. "And I will be sent to the gulag as the wife of a traitor and my children raised by the state, forever tarnished by being the children of traitors."

Louise realized Natalya was trembling.

In a whisper, Natalya said, "You have no idea what they can do to you."

Louise felt like a fool. It was as if she'd woken from a dream to some heretofore unseen reality. In her naïve enthusiasm for her brilliant money-raising idea, in her desire to look good to Kaarina, she'd made a serious blunder, not seeing the world through the eyes of women like Natalya and Kaarina. Their world was very much more frightening than the protected world Louise had, before coming to Finland, believed was normal.

"I've been an idiot," Louise said, quietly. "I'm so sorry. Of course, I won't take this to the papers. We can come up with something else."

Natalya was silent, uncomfortably silent.

Then she said softly, "Luckily, no harm has been done." She smiled. "Would you like some tea?"

When Louise got back to the church, it was dark. Kaarina must have gone home. Maybe she'd stayed too long having tea. Anyway, there was no urgency. The whole idea of a raffle based on the race's time spread had been scrapped. Suddenly weary, she walked back to the flat. She consoled herself that at least all the raffle tickets had been made and went to bed, turning over other ideas of how a raffle of some kind might still be used to raise money. The bed felt cold. She missed Arnie.

Monday Morning, February 3, 1947
Helsinki

L ouise woke up to someone pounding on the door. Fumbling into a robe, half-awake as usual first thing in the morning, she went to the door and asked who was there.

"Natalya." The answer was curt and cold.

Louise opened the door. Natalya thrust a copy of *Helsingin Sanomat*, Finland's largest daily, directly in her face. "How could you? How could you?" Natalya was shaking with anger. "You lied to me!"

Confused, Louise took a small step back so she could read the headline. It was in Finnish, but the headline had one word she understood well: AMERIKKALAINEN. Shocked, she rapidly searched through the rest of the article. Even with her rudimentary Finnish she could see that it was all about the raffle and Arnie's race.

"Honestly, I didn't do it. I . . ." Her confusion cleared. "Oh, my God, Natalya. Kaarina must have taken the press release to the papers. I asked her to translate it. I told her I would come back with any changes before the two of us took it to the papers. She wasn't there. I never in the world thought she'd do it on her own."

"Of course, a great puzzle," Natalya said sarcastically. "She gets money for her orphanage, and she hates Russians."

Natalya shook the paper in her face. "This is a capitalist newspaper," she hissed. "In the papers that are on our side *my Misha* will be the hero.

Your Arnie will be portrayed as a fat, out-of-shape, stooge of capitalism. Our side will have no problem representing it that way, unlike your side, which has to keep in our good graces or risk Stalin's anger."

"My side? Natalya, I'm not taking sides here."

"You are so stupid. There is no such thing as neutrality, just cowardice about choosing sides." Natalya turned her back on Louise and threw the paper down on the table. "If Misha loses, you've as good as killed us."

She sat on the couch, her eyes buried in her hands.

Louise looked at the newspaper, lying there, like a summons to judgment.

"We'll stop it," Louise said. "We'll get them to pull the story."

"Too late." Natalya looked up at Louise, tears forming, trembling with fear.

"Natalya, I didn't do it."

"You wrote it!"

Natalya picked up the paper, crumpling it together in a rage, and threw it on the floor. She turned her back on Louise and walked out the door.

Half an hour later, Louise was at the orphanage. She confronted Kaarina with the newspaper. "How could you go behind my back like this?" she asked.

Kaarina blinked. Then totally impassive said, "I didn't go behind your back. You yourself said it was important to get to the papers for the morning editions. I waited. It got late."

"I thought I made it clear I would come back if Natalya made changes."

"You didn't come back."

"I never thought you'd take it to the papers without me."

In the face of Louise's criticism, Kaarina had now gone completely cold. "So, the director of the orphanage who is putting on the raffle shouldn't try to make it succeed?"

"If Mikhail loses, the Russians will imprison him, maybe his whole family. They could even kill him."

"And I'm supposed to worry about what the Russians do to their own people?" Kaarina asked.

"Yes, you should. These *people* are Natalya's *husband*—and her family!"

"Hmmph." Kaarina dismissed Louise's comment. "Are you quite finished?"

Louise was surprised at how flat her appeal had fallen.

"No!" Louise said. "Did you take the release to other papers?"

"Yoh."

"How many?"

"All of them."

"Oh, my God. If Arnie wins . . . Oh, my God."

Louise rushed back to her flat for fresh clothes, some makeup, and hair repair. Half an hour later, she was waiting outside the office of the managing editor of *Helsingin Sanomat*, Finland's largest daily.

The editor's secretary spoke only rudimentary English. However, by showing her Arnie's card with the fancy American legation heading and the press release, Louise got an understanding smile and the woman had disappeared into an inner office.

She returned holding up five fingers. Louise acknowledged the five-minute wait with a smile. She put the press release in her purse, straightened herself, and put her purse on her lap.

Soon, a distinguished-looking man of around fifty emerged. He smiled as he walked toward her with an awkward limp and indicated she should enter his office. "I am managing editor Aapo Kari." The man spoke English. Louise breathed an inward sigh of relief. Once in his office, he held a chair for her in front of his desk, all without any further speaking. Louise could just make out the evidence of a crude prosthesis beneath his crisply creased trousers. His right leg had been amputated below the knee.

When she'd settled in front of his desk, she blurted out, "There's been a terrible mistake."

Kari waited. "A mistake?" he prompted.

Louise brought out a copy of her English version of the press release. "I assume you or someone received the Finnish translation of this and printed the story."

Kari motioned for her to give him the release. He glanced at it, then said. "It was me. Kaarina Varila brought it by, along with several hundred tickets. Good story. Good idea. A person can buy a ticket for two markka and that allows them one prediction of the time between the winner and the loser. Whoever guesses the closest to the actual time difference will win one thousand markka. That's around three hundred American dollars." He pursed his lips in a silent whistle. "That's a lot of money. Over a month's wages for most."

"Yes. But we must stop the raffle."

Kari was silent for a moment. "Why?"

"The way your article reads, it will be interpreted as a symbol of the rivalry between Communism and democracy, not two friends who are just doing it for sport."

"Yes, very likely. And why is this a problem? One would think it would sell a lot of raffle tickets."

"It's a problem, because I have it on good authority that if Colonel Bobrov, the Soviet skier, loses the race publicly, it will embarrass the Soviet Union and they will," she paused, searching for the right words, "take punitive actions."

"Yes, they probably will. Siberia if he's lucky. More likely, they'll accuse him of colluding in an attempt to embarrass the Soviet Union and execute him."

"So, you'll pull the story? I mean, not cover the race?"

Kari, however, was looking at the press release again. He looked up at her. "You say *we* must stop the raffle. So, does Kaarina know about pulling the story?"

"She doesn't." Louise looked down at her lap.

"At least you're honest," Kari said, "as well as a little impetuous." He smiled, letting her know he held nothing against her. Then he said, "You realize that I run a newspaper, not a charity."

"Yes. Of course, but—"

He stopped her short. "We will still want to cover this race as news, particularly since you've already gone to some of our rivals. Then there's the issue of all the lottery tickets already at our newsstands."

He was looking at her with unblinking eyes. She sat, silently feeling the floor dropping from beneath her.

"Mrs. Koski, if I may explain."

"Of course."

"Personally, I am not a fan of the Soviet Union. Or Communists." He reached down and knocked on his artificial leg.

"I'm sorry," Louise mumbled. "Of course, I understand."

"I would like nothing better than to write explicit articles every day extolling the virtues of democracy and attacking the horrors of the Soviet system. However, we Finns unfortunately find ourselves in the middle of a battle between the East and the West for Finland's loyalty. If we go with the Americans, the Soviet Union will invade, and we will lose our freedom. If we go with the Soviet Union, we will forgo all American aid and investment, and still lose our freedom."

Louise said nothing.

Kari watched her for a moment, making her feel a bit uncomfortable under his clear and unemotional gaze. "Perhaps I can explain better. My newspaper must be as nonaligned as my country, so we will cover this story evenly, strictly a race between friends, probably in the sports section. How the story is interpreted I'm afraid is beyond our powers."

"But surely, if you just don't publish anything, the race will be forgotten and Mikhail—Colonel Bobrov—will be in less danger."

"You have forgotten. This story is already with other papers."

"Of course."

"My nation is divided, Mrs. Koski. As, I am afraid, the world will also be divided in too short a time. As you must know, Finland had a bloody civil war between Communists and non-Communists less than thirty years ago. Terrible atrocities were committed by both sides. That's within living memory of about half of this country. Many of my countrymen are still ardent Communists. Many of them went over to the Soviet side during the war. Many of those returned from the Soviet Union and, with its backing, have taken positions of power in our government. Others in our government have been trying to remove them, but that is a very delicate and dangerous game. There are always Russians, hovering in the wings shall we say."

"But . . . I know there's tension, but surely you can let the story die. It's not news. It's a race between friends—just sport, not politics."

"One could say the same about the Olympics," Kari said.

Louise nodded, conceding his point. "Pardon me, Mrs. Koski, I am a Finn. As you must be aware, we are somewhat disposed toward bluntness."

Louise nodded. "I'm married to one."

Kari smiled, then went on.

"As a result of your press release, I can assure you that there are several newspapers at this moment thinking about how to cover this race to extol the virtues of Communism. As for this newspaper, your press release provides us a perfect opportunity to get at the Russians without saying a word about this struggle for Finland's loyalty, perhaps you might even say, its soul. Our readers certainly will see it that way." He let that sink in. Then he added, "And so will the Russians."

Louise had no answer. She considered getting down on her knees but instead leaned toward him across the desk and said, "I understand everything you're saying. What you're saying is true, but it is irrelevant to the lives of the Bobrovs. Will you please, *please* stop covering it?"

"I'm sorry, but no. The story is with rival papers. We've probably already sold quite a few tickets. We have already promised money to several, what is the word, people who work for us but not full-time?"

"Stringers."

"Yes. We have committed to several stringers up north who live near the probable race route. I've asked them to see if they can determine who is winning."

"Can't you just choose not to do the story they turn in?"

"Yoh." Kari looked at her face solemnly. "I could, but I won't."

Louise was dismayed by his unsympathetic demeanor. "Don't you feel *any* moral responsibility for this woman and her family?"

There followed one of those silences that to Americans are awkward but that to Finns are a part of normal conversation. Kari's face had become as cold and fierce as Arctic night.

"Mrs. Koski," he said very quietly, making sure she'd have to hang on his every word. "My *newspaper* must be careful not to offend the Russians. *Personally*, I have no such restriction. I hate Russians. They killed my brother." He gently pounded his fist on his right thigh. "They took my leg. They bombed us. They took eleven percent of our land and are raping the other eighty-nine percent to squeeze us out of three hundred million dollars of what they call 'war reparations.' *We* must pay reparations for a war *they* started. You think I care how these bastards interpret this ski race?"

The stereotype of Finnish emotional control was briefly shown to be just that, a stereotype.

After a moment, Kari did regain control. "I apologize."

"But Mr. Kari, these *bastards* are a husband and wife with two small children."

"Did they think about Finnish husbands, wives, and small children when they invaded us?"

"But the Bobrovs are just four people. *They* didn't invade Finland."

"Colonel Bobrov fought in Karelia, on the Lake Ladoga front with their Eighth Army in 1939 and 1940. I asked around. Colonel Bobrov *did* invade us."

Part Two

Monday, February 3, 1947
The Näskänselkä-Isoselkä System
Race Day 3

On the third day of the race, Mikhail and Arnie were skiing on a long, generally south-trending group of lakes and interconnecting streams east of the municipality of Ranua called the Näskänselkä-Isoselkä lake system. They would hit a small lake, making good time on the ice. Then they would leave the lake and have to plow laboriously through snow, trees, and brush until they either found a streambed or another small lake. Unable to see farther than they could throw something, neither could see the other. However, they both knew without seeing where the other was. They were evenly matched in skill and endurance. To win, it would come down to heart—and what one was willing to risk.

Monday Evening, February 3, 1947
Helsinki

Wracked with guilt, Louise walked back to her flat in the gathering dark, shaken and defeated. Even though she hadn't taken the press release to the papers, she was the one who wrote it. She was responsible and she needed to do something to right her wrong. She nearly bumped into a woman coming her way on the sidewalk. Mumbling an apology she stumbled away. A cold gust of wind hit her, and she crossed her arms, trying to hold in some heat. She became aware that she was angry. At the shallow State Department briefings for assuming all she needed to know was how to manage a cocktail party. At the Oklahoma education system for isolating her from any history beyond her own country. At America, for sheltering her from the stark and grim reality that Natalya faced every day. The horror of living in the Soviet system was no longer some textbook description. The reality now filled her with dread.

She nearly walked in front of a car as she crossed the street. How had she missed the subtext that everyone else seemed to be able to read? Her mind kept replaying the many conversations of the past few days that had an implicit meaning that she'd missed.

You didn't get it, Louise, she said to herself. You ignorant naïve American, welcome to the world outside of Oklahoma.

* * *

Her first thought was to tell Arnie. No matter how crazy the situation or what emotional state she was in, Arnie could somehow put all that aside and think and act. He could always figure out what to do. He was always there to help. But Arnie was gone. Gone where? Somewhere between Rovaniemi and Kuopio. Somewhere nobody knew. She wanted to pound her forehead with her fists, but her forehead was covered with a wool stocking cap and her hands with wool mittens. She tried to talk herself down from the panic, but some inner finger-waving demon wouldn't let her escape her feelings of guilt and shame. How could she have missed the signals? Kaarina's shifts in tone of voice and volume, the occasional quick, almost furtive look. Had Natalya herself hinted at the problems with making the race public? Then she realized that she'd heard and seen everything as if she was still in Oklahoma, that the rest of the world was like home. Now she knew a grim truth: naiveté was not an excuse; it was a flaw. And it was a flaw that hurt people.

She saw an empty bench at a bus stop and sat down, feeling the cold through her wool skirt and stockings. Bringing her head down and her mittens up to her face, feeling them scratch her cheeks, she started shaking with sobs.

Feeling frozen snot beneath her nose brought her back to the present. The crying had calmed her.

She remembered the time she'd lost a considerable number of lumber orders by carelessly failing to file them properly. She suspected that she'd somehow mixed them with scrap papers that she'd thrown into the office's potbelly stove. The orders represented a serious amount of income. After several hours of frantic searching, she'd gone to her father in tears and confessed. He was angry but calm. He'd made it clear just how much money was at stake and what that meant. After he'd let that sink in, he said, "There's an old expression: you've made your bed, now lie in it. I never liked that expression. It should be you've made your bed *badly*, now get the hell up and remake it." Then, he pointed to the telephone and walked out of the office, leaving her trembling. Three days of telephone calls, and several months thereafter to pay for the long-distance charges from her allowance, she'd remade the bed.

She rose from the bench and drew her coat in tightly, comforting herself. This bed could be remade. It *had* to be remade.

Mentally throwing her shoulders back, she began to think. The story was out. There was no putting that genie back in the bottle. She briefly thought of writing another release saying that the race had been canceled. That, however, would quickly be seen as a lie, making things worse.

Finally reaching home, Louise collapsed crying on her bed, kicking and pounding at the bedding in frustration and impotence. Then, the storm over, she carefully brewed a pot of tea and sat down to think. The papers weren't going to back off. Since the race would be well publicized, it made no sense to try to call off the raffle. Be practical. It was sure to bring in a good deal of money.

She kept at the kitchen table, scratching out various alternative plans to fix the problem, drinking cup after cup of tea.

Her first rejected plan involved Sokolov. He'd seemed so friendly; then she found that he'd bugged their apartment. Sokolov also seemed friendly toward Natalya and Mikhail. However, she also now knew that nothing about Sokolov—or most of the Russians she'd met—was necessarily aligned with what appeared on the surface. She still didn't know if Natalya knew about the bugging. She no longer cared. If Natalya knew, it meant nothing about who she was or their friendship. Who knew what pressure Sokolov could apply to both Natalya and Mikhail.

Plan two was to get asylum for the Bobrovs. The American legation in Helsinki, however, wasn't internationally recognized as a full-on official embassy, which by international law would make the building and grounds the sovereign territory of the United States, not Finland.

The nearest true American embassy was in Stockholm, nearly impossible to reach. It was 250 miles away and would require getting on a boat or ferry. They would be unlikely to escape without being seen by one of the many Communist sympathizers who would happily inform the Russians. Besides, she had no reason to think that either Natalya or Mikhail would want to defect, even if uncertain about their own lives.

Plan three was to try to stop the America-versus-Russia, freedom-versus-totalitarianism emphasis the newspapers were giving the race. Given Kari's reaction to that, plan three was probably a non-starter. Besides, not all the papers were published in Helsinki, and she couldn't reach them in time. The strongly pro-Communist *Kansan Lehti* was published in Tampere. News of the race could soon be all over Finland.

Then a cold chill enveloped her. Why not other papers in other countries? The story was out, sure to be carried by all the newswires. It was as if she'd released a virulent virus, and there was no stopping it until it ran its course. She grew desperate with the thought.

Of course, she could just do nothing, hoping Mikhail would win. Doing nothing kept the raffle money coming in. That would help the orphans and keep Kaarina happy. She, however, knew how good Arnie was at his sport. In most sports, the odds start to work against anyone over thirty. In endurance sports, however, like mountain climbing, something else kicks in besides sheer physicality: mental toughness. This grew throughout a man's life. The combination of slowly declining strength and increasing grit peaked around the mid-thirties.

Only she and Arnie really knew how good he'd been even before all the training with the Tenth Mountain. Had it not been for the war, Arnie would have been a serious contender for a spot on the US Olympic team. Of course, Mikhail had skied the entire war. Just looking at him, she could see he carried himself the way good athletes do. His fluidity and strength were apparent even in the way he drank and talked with Arnie. They were peas in a pod.

Both men were in their thirties, and both had been in office jobs since the war, so neither was going to be as good as they were during the war. Arnie, however, exercised hard every morning before work. Risking a family's life on hope that Mikhail would win didn't seem like a good idea. She also knew of what stern stuff Arnie was made. He'd had something he called *sisu* driven into him since he was a toddler. Arnie would put in one of the best performances of his life. The only physical failing that would stop him from giving it everything he had was death.

After far too many cups of tea—thinking, rejecting, thinking again—she realized that she had only one workable option. She had to find Arnie and get him to throw the race. But how?

Monday Evening, February 3, 1947
The Näskänselkä-Isoselkä System
Race Day 3

While Louise was walking home, Arnie was digging out a sleeping trench in the snow. Three of the most important rules of winter survival are stay dry, stay out of the wind, and stay well fed. Digging a sleeping trench satisfied the stay-out-of-the-wind rule. It had been dark for several hours and the temperature was still dropping. He felt like his body heat was being sucked away into a black vacuum.

All that day, he'd been making his way south, hitting good skiing on the lakes and rivers of the Näskänselkä-Isoselkä system. He had been playing the trade-off game between speed and safety. Speed required effort, which made a skier sweat. Sweat would soak clothes, from underwear out. The outer layers of clothes would freeze to ice, making the rest of the clothes beneath cold. The cold clothes would suck heat from the body and the skier would die of hypothermia.

Arnie, however, knew that the winning tactic was to keep pushing steadily, to keep his body heat up, but not push too hard. If he made a mistake by pushing himself too fast, he could fall, break a bone, and die from hypothermia for sure. If he slowed down to stop sweating, it would put him behind Mikhail. So, he sweated. There was no way to keep his underclothes dry. He relied on heat-generating fuel and physical effort to keep him from hypothermia during the day. That meant that his clothes had to be dried at night in his sleeping bag.

The whole situation filled him with satisfaction and purpose. He was once more living only in the present moment, with death over his shoulder. It felt right.

For three days, he'd caught glimpses of Mikhail. Clearly, they were evenly matched in terms of speed, skill, and endurance. This left an edge to the one who could get by on the least sleep. It was never fully dark if the sky was clear, because the moon was still growing toward full on February 5. However, around four in the afternoon, clouds had come in just as the sun was setting. This cut twilight nearly in half and it was dark by six o'clock. He'd packed a right-angle military flashlight with its standard issue red lens filter for maintaining one's night vision, but he only used it occasionally to read the map, not wanting to waste the batteries. He'd slowed to a crawl in the darkness, feeling his way forward. He knew he could cover the distance he'd traveled for several hours in the dark within minutes when morning twilight arrived around five, depending on the cloud cover. The problem was that if Mikhail chose to crawl forward in the dark while Arnie slept, then that small distance might mean the loss of the race. On the other hand, he knew that neither of them could go without sleep for more than a couple of days because doing so would result in not only skiing slower but also the possibility of making a fatal, poor decision. He ended up assuming that Mikhail was making the same calculations, and if he was, then he'd stop when Arnie stopped. So, by the third night, Arnie had settled into a pattern of skiing until around 2200, then making a shelter and sleeping until 0200. He'd been vindicated in this decision by glimpsing Mikhail several times that day. He had gone through most of the war on four hours of sleep—mostly two hours at a time—so this wasn't a major hardship. In the war, however, there had always been times and places where he could snatch fifteen or twenty minutes of sleep in safety. Someone was always around and on guard.

Now, a twenty-minute nap could cost him the race. Of course, not getting enough sleep could also cost him the race. With his practical engineering mind—inherited from his father, a superb logger, which meant a superb back-of-the-envelope engineer—Arnie enjoyed playing with these trade-offs. The enjoyment was further seasoned by two spices: not losing the race and not losing his life.

When he finished digging out the sleeping trench in the snow, he took out his small hatchet and made a small frame of limbs that he filled with pine boughs to slow the drain of heat from his body into the snow beneath him. Changing into dry clothes, he stuffed those he'd been wearing, damp with sweat, into the sleeping bag so they could dry. He fell asleep almost instantly.

Something woke him. It could have been an animal, or a change in the wind direction—or even a change in air pressure. In his heightened state, he was keenly attuned to his surroundings, unlike "normal" life, lived inside four walls or on four wheels, cut off from nature, which all people are part of, if only they could remember it.

He checked his watch. It was only 0030. Again, the trade-offs to calculate: get an early start but risk falling apart and needing sleep later or get in another hour and a half now but risk falling behind. It was a problem to which knowledge and experience could be applied but one that ultimately would come down to wilderness intuition. Those who had it survived.

Pulling into as close to a ball as he could get in the mummy sack, he wondered if Louise was asleep. He thought about the many times he'd awakened to find her propped up against a pillow reading. He would reach out, stroke her thigh, and she would smile. Then he'd wake up two hours later and she'd still be reading. When he got up for work, she was often in a sleep so deep he sometimes made it out the door without waking her. If she did wake, however, she'd always fix breakfast. He'd watch her sleepily scrambling eggs, a coffee cup in one hand, her body just outlined beneath her bathrobe. In the summer, she would sometimes make him breakfast wearing the robe and negligée set she'd worn on their honeymoon. In winter, it would be the silk robe he'd bought her for Christmas in 1940. A year later, the United States was at war and all the silk was going into parachutes.

He rolled to his other side, pulling his head inside the bag, leaving just a small hole for his nose. Shivering slightly—not enough to worry about, the bag would soon warm a bit—his mind drifted back to another time when he found himself lying in snow.

He'd asked her to come out to Fort Lewis over her Christmas break. She did. He'd gotten leave and they went skiing at Paradise on Mount Rainier, site of the 1936 Olympic tryouts, which he'd missed because he was still a cadet at West Point. They both had fallen into deep snow and wound up with their skis tangled together, laughing, then kissing. Then he'd blurted out, "I want to be tangled up with you the rest of my life."

She'd stopped laughing.

He remembered awkwardly struggling to get upright, but his skis were still attached to him by their leather bindings, making it impossible. He remembered grabbing her hands, still lying on the snow next to her and saying, "I can't get on my knee. Will you marry me?"

She'd clearly not expected it, at least right there and then. What she said after an agonizingly long pause was, "You Finns sure know how to be romantic."

Then the joy came bursting through her like sunrise at the summit. "Yes!"

She lunged for him, and they'd both gone flailing back in the snow, rolling, skis, arms, and legs entangled, Louise shouting yes to the clear cold Cascade sky.

Arnie fell asleep, smiling.

Tuesday Morning, February 4, 1947
Sokolov's Office

Natalya got to Sokolov's office before his secretary, Julia. When Julia arrived, Natalya pleaded to be able to see Sokolov first thing. Julia shrugged and nodded to an empty chair next to Sokolov's door. It was twenty minutes of nervous tension before Sokolov arrived. He carried a briefcase and had several newspapers tucked under one arm.

Natalya stood.

"Mrs. Bobrova," Sokolov said. "I'm *not* surprised to see you."

No "comrade" this morning, Natalya thought.

Sokolov turned to his secretary. "Another cup for Mrs. Bobrova."

As Julia went to get Sokolov's usual morning tea. Sokolov indicated Natalya should precede him into his office.

"Sit," he said.

She did.

He threw in front of her the same edition of *Helsingin Sanomat* that she had shown Louise. Saying nothing, he put two additional papers next to it, one sympathetic to the Soviet Union and the other unsympathetic. "I assume you've seen these," he said.

Natalya nodded. "Yes, Comrade, I have."

"As you must know, part of my job is making sure we keep the press honest."

"Yes, Comrade."

"Now, at home honesty is totally assured. Here, however, we must keep the illusion of strict neutrality. While we cannot guarantee honest reporting, as we can at home, we can, shall we say, apply certain incentives to the Finnish government to make sure *they* keep their newspapers honest."

Natalya knew they both knew the Soviet definition of honesty meant adherence to presenting correct political thought, not facts. "Yes, Comrade." What else could she say?

Sokolov studied her. "Your hero husband has done something very foolish."

"Yes, Comrade." She looked down at her lap to show contrition.

"When did you know about this?"

Her mind reeled off several answers and the possible consequences. If she told the truth, that she knew the night of the legation party, then he'd want to know why she didn't tell him. That would mean she was keeping a secret. That could mean Lubyanka. In fact, admitting to knowing about it any time before these news stories could lead to the same fate. On the other hand, if she lied and said she knew nothing about it, and he found out—somehow, they always do—same fate. Still, lying had a better chance than telling the truth. The whole system worked that way.

"The first I heard of it was last night when I saw the article in *Helsingin Sanomat.*"

"Yes, I know," he said.

Of course, he knew.

"Mikhail said he was going north to look at, what did he call them, egress and entry routes, something like that."

Sokolov looked at her with those eyes seemingly carved from glacier ice. "That's what he told all of us."

She sighed an inward sigh of relief. At least her story was consistent. Any lie at all could suffice to keep you safe, but a lie that fell apart because of some internal inconsistency could get you killed. Silence was also a good strategy, particularly if you haven't been asked a question. She felt she must be reliving her own mother's last days—the fear of the late-night knock on the door.

Sokolov poked at the newspapers, moving them slightly. "How well do you know your husband?" he asked.

"He's a patriot. He's dedicated his life to serving the Party."

Sokolov's eyes lidded slightly, and a tiny smile appeared.

"Yes. Of course. We are all patriots and dedicated to serving the Party."

He left that in a long silence. "I am going to ask again only one time. How well do you know your husband?"

How well do any of us, she thought. She gulped. "He can be impetuous," she said. That couldn't be construed politically. Could it?

"Yes," was all Sokolov answered. "I understand," he said, his whole tone changing to one of comradeship. "This foolish race started as a typical and childish army brotherhood of warriors." He did not restrain the sarcasm and disdain. He was digging into his briefcase. "Had it not been for this," he laid a carbon copy of Kaarina's translation of Louise's press release on the desk, "it would have remained so." She couldn't translate it word for word, but she got a very good sense of it. Even in Finnish, it had Louise's bubbly optimism all over it.

"The best interpretation of this, for your husband's sake, is that it *was* akin to a schoolboy stunt, although this might prove difficult given that your husband has been out of school over fifteen years and has been a commanding officer in combat, someone people looked up to for leadership and sound judgment." Natalya was nodding. "However," Sokolov went on, "there is a second interpretation." He made her wait to hear what that was. "We have reason to believe it was all engineered. Lieutenant Colonel Koski entices your husband to race, saying it is just between *warriors*," again, the unveiled sarcasm, "when in reality Koski has won national championships." She could only keep nodding, going along with his theory. "All the while, his 'wife,'" he made sure she heard the quotation marks, "very likely an intelligence agent like him, turns this 'innocent' and private race into a Western publicity stunt to undermine the reputation of the Red Army and the Soviet way of life. Do you really believe that 'Louise Koski,'" again the quotation marks, "is as naïve as she lets on? Do you believe that she cares about a Finnish orphanage, an orphanage in a country that fought for the Fascists? Do you think a true friend would do this?" He held the press release up to her eyes. "Callously disregarding how it would impact her 'friends,' like you and your husband?" He leaned back slightly. "What kind of friend is that? Hmmm?"

She knew better than to answer the rhetorical question.

"This whole innocent, corn-fed girl-of-the-prairies persona," Sokolov went on, "was the perfect cover to suck you and Colonel Bobrov in. I believe this whole orphanage money-raising effort was simply a setup. We are looking into this 'relative' of Colonel Koski, Kaarina Varila. We know she lost sons and a husband in the war. We have had an eye on her youngest son, Pietari. He is known for his anti-Party talk and hatred. That and a few American dollars would be quite sufficient motive for both of them to cooperate in this, I must admit, rather clever operation."

Natalya's mind was in turmoil. She felt simultaneously betrayed, vulnerable, and foolish. Could she have been so blind as not to see that Louise had been playing her just as Louise's husband had been playing Misha? Were Arnie and Louise even married? Their "marriage" could just be a cover. To think that Louise was a fabrication, that she was someone else entirely, felt like being stabbed as someone was knocking her legs out from beneath her. No, she thought, forcibly blocking her doubts. What Sokolov was saying just couldn't be true. She had to trust what she saw and felt, not what she was told by people like Sokolov. But the intrusive thought remained. What if she had been a total fool?

She struggled to keep her composure. She knew well that she lived in a world where "facts" could be true or untrue, where the interpretation of "facts" could be as changeable as political leadership. "Facts" being true or untrue depending on the needs of those in power didn't just impact politics; it undermined the bedrock of civilization: love, relation, family, and friends.

"Why would the Americans want to even do such a thing?" she asked.

"I am sure you are aware that the Soviet Union is in a not-so-subtle battle to show that our way of life is superior in every way to that of the capitalist West." He'd taken the tone of an adult lecturing a child.

"I am, Comrade," Natalya said.

"I am sure that you are also aware that any shift in public attitude of our Eastern European neighbors toward the Western way of thinking is a danger to the revolution and could damage our goal of securing our borders with nations that are friendly to the revolution. That's why."

It was clear that Sokolov wasn't through lecturing but was just waiting for her to take in his lecture up to this point. She shifted uncomfortably in her chair.

"So, explanation one"—he held up a single finger—"it *was* a schoolboy folly. Explanation two"—a second finger joined the first—"your husband was duped by a very clever intelligence operation." His hand lowered. His lidded eyes had the look of a cobra. "I'm sure you can figure out explanation three."

Natalya gulped down cold fear. Explanation three: Misha was a traitor.

Sokolov saw that she understood. "Yes. It would not be a stretch to believe your hero husband has colluded in all of this."

"No, Comrade. I swear. He loves Russia. And the Party. We knew nothing about this. On the lives of my children," she pleaded.

Sokolov's eyes were dead. He let her squirm a moment, leaving the "lives of my children" hanging in the air like a noose.

"And Louise Koski is really an innocent flower of the prairies?" He raised his eyebrows, clearly indicating what he himself believed—or wanted her to believe he believed. It was Russian dolls again.

Natalya's mind was racing, creating and rejecting answers and possible explanations. If Misha wasn't being duped by a clever American operation, then those unseen judges, the state, the Party, weighing his life—and hers—had to conclude he was either a reckless fool or a traitor. It was highly unlikely they'd select the reckless explanation. That would mean a Hero of the Soviet Union was irresponsible and dangerous and that those who selected him as a military attaché were themselves careless. She could only eliminate the accusation of treason against her and Misha by denouncing Louise as a spy. Nothing, however, indicated that she was. What evidence could she come up with that would convince Sokolov and his superiors that Louise, Coca-Cola personified, was an American Mata Hari? None. But she had to say *something*. Sokolov was sitting there like a spider watching his web.

He leaned forward. "We both know that your husband is not a fool."

But he *is*, she wanted to scream. No, not a fool, but a soldier whose actions could look foolish to people who weren't soldiers. *That* is the explanation. He and Arnie Koski were racing for the honor of their services and to test their hearts. How could any politician or bureaucrat like Sokolov ever understand this? She realized that Sokolov had stopped short of saying Mikhail was a traitor. Had he spoken it aloud, there would be no possibility of proving Mikhail's innocence once the judgment had been rendered. Just being *suspected* of being a traitor in the Soviet system was a crime punishable by death.

She could feel her heart in her throat. She fought to calmly say, "Perhaps we have been played."

"Ah," Sokolov said. "Perhaps *you* have." Then, changing his whole demeanor, he said quietly, "Comrade Bobrova, I know you must feel frightened for your husband's welfare. Are you frightened?"

"Yes, Comrade."

"You should be." He sighed, then silently began organizing the newspapers. When he'd finished, he placed the press releases on top of the neat pile and looked up at her. His expression changed from one of condemnation to one of fake genial support, the standard we're-all-comrades-together-here of the Soviet bureaucrat. "I don't want anything bad to happen to your husband. He is, after all, a Hero of the Soviet Union." The way he said hero made her think of someone holding their nose over a dead fish.

"For now, we will try to keep the story local," he said. "If we can keep it out of the major Western newspapers, the damage to Socialism will be contained. It is unlikely then, that we will have to take measures to ensure the story remains out of the newspapers of our Eastern European neighbors. I, of course, will have to report this to my immediate superior in Moscow. However, if it remains purely local, then it need go no further up the line from there." He held his hand up, as in heaven forbid. "I will do my best."

"Thank you, Comrade Sokolov."

"You had better pray your husband wins."

"But if he doesn't, Comrade Sokolov—" Just speaking the possibility aloud stopped her. "You must believe me. He would never intentionally undertake any activity detrimental to the Soviet state."

"Comrade Bobrova," he said softly. "We will of course investigate and get to the bottom of this. But you must realize, our findings about your husband's intentions are of little consequence." He paused, then added, "Other than the form of punishment." Natalya bit her lower lip. Sokolov leaned toward her. "Losing this race, now that Soviet prestige is at stake, is of enormous consequence."

"Comrade, you are an important person." Natalya leaned toward him, reaching one hand across the desk in front of her in supplication. "You, surely, can do something so Mikhail won't be unjustly punished for, as you yourself put it, a schoolboy stunt." She forced a smile, feeling slightly sick, knowing that her gesture of supplication would most certainly be interpreted as an offer. "What can I do to prove his . . . our innocence?"

He smiled, looking down at her hand on the desk. She saw the spider coming down the threads of the web. "I'm sure something can be done, Comrade," Sokolov said. "And who knows? He could win. I hear he's a good skier."

"Comrade Sokolov. I am sure he'll beat the American. It is the Americans who will be publicly embarrassed, shown to be pampered and effete. It will be a publicity success."

Sokolov smiled. "If you are so sure, why are you here?"

Natalya gave him a wan smile. "Because you asked to see me, Comrade Sokolov." She pulled her hand back into her lap and clutched it with her other.

Sokolov nodded, with a self-satisfied smile. If the spider had a hand at the end of one of its eight legs, it would have been patting her condescendingly on her head. Sokolov looked at his watch. "We need to discuss this further, perhaps make some plans. I'm very busy this morning. In fact, the rest of the day." She watched his eyes flicker just briefly down from her face to her lap, then back up again. "Perhaps we can get together later. Work something out."

Despite a sinking sick feeling in her entire body, Natalya didn't hesitate. She was a Russian woman. She could look at the clock and tell the time. The same set of skills that so pleased the man she loved could also be used as currency to pay for protection. She tilted her head and smiled warmly at Sokolov, making her eyes brim with gratitude. "Of course, Comrade Sokolov. I would be most grateful for any time you can make for this."

Courage takes many forms.

Tuesday, February 4, 1947
South of the Näskänselkä-Isoselkä System
Race Day 4

Both Arnie and Mikhail were nearing exhaustion. They'd been off ice for several hours. That meant breaking through snow in a frustratingly slow and demoralizing slog. Get a ski up on fresh snow from where it had been over a foot below the surface. Push forward. The forward ski breaks the crust and sinks. This leaves behind the other ski still buried from the previous effort. The thigh muscles quiver with the exertion. The hind ski is lifted, putting more weight on the forward ski, sinking it farther into the snow. Balance is thrown off, requiring exertion to regain it. Poles are pushed deeper, requiring more exertion to pull them clear. The floundering is repeated. And repeated. And repeated.

Arnie was frustrated. He'd gotten a glimpse of Mikhail about a kilometer off, looking to Arnie to be slightly ahead. The terrain had changed to what in summer would be marshy, boggy ground. Now it was frozen over. Almost all of Arnie's experience of cross-country skiing had been in mountains. When he saw the flat frozen surfaces of the marsh, with puffs of plants pushing above the ice, it looked nearly as good as a frozen lake or stream. He shoved off over the marsh before him, thankful to be once again moving rapidly, piling on as much distance as he could before darkness and exhaustion stopped him. He took his first Benzedrine pill.

*   *   *

Mikhail, too, had entered the same marshy, boggy terrain. He, however, had skied similar ground in Finland, in Belarus, and in Poland. He knew that organic material in the bog bottoms constantly generated heat. The heat had to escape somewhere. In winter, it came through what the local Finns called bog eyes. During the 1939–40 winter campaign in Finland, while negotiating a bog much like the ones he was encountering now, he'd watched his friend, Ivanov, vanish. There was a cry, a crunching and splashing sound, and then Ivanov was gone, taken down by his heavy gear. The Finns had been pressing them on their flanks, so after only a couple of minutes of lying spread out on the ice and fruitless poking with tree branches, hoping Ivanov would grab one and be pulled free, he had to make the decision to move on. Ivanov's body might still be there, a skeleton, wrapped with straps and a rifle attached. He tried to shake the image. The memory, however, recalled that this year, the winter had been late. Although late arriving, when the snow came, it came hard and heavy. This meant less chance for ice to form.

He and Arnie were also moving steadily southward. Every kilometer farther south, the more likely they were to encounter areas where the snow simply covered water or very thin ice, forming a dangerous snow bridge.

He began to modify his route when he hit bogs, moving more elliptically instead of straight across, so he'd be near solid land if something went wrong. It was safer but slower.

Tuesday Afternoon, February 4, 1947
Soviet Legation

While Arnie and Mikhail were pushing slowly through the deep snow, Arnie crossing over the bogs and Mikhail avoiding them, in the economic section of the legation, Natalya was pretending to work. She was laboriously going over Finnish government tax records to locate businesses that might have used or were currently using capital equipment that could be more useful back in Russia. Her rudimentary Finnish made it slow going.

She struggled against anxiety, wondering where Mikhail was, if he was winning, wondering if Fanya had just locked her kids in their bedroom and gone out shopping. She shook the anxiety off as typical mothers' insecurity that happened to all mothers when they were separated from their children. Underlying all this anxiety was dread about what she'd promised Sokolov and rage that this creepy son of a bitch held such unassailable power.

When the afternoon papers were dropped on the big common table near the economic section's door, the anxiety and anger turned to cold fear. All the Finnish dailies had a story about the race. One had even published a guessed-at route.

Fellow workers made a few wisecracks about Mikhail. Some wondered aloud what Mikhail was *really* up to, spinning yet another fantastic conspiracy theory. Natalya was used to conspiracy theories. In recent history, many were proven true. She knew such theories were a way for people to make sense out of senselessness. To ordinary people, it just didn't seem possible that their political leaders could be as stupid, self-serving, or greedy as their actions made them look. There *had* to be some explanation behind the story, otherwise people would have to admit that their fate was in the hands of stupid, self-serving, greedy people. Who would want to believe and accept that? So, people maintained hope and the will to carry on with difficult lives by believing virtually any conspiracy theory that explained the decisions of their leaders, other than plain evil or plain stupidity.

Waiting in line during the afternoon tea break, Natalya watched the two Finnish women who were serving everyone. They both spoke Russian, so she guessed that they'd been two of the many Finnish Communists who'd fled for protection to the Soviet Union when the Winter War broke out. They were now reaping their reward with a good, secure Soviet government job.

When one of them poured Natalya's tea she said, "We are all rooting for your husband."

Natalya smiled and nodded.

"We don't think the American will even finish. Their elites, like this guy, are too soft. They live off the hard work of exploited Blacks and starving workers." She smiled, showing teeth darkened by tea and two noticeable gaps where teeth had been pulled. "Their soldiers drove to war on tanks built by Cadillac. They sit back and bomb civilians from the air. They drank and raped their way no more than a few hundred kilometers from the French coast, while our soldiers fought and bled over several thousand kilometers doing all the fighting and dying."

Natalya nodded, reaching for the sugar cubes. Another perk of working in the legation. "Yes," she said, smiling at the woman. "I know. By our soldiers," she said carefully, not quite sure of the politics, "I presume you mean the Soviet Union's."

The woman's head jerked back slightly. "I mean the Red Army. The army of the People. Of the people of the whole world."

"Oh, of course. Yes, I see. Yes, our army . . . of the People."

As Natalya returned to her desk with her cup of tea, she was mulling over the whole concept of "we" and "the People." These concepts were just that—concepts—not fact, not reality. She and Mikhail and her children were reality. What were "the state" or "the Party" or, for that matter, "Communism" or "capitalism"? How could you love anything other than another human? Why would you die for anything other than another human who you loved? All her life, at least since the orphanage, she'd heard about the Party, and the People. She now had a vague, uneasy feeling. About it all. Maybe the concepts had been oversold. It, of course, wasn't right to have these feelings. She tried to stop having them.

She held the cup of tea, staring at it, warming her hand. This cup of tea was reality. She took a sip, but even with two lumps of sugar, the tea tasted bitter. The race was clearly between *us* and *them*, not Misha and Arnie. What before had been a vague fear was now reality.

Tuesday Evening, February 4, 1947
The Orphanage

That evening, Kaarina, Natalya, and Louise met at the orphanage.

News of the race and raffle had spread to churches, where the bets were mostly on Arnie. It spread to labor unions, where the bets seemed about even between Arnie and Mikhail. It spread to organizations dominated by the Communist Party of Finland, where Mikhail championed the People and a future free of religion and imperialism. When Louise asked for the numbers, a smiling Kaarina Varila announced that raffle ticket sales were nearly double what they'd initially hoped for. Had Kaarina been American, she would have been clapping her hands and popping champagne.

Louise took in the news with mixed feelings. On the one hand, the money was flowing in. On the other hand, as each ticket and its money were counted, she could see that for Natalya, the more successful the raffle the more people knew about the race, and that she was just another step closer to the punishment her husband and children would endure if Mikhail lost. Natalya's eyes had a deer-in-the-headlights look, and she was occasionally chewing on her lower lip. Louise wanted to reach across the table to touch her but worried that would be inappropriate. Instead, whispering in French she said, "It will be alright. We'll find Arnie and get him to throw the race."

Natalya's eyes darted from Louise to Kaarina and then back. She whispered fiercely, "*We* don't know where *he* is."

Kaarina was giving Louise a puzzled look, not understanding the French.

Not wanting to be rude, Louise quickly said to Natalya, "Let's talk about this on the way home." Natalya nodded and leaned back in her chair, holding her upper arms, as if comforting herself.

Louise hesitated, glancing at Natalya, before she explained to Kaarina, "Natalya is very worried what will happen to her family if Mikhail loses." She glanced at Natalya, who didn't understand the English. "I feel terrible," Louise added.

"You have no responsibility for the action of a totalitarian government."

"But I didn't think—"

Kaarina's face was a stoic mask. "It is a lot of money. A lot of orphans will be better off. You are responsible for that."

"I know. But it's a Pyrrhic victory."

"No. A real victory."

Natalya was looking between Kaarina and Louise, wanting someone to explain what was going on.

"But surely, we must consider Natalya and her family in this," Louise said. "It's my fault."

"And you want to assuage your guilt."

That stopped Louise. Her eyes flared. "It's more than that. You know it."

Kaarina sighed. "Yes. It's become America and freedom versus Soviet totalitarianism. Whether they're Reds or Whites, Finns all over the country will be rooting for their side. But you yourself said controversy is good for fundraising. The more people we get to buy tickets, the more money we get for the orphans. Perhaps you should consider that some sacrifices are worth making."

Louise firmly but quietly said, "I do not want to be responsible for knowingly sacrificing a family for all the money in the world."

A Finn would see no need to speak and Kaarina did not respond.

Louise broke the silence. "We have to find Arnie and get him to throw the race."

"Not even the newspapers know where he is," Kaarina said.

"Arnie gave me a general route," Louise replied. "What if I gave that to your son, Pietari? He was a ski trooper. He must have friends. If we get enough of them out there, I'm sure they'll find him."

"What is she saying?" Natalya finally asked Louise in French.

"She was just thinking out loud about how to find Arnie and Mikhail."

Natalya went silent, obviously hoping Kaarina and Louise would come up with some sort of plan.

Louise turned back to Kaarina. "What do you think?"

"About Pietari?" Kaarina shook her head. "Louise, you see Mikhail and Natalya here as a husband and wife, as friends. Do you really know anything about them? How many orphans did Mikhail create? How many German women did he rape? How many Finnish women? Don't forget, it was the German soldiers, not the Russians, who were our staunch allies."

"Mikhail would never rape someone."

"You don't know that. Natalya and I have lived through a war. You were alive when a war was going on. Those are two different experiences."

Louise felt as if she were wading through mud.

"What are you two talking about?" Natalya asked again.

Louise wanted to shout at Natalya, *She hates your country and she doesn't give a shit if your husband is sent to Siberia or what happens to you and your children.*

Louise's thoughts were stopped when she saw tears in Natalya's eyes. "Oh, Natalya," she said. She could see that Kaarina had also been moved.

"Maybe we could try other ways to get a note to Arnie besides Pietari and his friends," Louise said to Kaarina. "We could give notes to any reporters covering the story."

"Why would those reporters who would be rooting for the American even deliver the message? Those rooting for the Russian would see a thrown race as potentially embarrassing to their cause, particularly because the pro-Western reporters would all have notes asking Arnie to throw the race. They could use those notes to discredit Mikhail's victory, even if he did win the race fair and square."

"What about an airplane? The US Army Air Corps has airplanes all over Europe."

"Sure, but none here."

Louise wanted to scream at the way Kaarina kept coming up with objections—objections she couldn't counter. It was like talking to Arnie's mother. Was it some sort of Finnish gene? "What if we hired a Finnish pilot to find Arnie and drop a note?"

"He'd take your money and say he will," Kaarina replied. "You have no guarantee he'll actually do it, even if he does manage to find him. There's a lot of land between Rovaniemi and Kuopio and a lot of that is covered in forest."

Louise felt herself sinking even deeper into the mud.

She made one last appeal. "Kaarina, I know you've lost sons and your husband. I know the Russians ravaged this country. Millions have suffered. Still, if we are ever to get free of all this numbness and hatred created by the sheer numbers and horror, *someone* has to start valuing individual human lives over history and politics."

Kaarina studied her. Then she grunted. "Maybe."

Louise felt a bit of hope. Now she had to appeal to Pietari directly.

*   *   *

As soon as they were outside, Natalya grabbed Louise's arm to stop her. "What were you two talking about?"

"How to get a note to Arnie so he'll throw the race."

"How do you know he'll do what you ask, even in the remote chance that you do get a note to him? Do you actually think a professional soldier will choose to dishonor himself or even the US Army because *maybe* a Russian family will get sent to the gulag?"

"For your family, yes, I know he will," Louise said.

"In your mind," Natalya said. "In Arnie's and Mikhail's minds, honor is what they live on. You think they serve their country for the pay and easy working conditions?"

"Your point?" Louise prompted.

"Asking Arnie to throw the race, to surrender without a fight, would be like asking him to dishonor every member of his unit who he watched die."

"Natalya, I promise you, and I know Arnie is a warrior as you say he is, like Mikhail. But I know he'll do it."

Natalya gave a typical Russian shrug of her shoulders. The shrug of *who knows?* The shrug that spoke of years of endurance under hardship and repressive governments. The shrug of *I don't care. It's beyond me, what can you do?* The shoulder shrug of *I'm a Russian. I will endure this as we have done for centuries.*

Louise did not have a shoulder shrug like that.

Wednesday Morning, February 5, 1947
The Pudasjärvi Waterways
Race Day 5

Mikhail was out of his snow burrow and moving swiftly hours before dawn. He felt a satisfying, almost hypnotic happiness. The snow muffled all sound save that of his skis. It reflected the light from a full moon. In good weather, even without a moon, snow on the ground provided ample light for moving efficiently at night. With a full moon, it was like skiing in daylight.

He was in a bubble of light and silence. His body was operating at its peak. His mind was clear of distractions. Here, he was beyond organizational politics. Gone was the constant underlying anxiety that he wasn't performing well—which could lead to the dreaded knock on the door in the middle of the night.

He was moving on ice again, heading south on the Pudasjärvi waterways, making good time. If someone asked him if he was having fun, he would answer that what he was doing was too deeply satisfying for such a lighthearted word—or feeling—like fun.

He came across Arnie's ski tracks. This was not a good sign, as it meant Arnie was ahead of him. He knelt briefly to examine the edges of the tracks, to see how fresh they were. He figured he was no more than half an hour behind. He picked up the pace.

He moved easily and quickly, taking advantage of small lakes, their solid and safe ice clear of snow, making the skiing fast and easy. In between lakes, he'd have to plow through more difficult snow-covered ground. He occasionally encountered bogs but avoided them.

Coming off one of the lakes, he saw that Arnie's tracks went right into an adjoining bog. The fact that Arnie was cutting directly across bogs probably explained his lead. He smiled grimly. Know your opponent. Though he could never think of Arnie as an enemy, even if they might end up fighting each other someday. To Mikhail, Arnie was a typical Finn: taciturn and hotheaded. It was that Finnish hotheadedness that might be moving Arnie to risk crossing bogs as he was doing. Or it could be American ignorance. It could also be American soldier's two-edged sword of "can do." Get it done, even if you break a few rules. More relevant in Arnie's case, however, was get it done, even if you take more risk than is wise. Mikhail's grim smile came back. He knew he was thinking in stereotypes—and that could be a terrible mistake when trying to make an intelligence estimate of an opponent. On the other hand, stereotypes existed for a reason. Most Germans *were* meticulous. They were also militaristic. He had no doubt the Germans had the best army in the war. They fought under the handicap of crazy political leadership and the usual mix of incompetent generals—combined with extremely limited resources—against the greatest powers on earth and yet held them at bay for years. Any other army would have collapsed long before the Germans did.

He chuckled and headed slightly off course to skirt the edge of the bog. Arnie was classic. Mikhail really liked him and had a lot of respect for him as a professional soldier. As an opponent in a ski race, he was a highly skilled athlete and tough. However, Arnie was also a risk-taker, perhaps ignorant of Finnish winter terrain. Then, Mikhail thought of the motto of the British Special Air Service: *who dares wins.* Dare too little and you lose; dare too much and you die. He set his jaw and increased his pace.

Wednesday Morning, February 5, 1947
Soviet Legation

When Natalya arrived that morning for work at the legation, she was surprised to see an old friend of Mikhail's who had served with him in the GRU, military intelligence, during the war. The man put down his small traveling bag and briefcase and reached out to give her a hug and kiss her on both cheeks.

"Grigori, what are you doing here?" she asked.

He shrugged. "Don't know. Orders. Left Leningrad several hours ago. Was told to report to a Comrade Colonel Sokolov. You know him?"

Natalya could not speak. She could only put on her tight smile and nod.

"What's wrong?"

"Nothing. Nothing."

"Is Mikhail around? It would be great to see him."

"No. He's . . ." She hesitated. What did Grigori know? Was asking if Mikhail was around a cover for why he was really here? How should she answer? Was he even really a friend? "He's doing some research up north on invasion routes to and from Sweden and Norway."

The man laughed. "If I know Mikhail, he's probably up there mooning about the romance of the Arctic and watching reindeer."

Natalya smiled. It's what you did with fear when you couldn't show weakness.

* * *

She left her desk for tea often that morning, trying to figure out what was going on in the MGB section of the legation. More army officers came in. That was unusual. The MGB and the army were generally bureaucratic rivals. She tried to think of reasons that did not involve Mikhail why the army, particularly Mikhail's friend from army intelligence, had been flown in from Leningrad. Then even more MGB officers arrived, ones she hadn't seen before. The free-floating fear now coalesced in her stomach.

The arriving officers all crowded into a single conference room. The door was shut. An MGB guard stood in front of it. This meeting was not ordinary.

The meeting broke up after only an hour.

Natalya had been waiting. She hurriedly made her way to the hallway where she could intercept Mikhail's friend Grigori. When he saw her, he made an almost imperceptible shake of his head. His eyes flicked toward the side of the building facing Itäinen Puistotie, the eastern park road. She fought down a rush of panic.

A few minutes later, after telling her fellow staff members that she needed an outdoor smoke break, she found him by a tree leaning on the iron picket fence on the southwest corner of the grounds. They were near a large park that in summer had a lawn and shady trees, perfect for picnics. Now, the trees were stark structures, silhouetted against snow-covered ground and standing like lone sentinels watching over times past.

Grigori gave her a bear hug, kissing her on both cheeks. Then he offered her a Lucky Strike cigarette, popping it up by striking the bottom of a khaki cardboard US Army C ration minipack. She took it, giving him a conspiratorial smile, clearly declining to ask how he got it. He lit it and then lit one of his own. Two guards on duty in front of the legation could clearly see them, so in a way, it would look like old friends sharing a smoke.

Natalya pasted on a happy smile and moved her head and arms as if delighted to talk to an old friend. She asked quietly, "Was it about Mikhail?"

The friend nodded.

"Is he in danger?"

"I don't think so," he said. "In a bit of trouble, yes." He looked at her kindly. "Try not to worry."

She took another nervous drag on her cigarette. "Easy to say."

"It was a meeting to inform, not plan actions."

"Meaning?"

Grigori sighed. "The army has now officially been *informed* that the activities of one of its top intelligence officers has come to the attention of the MGB. Any action taken will of course be in accordance with established protocols that had been worked out between the old NKVD and the army during the war."

"Protocols," she repeated.

"Protocols, for when an army officer comes under suspicion of espionage."

Natalya winced. They both knew that there was no defense against suspicion of espionage. Once suspected, you were automatically convicted of being suspected.

Glancing briefly at the guards, Grigori leaned in a little bit. "I'm sorry, Natalya. I can say no more." He ground out his cigarette on the sidewalk, saying as he did so, "We both know that Mikhail's, shall we call it, exuberance had him in a couple of scrapes with the NKVD during the war. He managed his way clear of those. He has powerful friends in the Red Army."

"That was during the war," Natalya said, "when Stalin needed the army as much as he needed the NKVD. Maybe Misha's friends are no longer so powerful."

"You must know how we all respect him. Even many in the MGB." He held her shoulders and looked directly into her eyes. "We'll do the best we can." Then he kissed her on both cheeks again and set off down the street, leaving her feeling very alone.

Wednesday Morning, February 5, 1947
American Legation

A t that moment, Louise was entering Max Hamilton's office. Finding Arnie through Pietari Varila and his friends was possible but not even close to a sure thing. She needed as many possible ways of finding Arnie as she could think of. She was sure—once she explained to Max Hamilton how important it was—that he would want to help.

After exchanging pleasantries with Hamilton's secretary, Helmi, and the usual three-sentence conversation with Pulkkinen, who was sitting in a chair with a newspaper waiting for an assignment, she waited until Helmi ushered her into Hamilton's office.

Hamilton nodded to the chair in front of his desk. She sat. She started to speak, but he held up a finger and said, "Before you go any further, Louise, I'd like you to read this cable." He moved the cable across the desk toward her. "It just came in. If you hadn't initiated this visit"—he paused and looked at her over the top of his glasses—"I would have." He settled back in his chair. "Perhaps you can clear things up a little for me."

The cable was from the State Department in Washington, DC, in fact from the Office of the Secretary. In dry, bureaucratic language, it asked if the envoy extraordinary minister plenipotentiary of the American legation could shed any light on the below excerpts from the *New York Times*, the *Chicago Tribune*, the *Washington Post*, and the *Daily*

Worker. It further stated that a request for information had come from the Soviet embassy in Washington. In addition to Hamilton's name on the address list, there were two names she did not know but whose address was the War Department. The news stories were all similar, probably picked up from the AP or Reuters. They were about the highly decorated former Tenth Mountain Division expert skier who was neck and neck "somewhere in Finland" with a Communist opponent. All the stories were about America racing the Soviet Union, not Arnie racing Mikhail. Only toward the end of just one story was there any mention of a raffle and attempt to raise "international relief money" for Finnish orphans.

She looked up when she'd finished reading.

"I've made some calls," Hamilton said. "All of this started with some press releases?" He left the "written by you" unsaid. "Since you seem to be the public relations expert, what should I tell Washington?"

"The newspapers are blowing it out of proportion."

"Oh, God, Louise, what in the world did you expect?" Hamilton placed his hand on the cable. It would be out of character for him to slap his palm on his desk, but the anger was clearly communicated. "What Arnie did was foolish. What you did was exceedingly foolish. If you'd at least have had the courtesy—" He stopped. His left cheek showed a slight tremor. "Why didn't you come to me first? I could have spun it as an American-Soviet goodwill stunt. Included all sorts of sad orphan stories." He sighed loudly. "Now we've totally lost control of the narrative." He was still clearly angry but was now speaking to her in a kinder tone. "It's a diplomatic mess, Louise. Not my first, but I usually don't get them landed on my desk by my own people." Louise just worried her lower lip with her teeth. "Instead of allies working together to help Finnish war orphans," Hamilton continued, "it's democracy versus Communism. Worse, it's Finland versus Russia and the Russians are probably looking at these same news articles and fuming." He gathered the cables back. "It is not in the interest of the US government to have the Soviets fuming."

Louise, who'd been looking at the desktop, raised her eyes to his. She wanted to shout *I only had the idea and wrote the release; Kaarina caused all the trouble.* Instead, very softly she said, "I'm sorry."

Hamilton shook his head. "I'm afraid we're beyond apologies."

"I know that," Louise said. "That's why we've got to find Arnie and get him to throw the race."

"What? You think *losing* the race is going to smooth things over in Washington? Louise, we don't like our Soviet allies fuming, but we *really* don't like losing to them, no matter what the contest."

"If Mikhail Bobrov loses, I'm worried they'll punish his whole family."

"It's certainly a worry, but why is it *my* worry?"

She lost control. "They could kill him. Natalya and the children would be—"

He held up his whole hand this time. "Stop right there. Yes, the Soviet Union is a brutal dictatorship that punishes its people with little regard for their lives. We are trying to help those Finns who don't want to live under such a dictatorship. This"—now he slapped the cable—"is not helping those Finns."

She bit her lip. "Mr. Hamilton, I know. But if we can find Arnie and get him to throw the race, it will help four innocent people. Please." She started to plead using her hands, but then put them back in her lap. "I messed this up. It can't make any difference to . . . The Soviets would be happy if Arnie lost the race."

Hamilton softened. "Louise, I'd like to help, really, but—"

Louise blurted, "There must be something you can do to find him. You must be able to get an airplane. We have thousands of them over here."

"*We*, Louise, is the United States Army Air Corps, not the State Department."

"But surely, the army is there to support State."

"That's the way it used to be, yes, before the war. It's the other way around now," he said. "The nearest Air Corps field is in Germany. They'll calculate the fuel and maintenance costs and stack that up against a mission of finding a single army skier, presumably on his own time, in a country with which we're still officially at war. Oh, and just a small detail, they'll have to get permission to even fly over that country, from a massive bureaucracy called the Soviet Union. I give it two chances. Slim and none."

"What about the Finnish government giving permission? It's their airspace, not the Russians'."

"One chance. None. It is their airspace only in theory. Also, they would never say it aloud, but many of them will be rooting for your husband."

"A private plane?"

"And, what? Drop him a note tied to a rock? There's a good chance he'll never find it in the snow. There's even a chance that the pilot could drop it to Bobrov, thinking he's your husband. And if Arnie does get it, I can just see your husband sharing cocktails at the officers' club back at Fort Bliss, explaining why he purposefully let the US Army get beaten by the Red Army."

"It's just two people, Mikhail and Arnie, not two armies," Louise said.

"It *was* just Mikhail and Arnie until it went to the papers."

Again, Louise had no answer.

"Louise," Hamilton said, making sure he had eye contact. "You do know why your husband is here, why I'm here."

Louise had never thought about it much. "To represent us in Finland? To get military intelligence on Soviet and Finnish forces?"

Hamilton looked at her without emotion. Then, as if struggling to make something complex clear to a child, he said, "We are here for two things. One is to keep Finland from disappearing behind what Winston Churchill last year called the Iron Curtain. If Finland goes Communist, into the camp of the Soviet Union, this legation will have failed, and the world will be just that much more dangerous for the United States. Make no mistake, the only thing that keeps the Soviets from taking over all of Europe is convincing them that they'll lose the war."

Louise nodded. Hamilton was silent, watching her. "And two?" she asked.

Hamilton nodded slightly. "The second," he said, "is to secure free markets with transparent and fair rules for Americans to do business in."

Louise nodded again. It was fundamentally quite simple in concept. Up until the past couple of days, she'd somehow seen international relations as the government equivalent of making friends. "I see," she said quietly.

Hamilton let out a breath. "Given that we can't stop the race, and I wish to God we could, can you please explain how getting your husband to throw the race can lead to either of those goals?"

Louise simply looked down at the desk.

After a moment, Hamilton asked, "Do you need a ride home? You can use Pulkkinen."

She smiled, nodded yes, and felt like crying.

Hamilton followed Louise out to ask Pulkkinen, who was already standing and putting on his coat, to take her home. This made Louise wonder if Pulkkinen heard everything that went on in Hamilton's office, but she was too tired to care. She slumped into the back seat weary and discouraged, saying nothing.

When they arrived in front of their building, Pulkkinen didn't immediately rush around to open her door. Instead, he looked at her in the rear mirror. "I've read about Colonel Koski's race with the Russian," he said.

"Yes," Louise answered. "It's in all the papers." She smiled ruefully.

"I hope he stays safe," Pulkkinen said.

Louise perked up. "Not the Russian?"

"The Russian, too," Pulkkinen answered.

Louise hesitated. "Pulkkinen," she started, "can I ask you a personal question?"

"Yoh."

"Did you fight in the war?"

"Yoh."

She was used to this.

"You must have been quite young."

"Yoh."

"How old are you?"

"Twenty-three."

She did the math. If he started with the Winter War, he'd have been sixteen.

"That's young to be in the war."

"You age," he said.

She waited a moment after that. "You must not like Russians."

Pulkkinen's chin raised as he looked back at her in the mirror. In that narrow slit of a mirror, in the dark interior, she couldn't read him. He didn't answer.

After a beat, she started to open the door and he scrambled to help her out. She looked him in the eye—and he looked right back. She took a chance. "I know that if I ask you if you're a spy and you are one, you'll answer no, and if you aren't one, you'll answer no."

Pulkkinen actually smiled. "Yoh," he said. Then he shut the car door behind her. "Good morning, Mrs. Koski."

She didn't go into the building but rather stood there, watching the car pull away down the gloomy street. She reached into her purse and pulled out a pack of Chesterfields. She lit the cigarette, taking in its hot, acrid smoke. She coughed, unused to it, steeled herself to take another puff, did so, and coughed again. She tossed the only partially smoked cigarette on the sidewalk. It wasn't the smoking that gave her courage. It was the not smoking.

The words of her grandma Lowe had come to her. "When one door shuts, another one always opens."

She went directly to the orphanage.

She outlined her idea of trying to find Arnie using Pietari and as many friends as he could get to Kaarina. "It's our only hope," she finished.

"It's your only hope," Kaarina said, somewhat clipped.

"It is Natalya's and her children's only hope," Louise answered.

That softened Kaarina. "OK. I'll talk to Pietari this afternoon. Why don't you come over this evening? I made fresh nisu last night."

Wednesday Evening, February 5, 1947
Helsinki

At seven thirty that night, Louise was in front of Kaarina Varila's apartment building. A man was standing across the street, about a block down. He was either very sloppy or didn't care if she knew she was being followed. Who did he work for? The obvious choice would be Sokolov. Now that the whole thing had been blown up and made public, he'd want to be on top of absolutely everything. *As if his life depended on it*, she thought ruefully. But then maybe Hamilton wanted to keep tabs on her as well. It felt like she could find no place where she was safe, where she wasn't watched—including her own bugged home. But she had chosen to marry Arnie, knowing he was a career soldier. She had celebrated with him when he was offered the post in Helsinki and had been excited to come here with him. In short, she'd chosen all the steps that led up to now being watched by an unknown man, to realizing that the world wasn't safe unless someone was making it safe. She straightened her shoulders, turned, and waved at the man. Then she went into Kaarina's building.

Louise's hopes were buoyed when she found Kaarina Varila's little living room packed with young men. She counted ten, including Pietari. If that many of her sorority sisters had been packed that tightly in a single room, there would've been a wall of sound and at least five separate conversations. Kaarina's living room was four walls containing palpable wordless Finnish male energy, like a car tire, pumped tight. Whether that tire would roll and in what direction was up to her.

She made her appeal to the whole room, with Kaarina translating. "A terrible mistake has been made by publicizing this race. I initiated the mistake. I need your help to fix it."

"No need to hide me behind your skirts," Kaarina said. "I'll tell them I took it to the papers." She then translated.

Louise looked from face to face. "The lives of two parents and their children are in danger because if the Russian loses, the Soviet Union will take revenge on him and his family." She could see hard faces. "Yes, they are Russians." She paused. "But they are two children and two people who love them. I'm helpless to fix this. Please, I've tried everything. I've gone to *Helsingin Sanomat*. I've gone to the American legation. You are my only and last hope. These two children are innocent. They are as innocent as I am guilty. Help me. I need you to find my husband and turn this around." She looked at the circle of solemn, stern faces. "Please."

She was met with more silence. Then one of the young men said, "We'll lose work."

Louise agreed with him. Then she held her tongue. She had learned a lot about men since, as she put it, she'd joined the army, especially young men. "Losing work" was the last thing they cared about in the face of a potential adventure. She would wait for the real objection, which she knew was coming.

After "it's a long way up there," and "the weather may not be so good," and "there's a lot of ground to cover," and "needle in a haystack," Pietari asked the truly loaded question, "Why should we help a god-damned Russian?"

"You're helping his wife and children."

"Why should we help four goddamned Russians?" another man asked. His face was horribly burned. One eye was covered with a patch. There were several chuckles.

Louise remembered her father telling her one day at the lumber-yard that power was the ability to reward or punish. She, however, also remembered her mother telling her when Louise oversaw decorating for the junior prom in high school that power was getting things done through other people. A less capable leader than Louise would've thought she was without any power here—and about to fail. Louise, however, knew that she had the gift of a power over men that few of her sorority sisters recognized. It was a power that combined both her father's and her mother's definitions. Men who took their manhood seriously would do nearly anything to help a woman who simply asked for help. A woman could reward a good man with a feeling of pride and the pleasure of helping her when she said that she needed him. Her mother said it was part of a healthy man's psyche.

With Kaarina translating, she said, "You'll also be helping me. And I need your help. I know it won't be easy for you." Louise looked directly at the disfigured one-eyed young man and said, "I assume you lost your eye fighting the Russians."

Kaarina relayed his answer. "I wasn't lighting firecrackers on American Independence Day."

No one laughed.

She appealed directly to him. "I know how impossibly hard . . . how unimaginably difficult it must be not to hate the people who took your eye. But it was some Russian soldier who took your eye, not this mother and her two children."

There was silence, the young men silently searching each other's faces. Then, still without speaking, they seemed to come to some sort of agreement. They all turned to face Louise. The one with the burned face turned to Louise. "Do you have the approximate route?"

By the time she left, a plan had been worked out, including Louise's promise to pay for all the train fares to Kuopio. The group could probably get there by dark on Thursday evening. They would fan out, moving in a long line northward Friday morning. They'd reassemble at a small town north of the search area called Siilinjärvi so they could maximize their time in daylight and not have to return to Kuopio in the dark. There had been a long, quiet tactical discussion. If they kept close enough to see each other, they couldn't cover the width of the possible routes. If they covered the widest likely route, there would be gaps through which Arnie could pass unseen.

Either way it was a gamble. They decided to spread out, skiing out of sight of each other. It was their best shot. For Louise and Natalya, it was their only shot.

When Louise left Kaarina's building it was after nine o'clock. The man tailing her was still there. Did the Russians think *she* was some kind of spy or something? She walked briskly to Natalya's flat, wanting to tell her the good news about Pietari and his friends going to help find Arnie. When she entered the foyer of Natalya's building, the man behind the desk asked her name, although he knew perfectly well who she was. She answered his question and watched him put her name and time down in a logbook, his face expressionless.

When Natalya asked her to come in, Louise noticed Fanya reading one of her fashion magazines in the big armchair. She knew she could not talk straight to Natalya, so she chattered on about the orphanage project, the raffle sales numbers, and about the children. Natalya served tea. When they finished tea, Louise began putting on her heavy coat. Natalya said she'd escort her down to the lobby and see her out the main door. When they reached the head of the stairwell, Natalya looked over her shoulder and whispered, "Why did you really come?"

"Pietari Varila and some of his friends and relations are leaving tomorrow for Kuopio. They are going to look for Arnie. When they find them, they'll tell him the situation and give him a letter signed by me, also explaining what is at stake and asking him to throw the race."

"Do you think they'll actually try to get an American to throw a race to a Russian? They may not even try to find him, just go to Kuopio and have a party."

"We don't know for sure, but I think they will try. I had a good feeling about them."

"Hate is also a feeling."

Louise had nothing to say to this. Finally Natalya let out a sigh. "Good news," she said. "Thank you."

As Louise walked into the cold night, she felt a bit guilty for not telling Natalya that the major American newspapers had now also picked up on the story. Why tell her? Leave the poor woman with the good news—and a little hope.

Thursday Morning, February 6, 1947
South of Pudasjärvi
Race Day 6

South of Pudasjärvi, Mikhail once more ran across Arnie's tracks. The wind had picked up just enough to make him wonder if worse weather was on its way. It was already snowing lightly. The overcast sky would slow the radiation heat loss at night, which was good. Visibility, however, was cut considerably, but that made little difference skiing through forest since he could see no farther than ten or fifteen meters even on a clear day. The key piece of information was that there was barely any accumulated snow in Arnie's tracks. He was tempted to cheat, gain speed by following in Arnie's tracks, letting Arnie do all the heavy work of moving through fresh snow. His code of honor and fair play, however, wouldn't allow him to cheat. It wasn't sport if victory was won at any cost. Sport had rules. Abandon rules to win and everyone loses. You may as well not have had the contest.

He slogged on, breaking his own trail, his mind wandering with the monotony of it, turning over unrelated thoughts. Humans were such a potent mixture of good and bad he thought. People followed rules because people were good. However, they broke rules because people were bad. That's why there were other rules that promised shame or punishment, which helped keep rules from being broken. He knew this human dichotomy from his years of combat. He had watched men unhesitatingly throw themselves on a German grenade to save their friends. His own medal had been earned because he cared more for others than himself—he chuckled aloud—at that particular time. The memory, still vivid, of waiting before the assault on the day he'd won that medal rose like a ghost from a grave. All of them, waiting for the order to go, scared shitless. An interesting figure of speech. He'd heard of men shitting themselves from fear but never knew anyone who had; nor had it ever happened to him. Maybe it was just another of those fictions that writers come up with to try to communicate what is impossible to understand without direct experience. Or maybe civilians thought it might be that way, so they said it was. Maybe it happened. He remembered wanting nothing more than to turn around and run until he was in Natalya's arms. But he knew that just behind the assault troops were the troops of the NKVD, waiting to round up deserters and cowards. And the penalty for running was death.

Once the fighting started, something took over, something beyond himself. It was that something good that put the lives of others above his own operating at the same time he was killing people. It seemed impossible, but he'd lived it.

He became aware of the snow falling harder.

Arnie was trying to control his feelings of frustration as he worked his way around trees. To get speed, one had to glide. To glide, one had to stay on top of the snow and have gliding distance. He had neither.

Being in forest cut the chances of sighting Mikhail directly, but Arnie had seen no other signs of him, such as tracks. He assumed Mikhail was behind him.

Arnie suddenly came upon a clearing. It was only a couple of acres in size and clearly the result of human effort. Stumps still poked above the snow. From the looks of the stumps, the trees had been cut long ago.

He passed through the clearing and reentered the forest, resuming his steady rhythmic push and glide or, too often, push and sink.

His mind wandered in the sameness of the white snow, gray sky, and unchanging gray-green and silent trees, switching randomly between thoughts and memories. Why would someone have been way the hell out here cutting trees? Then he remembered that Finland had gone through periods of famine and many farms had been abandoned over the years. Most Americans thought farms were permanent. That was because most American farms were new. Arnie remembered the ski trip he took to Vermont in his First Class year. He'd come across stone walls in the middle of forests with nothing near the walls at all. In the nineteenth century, Vermont had nearly double the number of farms it had previously. Vermont farmers had abandoned them, just as Finnish farmers had abandoned the house that at one time must have stood in this clearing. Maybe there were foundations of the old farmhouse beneath the snow. Big difference, though. Vermont farmers left to find factory jobs—or bigger farms out West. Few farms in America were abandoned because of starvation. Had to make a difference in the character of the two countries. He'd tuck that observation away when assessing Finland's current fighting capacity. Nonaligned now, but which way would they go if forced to choose? He needed to spend more time with Pietari and his veteran friends. Intelligence was also about gathering information on the character of your potential enemies as well as your potential allies. How willing were the Finns to starve and even die for their country's cause? Ever since the big successes by the navy using signals intelligence to figure out that the Japanese were heading to Midway, signals intelligence was all the coming rage. But how tough was someone? How willing to sacrifice? How ruthless? How compassionate? You got none of this from radio waves.

Maybe it wasn't a farm. Maybe it was just a simple logging operation —or whatever Finns called gyppo logging operations, small family owned, fiercely independent. Maybe someone got the timber rights, and they dragged the logs down to one of the many lakes, and from there to a river, and from there to a mill. He remembered his first day on the job at 200-Foot Logging, his dad's gyppo logging company. Sixth-grade summer. He was twelve. He remembered his mother and father talking about it—openly—at dinner one night. He's too young. He's old enough. He'll get hurt. Only if he's stupid. He's twelve! No excuse for stupidity.

His dad kicked him out of bed at four thirty the next morning and told him to put on his work boots. All day he hauled stuff. He washed stuff. He put up with practical jokes. He would never forgive that goddamned Heppu Reinikka for making him look for a left-handed peavey, which he learned the hard way was a tool that didn't exist. Now *that* was a crew, he mused, those old World War I veterans. People call them the Bachelor Boys. All sorts of rumors about bootlegging. Axel Långström, his father's best friend. They'd logged the Middle Fork of the Nemah by themselves. People still talked about it. Axel was famous for pulling a Tommy gun during a fishermen strike. Dad had done well during the recent war, like most good loggers. Axel had also done well because he owned his own gillnet boat. And now all those returning servicemen were having babies. That meant houses and *that* boded well for 200-Foot Logging. Dad was in the Astoria Country Club for Christ's sake. War. Not all bad. For some. The ones not fighting it. Or the ones sitting on their asses back at headquarters thinking to themselves that they actually *were* fighting in the war. Or telling that to everyone back home. Hell, they were *directing* the war. That's real different than fighting in it.

If he did well here in Finland, he'd make colonel earlier in his career than most. That gave him a good shot at a general's star. Of course, with no war, the army was shrinking. Promotion was going to be slow. God, I hope the politicians don't pull us back down to prewar levels. If they do, I'll be lucky to be a captain. I'll have twenty years in June 1952. Retire on half pay. Dad wants me to take over 200-Foot. So does Mom. What would Louise do in Astoria? Hopefully, have a bunch of kids. *That* problem. Was he shooting blanks? He didn't think so. He'd masturbated and looked at his semen under a microscope when he was in high school. Weird. No, hell, scientific. Anyway, lots of sperm.

A sudden fall of snow from a branch showered his face. He snapped back to consciousness, but for a moment didn't know where he was or what he was doing. He knew that mind wandering was dangerous. There seemed to be some sort of trade-off between the body's energy requirements and consciousness. Willpower. Sisu. Better focus on skiing. Focus on what is directly ahead. No telling where Mikhail is. That's wandering again. Yes! Here's another of those frozen marshes. No trees or brush to slow him down. His frustration lifted, along with his spirits. Now he could make time.

Late Afternoon, Thursday, February 6, 1947
Porkkala Naval Base

L ate that afternoon, Sokolov was pacing nervously in the small waiting room at the airfield of the Porkkala Naval Base. The large, formerly Finnish base was located at the southern tip of the Porkkala peninsula, which lay just west of Helsinki, pointing like a finger at Soviet Estonia and protruding into the Baltic, where it choked off the seaward approaches to Leningrad.

Sokolov had received a cable saying Lieutenant General Pyotr Fedotov, head of the MGB's First Main Directorate, was flying in from Moscow. Fedotov reported directly to Beria.

Sokolov couldn't be sure what it was about, but he could guess. He'd already submitted a report, so he wouldn't be accused of hiding bad news. It was unlikely that it had already worked its way up to Fedotov, but it would be working its way up the chain of command. The race had probably come to the attention of the Kremlin through one of their operations in Europe or the United States. He, however, could still be blamed for not having things under control. The ever-present undercurrent of fear surfaced. In the purges of the 1930s, too many of his friends had been tortured and then killed for far lesser crimes than not having things under control.

The plane landed, and Sokolov rushed out to be waiting with the legation limousine, a ZIS-110, made in Russia, but a shameless copy of an American 1942 Packard Super Eight. He'd once ridden in a real

Super Eight in West Berlin just after the war. It made the ZIS look like a heavy turd.

When the plane taxied up, Fedotov descended the stairs, barely acknowledging the saluting reception party. Fedotov was curt with Sokolov as they got into the limousine. Not a good sign. He felt his heart rate quicken and he fought to bring it down, taking deep but he hoped unobservable breaths. Looking nervous was also not a good sign.

Fedotov said nothing during the ride into Helsinki probably because he didn't trust Sokolov's driver. One didn't get to Fedotov's position trusting people.

Sokolov's people were all waiting outside the legation entrance. Sokolov couldn't help but think of some grandees coming home to their estate before the revolution, all the household staff waiting outside in the carriageway, freezing their asses off, so they could bow and curtsy to the great lord and lady. We got rid of all that nonsense with the revolution. Right?

Fedotov, two stars on the finely braided gold shoulder tabs of his MGB uniform and his big hat—always the big hat—with the blue top sitting over a red band, sailed past the line of welcome, again barely acknowledging its existence. He was carrying a briefcase.

Sokolov had arranged a conference room. Fedotov jerked his head toward the door. Sokolov nodded to him and an MGB enlisted man who in turn almost bowed his way out the door, closing it behind him.

"Comrade General, can I take your coat?"

Fedotov grunted, turned his back, and let Sokolov help take his coat off. He opened his briefcase. He laid a newspaper clipping from the *London Times* on Sokolov's desk. He said one word: "Read." When Sokolov looked up, he laid another one from the *New York Times* in front of him, saying nothing. One by one, he slowly, silently, and deliberately placed clippings from the *Daily Express*, the *Manchester Guardian*, the *Los Angeles Times*, *L'Humanité*, *Le Figaro*, *Combat*, *Die Welt*, *Süddeutsche Zeitung*, and even the American Communist Party's paper, the *Daily Worker*.

Sokolov finished reading and looked up. There was no doubt about it, news of the race had gone international. As far as the West was concerned, the United States was in a ski race with the Soviet Union that was a metaphor for the competition between Communism and capitalism.

"I assure you, Comrade General, I was unaware of this race until it was made public by the supposed wife of the American, Lieutenant Colonel Koski. She used the guise of a raffle to raise money for an orphanage. Lieutenant Colonel Bobrov acted entirely on his own, without asking for our approval."

"Did Bobrov ask for and get army approval?"

"I assume not, Comrade General."

"You *assume?* You don't know?"

Sokolov looked at the floor, his heart racing. He hoped the electric quivering in his knees was not noticeable.

Fedotov's voice became soft, almost gentle. "*I* assume, Comrade Sokolov, that if you are doing your job, you *know* such things."

"Yes, Comrade General."

"I realize, Comrade Sokolov, that during the war, we couldn't supervise every activity of our army. However, I'm sure that you're aware . . ." He paused and then bellowed, "*The war is over!*" He brought his voice back down. "We cannot afford to have soldiers such as Bobrov doing *anything* without us knowing about it."

"Yes, General Fedotov."

Fedotov smiled. He put his index finger on the pile of clippings. He looked up at Sokolov. "You must know they've been translated and summarized in the daily briefings for both Comrades Stalin and Beria.

You surely cannot think that I would travel to"—he raised his palm upward—"*this place* on my own accord."

Hearing both names spoken aloud was like a cold NR-40 combat knife to the solar plexus. Sokolov scrambled for some line of defense. "They are the result of the American's wife. We suspect she is one of their intelligence agents. Bobrov may have been played."

"*May* have been!" Fedotov roared. He leaned over the table with his weight on his knuckles, making Sokolov think of a gorilla. Sokolov tried to get the image out of his head. That sort of thing happened when he was scared. "Your job, Comrade Sokolov, is to keep our goddamn stupid army officers from shooting themselves in the foot and embarrassing Comrade Stalin."

"Yes, Comrade."

"Should I assume that you cannot do this?"

"No, Comrade. I assure you—"

"Spare me your excuses. You need to fix this."

Sokolov wanted to plead with Fedotov, tell him none of this was his fault. He, however, knew that such pleading would be futile and only make him look even less competent. He waited nervously in silence.

Finally, with an exaggerated sigh, Fedotov broke the silence. "*They* say," Fedotov said, pointing to the newspaper clippings, "that the American has won several civilian championships."

"That's true, Comrade."

"So, this idiot Bobrov's chances of winning?"

"I understand he's a good skier. He served with the Fifty-Fourth Mountain Rifle Division."

"His chances of winning?"

"I really have no idea."

"Precisely, Comrade Sokolov. Precisely. You see the Party's problem here."

"Yes, Comrade. We must be certain that he will not lose."

"Precisely," Fedotov said, as if Sokolov were a student coming up with the right answer. He pointed to his coat and Sokolov hurried to get it and help him on with it. As he buttoned his coat, Fedotov said, "You earned a fine reputation during the war for doing what needs to be done."

"Thank you, Comrade General."

Sokolov knew, from years of experience, that it didn't matter what motivated an act. Stupid choices needed to be punished, especially when *not* punishing them could make you yourself look either weak or treasonous. Sokolov's very life depended on remaining someone who did what needs to be done and *not* looking like a sympathizer. He started scrambling.

"We have already formulated a plan," he lied. "First, we need to find him. That will take aircraft. I presume we can lean on the navy at Porkkala?"

"We can lean on the navy."

"Of course." Sokolov cleared his throat, thinking fast. "Once we have aircraft, we can spot him. Then, I suggest one of our MGB parachute units could deal with this. We will need to get them up here as soon as possible."

"That can be arranged." After only a slight pause, Sokolov continued. "Of course, dropping MGB parachutists onto sovereign Finnish territory will take clearance at the highest level of the Finnish government. That would mean President Paasikivi."

"I will make the necessary arrangements," Fedotov said. "As you know, the Control Commission is over the Finnish government, which means that Paasikivi reports to Andrei Zhdanov, who reports directly to Stalin. It will be made clear that it would be unfortunate if the Control Commission found irregularities in Finland's compliance with the 1944 armistice or shortfalls in Finland's reparation payments. I'm sure the economic staff here can easily help provide evidence for the latter."

"Of course, Comrade."

Sokolov knew that an accusation of a shortfall—or heaven forbid an active deception—would be sufficient reason for the Soviet Union to unleash the Red Army under the legal cover of Finland defying the Moscow Armistice, giving the Western powers the cover to stay out of the fight.

"We are fully aware that Paasikivi holds unstated leanings toward the capitalists," Fedotov went on, "but he's kept quiet about them so far to keep on our good side. He will not risk being on our bad side." He smiled grimly. "We will tell Paasikivi that we are simply going to pick up Comrade Bobrov and take him back home, an entirely internal Soviet affair that no one will see." Fedotov laughed. "If we keep quiet, so will he."

Fedotov turned to the door. Sokolov hurried to open it.

"I will lay out the options to Paasikivi's staff before I go back to Moscow," Fedotov said. He paused. "Then, after he's been briefed by his staff, Paasikivi himself will be contacted by the appropriate representative of Comrade Stalin. When Paasikivi assures us, as I am sure he will, that there will be no mention of Soviet activity in a remote part of Finland concerning only the internal security of the Soviet Union, I will leave the rest to you."

He pointed to the newspaper clippings on Sokolov's desk. "You may keep those as souvenirs. When we do decide to compete in sports against the Americans, it will be after we've had time to prepare our athletes to compete"—he hesitated and then smiled—"with all possible advantages." Sokolov chuckled to show he understood the reference to the addition of synthetic testosterone to the training regimes of both male and female Soviet athletes. "I hear we are already preparing the groundwork to have them here in Helsinki in 1952," Fedotov said. "Sport is a wonderful way to compete peacefully, is it not?"

*　*　*

Sokolov saw Fedotov off in the ZIS-110 and immediately turned to two tasks. The first was planning the operation to do what must be done. The second was to see Natalya Bobrova while he still had maximum leverage—that is while she thought her husband was still alive. He could make it clear, without saying anything directly, that he could greatly influence how Mikhail's actions would be interpreted in Moscow. He could hint at writing a report that could have Mikhail transferred to some frozen military base, sparing his life. He smiled as he walked back into the legation, anticipating Natalya's reaction to his carrot and his stick. He laughed at his pun, already feeling some of his power returning after Fedotov's departure.

Thursday Afternoon, February 6, 1947
Soviet Legation

Natalya had seen the three stars on the epaulets of the visitor's MGB uniform. Three stars meant the head of a main directorate.

She didn't need to know the man's name, and she didn't want to ask. It would only show that she was in some way concerned about the man's visit—which would only result in someone being suspicious of her motives. Part of life was behaving correctly so suspicion never arose.

The rumor mill soon identified the man as Lieutenant General Pyotr Fedotov, head of the MGB's First Main Directorate, responsible for all foreign intelligence. His remit included keeping surveillance over all Soviet diplomatic personnel. More chillingly, he reported directly to Beria.

The rumor mill also had several theories about why Fedotov would be visiting Sokolov. Any of them could, of course, be true. Conspiracy theories were only as good as their plausibility. Natalya could hope desperately that one of them was indeed true and not the one she held to herself—that the visit was about Mikhail. She was flooded with fear for Mikhail and her children.

She steeled herself to find out at the "planning meeting" with Sokolov if Fedotov's visit was about Mikhail. For now, all she could do was wait for Sokolov to tell her when and where that meeting would happen.

Thursday Evening, February 6, 1947
Natalya's Flat

Natalya left work as soon as it wouldn't cause people to wonder why she was leaving work early. Walking hunched against a cold wind, bundled in her scarf and heavy overcoat, she felt like a moving cocoon, a loan chrysalis, invisible to the world, a pupa that could never get out. With Mikhail gone, all she wanted to do was hug her children for comfort. However, she needed more than hugs. She needed to talk to someone. The only person she could think of was Louise.

She realized that Louise also lived in a cocoon—a cocoon of American safety and wealth, a cocoon of rule by law. Louise had every possibility of emerging from her cocoon as a butterfly. In fact, Louise was a butterfly already but didn't know it. A butterfly was free. The image nearly overwhelmed Natalya. All her life, she'd been wrapped in her private little world, keeping her true self secret. Now, she wanted to claw her way free of the surveillance, the whispering, the threat of the knock on the door, the inability to trust the news or the truth of a conversation. She wanted to be free of the constant vulnerability to injustice: living in a hierarchy where the only recourse against injustice was to ally with someone in the hierarchy more powerful than those who would oppress you—which only gave that person more power over you.

She was nearly running now, wanting to see her children. She would hug them and then she would bundle them up and take them with her to see Louise. And she could feel the warmth and love of her children. How simple. How different from work. How wonderful. Her spirits lifted.

After nearly suffocating Alina and Grisha, Natalya helped Fanya feed them. After dinner she began dressing them to go out.

"Are you going out?" Fanya asked. "With the children?"

"Yes," Natalya said brightly. "You know how my friend Louise loves children. I thought I'd go over for tea. Well, in her case, coffee."

"I'll come with you," Fanya said. "Let me get my coat."

"Oh, no. You take some time to yourself. I'll be fine."

"No bother. I'd love to come."

Natalya hesitated. What was going on? "But you're sure you don't want to . . . I don't know. You're young . . . Go out? Have fun?"

"In Finland?"

Natalya laughed. "It's not that dreary," she said, still dressing the children. She looked up. Fanya was clearly in some discomfort.

"No," Fanya said. "It's my job to help you with the children." This was new.

"But I don't *want* any help right now, Fanya."

Fanya looked at the floor. Then she looked around the room. It was as if she was seeking some way out. "It's my job," she muttered.

The constant underlying anxiety once again turned into fear. Clearly, Fanya had been told not to let the children out of her sight. They were already hostages. Natalya fought the fear down. If Fanya had been told not to let the children out of her sight, then Fanya knew Natalya had come under suspicion.

"OK, well," Natalya said. She forced a smile. "I'd really love some girl time with my friend. It would be so kind of you if you could put them to bed. I won't be long. Just, you know, catch up on gossip. Louise really can be quite a lot of fun."

The two women looked at each other. They both knew that they both knew. Neither could say it aloud, both wrapped in silken threads of silence and fear.

Thursday Evening, February 6, 1947
Louise's Flat

When Natalya left her flat to see Louise, she saw the man behind the desk look at his watch as she went by. The time she left would be recorded.

Anxiety walked with her through the dark streets. She went through the checklist of what to do to keep above suspicion. She had told Fanya where she was going. She had been clocked out and would be clocked back in. She was on assignment from Sokolov to pump the wife of the American military attaché for information. The visit would be totally appropriate and explainable. The greater source of her anxiety, however, was that she was thinking thoughts that would immediately put her under suspicion if they were public. She was desperately thinking of and then rejecting contingency plans to save her children.

One major problem with all the plans was that if she acted now, whether it was grabbing the children and running for Sweden or having sex with Sokolov, she would be acting on nothing more than an unsubstantiated fear that the MGB would kill Mikhail if he lost the race. If Mikhail won the race, any preemptive action of hers would have been a foolish choice, with terrible consequences for all of them. If, however, Mikhail lost, and she hadn't played Sokolov's game, she would lose Mikhail.

She needed to see Louise because she needed to talk to a friend, freely and without fear—and without Fanya eavesdropping. She needed to talk about her dilemma. However, she knew that Sokolov must have bugged Louise and Arnie's apartment. She was sure that Sokolov had set her up to tell Louise about the family leaving the apartment vacant. Ahh yes. Comrade Sokolov. Ever helpful—ever hopeful. He'd probably ordered the family home to free the space. On the other hand, Sokolov was just self-centered enough to think that finding the apartment was enough to get into Louise's good graces, and he hadn't bugged the apartment. He would certainly be attracted to Louise and her wholesome looks, not to mention an equally wholesome figure. Surely, Sokolov wasn't fool enough to think Louise would let him sleep with her because he helped her find an apartment? Louise would be grateful for his help but not that grateful. Sokolov probably dwelled in a hazy unconscious fantasy of eventual sexual fulfillment with most beautiful women he met. With her, however, if she was going to save Mikhail, Sokolov's fantasy would become reality. But, what if Mikhail won and none of this needed to happen? What if Sokolov was leading her on? She was in a turmoil of indecision and needed to talk it out with a friend. But who could she trust when she lived in a system based on lack of trust and in which lies were accepted as fact? To trust was to risk. She decided to take the risk.

When Louise responded to the knock on her door, she was delighted to see Natalya had stopped by unannounced. It was what friends did at home. However, when Natalya started taking off her first layer of clothes, she jerked at the buttons, unlike her usual careful and measured way of moving. Louise could see that she was upset about something.

"So, how was your day? Did you stop by the orphanage?" Natalya asked, once she'd sat down. She was trying to signal Louise by cupping her ear and looking around the room in an exaggerated manner. Louise immediately caught on. She quietly showed Natalya the hidden microphone as she was answering her. Then, chattering about her day, she handed Natalya a piece of paper and her pen, the Reynolds Rocket ballpoint Arnie had bought for her birthday. Natalya held the ballpoint up and raised her eyebrows. Realizing that they probably didn't have anything like it in Russia, Louise felt an unexpected pride in American enterprise.

Natalya had scratched out, *Did Pietari agree to look?*

Louise took the paper and pencil and wrote, *He and friends probably already in Kuopio.*

She watched as Natalya's face moved from long-accustomed stoicism upon being shown the hidden microphone to hope at the news that Pietari and his friends were looking.

"Do you want to go over to the orphanage and see how much money's come in?" Louise asked, putting her finger on her lips. "Kaarina always has pulla and something hot to drink." She was writing, *Careful, being watched* on the paper.

"Well, OK," Natalya said, nodding that she understood. She then wrote, *Must go orphanage. Confirm this conversation real and innocent.*

Louise understood and nodded agreement.

When they left the building, Natalya glanced around and immediately spotted the man across the street. When Louise joined her, Natalya linked arms with her and whispered, "So, is it your Central Intelligence Group that is monitoring you and Arnie?" She needed to appear innocent but knew the man was more likely Sokolov's.

"Heavens, no," Louise said, looking down at the sidewalk as they walked along. "The US government would never spy on its own citizens. It's your people, the MGB. I'm sure one of them is across the street." She stopped talking. Natalya didn't look behind them. "Arnie was so angry with me for accepting Sokolov's help," Louise started up again. "He suspected why and found the bug."

"And left it, so you could pass false information," Natalya whispered.

Louise's stomach dropped. Her hand went to her mouth. Oh, my God. Why hadn't she been cagey and told Natalya it *was* the US Central Intelligence Group? Now, Natalya could tell her people that Arnie and Louise knew about the bug, nullifying Arnie's false information.

She watched Natalya's stoicism replaced by a flash of quickly controlled anger. "First you endanger my family with your stupid attempt to publicize the race," Natalya said. "And now you put me in the position of having to betray you and what I thought was a friendship by telling Sokolov that you know about the listening device. Or I can betray my country by not reporting it."

"I'm sorry."

"Sorry!" Natalya stopped walking. She looked up at the dark sky. "Sorry," she muttered. She let out a long wail, then reached up and started yanking her hair, bawling, "Sorry? Sorry?"

Louise was stunned. She reached out to touch Natalya. Natalya jerked away. Louise could see Natalya's face was mottled even in the darkness of the deserted street. "I can't do it anymore! I can't do it. I can't talk to Fanya. I can't talk to Mikhail. I can't talk to you. I can't talk. I can't talk!" Her voice had been rising in intensity. She now dropped her voice. "Because *he* is behind us, I can't even scream." She subsided into choked quiet sobs.

Without thinking, Louise grabbed her, hugging her close.

The two women clung to each other separated by their heavy coats, forming a single dark lump on the cold street.

Natalya regained control and Louise relaxed her hug. "You can talk to me," Louise said gently.

Natalya took two deep breaths. Then she said, "Big hat from Moscow. Really big hat. He and Sokolov met with local intelligence officers. There were clippings from Western newspapers about the race."

Louise started to say "I'm sorry" but caught herself. "I don't know what to say."

"Say nothing," Natalya answered. "I'm not making sense."

"But you are. You're making perfect sense."

Natalya gave a brief sarcastic laugh. "What logic system do you use in Oklahoma."

Louise looked her in the eye. "The logic that you're scared because you might lose the man you love, your children might be taken away, and angry because your stupid American friend caused all this and doesn't have a clue about what you're facing. It doesn't matter what the words say. I understand."

They walked alongside each other in silence for some time. Louise once glanced back to see if they were still being followed. They were.

Louise said quietly, "I'm so stupid. Can you forgive me?"

Natalya stopped. "You're not stupid," she said. "And you know it." She smiled weakly. "Trusting and naïve, I can make a case for."

Louise shook her head, smiling.

Natalya hesitated. Then she said, "Sokolov wants me to believe he will protect Mikhail if I sleep with him. I don't know what to do."

Louise stopped walking. "Oh, Natalya! That slimy bastard. Don't do it. We'll find Arnie and I just know he'll throw the race if he's ahead."

Natalya didn't respond.

"You're not going to do it, are you? Suppose you do and then we reach Arnie?"

"You think I've not thought about that?"

"But, even if you do, there's no guarantee that Sokolov will deliver."

"That is indeed the risk." Natalya was stating the obvious and delivered it that way.

Louise looked into Natalya's eyes. She saw the sadness of a thousand years of the suffering of the Russian people.

"But would you not take that gamble for Arnie?" Natalya asked.

The thought flashed through her mind that because she'd been the cause of all this mess maybe she should offer herself to Sokolov in

Natalya's place. The thought was replaced by repulsion. She could never do it. Not for Mikhail, not for Natalya, not for their children. She realized that she simply did not have the courage. She didn't even know if she'd do it for Arnie until she was confronted with it. And yet, here was her friend, confronted with it. She was in awe of what Natalya was willing to do to protect her family and loved her for it.

"Can't you at least switch things around? Promise him sex after Mikhail is safe. Keep him on the hook, but don't go all the way."

"Can't you just say 'fuck him'?" Natalya said harshly. "That's what it is."

"I don't like to use that word," Louise said quietly.

The two walked on in silence for about a block.

"I know," Natalya said. After more silence, Natalya said, "The other problem with you Americans," she was smiling gently, "is that you're still Puritans."

Louise had no rejoinder, but she smiled. Both women looked ahead into the darkness.

They passed under a streetlight and Natalya turned to look at Louise. Natalya's eyes had changed. They now showed a thousand years of Russian resolve. "I ate rats to survive the siege of Leningrad," Natalya said. "I can certainly fuck one to save my family."

Friday Morning, February 7, 1947
Soviet Legation

S okolov was looking out of his office window. He tended to find something good in all the seasons of the year, unlike some of his comrades who would say things like, "I hate winter."

He didn't love—or hate—winter. He did, however, like getting to work in the dark and then watching his office window gradually turn from reflecting his image and that of the room to becoming transparent to the outside world as the outside light grew. He remembered doing this in school. That was a lot of sunrises ago. He also liked staying in the office until after dark. It meant less time in his empty apartment.

It also meant less time alone to think about the parts of his job that he didn't want to think about. He liked Mikhail Bobrov. He was a brave, honest—also naïve and romantic—soldier. But it was now his job to liquidate Bobrov for the good of the People and the revolution. If he didn't, then he would have failed the revolution himself, and someone would have to liquidate him.

He was disturbed by a gentle knock on the office door. It opened and his secretary peeked in. "Comrade Bobrova asked if she could see you."

His immediate reaction was happiness, maybe even a little joy. It occurred to him that in such a bleak existence as his, even a little happiness could be interpreted as joy. "Five minutes," he answered. It would look bad to appear eager.

He turned back to the window, which still could reflect a hazy image. He smoothed back his hair. He wished he were taller and had pushed himself to stay in better condition. He sighed and straightened his tie. He threw back his shoulders and grunted a sort of *I guess that's the best we can do.* He went to a locked filing cabinet, opened it, and took out two files. Then he returned to his desk and placed them such that the names on them could be seen. Then, he spread other files and papers out, making sure it would look like he was very busy and important when his secretary announced Natalya Bobrova.

She came in and he stood, almost involuntarily. To receive beauty like this sitting down would be uncouth, almost sacrilegious. And she *was* beautiful. If he were a religious man, she would prove the existence of God.

He saw that Natalya had taken God's work one step further. She had let down on her Socialist standards and used some makeup. It also was not lost on him how tightly the skirt of her suit hugged her lower body. She had that exotic elegance of the former Russian aristocracy. It was incorporated in the very way she held herself and moved—lots of ballet at a young age.

He knew that from reading her file, as well as the files on both of her parents. Both had indeed been minor aristocrats, the sort left after decades of an original large estate being broken into smaller and smaller pieces for each successive generation. Even that signified Natalya's mother and father both had come from families with more moderate attitudes— overthrowing primogeniture that would have kept a large estate and its power concentrated in a single offspring. Natalya's father had served as an officer in the 1914 war. He and her mother had been spared the brutal retaliation and justice of the revolution because he had sided with the Bolsheviks, bringing his unit to their side. They'd both given up their estates and served in Trotsky's Red Army, again with distinction, during the Civil War. Both had remained loyal followers of Trotsky.

So, Natalya had spent her formative years with her aristocratic parents. Of course, after Trotsky was exiled to Turkey in 1929, her parents had been rounded up and shot. Natalya was thirteen.

She had been sent to a state orphanage and had done well in school. It was all in the files. What was missing, he mused, was a picture of her mother. She must have been a beauty, too.

He graciously, at least he thought so, moved around his desk, and held the back of a chair for Natalya to seat herself. Leaning near her shoulder, he could smell that she'd put on perfume. Another good sign. He glanced past her neck and saw that he'd placed her parents' files just right, so she could see their names. He guessed that she would glance at the names as he moved back behind his desk. When he had seated himself again, she was smiling politely, showing nothing. "Comrade Bobrova," he said brightly. "How can I help?"

Natalya was smiling, but it was like winter sunshine. "I thought we should spend a little time together to discuss some ideas about Mikhail."

So! His heart lifted. Up until now, he'd not been sure that she would go through with it. He would get caviar! He was sure she almost never got that. And American cigarettes. It could be at his place. No, too closely watched. He knew his driver reported to someone in Moscow. But then several packs of American cigarettes—maybe even a bottle of champagne. Yes. The French embassy had had tons of it in their cellars left over from before the war. Of course, the Control Commission had looted it all within a day of arriving in Helsinki. And the NKVD had taken it from them three days later. Yes, give the driver a bottle, maybe two. Then it was just a wink and a nod—and an understanding that there would be no more cigarettes or champagne if the driver talked. It was how life worked.

"Of course. I thought perhaps the Hotel Kämp?" Sokolov asked. "I could send my driver. He could drive you there to a scheduled meeting. I'll take care of that. It would be concerning your work on locating assets for war reparations. As you probably know, there is a door with a plainclothes MGB guard that we use occasionally when we don't wish to be seen leaving the legation. The guard works for me."

"Of course, Comrade."

"Good. Shall we say nine o'clock?"

Natalya was hesitating.

"Does that not work?"

"Comrade, Sokolov," Natalya began carefully. "How am I to know that you would be able to"—she searched for the right words—"do what you say you will for my husband?"

Of course, she didn't trust him Sokolov thought. He hadn't found his way to the top of this particular greasy pole because he didn't see the real questions hidden by the stated questions. A brief fantasy of a widowed Natalya seeking solace flashed through his mind, quickly replaced by more thinking. Comrade Lieutenant General Pyotr Fedotov had basically said to kill Mikhail Bobrov. Doing what needed to be done was not a direct order, but what was clearly understood was if he didn't liquidate Bobrov, he would share Bobrov's fate.

His challenge was to make sure that whatever he did, it had to look—to Natalya—like he was trying to protect her husband. A major part of true power was perceived power. A major part of perceived power was how one's actions were interpreted, not what resulted from the actions. Hitler had given everyone in Germany a free radio as soon as he had control of all the stations. Now that man knew what he was doing.

"Rest assured, Comrade Bobrova, I will deliver my part of the plan. I give you my word."

"Yes, Comrade. Of course. A man of your position . . ." She hesitated again.

This one was not only a beauty but also a thinker. She'd have made a fine operative.

"I am not at all doubting your ability to carry out your part of the plan," she said and left it there.

No fool this one. She didn't trust that he would—or could—deliver. Now was the time to make her feel more secure. He pushed her parents' files across the desk toward her. She looked up at him, questioning. He cocked his head, indicating that she could look at them.

It was a gesture, to be sure, but it was the best he could do to ease her distrust. She, of course, could never be assured of help from anybody in the political game. When the only constant was getting ahead, things like promises were changed constantly.

A sudden fantasy of Natalya on her knees looking up to him intruded. Then thinking returned. She must know that he wanted her, if not to love him at least to like him enough to be with him. This meant she must also know that he would turn heaven and earth to make sure she would keep seeing him. So, she had every incentive to make sure that he believed this. Yes, she would meet him at the hotel. He knew that she must have already worked all of this out for herself. She was, after all, Russian.

She took the files and began reading. He watched her. He could see pulsing in her throat. He wondered what that warmth was adding to the perfume she wore. She closed one file and started on the other. When she'd finished, she closed the files and pushed them back across the desk.

"They were killed because they were suspected of being Trotskyites."

"Yes."

"There would have been no need to be informed on. Their association was clear from my father's position in Trotsky's Red Army."

"Yes."

She let out a sigh, its unsteadiness showing her only emotion. "Thank you, Comrade Sokolov," she said, her face calm. With sufficient training, he thought, she could operate anywhere in the world.

"Olezka," he said, smiling his best reassuring and gentle smile. "May I call you Natalya?"

"Of course, Comrade."

"Olezka, please," he interrupted.

"Olezka."

"If our planning meeting goes well, we could of course continue to plan." He paused to make sure the next words were clearly understood. "As long as there is a reason to keep planning."

There it was. The deal. He promised to protect Mikhail as long as she kept seeing him. Saying it aloud made him almost feel like he wasn't going to do what must be done.

He watched her eyes to gauge her reaction. She seemed to be looking through him, beyond him. Then her eyes shifted to the window, to the outside world, clean, cold, and clear.

"Of course, Com . . . Olezka," she said, her eyes returning to him. She smiled. "I shall be waiting for your driver at nine tonight."

He thought that he'd be happy when he heard her say what he wanted her to say. But he was not. There was no light in her eyes. He thought of the old jokes about the frigid upper-class Englishwoman shutting her eyes and doing it for England. He stood. "Wonderful. Nine o'clock then. I shall be looking forward to it."

He walked around his desk. As she stood, he put his hand on her arm. She looked at his hand. She did not move her arm back. "Natalya," he said. "Don't worry. We will get Mikhail out of this situation."

She looked at him, searching his face, but didn't move her arm. He awkwardly withdrew his hand.

"Of course, Olezka," Natalya said. "Nine o'clock."

"Nine o'clock."

He escorted her into the outer office. The secretary looked up briefly from her typing and quickly looked back down. He watched Natalya disappear into the hallway. Sokolov returned to his own office and shut the door behind him. He stood behind the chair she'd been sitting in, his hands on the backrest pretending she was still sitting there and breathed in the lingering smell of her perfume.

She had worn perfume—for him. He walked to the window. He realized wanting her to love him was like wanting a prostitute to love him. There would be all the sex he wanted, but she would be doing it for Mikhail. But what happens after it becomes clear that Mikhail had met some fatal accident. Would the deal be off? Not necessarily. He could still hold the safety of her children over her head, or offer her many things that she couldn't get otherwise, Western things that women liked and couldn't get in Russia, perhaps even trips to France? He hurriedly straightened the files. Face reality. This was not some Turgenev novel or Pushkin poem.

From long practice, he placed a tight box around the longing but not around the excitement of conquest. He doubted that she'd ever given herself to anyone but her husband. Such a prize. And Bobrov had already won it. She wasn't *giving* anything of herself to him. It was a transaction. The forlorn emptiness returned.

Friday Morning, February 7, 1947
The Oulunjärvi Lake System
Race Day 7

Mikhail was making good time on brush-free frozen lakes of the Oulunjärvi lake system. The early morning air was still. Without wind and the muffling of snow the only sound was his own fierce breathing and the swoosh of the skis.

He knew that Arnie was also making good time by taking more risk crossing frozen marshes. Americans took risks. Their country had never experienced any great loss, so of course they were optimistic and adventurous. So were teenagers. Russians were an essentially conservative people, slow to change, steeped in centuries of history—and tragedy. Even the success of the revolution had depended on their innate conservatism, a population that did what it was told by higher authority. He thought of his country as Mother Russia. The Americans thought of their country as a cartoon character called Uncle Sam. Arnie Koski was an American and would take risks. To a people without history, there are few examples of things gone badly wrong.

Friday Morning, February 7, 1947
North of Kuopio
Race Day 7

Pietari Varila was also musing that morning as he skied alone northward from Kuopio. Two things were on his mind.

The first was trying to guess where the American might be. Pietari and his friends had years of experience skiing across primitive landscapes, as children and in the war, so they had a fairly good idea of where in general they'd find Koski. Still, *in general* covered a lot of territory. Pietari was roughly in the middle of the dragnet he and the others had planned out on the train the day before, giving him a good chance of being the one to find one of the racers. Then, it was a fifty-fifty chance that it would be the American. They'd all agreed that the most likely scenario was meeting the racers on the next day, Saturday, but that depended on how fast the racers had been moving south. In any case, it was almost certain they'd have to spend Friday night in the open, to all of them, more of an inconvenience than a hardship.

The second thing on Pietari's mind was that if he did intercept the American, what he was going to say to him. His mother had done the usual mother thing of eliciting his sympathies, this time for the wife and kids of the Russian. Certainly, if the Russian lost the race, it would go very badly for him and his family. To hell with *him*, and he'd told his mother that. He couldn't, however, bring himself to feel the same indifference for his innocent children. Yes, his mother had gotten to him. The American's wife, on the other hand, Louise—he chuckled to himself—she'd simply bowled them all over with American enthusiasm. *Of course,* he would find her husband. There were only countless square kilometers of wilderness. Just go out there and tell her husband the problem and the problem would get fixed. *Can do,* he thought, the American version of sisu. Sisu was about toughness in the face of what other cultures would call hopelessness. It was about enduring. As the Finns had done for the past seven years and would continue to do for as long as the Soviet Union threatened their border. Those years of death, starvation, and terror at the hands of the Russians would never be forgotten—or forgiven.

Everything he'd heard about Americans was that they could hardly endure anything for long, but they were very good at changing things so that they didn't *have to* endure anything for long. He snorted aloud in grudging admiration, moving gracefully, alternately pushing off the skis' inside edges. But now that he was out here, he was feeling, not just remembering, the war again. Why should he give a damn about the life of this Russian or his family? What were his mother and this wife of a shirttail relative thinking? Forgive the Russians for giving him the constantly intruding memory of digging the body of his friend Toivo from the snow, one leg blown off, the blood frozen solid, mixed with snow? They'd only found Toivo because the platoon's dog had smelled the body.

He shook the image away, focusing on the horizon, a low line of hills. Stay present. Don't slip back. Focus on efficiency and speed. They thought he'd want to save a Russian? Why? The childhood Lutheran in him said because it's the Christian thing to do. The thinking adult in him said that it was time to get along with the Russians for the sake of a free and prosperous Finland. But the warrior in him wanted every Russian he encountered to feel pain before he killed him.

Friday Afternoon, February 7, 1947
The Orphanage

At the orphanage, Louise kept herself busy to avoid the anxiety of waiting for the telephone call that would tell them that Pietari had reached Arnie and this nightmare she had caused would go away. She was stirring soiled diapers in a large bucket of boiling water, moving the stick up and down, trying to imitate the action of one of those new washing machines that were selling like hotcakes back in America now that the war was over. Not in Finland, it seemed.

All Arnie had to do was lose she mused. She was sure he'd do it. Yes, yes, in spite of the pride of the Tenth Mountain, the US Army, all that. She also knew that deep down, Arnie Koski was a decent man who would do the right thing. He would never betray his friend or fail to respect him as a fellow warrior—or himself. But, what about Kaarina's son, Pietari, or his friends? In Arnie's war, the Russians were allies; in Pietari's war, they had been enemies and they remained so.

She held up a diaper on the end of the stick, watching it steam in the cold air of the orphanage utility porch. Mixed with the steam was the smell of poop. *And he who was seated on the throne said, "Behold, I am making all things new."* She smiled wryly. Somewhere in Revelations. Yeah, but people who sat on thrones never washed dirty diapers. She dropped the one on her stick back into the hot water.

She knew it was silly to go ask Kaarina, probably for the third time, if Pietari had called. Kaarina would surely tell her when it happened. Still, after a few more minutes of pounding the washing, she walked into Kaarina's office and gave her a questioning look. Kaarina shook her head. Louise went back to the cold utility porch and stabbed repeatedly at the mass of diapers, trying not to think.

Friday Afternoon, February 7, 1947
A Bog Near Oulunjärvi
Race Day 7

It was two in the afternoon when Mikhail once again picked up Arnie's ski tracks. Damn. Arnie was still ahead of him. Grimly determined, he pushed on next to Arnie's trace. The tracks were clean, no sign of drifting snow in them, no sign of melt and refreezing. He couldn't be more than half an hour ahead of him.

The tracks once again disappeared into a frozen bog. He kept to his plan, although he was a little less sure about it. Koski was beating him by taking risks. He'd have to beat Koski by more than matching his speed or start taking risks himself. The former he wasn't sure he could do, the latter he didn't want to do. He could still hear Ivanov's startled shout just before he went under the ice.

Mikhail left Arnie's tracks to stick to the bog's edge.

An hour later, the temperature was dropping rapidly. Sunset would be around four. That left only an hour of daylight and maybe another hour of twilight. The bog was in a swale that headed north-south. On the southern end, the ground rose, ending the bog, but the landscape continued in a long shallow valley, flanked by gentle ridges.

Mikhail swung into the valley with a fury. Darkness would stop him, but he knew he'd have to be at least even with Koski before it did, or the race might be lost. Five minutes into the shallow valley, it occurred to him that there were no ski tracks. He began casting his eyes, sweeping the ground before him as best he could. From one gentle rise on the left to another on the right, the snow had not been disturbed. Koski must have been making faster time taking the risk of skiing on the bog. So, why no tracks coming out of it into this shallow valley? It was inconceivable that Koski would not take advantage of the terrain and ski between the hills. Mikhail stopped. Maybe Koski just hit a patch of trees or brush and was truly behind him? Then he thought maybe Koski's gamble had failed, or he wasn't aware that he was gambling. Then the thought struck him—maybe he'd fallen through thin ice.

Mikhail spun on his skis to look behind him. He listened. Wind. The beautiful silence of a vast forest blanketed with snow. No sounds of struggle or cries for help. He spun around and headed off. After about five kick and glides, he stopped again. If Arnie had fallen through the ice, he'd be wet through and dead within the hour. If he turned back to find out if Arnie was in trouble, he'd throw away the clear lead indicated by there being no tracks. But, if he kept heading south, he might be leaving a fellow soldier to die.

Arnie had felt elated to be making such good time, but the elation vanished when he felt his left ski suddenly sink through the snow, encountering—no resistance. He was flooded with fear as he felt his left ski pass through thin ice and into water. As his ski and foot continued down into the water, Arnie desperately flung himself to the right to spread his weight as much as possible. His instincts were good but not good enough. His left ski and leg were caught in a hole now edged with thin and breaking ice. Arnie's body, hitting the thicker ice around the hole, caused cracks to radiate from the hole, further weakening the ice beneath his body, which had been twisted sideways because of the stuck ski. His heavy pack, normally centered and balanced, now became an off-balance anchor, making it impossible to turn onto his stomach so that he could spread his arms and legs to distribute his weight. His weight instead was concentrated over a smaller area, causing the radiating cracks to continue to lengthen and widen. All of this happened in about two seconds.

Now, water was pushing up through the widening cracks, spreading through the thin layer of covering snow. Foundering, trying to get the ski loose, Arnie twisted out of the pack, which had already taken on water. As water oozed up around him, the hole widened beneath him as he sank. He managed to loosen the bindings and free himself from the skis. Holding on to both ski poles with one hand, he flung the skis back on his own trail, knowing it more likely to be safe in that direction since he'd not fallen through until this point. He looped an arm through one of the pack's shoulder straps and then stabbed both ski poles into the ice between him and the skis. Kicking furiously and pulling at the same time, he managed to get free of the hole. He lay there, breathing hard, soaking wet.

If he stood, he would concentrate all his weight into a small area and go through the now-moving ice. He rolled over on his belly, his only alternative. This submerged the front of his parka and clothes beneath it. Dragging his pack from his elbow pit, he low crawled toward the skis, stabbing his poles in front of him, making sure every ounce of him was spread as wide as possible.

He reached his skis. The ice seemed firmer. Still panting, he thanked God.

Then came a deeper, longer-lasting fear. Alone. Hypothermia next. Then death. He went through the mountaineer's checklist. Get out of the wind; that meant find shelter. Get dry; that meant get out of his wet clothes, but the change of clothes in his pack were probably soaked. Get warm; *that* would be nearly impossible. The nearest wood for a fire was a tree line several hundred yards across the bog from him. To gather wood and build a fire would take time, time he didn't have. He couldn't shake the image of the man in Jack London's *To Build a Fire*, fumbling to strike a match with frozen hands—and failing.

He began pulling off his wet clothes. The numbing, bone-chilling cold flailed his bare skin. He wrung his clothes as dry as he could and was shivering as his body tried to generate heat from his muscles. His toes were now going numb as his body struggled to keep what heat remained near his vital organs.

His hands and feet, not just his fingers and toes were rapidly going numb. His fear grew as he realized that his hands would soon be useless, that he was already dying from hypothermia.

He fumbled with his damp long johns. His trousers didn't want to go over his feet. Then his feet didn't want to go into his socks and boots. His hands now nearly useless, he managed to get his skis on.

Arnie headed for the nearest line of trees where he could get out of the wind. He felt like he was trembling violently but in a slow-motion film. Nothing worked. His legs felt like logs with dead weights tied to their bottoms. Try as he might, one ski seemed to go somewhere he didn't want it to. He floundered toward the trees. He'd lost all feeling in his feet. He panicked, afraid his toes would be lost. Then he caught the panic. That would get him dead for sure. He lost track of where the tree line was. Yes, over there. But it seemed so far. He wasn't so cold anymore . . . There was a really great burger stand there in the trees by the beach. Maybe he'd rest a bit . . . Yes, rest. It made sense to sink on his knees into the snow. He felt his mother tucking him into bed.

Skirting along the same tree line at the edge of the bog, Mikhail saw Arnie just as he went down on his knees. He saw the now-exposed water of a bog eye toward the center of the bog and the ragged trail Arnie had formed trying for the shore. Knowing that the ice must be supporting Arnie where he lay, Mikhail shed his pack and rushed across the bog, hoping that if there were other bog eyes, his speed and momentum would carry him across. He didn't think about the race—winning or losing or the risk to his own life. He didn't think at all. It was the warrior's instinctual response to save a fellow warrior. It had been this way ever since men have hunted in packs.

When he reached him, Arnie was smiling, lost in a dream.

He immediately checked Arnie's clothes, grunting with satisfaction that at least Arnie had enough sense to have wrung them out. Still, ice was forming on Arnie's parka and trousers. He got Arnie's skis off and squatted down, balancing as best he could on his own skis, and threw Arnie over his back in a fireman's carry. Leaving Arnie's pack and skis where they lay, he retraced his steps, knowing full well that now, because his weight was doubled, what was proven safe before was no longer proven.

It was just after four o'clock and the sun had set. He had about an hour before total darkness set in.

He dumped Arnie and retrieved his own pack, which took only a minute. Unrolling his sleeping bag, unzipping it to form a single blanket, he threw it over Arnie. He pulled out his snow shovel and began digging, fueled with adrenaline. When he'd made a shallow hole just big enough for him and Arnie to lie in, he laid pine boughs on the bottom. He opened his parka and hugging Arnie close wrapped them both in the sleeping bag and rolled into the shallow hole, out of the wind. He began vigorously rubbing Arnie's limbs and core to generate heat from friction.

Arnie moaned beneath him.

"Arnie. Wake up," Mikhail shouted in Finnish. He slapped Arnie's face, barely seeing it in the diminishing twilight.

Arnie grunted. Mikhail shook him. "Wake up. Goddamn it, wake up." He could see Arnie looking at him with wonder. He slapped him across both cheeks again.

"Wake up, you dumb fucking American." Now he saw Arnie get mad. He slapped him again. "Wake up!"

Arnie shook his head. His eyes came clear.

"Mikhail," he said with a dreamy smile. "Vaseline cotton balls."

"What?" Arnie was hallucinating.

"Mikhail," Arnie repeated more slowly, as if confirming something. "Fire. Vaseline." Then he came completely awake. "Mikhail, goddamn it, Mikhail."

"You're so articulate," Mikhail said.

"Yeah, no Russian eloquence," Arnie mumbled. Then he lifted his head and grinned. "But I was ahead when I went through the ice."

Friday Night, February 7, 1947
Helsinki

Standing inside the door to the apartment building, where she could see the street and shelter from the cold, Natalya waited nervously for Sokolov's driver. It had taken considerable planning—and risk—to get there. She had to leave the children with Fanya, most likely for the night, which meant explaining herself when she got back. She left the apartment dressed as if she were going into the legation for a work emergency, which she'd told Fanya. She knew, however, that she had to look good for Sokolov.

She wore her usual wool stockings out the door so as not to tip off Fanya, but she'd carefully packed her one pair of American nylon stockings into her largest briefcase, along with all her seldom-used makeup. All she had were sensible shoes, but at least they were for indoor work, so not completely gauche. Then, there was the problem of where to change.

She decided the driver knew everything anyway, so she directed him to pull to the curb on a darker street and keep his eyes off his rearview mirror. The last time she'd put on her nylons was for Mikhail's birthday. It had given both of them pleasure. Now, she felt like she was decorating a roast chicken that was about to be served.

She finished putting on her lipstick and snapped her compact shut. The sound made the driver involuntarily look up at the mirror.

The car pulled up in front of the hotel. Sokolov was waiting by the curb. He opened the door and smiled at her. Then she went numb.

Saturday Morning, February 8, 1947
Near Oulunjärvi
Race Day 8

T o say the night Arnie and Mikhail spent wrapped together in the snow hole was difficult was like saying war is hell, an expression that is meaningless to anyone who has not experienced it.

As soon as Mikhail had Arnie naked and shivering in his sleeping bag with his hands tucked in his armpits to save his fingers, he had started scraping snow down to bare ground. He found a flat stone that was next to a tree, just exposed enough to be visible. He put it on the cleared spot, where it would keep the fire just above the snow that was sure to melt around the fire once it got going. He kicked snow away to find branches, snapping and listening to them to make sure they were still dry. It was while doing this that "Vaseline cotton balls" suddenly made sense. He was going to use a thick candle to start the fire. He rummaged through Arnie's pack and pulled out a tin of cotton balls that had been soaked in Vaseline. They burned hot and long, and he piled the branches on them. He smiled wryly, American know-how.

When the fire was roaring, Arnie's wet clothes hanging on sticks as close as possible without burning up, he rolled out his sleeping bag. He got in and pulled Arnie—bag and all—in close to him, only breaking the connection long enough to keep the fire roaring.

*   *   *

Several hours later, the two of them crawled out of their bags, shaking off the snow and thin ice that had formed on them. The sun was not yet up, but faint light reflecting from high clouds showed its presence beyond the hills to the east. Neither spoke. They both knew there'd have to be some sort of arrangement to get the race started fairly again.

Arnie dug into his pack, but he was shaking so badly he had to use both hands. He dug out a Hershey bar and thrust it at Mikhail, wedged between his mittens.

Arnie was trembling. "My hands and legs hurt," he said, the words coming out almost as if he'd had too much to drink.

Mikhail nodded. They both knew shivering was unpleasant but good. Blood was returning to Arnie's extremities, and they were still functioning.

Mikhail unwrapped the Hershey bar and slowly began eating, savoring it as it melted in his mouth, his eyes on the dawn. "Americans make good chocolate," he said quietly.

"We do," Arnie answered.

Arnie was unwrapping his own Hershey bar. His last. Unwilling to mar the pristine snow, he stuffed the paper into his pack, then held out his hand to take Mikhail's Hershey wrapper.

Mikhail unwrapped the rest of his chocolate and handed the paper to Arnie. He'd never seen anyone save a candy wrapper out in the middle of nowhere.

"You won," Arnie said. He stuffed the wrappers in his pack.

Mikhail looked away to the brightening skyline. "You were ahead until you fell through."

"Dead ahead," Arnie deadpanned.

Mikhail nodded and smiled.

"Really," Arnie said. "If you hadn't come back for me, you'd be the winner. I'd be dead."

Mikhail stared at the horizon, not wanting to openly acknowledge Arnie's debt.

Arnie put out his hand. "You won."

The two men looked away from the dawn and at each other. Mikhail shrugged. "Yes. I accept," he said. He took Arnie's hand, a firm meeting of right hands with no weapons in them.

They dropped their hands. Both started to put on their packs. Their breath was becoming more visible in the increasing light.

"How about we race again?" Mikhail said.

"Again?"

"Yes. We race from here to Kuopio," Mikhail said. "When you lose, again, you make a public announcement that Russian ski troops are the best in the world." The challenge made.

"Like hell. That'll never happen." And accepted.

Mikhail knew that Arnie was probably right; it wouldn't happen. Arnie was simply faster. With only two full days of racing left, any advantage Mikhail held because of his experience skiing in this kind of geography—and skiing in Finland in particular—would count little.

"I propose we each ski to opposite sides at the middle of the next lake," Mikhail said. "We can see each other across the lake. We wait until oh-six-hundred." He paused. "You won't see me after that."

Arnie chuckled at that. "You're on." He held out his hand. Mikhail took it. A quick firm grip. "You saved my life," Arnie said.

"How else was I going to beat you fair and square?"

And release.

It felt good to have saved a man's life, especially now, here, where there were only two men in the whole world.

The two quietly waxed their skis, debating a bit about which wax to use given the weather and snow conditions. When both were standing on their skis, Mikhail nodded and headed off, Arnie in his trace.

At first Arnie was very slow. Mikhail was patient, knowing it would take time for Arnie's body heat to make his legs feel like they belonged to him again. After about half an hour of good steady skiing, Arnie came alongside, breaking his own track alongside Mikhail.

"You back?" Mikhail asked.

"Will be."

Still, Arnie fell back to take advantage of Mikhail's tracks.

Half an hour later, at the head of the next lake, Mikhail turned to look back at Arnie. Arnie nodded. Mikhail veered off to the east, briefly raising a ski pole in salute. Arnie answered with his own and veered off to the west. Nothing was said. What had happened between the two men was beyond words.

Saturday, February 8, 1947
The Kallavesi Lake System and
Porkkala Navy Base
Race Day 8

That afternoon, Pietari was just south of the Kallavesi lake system. He and the others started before dawn with high clouds overhead. All morning, the clouds kept coming in lower, and now it was snowing lightly, the visibility diminishing with every hour.

Breathing through his nose to warm the air, he could feel his lungs pushing against his parka. It felt good. It felt clean out here, away from Helsinki, away from politics and money—and memories. The shushing of his skis was meditative. The rhythm was meditative. Even though reaching the American was the reason he was out here, he didn't want to end the reverie by reaching him.

He came over a small rise and was just beginning to glide down the gentle slope when he thought he caught movement to his immediate north. He swung his skis parallel to the hill and twisted, trying to see through the snow. A lone, fast-moving skier was heading south. Pietari glided forward toward the skier, nodding his head to no one present and accepting the end of the silence. It was Koski. Part of him had hoped it wouldn't be. Not being the one to find Koski would have precluded what he was planning to do if he were the one to find him. He would do it for his dead brothers, his mother's sons, and the tens of thousands like them.

* * *

Sokolov was also planning, but it was much more involved. Fedotov had informed him that there would be no interference from Finnish authorities on the question of Finnish sovereignty and airspace, but care must be taken not to alert the Finnish police. They couldn't be trusted to obey orders, even those coming from Paasikivi, if they went against their reactionary politics.

It hadn't taken but a few hours to get a small, elite team of MGB parachute-trained agents to Porkkala from Moscow. A quick telephone call from Fedotov to the commander of the base placed all the base's assets at Sokolov's disposal. Sokolov had asked for and received two navy Ilyushin-4 long-range torpedo bombers. He'd had them in the air before the parachutists arrived, an MGB agent with a camera aboard each in the place of the rear machine gunner. They'd been warned to locate both skiers without raising any suspicion by flying to the east and west of the assumed course, just close enough to spot the skiers without them noticing. If they did notice, they'd be unsuspicious of a single Russian airplane they'd assume was on some kind of mission from Porkkala. The instant one or both skiers were spotted, the agent aboard would take a photograph with a telephoto lens, the Ilyushin-4 would continue on its way and the other plane would be warned to veer off course.

Sokolov briefed the team of eight. They had very few questions. They didn't ask, and they didn't want to know why their superiors wanted them to find a Russian army officer in the middle of nowhere. Asking questions would only raise questions about their loyalty. They settled into their most frequent activity—waiting.

Arnie caught a glimpse of movement before he made out the somewhat obscured figure of another skier coming north toward him. Whoever he was, it wasn't Mikhail who would be heading south. Only mildly curious as to why someone else would be skiing in the area, he kept to his course, not wanting to waste any time going to say hello to some stranger.

Then, it appeared that the stranger was coming his way. Arnie fought another battle in his lifelong war between just wanting to be left alone and having to get along in the world, which required talking to people when he didn't want to. It wasn't that he disliked people, far from it. It was just that there was some pull, some inertia, intensified since the war, to keep his distance. One could observe a pack and its inherent dangers from a distance far better than from within it.

The distant skier kept coming his way. Now puzzled, Arnie stopped. Standing straight, he watched the skier, a man clearly at home on skis who was coming steadily for him. The man stopped about ten feet away and lifted his snow goggles. It was Kaarina Varila's son, Pietari. *What in the hell?* Arnie's first thought was that something had happened to Louise.

"Päivää," Pietari said with the usual reserved dignity of the Finnish male. It was the informal "day" half of the more formal greeting, *hyvää päivää*, good day. Arnie knew, since childhood, that watching another Finn's face for any indication of what was going on in their head was futile.

"Päivää," he replied. Then he waited. What was going on? Was Louise OK? His own dignity required he conform to Pietari's dignity. He'd wait stoically until the man delivered his message.

"Everything is OK at home," Pietari said. "Louise wanted you to know several things, so she sent me." He stopped talking.

Arnie nodded.

"But first, she wanted to know if you were winning."

Arnie shrugged. "It's pretty tight right now," he said. "We were dead even this morning." He didn't think it necessary to go into the fact that Mikhail had saved his life, given up a sure victory doing so, and that he had conceded the victory of the long race to Mikhail. That could come later by a warm fire, and if he spent too much time talking, he wouldn't win that one either.

"How did you find me?"

"There are ten of us, spread across several kilometers. I figured you'd be around here and took the center spot. Still, mostly luck. But with the snow starting . . . not easy to find either of you."

Arnie grunted an acknowledgment. *Ten? What is going on?* He waited impatiently for the second part of the message, aware that he was losing time.

"Louise also wanted you to know that there has been some publicity about the race."

Arnie furrowed his brow, questioning.

"She is raising money for Äiti's orphanage."

Arnie nodded.

"She has formed a sort of raffle. People buy a ticket for one hundred markka and try to guess the difference between your time and the Russian's. The one who gets closest wins one hundred thousand markka."

Arnie took this in, not wanting to believe Louise had made the race public.

"She got the local newspapers to promote it."

Arnie tried to suppress his growing anger. He surely must have told Louise that the race was a private affair, but he hadn't specifically said to keep it quiet. Still, it was that damned impetuous go-get-'em attitude of hers. Of course, she'd come up with some scheme to bring in money for the cause. To cover the anger, he asked, "Is it working?"

"Yoh." Pietari paused. "Big success. Thousands of markka coming in."

Again, Arnie furrowed his brow.

"The articles got picked up in London and New York." Pietari paused. "And Moscow."

Arnie's anger turned to a sinking feeling that went straight to the bottom of his gut. He compressed his lips very tightly, struggling to sound calm. "So, this race has become"—he couldn't find a Finnish equivalent for "cause célèbre"—"a big deal."

"Yoh."

Arnie allowed himself the indulgence of stabbing a ski pole into the snow. "And she sent you out here to tell me that?"

"Yoh. She said you hate surprises and would want to prepare yourself for questioning by news reporters when you get to Kuopio."

You're goddamned right I'd hate a surprise like this, Arnie thought. Louise had cajoled ten of them to find him. He knew her well enough to know that most likely she had made the race public feeling the cause outweighed any consequences. She was now probably trying to soften the blow of facing his anger over what she'd done.

Arnie started moving his skis back and forth, anxious to get moving.

"She also thought it would be important for you to know that because the race is no longer just personal, you are skiing for the honor of the Tenth Mountain Division and the US Army. Of Finns and Americans everywhere."

"She's such a cheerleader," Arnie said without humor. He looked up, trying to see where the sun was behind the high clouds. "Tell her thanks. I've got to get moving."

"Yoh." Pietari pushed his goggles back down and Arnie followed suit. "We all agreed to rendezvous in Siilinjärvi. I'll telephone from there that you're in good shape."

"I just saw Mikhail this morning. Get word to his wife he's in good shape, too."

"Yoh." Pietari pushed off.

Arnie set off south, furious, stabbing his poles with unnecessary force until he realized he was wasting energy. Louise could be so goddamned headstrong, single focused on one of her causes with blinders on to avoid seeing anything that might get in her way.

After about ten minutes of hard skiing, Arnie started thinking. Convincing ten Finns to go looking for him? Louise must have been feeling exceptionally bad about ignoring his request—their agreement—to keep the race just between him and Mikhail. But *ten*? That's asking a lot to just avoid facing your husband after making him angry. Louise was probably feeling bad about making the race public, but she wasn't the type to turn heaven and earth to let him know she'd made a mistake. She wasn't afraid of him. That couldn't be the motive.

He kept working his skis, trying to make up for the time lost talking with Pietari.

And this stuff about the honor of the US Army. That didn't sound like Louise at all. The story of the race is being read in the major capitals. Paris, London . . . Moscow.

The penny dropped.

This was about Mikhail. Of course, the Kremlin would be reading about the race, who knows how high up. Stalin and Beria were not the kind of men who laughed at embarrassment. They were the kind of men who would kill you if you embarrassed them. That goddamned Pietari simply didn't deliver the real message. Why would he? He and half of the country would be happy about one more dead Russian.

He felt a stab of fear for his friend. What would happen to Mikhail if he lost? That could go two ways for him. It could be seen as a terrible disgrace because he was a Hero of the Soviet Union. The punishment could be severe. On the other hand, *because* he was a Hero of the Soviet Union, they could cut him some slack. After all, in America, a Medal of Honor winner could hardly do anything wrong for the rest of his life. Surely, Mikhail wouldn't be in any serious danger. Some trouble maybe, but—

He was skiing hard, focusing on the terrain, but he couldn't shake an uneasy feeling. Russians weren't Americans, and totalitarian dictatorships weren't democracies.

Pumping up a small hill, with his skis making a forty-five-degree herringbone pattern, Arnie's anger with Louise was being replaced by fear for his friend's life.

He crested the small hill. Squatting to lower wind resistance, he gained speed heading downhill. By the time he slowed at the bottom of the slope, he knew that he had to find Mikhail to warn him. Maybe they could come across the finish line hand in hand. That would look good in the papers. Hell, just let him win. Whatever Mikhail wanted.

But there was one problem. Where was Mikhail?

He set off nearly perpendicular to his original course to see if he could pick up Mikhail's trail. If Mikhail was in front of him, he'd come across his tracks. But Arnie knew now that he was the better skier. That would mean Mikhail was behind him, so he wouldn't cross Mikhail's tracks. He could wait for him, gambling Mikhail was indeed behind him, but then how would he spot him? The country was vast. And it was getting dark. And it was snowing.

Saturday Night, February 8, 1947
The Orphanage

Louise was in the orphanage kitchen watching the first perks of the light-brown coffee she'd managed to wheedle out of the legation supplies spattering up against the glass at the top of the percolator's central tube. It was meditative, watching the coffee get darker and darker until the aroma filled the room and she judged the coffee to be just right. When she was little, she used to watch the hot liquid slowly turn dark when she made coffee for her mom and dad on Sunday mornings, when they'd both sleep in. Sleep in, that is, until she would proudly come into their room with hot coffee to wake them up, usually around half past six. She smiled at the memory. There were probably mornings when they'd have happily shot their proud and smiling coffee-bearing child. But they always sat up in the bed and beamed with thanks as she handed them their cups.

The memory gave her comfort. She needed that comfort now. It was several hours after dark and no word from Pietari. So far, around five of his friends had found phones, calling in to say that their search had not been successful. Several speculated that they hadn't heard from the rest of the group because of the difficulty in finding phones.

They'd all expected someone would have made contact with Arnie sometime during the day. Was he still even alive? Of course, he was. Then again—

Louise shrugged off the thought and poured three cups of coffee, walking them into Kaarina's office, where Kaarina and Natalya were sorting through ticket stubs and money. Kaarina was beaming. They'd passed the breakeven of five hundred ticket sales to cover the prize money a couple of days earlier. Now, every markka was going to the orphanage. Louise set a cup down before each of them. She noticed that Natalya was not beaming but despondently going through the motions of counting stubs, recording names, looking numb.

Louise put a cup in front of Natalya, setting two sugar cubes on the saucer, thinking she couldn't bear giving her three, which she knew Natalya would probably prefer. Once, she almost said something about how Natalya could rot her teeth but caught herself. Now that she knew Natalya better, she had become aware of how Natalya only smiled with closed lips. Natalya had dozed off once, her mouth open, and Louise saw why. Her mouth was full of crude fillings. Several teeth were missing, and the remaining ones had an unhealthy dark look to them.

Natalya nodded, showing a small polite smile that quickly faded. Louise glanced at Kaarina. Kaarina returned the glance, acknowledging she, too, could see something was amiss with Natalya and quickly looked back down at the money.

Louise sat at the end of the table and started going through her own pile. No one spoke.

Finally, Louise had to say something. "Are you sure the telephones are working?"

Kaarina nodded. "Yoh."

More silence.

"Don't worry. He'll call," Kaarina said. "He's reliable."

"About calling," Louise said.

"Yoh."

They all knew the issue wasn't whether Pietari would call but whether he'd even found Arnie.

After more silent counting, Kaarina stood, stretched, and walked out of the room.

Louise put both of her hands on the table and looked directly at Natalya.

Natalya stopped counting. "What?"

"He'll find him. I just know he will."

"Know or hope?"

"Know," Louise said, perhaps more emphatically than she felt. Her father had told her, and Arnie had confirmed it more than once, that a leader never shows anything but optimism.

Natalya didn't seem to be reacting at all to the discussion about the hoped-for telephone call. Louise could see that Natalya's eyes were bloodshot and red, probably from lack of sleep—or crying? The numbness, the vacant nobody's-at-home stare. It was like Natalya's body was here but not Natalya.

Then Louise realized, Natalya must have done it. "Oh, Natalya . . ." Louise said.

Natalya looked away from Louise, lips tight. Then she looked down at her hands on her lap.

"I am so, so sorry," Louise whispered.

Still unable to look at Louise, she looked up at the ceiling.

There was an awkward and long silence.

Then Louise said softly, "I think you're the bravest woman I've ever met."

The two sat there, silently, two women against the gods.

Kaarina came through the door. Louise quickly said aloud, "He'll find him. I know he will."

Natalya regained control of herself and began arranging papers on the table.

Kaarina looked at them, her eyes moving from one face to the other and back and then proceeded to her chair to resume work saying nothing.

A tense hour went by.

Then, the phone rang. It was as if the room were being cut in two. All three stopped breathing.

Kaarina answered the phone.

"Yoh." Silence. "Yoh. Se on hyvää."

She hung up and looked at the two women without expression. "Pietari found him."

Louise jumped to her feet, clapping her hands. "Yes, yes, yes. Thank God. Praise God. Praise Pietari. Oh—" She looked at Natalya.

Natalya sat there, stunned. She looked up at Louise. Her eyes were blank, her mouth slightly open. "Pour rien," she whispered. "Pour rien."

Part Three

Early Sunday Morning, February 9, 1947
Near the Kallavesi Lake System
Race Day 9

Arnie had skied back and forth the night before until he was exhausted. He'd burrowed into snow to get out of the wind, caught a couple of hours' sleep, and then was up and moving in the dark, zigzagging across the route he thought Mikhail most likely to take. As it grew lighter, he was faced with a landscape devoid of any human, a blue-gray sky cover, and steadily falling snow. He shoved off, eating the last chunk of dried reindeer meat that he'd been saving for the final sprint to the finish. He wanted every ounce of energy to go into the search for Mikhail.

Two hours later, he was on a small hill sweating with the effort of climbing this one hill of many, all with the same negative result. Snow gently fell, beautiful to look at, close to impossible to see through. He fought despair. Even if he managed to cross Mikhail's route, he'd never see his tracks, buried under the snow. Mikhail could be behind him. He could have had an accident. Arnie could have missed him and Mikhail was already way ahead of him. Yet, there was no thought of giving up and heading for the finish line. It was the warrior's code. No one gets left behind—ever. You search until you know the person is safe, or you bring home the body.

Sunday Morning, February 9, 1947
Train to Kuopio

Louise was at Natalya's apartment long before sunrise to help her get everyone packed to go to Kuopio. Arnie had said ten days; that would be Monday. There was a small chance they'd finish this afternoon, but it was more likely they'd be a day late. Aware of Natalya's anxiety, Louise was trying to sit on her own excitement. Of course, Arnie would make sure to come in a very close second to Mikhail, so Mikhail's victory would look legitimate. Maybe they'd even contrive to come in together. That would make a nice picture.

She helped supervise the packing and transporting of Natalya, the two children, and the ever-present Fanya, to the train station. There was something warm and pleasing about the controlled chaos. Squatting down and helping little Grisha into his snowsuit, Grisha wiggling, looking around at his mother doing the same with his big sister, Louise again felt the sweet longing. She kissed little Alina on top of her head. Grisha, seeing Louise kissing his sister, wanted in on it. He tried to stand, but lost his balance, plopping down on his rear end. Louise picked him up, hugging him close.

Natalya, of course, was all business, looking at her watch, shooing them all outside to get the taxi for the station.

They left Helsinki in the dark, but now on the train halfway to Kuopio, they were rolling steadily across the frozen countryside, the steam and smoke from the engine whisking past their windows. Even though Louise was feeling more positive because Pietari had reached Arnie, she still felt awkward around Natalya, knowing what Natalya had been forced to do in large part because of her. The fact that the money was rolling into the orphanage, far beyond anyone's expectations, offered little solace.

She expected to see both Arnie and Mikhail tomorrow afternoon, racing toward the finish line. It would be a great show. She'd made sure all the papers were well informed about the approximate time of the race's end. She envisioned pictures of Mikhail holding up his ski poles in triumph with a good-natured Arnie beside him being a good sport about a close loss. It had been a close call.

She caught Natalya's eye and smiled at her, trying to encourage her, to help set things right between them. Alina was asleep on Natalya's lap. Fanya was walking Grisha up and down the aisle of the car, holding his arms above his head. Natalya smiled back with her closed-lip smile. Then she broke eye contact and looked out the window.

Sunday Morning, February 9, 1947
Porkkala Naval Base Airfield

At Porkkala Naval Base, Sokolov was peering out of the window of the airstrip ready room, worrying about the increasing cloud cover and snow. He'd had the two Ilyushin-4s up in the air before dawn, tasked with finding one or both racers without being detected.

The radio crackled and he heard the call sign of the pilot of the most easterly plane. The operator acknowledged. The pilot's voice came back strong, clear, and excited. They'd located Bobrov about six kilometers west of Lapinlahti. The pilot gave the coordinates and said he was dipping behind some hills, moving very close to the ground, making sure with just a few words that the people back on the ground knew the danger of flying this low in falling snow.

Sokolov took the transmitter from the operator and asked if either plane had seen the American. Neither had. They'd been lucky to even spot Bobrov.

Sokolov hesitated only a moment. Without knowing the whereabouts of the American, he could not know for certain if Bobrov was winning or losing. That justified making sure he didn't lose. And doing what must be done to protect the reputation of the Soviet Union would only result in him looking good. He ordered both planes to return to base.

The leader of the MGB parachutists had been dozing in a chair he'd leaned up against the wall, but he'd jerked awake with the burst of radio traffic. *Clearly a veteran*, Sokolov mused. They never missed an opportunity to sleep. One never knew when the next one would come.

He walked over to the man, who jumped to his feet and handed him the coordinates. "As we discussed, Comrade. He's probably behind. Do what must be done."

The man, in full combat gear, saluted and clambered out of the room. Sokolov watched him stride across the runway to the waiting aircraft and his men. The twin engines of the Lisunov Li-2 in which the team had flown from Moscow coughed to life.

Sokolov watched until the plane disappeared. Here he was once again in command of an operation to eliminate a threat to the Party. He sighed. How many had there been before? They were starting to blur. What was the most difficult about this one was having to lie to the man's wife about her husband's guaranteed safety. He'd even urged her to be at the finish line with her children to meet him, further reinforcing the story that Mikhail must have met with an accident. A flicker of guilt arose just above his consciousness. He'd convinced a wife that her husband would live, all the while giving the orders that would make sure he didn't live. With practiced ease, he pushed the feeling down and away. Yes, husband, wife. Not Mikhail and Natalya. Roles. We all play our roles. *That* was reality.

Sunday Morning, February 9, 1947
Kallavesi Lake System, North of Kuopio
Race Day 9

Mikhail squinted against the snow, looking to the east, puzzling a little as to why a Lisunov Li2 would be this far from Porkkala, flying dangerously low beneath the cloud cover. Maybe it wasn't navy, but he was almost certain the air force and army didn't have any Lisunovs in Finland. The plane had disappeared, and it seemed to Mikhail that it had altered course, another puzzle. But then he bent to his task. Given their second equal start, the race had now turned into a sprint, where speed and form became more important than strategy and endurance. Having now competed against Arnie for a week, watching his fluid and powerful technique, he had seen for himself why Arnie Koski had been a champion skier even before the war. He also knew that even though Arnie had conceded him the long race, he was probably behind Arnie in the short one.

Arnie, too, was puzzling over the appearance of a lone aircraft. It looked like a DC-3. Since the war, DC-3s were all over the place, rapidly being put to use by civilian airlines, both as passenger and cargo planes, so it could be one of those. But why would a commercial plane take the risk of flying so low under falling snow. He stopped for just a moment to take a quick compass bearing on two hills. Mentally estimating the azimuths, he located his position and jotted down the coordinates and time in the small notebook he always carried in a breast pocket. He set off again. The Russians had copied the DC-3 he remembered, and they made a lot of them during the war. So it was possible this was Russian military. If it was, what was it doing in Finnish airspace? Surely, it had obtained permission. He kept pushing toward Kuopio, alternatively angling to one side or the other from the direct line still hoping to catch sight of Mikhail.

The plane had disappeared over a ridge.

At that moment the plane passed over Mikhail, who watched it bank and turn toward him, flying at around three or four hundred meters above the ground. That puzzled him. He stopped momentarily before pushing off again, focusing on the race, not wanting to lose any time.

Then, he saw a body tumble from the plane. Another followed. Their chutes opened immediately. As the plane roared overhead, he saw the red star of the Soviet Union on the fuselage as more parachutists were strung out above him. What in the world? There couldn't be a military exercise without him knowing it. But who? Without him knowing? MGB? Why? All of his antennae were up. Something was wrong. Had someone denounced him? But who? Who could be an enemy? Was it the start of another purge? The first to go would be the intelligence officers, of course.

Whatever the cause, there was no doubt these parachutists were coming for him. He fought down his fear, frantically looking for some way to escape.

There was none.

Two parachutists had already reached the ground and were unbuckling from their chutes. Mikhail quickly estimated distances. One of the men was coming toward him. The other was moving to his west, cutting off any escape in that direction. Two more men hit the ground, and the same thing happened, one moving toward him, the other moving to cut off any route to the east. Three more men landed south of him, two joined the man on the east and west sides, and the third moved toward him. The plane banked, then dropped another man to his south and one to his north. He knew a well-planned operation when he saw one. Four two-man teams covering the four compass points. Should he try any direction, at least two teams would easily converge on him. The lone skier to his south kept coming toward him. Probably the leader. Nine to one, all armed with Shpagin submachine guns with seventy-one-round drum magazines. A Shpagin could fire a thousand rounds a minute. Mikhail had a pistol.

Even if he did escape, he'd have to make it all the way to Norway or Sweden by himself. The MGB would still have Natalya and the children.

There was no escape.

The fear left him. He was filled with an intense sadness and longing.

He tried desperately to picture Natalya, Alina, and Grisha. He wanted to reach them, touch them, smell them. He looked around him at the beauty of the snow-covered hills. He breathed, feeling every molecule, the biting clean, cold air. During the war, he'd often wondered, not morbidly, where he would die. What a cosmic joke. He would die in Finland at the hands of his own countrymen. He doubted he'd ever know why. Explaining why people were liquidated was not part of the deal.

He waited, watching the lone skier approach.

"Colonel Bobrov," the man said when he'd come within talking distance.

"Yes," Mikhail answered.

"You are under arrest."

"On whose authority?"

The man was pointing his Shpagin at Mikhail's chest, but his face was sad. "We understand the order has come all the way down from Comrade Beria."

"Well, second best is not bad," Mikhail said. "Too bad I didn't rate Comrade Stalin."

The man smiled at Mikhail sadly. "Yes, Comrade. Almost reached the top. Please pull out your pistol. Slowly. And drop it."

Mikhail pulled his pistol. It didn't even have a magazine in it. He dropped it on the snow.

"Move back," the man said.

Mikhail did and the man picked up the pistol and signaled to his team, who all started skiing toward them.

"And to what do I owe this honor of a visit from my MGB comrades?" Mikhail asked.

The man hesitated, then said solemnly, "The race has been in the newspapers. Big capitalist ones."

Mikhail involuntarily jerked backward.

"The *London Times*. The *New York Times*," the man added.

"And *Pravda*," Mikhail said.

"Yes."

"So, I am famous," he said sarcastically.

"Unfortunately, yes, you are. We don't often get orders from Beria himself." The man pulled out a pack of cigarettes and offered one to Mikhail. Mikhail declined. "Not in the mood," he said. "Don't want to be a cliché."

The man chuckled. "I've heard about you, Bobrov. All good, by the way. You don't disappoint."

"That makes me so happy."

The rest of the parachutists had gathered around them. "Can I ask why?" Mikhail said.

"You know, Comrade Colonel, we are never told."

Mikhail shrugged. "Yes," he said almost abstractly, looking at the land, the trees, the soft light filtering through clouds, reflecting from the snow. Looking, he knew, for the last time. The beauty. The beauty that he'd spent so little time looking at.

"Maybe I'll take that cigarette," Mikhail said.

The man nodded, sadness in his face. He knocked a cigarette from its case and handed it to Mikhail. "You will die a hero." He lit the cigarette with his lighter. "As you lived," he said sincerely. Mikhail pulled in the smell of lighter fluid. Even that seemed precious, like perfume that Natalya wore on special occasions. He breathed in the warm smoke.

"Anything in those orders about my family?"

"No, but I am ordered to convey to you that Comrade Sokolov will guarantee their safety if you agree to cooperate. That means no sign of a struggle."

"What guarantee do I have if I do?"

"Colonel, you know you have none."

Mikhail nodded.

"Comrade Sokolov is very high up, as you know. He at least has the power to make it happen."

"And if I don't cooperate?"

"The People should not be subjected to the presence of the wife and children of a traitor."

"A traitor! They'll paint me as a traitor?"

The MGB leader nodded sadly. "You know that they'll make it true."

"Wife and children of a traitor," Mikhail repeated softly. "I see." To not cooperate meant sure death for Natalya and orphanages for Alina and Grisha. To cooperate meant there would be a chance for them to stay together, relocated to Siberia somewhere but most likely together, maybe even not imprisoned.

"Colonel." Mikhail noticed the man had dropped the "comrade" and was addressing him by his military title. "We all here"—he nodded to those around him—"know you are no traitor. You've done your work for the People well. Now we, sadly, must do ours."

Several of the men nodded. "We are to make it look like you met with a tragic accident. This will be why the American won the race. The papers will indicate that you were well ahead when you met your death. At least that's the story for now."

"Well," Mikhail said. "I'll be sad to miss how it all came out." He pulled in another deep breath of smoke. "So. How did I die in the current story?"

"You unfortunately fell through the ice on that lake over there. You were trapped. Drowned. The desperate search will be in all the newspapers. It will, of course, prove fruitless. We'll see that you'll be found after the spring thaw and given a burial with full military honors." He looked sadly at Mikhail. "Which you deserve."

He handed Mikhail a cyanide tablet.

Mikhail looked up at the somber sky. Normally such a sky would seem to him to be featureless. Now it seemed limitless. Not big enough, however, to fill the aching hole in his heart for Natalya, Alina, and little Grisha.

Monday Morning, February 10, 1947
The Kallavesi Lake System
Race Day 10

Arnie had again skied until nearly two in the morning, making very slow progress, crossing his course as if tacking against the wind. Snow had been falling intermittently for two days.

He again slept curled in the snow in the open. Waking with the cold after only two hours, he brushed the snow that had fallen on him while he slept and set off again without eating. At the first small lake, he smashed a hole in the ice and filled his canteen. The cold water burned all the way to his stomach. Standing there that brief moment, the water cool in his stomach, breathing the undefiled air all around him, alone in a world of white silence and falling snow, he felt he was designed by nature to survive in nature. Striving to warn a friend of possible danger, he felt that once again he counted for something important. He hadn't felt this since the war.

He was now only a few hours from Kuopio. If he headed there directly, he might beat Mikhail. That couldn't happen. With Mikhail's tracks under snow, he was left with a simple chance decision. If Mikhail was ahead, all would be well. If Mikhail was behind, all would not be well.

Arnie began again skiing back and forth perpendicular to Mikhail's probable route. He'd do this until he intercepted Mikhail—or until he was sure he'd delayed long enough for Mikhail to reach Kuopio before him.

Monday, February 10, 1947
Kuopio City Limit

Louise woke early Monday morning in the sparsely furnished hotel room where she'd collapsed after the long train ride with Natalya, Fanya, and the children. There was a toilet and sink down the hall. To wash her hands, she had to break a thin layer of ice in a large pitcher that the owner had put out the night before. She took the pitcher back to her room to sponge bathe where it was marginally warmer.

As agreed, she met Natalya, the children, and Fanya for a typical Finnish breakfast of split whole herring, coarse brown bread, cheese, butter, and *karjalanpiirakka*, a pastry made of *talkkuna* flour, eggs, and short grain rice. The children, unsure what was going on, were subdued. They knew that they had come to meet their father, but their mother was tense and distant, speaking to them tersely for behavior that normally wouldn't even evoke attention.

Louise took Alina in her lap and helped her drink her cocoa while talking to Natalya in French. Fanya ate silently. Grisha was constantly toddling off to investigate other tables. He was mostly tolerated and sometimes even smiled at, until he tried to see what was on one of the tables, rocking it a bit. Fanya was on it instantly, rushing over to the table, scolding him in Russian. Hearing the Russian, the temperature at the table Grisha was visiting dropped a good ten degrees Celsius.

When Fanya returned with Grisha, Louise leaned over to Natalya and whispered, "Good thing we're speaking French."

Natalya, who had been constantly looking out the window, didn't seem to register what Louise was talking about.

"Maybe we should go to where they'll finish. Mikhail might get in early. We won't want to miss him."

Natalya shrugged the Russian whatever-happens-happens shrug, but her eyes showed her anxiety.

Up to this point, Louise had been confident that Arnie would be carefully and deliberately just behind Mikhail, whatever time they crossed the northern Kuopio city limits. Natalya's fatalistic shrug evoked a quiver of anxiety. She wouldn't be sure until she saw Mikhail crossing the finish first.

A small crowd had already formed in the lightly falling snow when they reached the city limits. Clearly, the publicity effort had worked, Louise thought somewhat ruefully. Someone had stretched a ribbon across the road, one end tied to the city limit sign and the other to a leafless bush across the road.

After about an hour, during which time both Natalya and Louise had been interviewed by a reporter from the local newspaper, the children had come to the end of their patience. Grisha had a runny nose and the snot had frozen to his face and chin. Alina had built a tiny village of little snow houses with twigs for flags but had started complaining, showing her mother her hands. When Natalya snapped something at her in Russian, she turned around and stomped all the snow houses back into the snow. Natalya sent them back to the hotel with Fanya.

Both women paced, keeping warm that way, constantly scanning to the north. Where were their husbands?

Around midmorning, an enterprising teenaged boy arrived with a large container of hot Chaga pulled behind him on a sled. He was quickly doing a brisk business. He would carefully wash the used ceramic cups in the snow and dry them with the towel that he kept wrapped around his neck. Louise remembered a State Department lecture that said that before the war, Finland had supplied a huge percentage of Europe's and Russia's lumber and paper. The war had ended that. How long, she mused, would it take to recover fully? No one in America thought twice about throwing away paper cups.

The morning was an anxiety-filled stupor of stamping their feet and slapping their arms for warmth. Spectators came, stayed until they got cold, then disappeared to someplace warm. Natalya and Louise wouldn't leave. At lunchtime, Louise volunteered to go back to the hotel to check on the children and get some lunch, leaving Natalya looking anxiously northward. Louise returned with some bread and cheese wrapped in newspaper that she'd stuck inside her coat, hoping to keep it from freezing.

The day dragged on, the crowd thinning. The sun, hidden behind the overcast sky, was slipping closer to the southeastern horizon when the crowd started building again, hoping to see a finish before dark. People were starting to speculate on why the racers hadn't yet shown.

Darkness in the east began replacing fading gray in the west. It had momentarily stopped snowing.

Louise wanted to hug Natalya to give her comfort but knew the gesture would be futile, given all their clothing, and besides, she wanted Natalya to hug her, for the same reason. Where were their husbands? Were they even alive? She no longer thought about who would win the race.

A young man came skiing toward them at a furious pace in the gloom. He was shouting something in Finnish. Louise's heart rose. Then it plummeted. All she could understand from the young man's excited shouting was the word "Amerikkalainen."

She looked at Natalya. Natalya stared into the distance, her face immobile.

"Oh my God," Louise whispered aloud. She didn't know what to do. A second skier was now visible, clearly Arnie, his style unmistakable. She looked at Natalya again. Natalya was standing very still, her mittens held close to her chest. If Louise didn't know better, she would have called it praying.

The crowd was now roaring; people were moving parallel to the road. Shouts were repeated up and down the road. "It's the American! It's the Finn!" Louise felt someone clap her shoulder. Then she noticed a smaller group of clearly disappointed Finns standing together, saying nothing. Some jubilant Finns made comments. A fistfight broke out, broken apart by one of several local police who were on hand.

Arnie was skiing easily, almost unhurriedly, toward the finish line, his breath condensing in the air, trailing behind him. The initial joy of seeing him safe was now being replaced by all the guilt that she'd pushed down while trying to fix the blunder of the press releases. How could she rush to hug Arnie, who was obviously unaware of what was happening, with Natalya standing silently beside her, stricken with grief? Should she hug Natalya? She could see that Natalya's world was crashing around her.

The crowd was cheering her husband—victory.

Louise saw Arnie looking around for her, then spotting her and pushing his way through the crowd to reach her. She made one last hopeful scan of the distant and now-darkening snow to the north. No Mikhail. She covered her face with her mittens. She felt like the inside of her body was whirling, draining into some vacuum beneath her legs. She had been so hopeful, hopeful to the point of almost certainty that Arnie would throw the race. She looked over at Natalya, not knowing what to say or how to comfort her.

Natalya didn't move.

Louise ran to meet Arnie.

After a hard but brief hug amid the backslapping and laughing of surrounding Finns, they both almost simultaneously blurted out, "Where's Mikhail? Have you seen him?"

The simultaneous questions gave them the answer they were dreading. He was still out there somewhere.

"Oh my God, I missed him," Arnie said. He looked back into the north. Someone offered him a glass of some liquor. He declined it. The man looked at him, puzzled.

"How could I have beat him?" he asked no one in particular, still looking to the north. "I spent the whole afternoon going in circles." He waved off two more laughing well-wishers. "He must be in trouble. We have to look for him."

Natalya had joined them, searching Arnie's face, not understanding the English.

Louise couldn't hold back any longer. "Pietari said he found you. You were going to let Mikhail win."

"He did. Told me about the raffle. The story making all the big papers. Gave me some BS about you wanting me to know the honor of the army was at stake."

"That's not at all what I—"

"I know. If I'd known right then you were worried about Mikhail, I might have found him. I didn't figure out Pietari wasn't straight with me until long after he left. With that delay and the snow. It's probably why Pietari's friends missed him, too." He looked north again. "I have to find him."

"That son of a bitch."

Arnie had never heard Louise use that word. He suddenly grew serious. "Has there been any, you know, reaction, statements coming from the Russians?"

"There has," she said quietly, looking at the ground.

Natalya was tugging on her coat sleeve. "Where is Mikhail? What is Arnie saying?"

Louise swallowed. "We'll find him," she said.

Natalya looked at her, her face paling, trying to take in what Louise was saying. Then she turned her face to the sky and howled like a wounded animal, "Au, bog na nebesach. Boze moi." Oh, God in heaven. Oh, God.

She knew.

Louise took her into her arms and Natalya broke down weeping. "We'll find him," Louise whispered in her ear. "We'll find him." Never show anything but optimism.

Arnie held up both arms, looking at the crowd, waiting for it to quiet. "You must hear me," he said. "Please. I have to say something."

When there was total silence he said, "Mikhail Bobrov is the true winner."

Natalya took her head from Louise's shoulder at the sound of her husband's name. Louise pulled her in tighter.

There was a stir, a murmur of question, but then everyone was again quiet. "On Friday, Colonel Bobrov was well ahead of me," Arnie said. "Then I fell through the ice and was totally soaked." He let that sink in. The Finns all knew that "totally soaked" meant death in these temperatures. The crowd grew more solemn. "He circled back. Somehow, he found me." Arnie choked up, then regained control. "He saved my life." There was silence. Arnie repeated, "He won the big race. I only won this last leg and I'm afraid it's because he's in trouble. We need to form a search party. Now. Who will help me find him? I'll wait for half an hour for you to get your gear."

Natalya had stopped weeping, trying to translate what Arnie was saying to the crowd, knowing it was about Mikhail. Louise's Finnish was totally inadequate to help.

When he'd finished, Arnie walked over to Natalya and Louise and told Louise the story. Louise translated it to French. Natalya nodded. "Yes. That would be Mikhail." Then she turned and headed in the direction of the hotel.

The light was nearly gone, and it was snowing again. Arnie waited by the finish line with several of the local men who'd already gone home and gotten their skis. They now stood in a circle around Arnie, discussing what possible routes Mikhail might have taken once he and Arnie departed from the lake. The group agreed on a search pattern. When the half hour was up, they strapped on their skis and headed north into the night.

By midnight, most of the searchers had given up and returned home, knowing that if Mikhail had managed to find shelter, they'd find him in daylight. If he hadn't, he was already dead. Arnie searched until two in the morning before he, too, gave up and wearily made his way to the hotel.

Tuesday, February 11, 1947
Arnie and Louise's Hotel

Anxious and alone, Louise waited in the combination dining room and lobby of the little hotel. She had gotten the hotel to fill a thermos with hot tea. Next to her on the sofa was the first edition of *Savon Sanomat*, the local morning broadside. An hour earlier, she had gone to the *Savon Sanomat* office to get the first printing off the press to see what was being said about the race. She couldn't understand most of the text, but she could see that the story about the race and Arnie's concession had been relegated to the bottom of the page by a huge banner headline: RAUHANSOPIMUS ALLEKIRJOITETTIIN PARIISISSA!! She grabbed the first person she saw. Pointing at the headline she asked, "What does that say? Do you speak English? French?"

The man grinned broadly. His face smeared with ink. "It say, Treaty of Peace Signed in Paris. It is official end of war. Now full peace with England, with Russia."

When she finally heard Arnie at the door she rushed to him, reaching her face up to kiss him. She pulled back, silently questioning him.

Arnie shook his head. "Not a sign. No broken ice. No tracks." He sighed, obviously deeply weary. "I don't understand," he mumbled again.

She handed him the newspaper. He read silently, going to a second page to finish the story. The United States, the United Kingdom, and the Soviet Union had signed the official peace treaty with all the countries that had fought on Germany's side during the war. This included Finland.

Arnie sighed. "They gave the Russians Petsamo. The Finns won't be happy."

"Well, they did fight for Germany."

"I'd say they fought for themselves, but with German help." He sighed and tossed the paper on a nearby table. "Right now, I don't give a damn about international politics. My friend is missing in action. Let's go to bed. I'm exhausted." He headed for the stairs to their room without waiting for her.

Louise followed. She shut the door and broke down crying.

He was still in his ski clothes. He pulled her in against his jacket and let her sob.

She became aware of the smell of Arnie's clothes, the result of ten days of hard physical exertion.

Arnie gently pushed her back and looked at her. "I may have gotten Mikhail killed," Louise said. "Natalya is sure that the MGB would make certain that he didn't lose the race. I set off a chain of events that has destroyed my best friend's family."

He gently moved her tears on her cheeks with his forefinger.

"You must be so angry with me."

Holding her close, talking over her head, Arnie said, "You thought you'd fixed it. We'll get through it."

Louise moaned. "Oh, Arnie. Natalya is afraid they'll arrest her, too. Their children will be raised by the state."

"Lulu Moppet," Arnie said, pushing her back gently so he could look into her eyes. "How can Natalya even think such a thing? Pure Russian paranoia." Then he stopped, his mouth slightly open.

"What is it, Arnie?"

"I don't know," he said quietly. "I mean. Maybe I'm wrong. But yesterday I thought I saw a DC-3 and wondered what it was doing up here."

"A DC-3 is American."

"Yes. But the Russian Lisunov Li-2 was copied from it. You can't tell them apart from a distance."

"But why is that anything?"

"Soviet paratroopers jump from modified Li-2s."

Louise put her hands on her mouth and sank to the floor. "What have I done," she whispered, looking up at Arnie.

Arnie knelt down to her. He took her head between his large hands. "Look at me."

She did.

"You tried to make money for the orphanage. And you did. You tried to alert us. Not your fault Pietari didn't come clean and not your fault it was snowing. If something bad has happened to Mikhail, you didn't do it. The Russians did."

She curled up in a ball on the floor.

"You couldn't have known," Arnie said, lying next to her to hold her. She turned away.

"Lulu, Lulu Moppet," Arnie said, stroking her hair. "He could still be alright. We don't know for sure *anything* about that airplane. I could have it all wrong."

She curled tighter in her fetal position.

"Louise, you've got to get up."

She didn't move. Arnie sat on the bed, looking at her. "Louise, just come here. It will be OK."

She didn't move.

Arnie sighed. He lay back on the bed looking up at the ceiling and was asleep instantly.

*   *   *

After about half an hour, Louise got off the floor. She took off Arnie's boots and struggled to lay him straight on the bed, then repaired her makeup and went to Natalya's room.

Fanya answered the door, bleary eyed and in a flannel nightdress. She said Natalya had gone out to the city limits.

When Louise found Natalya in the dark, a single man in an overcoat and Russian-style fur hat stood in the lee of a building, watching them.

"He'll come," Louise said softly.

Natalya didn't look at her but instead, staring into the night, said, "I think not." She slowly turned her head and looked at the man who was watching them. "They've been watching me since I arrived. They take defections very seriously. If they imprison Mikhail, or . . . maybe they've already killed him." She stopped.

Her voice dropped to a near whisper. "We know what happens to people."

The horror of it—the unfairness—stabbed at Louise. "He'll come."

The two stared into the night.

After some time, Natalya said, "They'll be organizing the fake search parties tomorrow morning."

"Oh, Natalya, don't give up hope."

"Louise, I gave up hope when they shot my parents." She was quiet. "We played by the rules," she said softly. "By the rules."

Louise was so stiff with cold she could barely walk back to the hotel with Natalya. She was so tired of saying, "I'm sorry." It sounded hollow and meaningless. She said nothing. The MGB man trailed behind them, not bothering to conceal his presence.

When they reached Natalya's hotel room, Louise reached out to hug her.

Natalya pulled back. She opened the door, then turned to Louise. "I have to think," was all she said. She closed the door quietly, so she'd not wake the children. Louise stood in the hall looking at the closed door for a full minute before she returned to her room.

Arnie was still asleep in his ski clothes, curled on his side.

Natalya had only started to take off her warm clothes when the door to her room flung open. The man who'd been watching her all night walked in. Another man stood outside in the hall. Natalya started trembling. She had no doubt they were MGB. However, she said coolly, "Yes, Comrade? You could at least have knocked."

"You're to come with us. Get your children."

The fear that had haunted her for days was now fully alive in her body.

"Can't we wait? We all need a little sleep."

"No. We have a car waiting."

Fanya had gotten out of her bed and was backed up against the wall. She looked at Natalya, almost begging forgiveness. Then Fanya started packing her things.

Natalya was scrambling, trying to think of a way out.

"Can I at least write a note to my friend? She'll be alarmed. You know her husband is with the American legation. You wouldn't want that."

The man thought about it. "Pack. Then you can write a note."

She packed, still leaving the children asleep. Then she wrote a note—in French. The MGB man looked at it, then over to Fanya, motioning her to come read it. Fanya looked at it. "It's in French," she said. "I don't know the language."

"Oh, dear Fanya," Natalya said in Russian. "And all this time, I was worried that you might be civilized."

Fanya looked away from her and continued packing.

The man took out a small camera, placed the note on the bed, and snapped a picture. "When this gets developed," he said, "you'll be very sorry if there's any funny business. So will your children."

"I'm just going to say goodbye. When the Koskis wake up, we'll be gone. There's no way there can be any funny business," Natalya said.

The man nodded toward Arnie and Louise's room, and Natalya slipped the note under their door.

Tuesday Morning, February 11, 1947
Arnie and Louise's Hotel

Louise couldn't sleep, resenting the fact that Arnie could, knowing she shouldn't resent it, which made her even more resentful. At some point, she must have dozed off. Some noise woke her. Disoriented for a moment, thinking she was home in Helsinki, she then remembered that she was in a hotel room in Kuopio. She thought someone must have been at the wrong door and fell back asleep.

Twenty minutes later, she jerked awake and rushed to the door. She opened it, peering left and right down the dim hallway. Then she noticed the note at her feet that must have had been shoved under the door when she'd awoken earlier.

She quickly opened it. It was from Natalya. *J'ai dû partir tôt. Bon va obtenir tant d'aide pour les orfelins. Rendez-vous à Helsinki.*

Arnie had woken up and was sitting upright. "What's that?"

"A note from Natalya."

Arnie waited a moment, then said, "You've been in Finland too long. What's it *say?*"

Louise looked at him, a puzzled expression on her face. "It says, 'Had to leave early. Good going getting so much help for the orphans. See you in Helsinki.'" She looked at it again. "Only she misspelled 'orphans.'"

"So?"

"Natalya's written French is close to perfect."

Arnie came over to her and she handed him the note. He shrugged. "Don't speak French." He looked at the note a little longer. "But I do know something about code. Anything out of the ordinary, if done on purpose. And you say she misspelled 'orphans,' but her French is flawless. So—"

Louise had grabbed him with both hands.

"What?" he asked.

"My God. She's going to try and get the children to the orphanage. We've got to help her."

Arnie was already searching for his boots.

Tuesday Evening, February 11, 1947
Helsinki, American Legation

The train ride back to Helsinki had been a nightmare of anxiety. At the Kuopio train station, they were greeted by headlines in *Savon Sanomat* saying, SOVIET SKIER FEARED DEAD. The story talked about Arnie's statement that Mikhail had come back to save him and would have won the race.

Natalya and the children weren't on the train. Arnie and Louise assumed she'd gone by car, most likely driven by one of the MGB watchers.

All Louise could do was express her anxiety to Arnie, who listened stoically, only once pointing out that nothing could be done until they got to Helsinki.

They got there just after dark. Arnie and Louise took a taxi to the apartment. After leaving their bags, Arnie immediately went to the legation to see if there was any information on Mikhail, and Louise went to see if Natalya had gotten safely to the orphanage.

When Arnie got to the legation, most of the staff had gone home for the evening, but Hamilton's secretary, Helmi, was still there, along with Pulkkinen. He was reading a newspaper, probably waiting to take Hamilton home. When Arnie came in the office door, Helmi walked over to him, and gestured with her eyes toward Hamilton's inner office. "He's not happy," she whispered. Arnie gave her a puzzled look. She merely nodded toward Hamilton's door.

The door was open, as it usually was. He entered, aware that Pulkkinen had followed him as far as the door and sat himself down next to it. Hamilton nodded toward a chair. Arnie, instead, kept on his feet.

"Colonel Koski," Hamilton said softly. "I'm afraid we have a problem." He pushed a copy of *Demokraatti*, the daily newspaper of the *Suomen Kommunistinen Puolue*, the Communist Party of Finland, across the desk.

Arnie quickly translated. The headline was shocking enough. HERO OF THE SOVIET UNION GIVES LIFE TO SAVE AMERICAN. The lead paragraph, however, made Arnie's stomach sink.

In a closely guarded ski race between Hero of the Soviet Union, Colonel Mikhail Bobrov, and the US military attaché at the American legation, Lieutenant Colonel Arnie Koski, Colonel Bobrov is believed to have lost his life after being abandoned by the American skier. Bobrov and Koski had met in Austria in the final days of Russia's Great Patriotic War against Fascism. The race from Rovaniemi to Kuopio was to be private, between the two military men. The government of the Soviet Union now believes this was a ruse to create a publicity stunt showing the defeat of a Soviet military hero at the hands of an American capitalist. Mrs. Louise Koski, now suspected to be an American agent masquerading as Koski's wife, shamelessly exploited Finnish orphans by using a common American system of gambling called a raffle to advertise the race.

Koski had won national ski competitions before the United States belatedly entered the war. The Americans assumed Bobrov would easily be defeated. They underestimated Soviet manhood. According to eyewitnesses at the finish in Kuopio, Koski himself stated that Colonel Bobrov was well ahead of him but had turned back because he suspected that the American had gotten into some sort of danger. Koski went on to say that Bobrov pulled him from where he'd broken through ice and revived him, saving his life. Koski further stated that after he'd been revived, he had conceded the race to Colonel Bobrov. Then he alleges that the two decided to race the short distance from the accident scene into Kuopio. Here the American's story falls apart. Searches by local skiers and even special teams of Russian parachuting ski troops, found no sign of Colonel Bobrov. Snowfall has covered any tracks that could provide a clue about Colonel Bobrov's fate or the activities of the perfidious American.

The head of Soviet security forces for the Soviet legation, Colonel Oleg Sokolov, told this newspaper that he suspects foul play. "We helped our American allies during the war. We continue to help all our allies. Here is sound evidence of our goodwill and good intentions. The Americans talk about 'deteriorating relations,' when they alone are responsible for this. We urge the American legation to investigate this incident and punish whoever is responsible. We also want to make clear that the Soviet Union does not appreciate the West in general interfering in the affairs of Finland and other Eastern European countries who have already or would like to voluntarily ally themselves with the Soviet Union."

The general secretary of the Communist Party of Finland, Ville Pessi, vowed that every effort will be made to bring the perpetrators of this crime to justice.

Arnie quit reading. The magnitude of the lie overwhelmed him, as did its plausibility to a credulous public. He stood there, stunned, the paper in his hand. "It's all lies."

"That's irrelevant." Hamilton pointed at the newspaper. "*This* is all that's relevant: bad publicity. Denying lies put forward by newspapers only increases the negative publicity."

"She meant no harm," Arnie said.

"I am well aware of her motives, Colonel. What concerns me are the outcomes."

Arnie took that in, silent for a moment. Then he said, "I think the MGB killed Colonel Bobrov. They were afraid he'd lose the race."

Hamilton said, firmly, "Sit down, Colonel."

Arnie sat.

"Now. Your wife explained her part in this mess a couple of days ago. I want to hear yours."

Arnie started with the legation party, ending with the unsuccessful search for Mikhail.

Hamilton quietly pushed several newspaper clippings across the desk toward Arnie. "You even made the *New York Times*," he said. "Most Americans tend to think everything is a game."

Arnie said nothing.

"Do you think everything is a game?"

Arnie hung his head. "No, sir."

"Do you even think?"

Arnie knew he was being chewed out, so he kept silent. It was a long silence.

Hamilton broke it with a sigh. "Bobrov was someone we could have worked with. Well. Pfftt. You screwed that up."

"Yes, sir."

Hamilton watched him for a moment. Arnie was looking at the edge of his desk. "Next time you get a diplomatic assignment, leave your military culture at the O club." He paused. "If you ever get another diplomatic assignment."

Arnie visibly winced.

"OK, Colonel," Hamilton said briskly. "Let's get to work. What makes you suspect that Bobrov has been murdered?"

"On Saturday I glimpsed what I thought was a commercial DC-3, somewhat off course. Didn't think anything of it at the time." He paused. "When Colonel Bobrov didn't show on Monday, I began to suspect it was a Lisunov Li-2. Many were modified to drop airborne troops during the war. The MGB has special operations teams, all jump qualified. There's no other reason a Lisunov would be out north of Kuopio. *Demokraatti* even mentioned ski troops."

Hamilton nodded very slightly, taking it in. "He's a Hero of the Soviet Union," he finally said. "They wouldn't want to see him lose."

"No, sir. And he's too good a skier not to have been within an hour of me, behind or ahead. And he's very savvy about operating in winter. Unlikely that he'd get himself into trouble." Arnie paused. "More savvy than me. He saved my life."

"So, at least that part of the story is true."

Hamilton listened as Arnie told him about Mikhail rescuing him.

"We need to try to find him," Arnie said. "Maybe I'm wrong and there's a chance that he's out there somewhere alive."

Hamilton looked at Arnie solemnly. "Unlikely. Comrade Beria has killed people who looked at him the wrong way. Same with Stalin. No, sadly, I think they killed him."

"To avoid embarrassment," Arnie spat out.

"To avoid tarnishing the Soviet system. To avoid losing Finland to the West. To make an example of Bobrov to send a message to the GRU about who's really in charge and what happens if you cross them."

"For politics," Arnie said bitterly.

Hamilton looked at him for a long time. "Yes, for politics." He lifted one of the news clippings and looked at it, but he was thinking, not reading. "Arnie, your dirty word, 'politics,' was invented to settle differences without violence. The Soviets want to control Europe without going to war. We want to stop them without going to war. The Finnish Communists want to control Finland without a civil war. The Finns who see things our way want to do the same. Republicans and Democrats want to run the USA but don't want to go to war to do so. *Politics* allows this to happen." A bit exasperated he sighed. "You, above all, should know that no matter how dirty politics gets, it's never as dirty as war."

"We agree on that, sir. I'm just sorry for the whole mess."

Hamilton sighed. He picked up a clipping from *L'Humanité*. "Of course, the pro-Communist press will be encouraging the conspiracy theory that he was abandoned after some tragic accident or, even more juicy, that he was murdered." He paused. "By you."

Arnie leaned forward. "That's why we need to find Mikhail's body and prove what really happened. I *know* it was the MGB."

Hamilton opened his palms upward. "And what then? Send Wyatt Earp to bring 'em in dead or alive?"

"But he's a friend! I can't just leave him out there. And what about justice? Doesn't that count?"

"Arnie," Hamilton said softly. "The days of stalwart military men, comrades in arms, gentlemen all, toasting downed enemy pilots at the officers' mess . . ." Hamilton looked sadly at Arnie. "Those days are dead. The Russians never trusted us, even when we were allies, but ever since we dropped the bomb, they've feared us. Make no mistake, we are now enemies. Given acts like what we think just happened, they should be our enemy. For the good of the world."

"I don't think of Mikhail Bobrov as my enemy."

"I'm sure you both felt that way, but it's irrelevant. If your masters get into a cockfight, it won't be them in the cockpit. It'll be men like you and Bobrov, with bloody spurs on your feet instead of skis."

"Let's hope it doesn't come to that, sir," Arnie said.

"Indeed. Hope is what we still have." Then, almost to himself he said, "Sometimes I think *it* is our worst enemy."

Arnie asked, "What about Bobrov's wife and children?"

"She'll be under surveillance, for sure," Hamilton answered. "She most likely knows too much and they'll want to get her out of the country. Or worse."

That hung in the air.

"Sir," Arnie said. "I think Bobrov's wife is going to try to get her children to the orphanage."

"How do you know that?"

"She left a coded note for Louise. We both think it's what she intends."

"Not much chance she'll even get out of her apartment building. If she does, Russians have informants everywhere. A single woman with two small children on the streets by herself in the middle of the night? She won't get far."

"I can't just do nothing. I'm going to the Russian legation to see if there's any news on Bobrov and to confront them with this story. We can't just let lies go unanswered, that's a sure way that they'll become facts."

Anger flickered briefly across Hamilton's face. "You can go to the Russians to inquire about Bobrov, but you will not confront them with this story. We will let any number of lies go unanswered if it means keeping out of a war with the Soviet Union. Am I clear?"

"Yes, sir," Arnie said. "Very clear."

Hamilton softened. "I'm afraid you'll get nothing from them, but OK. Go. I'll take care of the newspapers." Hamilton stood, clearly dismissing Arnie.

Pulkkinen was just outside the door. He stepped aside, nodding briefly, as Arnie rushed past him.

Tuesday Evening, February 11, 1947
Helsinki

When Louise got to the orphanage, there was no sign of Natalya or the children. Kaarina had already gone home. Louise knew the staff well but not well enough to trust them with what she was sure was Natalya's plan: hiding the children in the orphanage. Over a quarter of Finns were Communists or sympathizers and they were everywhere. If any of the orphanage staff were one of them, they'd instantly want to make themselves look good, contributing to the cause of worldwide Socialism by betraying Natalya and the children.

Louise ran to Kaarina's house. The door opened as she was pounding on it. She was staring directly into Pietari's face.

He blinked and said, "Hyvää iltaa," the formal "good evening." His face was stone-cold.

She knew that he understood full well what he'd done. He'd taken revenge. The hate and anger behind Pietari's stoicism was palpable. Why had she not seen this? She realized it was because she'd barged ahead, convincing him and his friends to go looking for Arnie, not wanting to see it, because it would have gotten in the way. Now, she fought wanting to take out her anger on him, to slap that expressionless face of his. But right now, she didn't have time for hate or revenge.

"I need to see Kaarina," she said.

"Yoh," he answered, stepping aside and opening the door wider.

Kaarina was darning socks. Louise had never seen her idle.

"What is it?"

"Surely you heard the outcome of the race," Louise said.

"Of course. We'll need to go over the stubs and time guesses tomorrow to find the winner." She smiled and said quite proudly, "We have made over fifty thousand markkas."

Shocked by Kaarina's seeming indifference to the outcome of the race and her focus only on the money, she blurted out, "I think they've killed Mikhail."

Kaarina stopped knitting. "Yoh," she said. That was all. That was it. She resumed knitting.

Her response had Louise nearly spitting. "Yoh? That's it? Yoh? How can you sit there, darning socks, while your son"—she turned and pointed a finger at Pietari—"your son tried to condemn Mikhail to death by not passing along my message to Arnie, telling him to throw the race."

Pietari looked at his mother and she translated. Neither showed anything. Then Pietari said something. Kaarina translated. "He says asking him to tell Arnie to throw the race was like asking him to betray Suomi." Kaarina used the Finnish word for their country. "You should never have asked that. The war is not over until Finland is safe from the Russians and for him, it won't ever be over. He is happy to hear about Russians killing their own soldiers." Then she looked at Louise hard. "My son killed no one. If Mikhail was murdered, it would be at the hands of the MGB. There is no Russian blood on this house's floor."

Louise struggled not to cry, to weep for the sadness and lingering bitterness of war. But she'd be damned if she'd break down in front of Pietari and Kaarina. She had to stay focused on Natalya and the children.

"I apologize," she said quietly. "Tell him."

Kaarina did so.

"Also tell him that Natalya's afraid for her life and her children's lives. Her children are innocent. They are not the enemy."

Kaarina did. Pietari walked out of the room.

The two women looked silently at each other for a moment. "Natalya will probably be arrested," Louise said, "perhaps executed as soon as the story about the sacrifice of her noble heroic husband is off the front page. She knows too much. Her children will become orphans raised by the state. She left me a coded note. Her plan is to get the children to the orphanage."

"How?"

"I don't know. Will you help?"

She waited, watching Kaarina intently. Kaarina's face showed nothing of what she was thinking. Then Kaarina said, "The children are not the enemy."

"Oh, Kaarina, thank you." Louise breathed again. "Natalya will have to do something tonight, before she's arrested. Will you go to the orphanage and be there if Natalya somehow manages to get the children there? I don't trust your staff."

"With good reason. Ava is a Party member and Mila leans in that direction. I will go there, tell them I can't sleep, and to take the night off. I will also do the paperwork that says the children were left on our doorstep without any identification." Kaarina said it with all the emotion of having been asked to set the table. "But why a Finnish orphanage? The Russians have plenty of them."

"It's not the orphanage, it's the country. I think Natalya wants her children raised where you don't constantly live a lie. Where you are not in fear of saying the wrong thing. Where saying the wrong thing, or even thinking it, is punished." She took a deep breath, realizing she was sounding truths that up until this moment she'd always thought were platitudes. "She wants her children raised here in freedom."

Kaarina took that in. "Yoh," drawn out, as in "I understand." Then she said, "I assume you are going to try to help her."

"Yes."

"How?"

"I don't know."

Late Tuesday Night, February 11, 1947
Outside Natalya's Building

Louise was hurrying to Natalya's apartment building when the big Chevy Fleetmaster slowly came up behind her. It slowed. She saw Pulkkinen nod his head sideways, his face stoic as usual. The car picked up speed. It turned into a side street. What did he want?

She looked around. For once, no one in sight. She rounded the corner of the side street and saw the car's exhaust barely reflecting light from one of the feeble streetlights on the street she'd just left. The passenger door opened, and she slipped in.

Pulkkinen was smoking, the red light on his face glowing a bit when he drew on the cigarette. He put the cigarette out in the ashtray. "You're up to something," he said quietly.

"No."

"I heard Colonel Koski in Hamilton's office."

"So?"

"What are you planning?"

Once again, the icy fear that saying the truth would get you or someone you loved killed. If she told Pulkkinen her plan, who would he tell?

"I can help you," he said. "The Russians will be all over the place tonight. They won't look inside an American legation car driven by someone they know well."

Yes, she thought darkly to herself, *know well because you work for them and not us.* Still, she asked, "You are proposing?"

"If you want to get Mrs. Bobrova somewhere tonight, she cannot go on foot with two small children."

Louise knew this to be totally true. However, if she told Pulkkinen she was trying to get Natalya and the children to the orphanage, it could be the end of Natalya and her children. But Pulkkinen already knew *something* was up. He could already have informed his masters, whether Finnish secret police or MGB.

She sifted through every memory of every conversation she'd ever had with Pulkkinen. Every flicker of his eyes. Every minute hand gesture. She drew on all her years of reading people, a skill that had gotten her far in college, as an army wife, but here, now, seemed so inadequate. It was a skill based on ephemerals, on nuances, without solid evidence. Hunches. What her mother called women's intuition. It wasn't magic. It was skill, honed over years. But could she trust it now when it was a matter of life or death? Even Arnie and Hamilton didn't know who Pulkkinen really worked for.

She swallowed. She looked into this man's eyes as deeply and as carefully as she'd ever looked into a man's eyes in her life.

Then she told Pulkkinen what she had in mind.

She watched Pulkkinen drive off, still not knowing for sure if he'd joined her plan or was about to reveal it to the MGB. Hoping for a reprieve from the problem of how to get Natalya to safety, she walked a second time to the orphanage to see if she'd already made it there. She had not. They still had to be in the apartment.

She hurried to Natalya's building, stopping behind the corner of a building just before Natalya's. She quickly looked toward the front door and pulled back. There was now a man outside the building in the usual long overcoat and hat. Still not sure what to do, unable to get into the building to reach Natalya, she did what she could; she waited, bouncing up and down, flapping her arms in the cold alley. She needed a clear sign confirming that Natalya was indeed trapped in her flat. She had a good idea she was. Why else would there be a guard at the door in addition to the usual man at the desk? But she also needed some sort of opening to get into the building. None appeared and she was running out of time.

Just before midnight, a Soviet legation car pulled up. A young, probably not yet twenty, uniformed MGB soldier got out. He had what looked to Louise like one of those guns she'd seen in gangster movies slung over his shoulder. Clearly, this was the changing of the guard and just as in the army, the crummy guard duty and graveyard shifts went to the lowest ranks.

She recognized the "clerk" as he came out the door. A good sign. The reception desk wasn't manned after midnight, probably relying on the outside guard to report any rare exit from the building. The clerk and the man with the overcoat got in the car and it drove off. The young soldier stamped his feet, beat his arms against his thick overcoat, and then started to walk back and forth. Then, the plan crystalized.

She hurried back to her apartment. Off went the heavy clothes and out came the lipstick, heels, dangling earrings, her tightest dress, and the perfume that Arnie would breathe in from those places she shared only with him. Taking a chance that a young Russian soldier couldn't read the Latin alphabet, she took out several of her old Oklahoma identification cards: the ornate scrolly one that identified her as a member of Alpha Iota chapter of Delta Gamma sorority. The rather plain but very official-looking Oklahoma driver's license. Neither had a photograph. She then slipped several barbital sleeping pills into her purse. She looked up at the ceiling. "Oh God, let this work. Please let this work."

She put on her heavy coat and again returned to her vigil across from Natalya's building. The fact that the overcoat hid the tight dress would have to be negotiated somehow. She'd improvise. She took in a deep breath and let it out. Then, somehow, it was like Arnie had said about the war. The worst fear is before the battle. Once the battle starts, you're too busy trying to win it to be afraid. She felt calm and powerful. She *was* calm and powerful. She had been designed to wield this power and by God she would.

She deliberately waited another hour, her feet gradually going numb because of the thin, leather soles. If she was cold, so was the young soldier.

She watched him make a turn at the end of the block and come slowly back to the front door. She took a deep breath against the cold as she opened her coat to reveal the dress. Then she hurried across the street, the tight dress and heels limiting her stride, but she knew that if that young guard was typical, he'd be totally focused on her and not on his job. One thing she knew well was how lonely and needy young soldiers were.

He stopped her just as she was going through the door. "Net," he said, and something else in Russian. Louise turned to him and spoke rapidly in French. The soldier couldn't have been twenty. His cheeks glowed with both the cold and youth. His eyes were the color of pale-blue forget-me-nots. She steeled herself. She was going to hurt this child.

He looked concerned, but still shook his head and said, "Net," then more Russian. Louise gave her best seductive smile, then finished it with touching one of his coat buttons and looking up at him, imploring him with everything she had. She pulled the identification cards from her purse. Pointing to them she said, "Frantsuzkaya. Frantsuzkaya zhenshchina." French woman.

He shook his head. "Net." She smiled again, her mouth just slightly open. She leaned her head toward the door, tilting her head, questioning.

"Ne dopuskayetsya," he said, almost apologetically.

She didn't know the word, but it clearly meant some kind of no as well, but the no was losing force. Louise did a little wiggle, putting her hand lightly on her mouth, then put one finger on the boy's lips. She put it back onto her own lips in the universal sign to keep something quiet. She rolled her eyes and looked up at the upper windows of the building. Then she made the other universal sign, forming a circle with her left thumb and forefinger and plunging her right index finger in and out of it. She knew the young soldier knew that only high-ranking legation people lived in the building. He wouldn't risk messing up a powerful man's sexual liaison.

The boy laughed. He made a sign like he knew the score. Then he made an inquiring face and nodded toward the side of the building, pursing his lips as if kissing. Louise smiled, then shook her head sadly. She touched her wristwatch and looked back up at the building. Then she made the face of an angry man and slapped the back of her hand, followed by her own sad face. Then she pointed her finger at the boy and wagged it. He looked up at the window, doubt on his face—and anxiety. There was no way he'd get in trouble messing with some big hat's big night, but clearly he had orders not to let anyone pass.

This was it. She leaned in close to him, and said, in French, "If you let me up, then afterwards . . ." She glanced meaningfully at the alley and pursed her lips in return. She knew he didn't understand the French, but she also knew he could hope he understood her promise of reward. Louise then pointed again to the upper floor and made a sign that she hoped would keep his hopes up.

"OK," he said very loudly, as if proud to know the universal "it's alright."

"OK," she said, beaming back at him. She opened the door and slipped through.

Natalya opened the door to her flat and peered through the narrow opening, fear on her face. Seeing it was Louise, she gasped, threw the door wide, and pulled her into the apartment. There, she started to cry, hugging her.

"The children?" Louise asked.

"Asleep."

"Fanya?"

"Gone. Work done." She hesitated. "How did you get in?"

Louise told her. Normally, such a story would elicit a giggle or two. This telling was done with clinical sobriety. Then Louise told Natalya the plan. Natalya nodded soberly, understanding everything. They both knew that success depended on a teenaged boy's hormones.

Natalya gently lifted each child's head and slipped half of the barbital sleeping pill Louise had taken with her into each mouth. Both mumbled, swallowed, and fell back asleep. Louise sighed with relief. Phase one accomplished.

She helped Natalya dress the children and they laid them in Grisha's old baby buggy along with several blankets. Natalya and Louise got into their coats.

"Ready?" Louise asked.

Natalya nodded.

Louise opened the apartment's door and looked up and down the hallway. She simply nodded and Natalya pushed the buggy into the hall. She grabbed the sleeping Grisha, snuggling him against her side with her left hand. Louise did the same with Alina, grunting with the effort. Together they grabbed the front and rear of the buggy and managed to get down the stairs. On the ground level they put both children in the buggy, covering them with the blankets.

Natalya slipped the buggy behind the reception desk, ducking down behind it herself at the end near the door where she could peek around the desk and see the street.

Louise looked at her squatting there with the buggy and her children. She realized this might be the last time she saw her if the plan failed and Natalya didn't make it to the orphanage. She wanted to hug her goodbye, but that couldn't be. She did something totally silly. She winked. Natalya smiled at that, shaking her head. She then blew Louise a kiss. Louise, about to do something that might cost her and her friend their lives, launched into Phase two wondering why she hadn't thought about blowing a kiss rather than giving a stupid wink.

The night air instantly made her legs cold. She saw the young soldier who was at the end of his beat perk up and come almost jogging up to her. Well, Phase two was starting off well.

"OK!" he said excitedly.

"OK," she answered as heartily as she could.

He looked up at the top floor and made a questioning face. Louise made the universal sign for intercourse followed by the one for sleep. The soldier grinned. He put a fist on his chest. "Ne budu spat," he said, lightly hitting his chest. She looked at him quizzically. "Net . . ." and he made the sign for sleeping. Louise laughed, trying to convey she thought the joke was hilarious. She then repeated "net," followed by the sleep sign. She took him by his gloved hand and gently started him toward the alley.

He started unbuckling the belt around his coat. She put her hand on the buckle, and smiling up at him warmly, shook her head. His blue eyes were shining with excitement and, could it be trepidation? Uncertainty? Oh, my God. He's a virgin.

Once off the street, she pulled him into her, getting his back to the street, and started to slowly kiss him. He grabbed at her, his submachine gun falling off his shoulder and dangling by the strap. She smiled, looking into his eyes, gently lowering the gun to the pavement with her right hand while touching the front of his trousers with her left. His breath smelled and he had serious body odor, but everything else was in total working order. She saw Natalya slip by the alley, pushing the buggy. Then she saw the American legation's Fleetmaster glide slowly by.

She continued gently rubbing her hand against the soldier's erection. He erupted in an orgasm, barely twenty seconds after she'd started rubbing him. *Thank God for nineteen-year-old boys*, she thought.

The boy looked stricken. Ashamed. Oh, my God. She touched his cheek. "C'est bon," she murmured. She held both cheeks and kissed him full on the mouth, breathing, "C'est bon." Then she whispered again, nuzzling his lips with her hair. "OK. OK."

He embraced her as if he'd never been loved before. Perhaps he hadn't. She tried to relax up against him, letting him feel that indeed everything was OK. She held him for a bit longer, then pulled back smiling, again making the sign for secrecy. He leaned back against the side of a building. She planted a kiss on her fingers and transferred it to his lips, then moved as quickly as she could back to the street. It was deserted.

Natalya and the children were gone.

Early Wednesday Morning,
February 12, 1947
The Orphanage

Louise woke at the orphanage with a start, still in her heels and dress. She had dozed off around four in the morning after settling Grisha and Alina in their blankets on the canvas and wood folding cots that the orphanage used for beds. She saw Natalya, still where she was when Louise had dozed off, standing watch over her two sleeping children.

This was where Louise's plan had ended, with the children safe in the orphanage, driven there by Pulkkinen.

She had no idea what to do next. Perhaps that was appropriate she thought. She'd gotten Natalya sprung from the flat and the children to the orphanage. Natalya now faced the gravest moral choice of her life. This part of the plan had to be solely hers. Louise felt her heart weeping for her friend, sitting silently and loving her children with her eyes—with her whole body—clearly grieving. The choice had already been made. It was clear that Natalya did not want this brief last time with her children to end.

Kaarina, face drawn from lack of sleep, walked into the room full of sleeping children. She saw Natalya sitting there. She motioned to Louise to join her outside the room.

"She's got to get out of here," she whispered. "The Russians will be looking for her as soon as they discover she and the children are gone. My guess is the young guard will be relieved at eight and someone will look in on Natalya around that time. God help that young man when they find them gone."

Louise felt a sharp spasm of remorse. The young guard would almost certainly be sent to the gulag if he wasn't shot. There was no escaping the situation. It was the kid—a stranger to her—or Natalya and her children. She felt good about getting Natalya out—and bad about very likely getting the young man tortured and killed. Arnie had once said that there were very few unambiguous moral choices in war, mostly because whatever you chose to do, someone died because of your actions. Louise now knew viscerally what he meant. The old adage that you can't make an omelet without cracking an egg came to her mind. She immediately rejected it. Talking about human lives in cooking metaphors should repulse everyone. Curious how it came to her mind so readily. Was it war that made people callous, or was it that people were callous, and they made war?

"We've got to find a place for her to hide."

"I'm taking quite enough risk keeping the children," Kaarina said.

"OK. I've got to find a place for her to hide."

"What about Arnie?"

"He's been beating down doors, trying to make a stink, hoping the MGB action will be exposed. He's also still hoping Mikhail might be alive."

Kaarina harrumphed. "We're talking Lavrentiy Beria and Joseph Stalin here." She looked Louise directly in the eyes. "He's dead."

"I'll get her to the legation. She can seek asylum."

"Louise," Kaarina said quietly. "The Russians will have every approach to the legation covered. She won't have a chance."

"Sweden then."

"The ferries will be covered. The Finnish police will probably have to help. It's seven hundred and fifty kilometers to the border. It's February. There are no towns up there. Few roads. Neither of you will survive. And who knows if the Swedes will let her in. They don't want to anger the Russians any more than the Finns."

Louise said nothing.

"Why do you think Natalya's saying goodbye to her children?" Kaarina asked gently.

It hit Louise very hard. "She can't," she whispered. She rushed back inside.

She knelt in front of Natalya, who seemed to be somewhere far away now. "Natalya, we've got to get you out of here," she said quietly.

Natalya's attention came back into the room. She smiled at Louise.

"Natalya, you've got to try."

Natalya looked wearily at Louise. "My dear innocent girl from Oklahoma. I have found our friendship . . ." She started to tear up but caught herself. "Nearly a quarter of this country are Communists. The word will go out. Something like a fleeing spy. Whatever. They're very good at storytelling, as you know. Anywhere I go, any direction I take, the MGB will be informed." She stood. "The one thing I must do is get captured as far from this orphanage as possible."

Louise gulped back a pain in her throat. "Natalya, you can't—"

Natalya smiled gently. "It's not hopeless, my friend. Maybe they just threw Mikhail in prison. Maybe they'll do the same with me. Who knows, a year, maybe five years, it'll all blow over. Kaarina can stay connected with them. They'll almost certainly get adopted." She smiled and gestured. "I mean look at them."

Natalya grabbed Louise, kissed her on each cheek, and walked rapidly to the door. Louise followed, but Natalya had disappeared into the February darkness.

Wednesday Afternoon, February 12, 1947
The Orphanage

That afternoon, Louise and Kaarina carefully went over the records and the stubs. By six that night, they'd agreed that a woman who lived in a northeastern suburb of Helsinki had won the raffle. Her guess had been the longest time difference of all the guesses.

Louise wrote the press release.

Then, before giving it to the papers, she and Kaarina went to the address on the ticket stub to tell the woman she was the winner.

Thursday Morning, February 13, 1947
Helsinki

On Thursday morning, Louise went to Natalya's apartment, hoping against hope. The man at the desk, the same one she'd seen many times before, gave her a deadpan look. She repeated Natalya's name, then Mikhail's. The man picked up a large ledger and methodically paged through it, expressionless. No, he said. No one by that name here. Sorry.

She rushed to the Russian legation. She wasn't sure what she wanted to find out, but just something, anything about her friend. She'd go straight to Sokolov. That's what she'd do. She'd go straight in and ask him.

The guard at the door, after she showed him her diplomatic identification, picked up a telephone. There was a brief conversation.

He shook his head. No.

Louise lost her temper. "What do you mean, no? I'm the wife of the military attaché of the United States. I want to talk to Mr. Sokolov."

The guard looked at her.

She pushed her identification papers in front of his nose. "Sokolov. Sokolov. You understand me?"

The guard picked up the telephone again. He hung up and stared at her, saying nothing.

Someone opened the legation door. She'd never seen the man.

In perfect English he asked, "I understand you want to see Comrade Sokolov? I am so sorry, but he's been called back to Moscow for a conference. Can I help you?"

"I want to know where Natalya Bobrova is."

"I'm sorry?" he asked.

"Natalya Bobrova. The wife of Colonel Mikhail Bobrov."

The man looked at her coolly. "I'm sorry. Was the colonel married? If he was, then his wife must not have accompanied him to Helsinki."

"Those are goddamn lies!"

The man said nothing, looking at her with soulless eyes.

"She was here. I know her. You can't believe I will swallow that. I'll . . . I'll—"

"If you want to make a formal inquiry, I suggest you do it in writing. We will most certainly attend to it." He glanced at the guard and said something in rapid Russian. Then he smiled genially at Louise. "Now, you must excuse me. I have my work." He turned. The guard held the door open for him. The man disappeared and the guard shut the door. He then stood firmly in front of it, his machine gun held by both hands across his chest.

Friday, December 9, 1949
Stockholm Ferry Terminal

Louise couldn't stop shaking her head. It seemed as if the three years since she and Arnie had first approached Turku, pushing slowly through thin ice, had flashed by as if in a dream. Now, she was standing alone on the deck of a similar ferry, watching the picture-book houses and buildings of Stockholm slipping by so close it felt like the ferry were on a lake rather than the sea. She watched the ferry's wake gently slapping the shore on both sides behind them. Being inside one of the many passages between the islands that formed the city felt safe.

In three more years, Arnie would have his twenty in and they'd retire. It had been made clear that there would be no chance of getting a star. He was coming to terms with it. His father also wanted to retire and had asked Arnie to run the logging company. Arnie said he would. They'd be back in the Pacific Northwest.

The massive and deep blast of the ferry's horn made her jump out of her reverie. She hurried down to the exit passageway where they'd debark and go through Swedish customs.

At the customs building, Arnie handed a happy-looking young man their passports and waited. The man peered at them, then looked around, trying to see over his desk. "And how many in the family, sir?"

Smiling proudly at his family, Arnie answered, "Four."

Louise felt Alina's hair, already showing yellow amid the nearly white blonde. She was a big girl and refused to wear a hat. With her other hand, she felt the wool of Grisha's stocking cap that she had knit for him. She pulled the children in close to her and looked back toward Finland. She felt the start of a sob and pulled the children in tighter to stop it, remembering their mother, her eyes blinking back tears.

Then, she turned and followed Arnie Koski into Sweden. In two weeks, they'd be in Oklahoma for Christmas.

ACKNOWLEDGMENTS

My wonderful wife and live-in editor, Anniki, for her comments and insights on all my books; Marcus Prest, for mapping out the ski race, skiing in Finnish winter, and Finnish history and culture; Julia Karpeisky for comments and insights on Russian culture and life in the Soviet Union; my daughter, Laurel, for her inciteful comments; Risto Penttilä, author of *Finland's Search for Security through Defence 1944–89*, for historic and cultural context; my agent, Sloan Harris, for all his support and early commentary; Matt Cook, for his early reading and great plot ideas; Karl VanDevender, Treacy Coates, Mike Harreschou, Vicki Huff, Mary Fellows, and John Russell for their early comments; Anne-Mari Paster, Tiffany H. Cabrera, PhD, the Office of the Historian, US Department of State, and Jyrki Runola, for historic Helsinki; the staff at Grove Atlantic, my editors Morgan Entrekin, Sara Vitale, and Zoe Harris; Eldes Tran for her meticulous proofreading; and especially my copy editor, Paula Cooper Hughes, who makes me look way better than I would look without her.